Boomer

a novel by

Jim Olson

Edenvale Glen Publishing   Minneapolis, 2007

Copyright @2007 James Olson. All rights reserved.

Edenvale Glen Publishing
15157 Patricia Ct.
Eden Prairie, MN 55346
www.edenvaleglenpublishing.com

Printed in the United States of America. No part of the contents of this book may be reproduced without the written permission of the publisher.

This novel is a work of fiction. Names, characters, places, and incidents are either the products of the author's imagination or are used fictitiously.

Cover by RJ Communications

ISBN 978-1-4243-2988-5

First Edition

Dedication

For my fellow teachers of English with whom I have read and written the past 35 years of my life. You always helped me believe there was a book in me.

For thirty years of students. Helping you with your writing struggles taught me to confront my own.

For Jerry and Gene who helped me through Vietnam and Don and Rick who helped me understand it afterward.

For my parents, both gone, who wouldn't be surprised that I have written a book, because they always believed that I could do anything.

For my wife, Judy, my partner in everything. Without her, anything I do would be diminished by more than half.

Introduction

In recent years a number of authors have been caught trying to pass their fiction off as nonfiction. That will not happen with me. Boomer is fiction. However, folks from my hometown and other places in my life will recognize much of what I have written as familiar. Many of the things in Boomer really did happen. They just didn't happen the way they are described in the book. My creativity depends heavily on the things that I have experienced.

None of the people in the book are real people. Well, that is except for Liberace. He was kind of real. I have drawn heavily on people I have known in the creation of the characters, but these characters never lived beyond the written page. For example, Glen Boomer runs a gas station, as did my own father. After that they have little in common. On occasion Glen will do something with his son that is like something my father did with me, but he does it in the Glen Boomer way, not my father's. Sure, I could have put him in a grocery store instead of a gas station to avoid the connection, but the gas station is what I know and how I remember the incredible atmosphere of small-town Midwestern life.

I suppose that Boomer is in some ways nonfiction. It is the nonfiction that all authors struggle to create. It is the truths of the real world that an author tries to reveal through fictional characters and events. In Boomer those truths lie in the dramatic changes that have taken place in Midwestern life in the past half century and in an event which has so much to do with those changes, the Vietnam War. The Vietnam segments are such a mishmash of fact and fantasy I can scarcely recognize the difference. So please, dear reader, don't you try. Just enjoy the story.

2004

I had come home for my father's funeral. It was less than a year since I had been there for my mother's funeral, which, according to my sister, Elizabeth, had been my father's funeral as well. Glen Boomer had been married to my mother for sixty years and evidently couldn't sustain a life without her. Marion Boomer was an incredible woman, although for a long time I failed to realize just how incredible. My father didn't take his own life, but in Elizabeth's analysis, just gave it up. Before my mother's death he had been a healthy man. Eleven months after, he was dead. In the twenty years before my mother's death, I had only visited Chandler for a few brief interludes. Still, I call it coming home.

My entire boyhood had been spent in that tiny Minnesota town as one of its four thousand or so odd occupants, less odd than some, more than others. I had played as the last man on Chandler High School's only basketball team to participate in the state high school championship, sung a weak tenor in the choir, and graduated 33rd of the 102 members of the class of '63.

~Boomer~

It was really Vietnam that took me away from Chandler. It was also Vietnam that made me uncomfortable when I returned. The ugly residue of that war seemed to coat the town with a film that slightly distorted it for me, as though I were viewing it through dirty glass. Sometime after I left Chandler, I discovered that the film was on my eyes and not on the town.

Away from Chandler I love it far better than when I am there. I remember the escapades of my youth with warm fondness. No, with downright ecstacy. Chandler was the perfect place to be a kid. I had been blessed with a solid family and four friends who grew with me like five trunks of a white birch tree. They are worthy of this story and not me. I just happen to be what they all had in common.

When I returned after the war, the birch tree was gone. The strong relationships I'd had as a child were replaced by sad substitutes. My hasty marriage to a Chandler girl, Deanna Westbrook, was a shambles from the start. Disagreements with my father about Vietnam escalated to a personal war, until we could not be in the same room without sniping at or openly attacking one another.

After several failed attempts to hold jobs in town, I escaped to the West Coast. My contact with Chandler dwindled to weekly, then monthly phone calls to my mother, who was outwardly more understanding of my absence than she must have been inwardly. For years I doubted if my father cared. Fortunately, I was wrong. Unfortunately, I was too late to realize it.

~2004~

I left my parents' care to my older sister, Elizabeth, who lived in Shelton, twenty miles from Chandler. In recent years she had tried over and over to urge them into a nursing home, but they had clung stubbornly to their own house, so stubbornly that my father had died there and not been discovered for two days.

That fact and others made me uncomfortable being alone in their house. It had never really been my home. My parents had moved there the year I left for college. When I returned on my first visit, I felt disconnected. Growing up I had slept north and south on Morse Street. That same bed felt unfamiliar pointing east and west on Harrison.

At some point during every visit since, I found myself walking past my real childhood home. It seemed that only through this ritual could I retreat beyond the messes of my later life to the joys of my childhood and a love for Chandler. Once again I set off toward Morse Street through the drizzle which had begun to fall. It occurred to me that this would likely be my last such journey. The burial of my father the next day would snip the final, fragile strand connecting me to Chandler.

The town looked withered to me as I walked up Brown Street. In my youth I had ridden my bicycle between towering elms, who like gentle giants, watched over my carefree play. They had dwarfed and shaded the white houses until disease had taken them. Their replacements were, as yet, poor substitutes, leaving the houses looking weak and unprotected. Those houses were the castles of my childhood memory. They had held my classmates, my adventures, my friends. Now, they were scarred by chipped paint and surrounded by moats of weedy grass. Nearly every block had at least one "For Sale" sign growing on the boulevard. It felt like a place from which others were escaping.

I jogged the last four blocks past the old high school to Morse Street. Those blocks had seemed so long as a boy. On cold days my brother, sister and I would beg my mother for a ride to school, and as a teen I usually drove, the bed of our pickup filling with friends along the way. Now the walk seemed nothing, a fraction of the five miles I do daily in California.

I measured my steps to avoid the sidewalk cracks, as into my mind came the old verse I had often chanted along this same stretch. "Step on a crack and break your mother's back." Would that I had been as concerned with my mother's heart in later years.

Each house along the way held a memory for me. At one time or another, I had delivered newspapers to all of them. Here was the Patch house. Old Irv claimed never to have smaller than a twenty; on collection day, I always brought a five and a ten to foul his plan to postpone paying. Mrs. Henshaw's house. She always called my father to complain if I accidently slammed the screen door on my early morning route. She was so deaf, I never understood how she could hear it at all.

Next came the Baptist Church, and beside it the parsonage, home of my close, boyhood friend, James Roberts, the minister's son. Pastor Jim Bob, as we called him, was one of the four friends with whom I passed most of the first third of my life. Four boys and one girl. Together we perpetrated more nonsense on the town of Chandler than Huck Finn had on the Mississippi during his legendary voyage.

I was glad to see that the garage, which we had twice nearly burned down, was still sitting alongside the parsonage. I was sad that it had long outlasted our friendship. As children we believe our friendships will go on forever. As I looked at Pastor Jim Bob's old house, the twists and turns that had wrenched the five of us apart hung on the edge of my mind like an impending migraine.

As always, a shiver ran through me as I approached the Fritz house. Denny Fritz, though somewhat older than me, had been a friend by geography. His house was simply so close to ours that coming outdoors at the same time brought us together. While it was not a close friendship, my stomach still nearly turned remembering how it had ended so badly.

And then I was at my house, 230 Morse Street. My first look produced disappointment. A later owner had stripped away the shrubbery, leaving the gray cement foundation naked. In my boyhood, my father had always kept the house a brilliant white with fresh green window trim. At some point this had been darkened to a sickly gray with a pink accent.

But the greatest violation of all was the enclosure of the front, screened porch. It appeared to have been done rather recently. The porch had been my realm. It had spanned the entire front of the house. On summer, air conditionerless days I would sit out there in one of the two

~Boomer~

enormous wicker rockers, creating my own breeze, waiting for life to grab hold and give me a shake.

Chapter 1
The Gravedigger and Other Childhood Tales

1956

For seven o'clock, it was way too hot, even for a summer evening. I rocked a little faster, trying to raise a breeze to dry me off. Out front on Morse Street a car crept by. It could only be Emil Sarcroft. Emil was Chandler's slowest driver. Whenever he drove past Ashcroft Park, all of us boys would rush to the sidewalk to see if we could walk as fast as Emil was driving. His concentration on the road was so intense that he never realized our mockery. Or if he did, his temperament was apparently as steady as his driving.

I methodically bounced a tennis ball against the wall in front of me below the screening. Again and again I made the toss. One thump on the floor, a second off the wall and back into my hand. Thump thump catch. Thump thump catch. I was able to keep a perfect rhythm of sound and motion, something that would have surprised my piano teacher. At eleven years old, and on this quiet Minnesota evening, I had nothing better to do.

When the ball returned this time, I swatted it across the porch and rocked myself out of the chair. Pressing my

~Boomer~

nose against one of the screens, I looked up Morse Street to the left to see an empty Ashcroft Park. It wasn't much, as parks go, a perfectly square block with a ragged baseball infield on the southeast corner and some functional, but uninspiring, playground equipment in left field.

As I looked back to the right, I discovered someone standing in the middle of the street in front of our house. It was Wayne Hoffart, one of my older brother, Tom's, best friends.

"Boomer," bellowed Wayne. "Ball in ten minutes. Be there!" While I could see Wayne clearly, the sun shining over the corner of the house kept him from recognizing at whom he was bellowing.

"Tom's still at piano lessons, Wayne." I didn't feel brave enough to call him Fart, as my brother would have. "He should be back pretty soon."

Wayne shaded his eyes. "Hey, Little Boomer. Does your mommy let you stay up this late at night? Tell that fathead brother of yours to get his butt to Ashcroft. There are home runs to be hit."

"I'll tell him as soon as he gets here," I said dutifully. "Hey, Wayne, can I play?"

"Sure Eugene. Come on over. We'll use you for second base. Bring a couple of bats with you, if you can lift them." Wayne jogged up the street to summon more players.

I gladly accepted Wayne's jibes as conditions for participation and headed for the garage to collect the bats. Nearly all of the boys in the neighborhood were about Tom's age, so I would be four years younger than most everyone else. The older boys were always looking for

~1956~

warm bodies to fill positions, so I almost always got to play.

Unlike many big brothers who would feel cramped having little brother on hand, Tom always encouraged me. He had even negotiated some special rules to compensate for my underdeveloped skills. Ashcroft was so small that the older boys could easily hit the ball well out of the park. To make it more of a challenge, the left-handers all batted right-handed and the right-handers left. Tom convinced the rest that I should bat right-handed, my natural side. It didn't really matter; I always made an out.

*****

I spit on my hands and re-entered the batter's box. The bases were loaded. I was so excited that my stomach hurt and I felt like I had to pee. I squeezed the bat and pictured myself driving the ball into the left field gap and sprinting around the bases as run after run scored ahead of me.

"Easy out here, Denny," called Wayne Hoffart from shortstop. "Just let him hit it."

My ears burned with the insult. I dug my feet into the dirt of the batters' box. Denny Fritz was pitching for the other team. Like me, he was younger than the other boys, but they had discovered he could throw strikes with acceptable regularity. Denny lofted the ball toward the plate. With my usual lack of patience, I lashed out at the ball considerably above my eyes. The ball rolled pitifully toward the second baseman. Denny Fritz slid to his left, cut it off, and before I had taken four steps from home plate, I was out.

"Crap," I muttered, tossing the bat to the side, narrowly missing Stretch Hanson.

~Boomer~

Stretch danced away from it. "Easy, Little Boomer. I want to live to bat another inning."

"Sorry."

I grabbed my glove and headed toward left field, where my teammates felt I could do the least damage. Normally, the weak link is placed in right field, but with almost everyone hitting left-handed, I seldom had to move, much less field a ball, in left. I found the spot that I had been matting down for the last five innings. Ashcroft didn't have the lush green grass of a proper outfield, but only tufts sticking up here and there from the brown clay.

I had been shagging flies off the bat of my brother earlier in the week, and I was almost to the point of wishing someone would inadvertently loft one in my direction. But until that happened, I was comfortable just standing and yelling an occasional, encouraging oath to our pitcher.

"Come on, Stretch. Throw him the dark one." I had been collecting a good supply of baseball lingo while listening to Dizzy Dean broadcast the game of the week on Saturday afternoons. "Rock and fire, big fellow. Rock and Fire." In my head I heard Diz breaking into his rendition of "Wabash Cannonball."

From center field Tom called to me, "Be ready, Gene. Deak likes to go the other way."

I took my glove off my head where it had been resting while I fished in my pockets for a stick of Juicy Fruit. No sooner was the mitt back on my left hand than Deak Turnbull whacked a line-drive toward left field. The sound of ball meeting bat told me immediately that the hit was solid and deep.

"I can do this," I said to myself. "I've been

practicing." Keeping my eye on the ball, I turned my back on the infield and began the chase.

"This is my chance to show Wayne Hoffart," I thought. I still had the ball in sight and was moving swiftly and gracefully (or so I thought) toward the spot where it would land. I felt the strength of Stan Musial propel my legs. My cap flew from my head. The ball seemed to accelerate and carry further than I had anticipated. I lengthened my stride to catch up.

At that moment, Emily Ashcroft, granddaughter of the man after whom the park had been named, was at her maximum forward peak in her swing in the left-center field playground, just one pendulum swing from disaster.

As I strained to make up ground, Emily was equally high in the other direction. I felt the ball getting just beyond my reach, so I leapt into the air with my arm fully extended, just as I had seen Mickey Mantle do last Saturday on "Game of the Week." So intent was my concentration that the warning shouts of my teammates went unheard.

As the ball hit the pocket of my glove and stuck, the feet of Emily Ashcroft hooked my left arm just above the elbow and continued upward to crash into my chin. In some odd equation of physics, our weight and momentum were equivalent; for a moment, we stopped one another, frozen in space and time.

That Emily didn't fly out backward, attests to how firmly a seven-year-old must grip the ropes of a swing. My glove, still clutching the ball, flew from my hand. I stood upright for an instant. Then my knees buckled, and I sank to the ground.

The next few minutes were a little fuzzy. My ears

were buzzing, but above that I heard a siren, and when Tom helped me sit upright, I realized it was Emily Ashcroft, wailing in a puddle of her friends. My teammates, used to their games ending abruptly because of personal injury or property damage, one by one patted me on the back and headed toward their homes.

Tom and Wayne Hoffart pulled me to my feet, and we slowly made our way across the park. In our front yard I felt a spell of dizziness, and Tom had to support me as we entered the house.

One look and my sister, Elizabeth, burst into tears, blubbering that her baby brother had been disfigured for life, and "Who would want to marry him now?" The crying and blubbering unnerved me slightly, but the prospect of escaping marriage had an oddly comforting effect.

Always calm, my mother adjourned to the kitchen to heat some soup, a wise choice, as it would be several days until I could chew comfortably.

My father took the occasion to once again tell the story of how he had dislocated his middle three fingers, crashing into the wall and robbing a Bancroft Iowa power hitter of a home run. I had learned to not expect sympathy from my father.

Tom helped me stagger to the bedroom we shared, as my father chuckled, "If you are going to run, you'd best pay better attention to what's ahead of you." In my foggy state, I kind of remembered having that thought just after Emily Ashcroft's knee smooched my nose against my cheek.

Later that evening Dr. Turnbull, Deak's father, stopped by to check on me. He doubted a concussion had occurred. He suspected that my nose had been broken, but

~1956~

since it had seemed to right itself, he recommended we leave it alone.

After the exam Dr. Turnbull said that Deak wanted me to know that he thought my catch was one of the best in the history of Ashcroft Park, and that no matter what happened after the collision, he considered the ball caught and himself out.

Nothing else mattered that night. Not the ringing in my ears or the throbbing behind my eyes or the puffy feeling in my nose. I had made one of the best catches in the history of Ashcroft Park!

*****

When my dad shook me awake the next morning at 6:00 A.M., I immediately wondered if Emily Ashcroft was as sore as I was. If I kept absolutely still, I felt fine, but over night my neck had stiffened, and any attempt to look to either side brought a sharp pain. I closed my eyes and tried to relax.

"Come on, Buster," my dad persisted. "Some people want to read their paper before noon." I delivered newspapers on the weekends. The route was really my brother's, but on Saturdays and Sundays I took over to give Tom a break and earn a little spending money.

My mother bustled into the room and peered at me over Dad's shoulder. "How you doing, honey? Is your nose sore? It doesn't look quite as swollen as last night."

"It's my neck," I whined. "It hurts to turn my head."

"Don't turn then," ordered my father. "Eyes front," he snapped, issuing one of the many military commands he enjoyed using on his children. "It'll loosen if you get up and move around a bit."

~Boomer~

"Oh, Glen, don't be silly. He can't deliver papers on a bicycle if he can't turn his head." It always amazed me that my gentle mother could stand up to and defeat my iron father. "Tom can do the route today. Can't you honey? You were in early last night." She moved to the other bed in the room. There was a groan as Tom rolled over and pulled the covers over his head.

"Thank you, dear," she said, as if Tom had enthusiastically accepted her gentle command. She returned to my side. "You sleep a little longer, Gene. The rest will do you good."

"It would do me good too," grumbled Tom from under the covers, but his plea went unnoticed.

My mother bent over me and adjusted my pillow. I appreciated the sympathetic gesture, but not the pain that shot down my spine.

"Do as you will," said Dad. "I'm off to the war. Tom, don't slam Mrs. Henshaws's screen door. She calls every time it happens, and I've got better things to do than listen to her gripes." There was a muffled grunt from Tom. Our father turned with military precision and marched from the room. He was not a man to dawdle or to kiss his family farewell.

"You go back to sleep now, honey," said my mom. "I'll probably be at work when you get up, so I'll leave some waffles in the fridge. Just heat them in the toaster. Come down to the store today and let me know how you are doing, if you feel like it." She gave me a peck on the forehead. "Tom, thank you for being the good big brother." I heard the door creak shut behind her.

Just before falling back to sleep I felt someone's face

close to mine. I opened one eye to see Tom's head looking at me sideways.

"You owe me one, Buddy. And I intend to collect," Tom said.

"Thanks, Tom," I mumbled, already half asleep.

*****

When I woke sometime later, it was with the strange sensation of being stuck to my pillow. My nose had evidently bled during my morning nap, and the blood had dried, securing me to the linen. I wasn't stuck very firmly, and a quick tug, accompanied by a slight sting, set me free. I was a little alarmed at the dark red stain on my pillow. I wasn't sure how much blood I had, but to make a stain that large, I must have leaked a sizable fraction of it.

I stumbled into the bathroom to survey the damage, which on first glance looked considerable. My nose appeared twice its usual size, and my lower lip wasn't at all the color it had been the day before. Splotches of dried blood decorated the bottom half of my face.

I turned on the cold water to begin the cleanup, but as I opened the cupboard to fetch a wash cloth, the phone rang. Tom was back in bed after his paper delivery, so I hurried to quiet the phone and let him sleep.

"Hello. Boomer residence," I said, immediately realizing that even my voice had been affected by last night's blow.

"Is this the Boomer Tobacco Emporium?" said a sort of distinguished voice. I recognized my good friend, Fud, being his usual dopey self.

As always, I played along. "Why, yes it is. How may we help you?"

~Boomer~

"Would you happen to have Sir Walter Raleigh in the can?"

"Yes, I believe we do." I looked at myself in the wall mirror and checked to see if I could still wiggle my nose. I could, but it hurt to do so.

"Well, could you let him out? He's suffocating. Ha, ha, ha."

"Very funny, Fud. That joke's as old as Gladys Dingman. What's up?"

"What's the matter with your voice? It sounds like you're talking in a tunnel."

"I got hit in the face last night playing ball."

"At least they got you in a spot that couldn't be made uglier. Anyway, get your face and your butt down to Sticks' house, man. We're having an early morning snack, and you are not going to believe what's on the menu."

"It'll have to be pretty good. Sticks' house is a long, dusty ride, and I am in considerable pain."

"Just get down here." Fud hung up. There was never really any question of my going. Whenever one of the five friends called, the other four gathered.

I retreated to the bathroom and gently dabbed the dried blood from my face, which I hoped would soon return to its former size and color. I knew that I was in for a good deal of kidding and little sympathy from the four friends I would shortly face. I gently twisted my head back and forth, happily discovering that my father had been right. A little movement loosened it up.

In the kitchen I scribbled, "Gone to Sticks" on a napkin and taped it to the fridge from which I grabbed two of my mother's waffles. I spread a generous layer of grape jelly between them. A cold waffle sandwich was one of my favorites. I donned my Boston Red Sox cap and headed for the garage and my bicycle.

My house was on a hill, and Kent "Sticks" Skulsky lived near downtown in the valley, so it was always my goal to travel between the two without pedaling. Our front yard had a short downward dip which set me rolling. If I took the right course, catching extra speed from the sloping, narrow alley beside the Lutheran Church, and if I encountered no cross traffic, I could coast the twelve blocks and dismount without so much as a single push of my feet.

This morning, however, I slammed on my brakes a block short of my destination. Lying on its side in front of Kent's house was a semi trailer, its contents of boxes strewn along the sides of Highway 17.

"Not again!" I said out loud. I took the last bite of my waffle sandwich and licked the jelly residue from my fingers.

The highway, which entered Chandler from the north, bent sharply to the right just at the bottom of a long hill. It had been rebuilt two years earlier. Upon completion, it was determined that the curve entering town sloped the wrong way. This was discovered after a cattle truck went off the end, badly damaging a fifty-foot elm tree, and landing on its side in Skulsky's front yard.

The only good result was, that except for one broken leg, the cattle were unharmed, and the town kids, unaccustomed to such chores, spent a happy half-day herding them into a make-shift coral in the parking lot next to the bowling alley.

Since then, a bread truck, a tire truck and a laundry

~Boomer~

truck had battered other trees on the Skulsky's boulevard, leaving only two oaks to protect the house. As I pulled into the yard, two men started chain saws. Now only one tree would be left to defend against runaway vehicles.

I wheeled my bike between two cardboard boxes with "Schlitz" on them. Liquid dripped out of both. I dipped my index finger into a puddle and touched it to my tongue. The bitter taste made my nose wrinkle and sting.

"Hey, kid! Get the hell away from there," yelled one of the men over the buzz of his saw. "This ain't happy hour."

I dropped my bike into Stick's yard and knocked on the front door. Nobody came to the other side. I banged several more times, each a bit louder, but with no result. Two chainsaws were now roaring at top volume, and I couldn't even hear my own fist meet the wood. I guessed that no one else could either, so I opened the door and stepped inside.

The kitchen was empty, so I wandered into the living room. "Sticks," I called out.

From up the stairs I heard a giggle and then a chorus of "Shhhs."

I went to the base of the stairs, "Fud? Gracie? You guys up there?"

"Boomer, is that you?" It was Sticks.

"Yeah. Can I come up?"

"Anybody with you?"

"Only Marilyn Monroe," I said.

From above me came a burst of laughter, much louder than my rather lame response deserved.

"Come on up. You can hang Marilyn's mink coat in

18

the hall." It was an uncharacteristic remark from the usually unfunny Sticks.

I bounded up the stairs, taking three at a time, and stuck my head sideways around the door frame. Seated in a circle on the floor were my four best friends in the whole world. To my right, at three o'clock, was Pastor Jim Bob, unfairly christened for his father's occupation. At six o'clock, her back to me, sat Grace Maculum, Gracie or Miss Mac or just Mac, depending on the formality of the circumstance. At nine o'clock, sat our host, Kent "Sticks" Skulsky, basketball, football and baseball star of the sixth grade. At high noon, with a rather crooked grin on his face, sat Fred Untiedt, Fud.

We lived in a time and place where every kid in every neighborhood had a nickname. We took great pride in playing with our friends' real names until we devised the perfect handle. Thus, if we pulled just the right letters out of Fred Untiedt, we were left with Fud, a name that perfectly fit our pudgy friend.

"Sticks" was a descriptive rather than a phonetic nickname. It described Kent Skulsky bony legs. And since it was those legs on which he could leap above us to shoot a basketball, or race a hundred yards in almost no time, "Sticks" stuck.

My name needed no adjustment. Boomer made as good a nickname as it did a surname. So, from the time I was in second grade, I had always been Boomer. My older brother Tom was Boomer too. For a while he was Big Boomer and I was Little Boomer, but as I got bigger, we became just Boomers.

The unfortunate one was my sister, Elizabeth. How

~Boomer~

my folks could have overlooked that everyone would call her Betty, is beyond me. And so, no matter how many times she corrected people that her name was Elizabeth, she was called the percussive Betty Boomer more times than not.

So here sat my oddly named friends, Sticks, Fud, Miss Mac, and Pastor Jim Bob. In their midst sat one of the cardboard boxes I had seen scattered across the Skulsky's front yard. Atop the box stood a dozen or so empty brown bottles, identical to those in the right hands of each of my friends, except for Sticks, who as a southpaw, held his in his left hand. I stood up into the doorway with my bruised mouth hanging about three-quarters open.

There was a pause when all four stared at me, their mouths one by one dropping open to mirror mine. Fud broke the silence. "Good grief, Boomer, didn't anyone tell you that a face-first slide doesn't actually mean you slide on your face."

"All right, all right, I know. I'm uglier than usual. Can we leave it at that and cut the sympathy short?" I said, taking a step into the room.

"Well then, welcome to Stick's Tavern," said Fud, raising his bottle above his head. "Can we interest you in a beverage?" Fud was by far the smartest of our group and the only one who would ever use a word like beverage. Such language was why, if you mentioned Fud's name to a school classmate outside of our group of five, the word "nerd" would usually enter the conversation.

"How'd you get this stuff?" I said, giving Grace and Pastor Jim Bob a shove and sitting between them. Gracie fell over onto her side and lay giggling, something I had

~1956~

seldom seen her do.

"Let me tell this time, Sticks, my friend," said Fud. He rose to his feet rather unsteadily and struck a dramatic pose. Already Fud was developing as an actor. "It was pitch dark when the fatal truck tipped this morning. It woke up everybody on the block when it hit that tree. Sticks and his dad were the first ones out there, but then people came running from every which way."

"You should have seen Paul Harrison's mom come out in this flimsy red nightie," said Sticks. "Jeez, you could see everything." Sticks was a really shy kid. It was obvious that the beer was making him more vocal than usual.

"While everyone was up by the cab looking after the driver, the sly Stickman hauled one of the cases of beer around back and hid it under the porch," continued Fud. "After his folks left for work, he brought it up here."

"I picked a lucky one," said Sticks. "Only two bottles were broken."

"So far the rest seem to be just fine," said Gracie. She looked through her bottle and giggled again.

"We gotta be careful though," said Sticks. "If my folks ever find out about this, I'll be dead."

"Oh, well, Now that we've got the hydrogen bomb, we're liable to all blow up anyway," said Pastor Jim Bob. Pastor Jim Bob had recently gotten a new chemistry set and was much into things blowing up. He pulled another bottle from the case, flipped off the cap with a bottle opener and offered it to me.

I received the bottle skeptically. "How long have you guys been at this?" I asked. The number of empties and the slurred voice with which Fud had told the tale,

~Boomer~

suggested that I was a very late comer. I took a little sip and flinched when the liquid burned my injured mouth.

"About an hour," said Sticks. "I called your place, but I got your mom. She said you got hurt playing ball last night and needed your rest."

"Are you all better after your nap?" mocked Fud.

"I guess, but this cut on the inside of my mouth really hurts." I turned to Gracie and pulled my lower lip down, revealing the swollen gash that had resulted from Emily Ashcroft's knee pushing my chin into my teeth.

A shocked look came across Gracie's face. "Oh, ick," she cried. "It looks like raw meat."

The sight of my bloated lip, in combination with the better part of two bottles of beer on an unaccustomed stomach, was too much for her. She leapt to her feet and sprinted for the hall bathroom.

Sticks raced behind her shouting, "Hurry, Mac. We just got the upstairs carpeted. My mom will kill me if you heave on it."

In the distance we heard Grace retching and moaning. Sticks returned to report that she had gotten accurately positioned above the toilet before losing both the beer and her breakfast.

"Shouldn't somebody help her?" said Pastor Jim Bob.

"Be my guest," said Sticks. "It smells gross in there. I had to get out or I'd be the next one losing my cookies."

We listened. All quiet. "You all right in there, Gracie?" I called. "You need any help?"

From the bathroom came a groan. "I feel awful. What do I do now?"

~1956~

"You can lie down on my bed if you want," Sticks called to her. "Just don't throw up on anything."

"Maybe later. Right now I think I'd better stay close to the john."

"Poor Gracie," said Pastor Jim Bob. "Maybe we shouldn't have any more beer or the same thing will happen to us." He set down his half full bottle.

"What do you guys feel like?" I asked. I had only taken two small sips from my bottle and wasn't feeling anything at all except a strong desire to get some lemonade to wash the awful taste out of my mouth.

"You know," said Sticks, "when you wake up in the morning and you slept all night on one of your arms, and you try to get out of bed, but your arm doesn't come with the rest of you? That's kinda what my head feels like."

"I'm really dizzy," said Pastor Jim Bob. "I'm not sure I can stand up. How long does this stuff stay with you?" He did stand, but staggered and wobbled before catching his balance.

"Hey man. Good moves," said Sticks. "You look like that rock and roll guy, Elvis Presley. Have you seen him yet?"

"Yup," said Pastor Jim Bob. "My father is getting ready to give a sermon on how he is the anti-Christ. I think my folks would rather have me drunk than listening to Elvis. I'm not feeling so hot either." He plunked back down into his place.

"You pansies," chided Fud. "That's called a buzz. That's the fun of it. If you didn't get it, you might as well have a Dr. Pepper truck tip over in your yard."

It was always Fud who drove us forward on these

~Boomer~

kinds of escapades. While all of us gladly took part, without Fud as our catalyst, our lives would have been a lot more like our parents probably wanted them to be, but a lot less fun. Whenever Fud began a sentence with "I wonder," it was a sure bet that we'd be into mischief before long.

Suddenly the entire room was filled with a strong, sickening odor.

"Oh gross," said Fud. "Who let one? That's the worst fart I've ever smelled."

Three of us pinched our noses and frantically fanned the air in front of us toward the two at our sides. Only Sticks sat motionlessly in a gesture of certain guilt.

"Holy Toledo, Sticks," said Fud. "Are you trying to peel the paint off the walls? Ugh, I can't breathe."

"I'm sorry. Jeez," said Sticks, "I think it's the beer. My stomach is starting to feel kind of funny."

"I know what you mean," said Pastor Jim Bob. "I'm about ready to cut one loose myself."

"Oh, no!" I complained. "Yours are bad enough on a normal day. Man, Sticks, between you guys and Gracie, you'll have to have the place fumigated before your folks get home."

Sticks stood unevenly, waddled to the side of the room and opened a window. "We'd better start cleaning this mess up. What are we going to do with the rest of the beer and all these empty bottles?"

"You know," said Fud, "you can light a fart."

"What?" I asked.

"If you put a lighter down by somebody's rear end and they fart, it looks like fire shoots out of their butt."

"You're crazy!" said Sticks.

"He's probably right," said Pastor Jim Bob, who seemed not to know much of anything, except in the field of science where he bordered on genius. "A fart is just gas, and if you set a flame to most any gas, it will burn."

"Well, I've got to see this," I said. "Who's going to let one rip for the good of scientific discovery?"

All eyes turned to Pastor Jim Bob. Even without the intake of beer, Pastor Jim Bob regularly added sounds and smells to the atmosphere in which we played.

One look at the three of us, and he could see that a protest would fall on deaf ears. "All right," he whined, "but somebody needs to guard the door so that Gracie doesn't see me."

"My sister has a lighter in her desk," said Sticks. "I'll get it while you lower your pants, J.B. I can't believe this is all happening in my bedroom. I'm going to get killed." He ran out of the room, while Pastor Jim Bob unbuckled, and Fud went to the bathroom to check on Gracie.

Pastor Bob started to lower his pants, when he suddenly jerked them to his waist. "I .. I.. I don't want to do this," he stammered. "One of you guys can."

Sticks came back in with the lighter in his hand, followed by Fud. "Gracie is laid out in the bathtub," said Fud. "She says her head feels like a watermelon and she's about that green."

"Pastor Bob's backing out," I said. "Says he doesn't want to double for a blow torch."

"Come on, Jim Bob," said Fud. "We gotta see this work. If it does, we could demonstrate it for science show-and-tell this fall."

"Very funny," said Pastor Bob. "Then one of you

guys can get all the glory."

Fud had by this time slid around behind Pastor Jim Bob, who in his dizzy state, was letting his pants sag a bit anyway. Fud grabbed them on both sides and yanked them to his knees.

For an instant, the four of us stood in silence. Then three of us burst into laughter.

"Are those boxer shorts?" Fud howled.

"And is that Old Glory I see?" I said.

"My mom got them for me for the 4th of July. I forgot I had them on. I didn't have any other clean ones this morning."

"Well, get that flag to half mast," said Fud, "and let's get on with the experiment."

"Let me shut the drapes," said Sticks. "I don't want to gross out the neighbors."

"And cut the lights, Boomer," said Fud. "We'll be able to see the flame better if it's darker."

We performed our chores and gathered back at Pastor Jim Bob's side.

"All right. Bend over and let her rip, Jim Bob," said Fud. "Just don't burn the house down."

Pastor Jim Bob bent down and grabbed his ankles. Fud took the lighter from Sticks, lit it, and held it two inches from the focus of our attention.

We all held our breath. Pastor Jim Bob gave a grunt and then a second, but no sound emitted from his other end. "I'm not sure I can do this under this kind of pressure," he said.

"Oh, come on," said Sticks. "In phy ed you do it any time you want to."

~1956~

The lighter went out and Fud had to flick it several times to relight it. "Come on, Jim Bob. This thing is running out of fuel."

"Maybe I am too," said Pastor Bob.

"Come on, J.B.," I said. "The scientific community is counting on you."

Pastor Bob re-gripped his ankles, took a quick breath, blew out his cheeks, and pressed to the rear. From his lower cheeks came a roar, and with it a burst of air which ignited in the flame and shot backward a good two feet, softly singeing my hand.

"Oh ick," I yelled. "I've been farted on."

"Wow!" said Sticks. "It really works. We gotta see that again."

"One of you guys do it," said Pastor Jim Bob. "I want to see it once too."

"Nobody else could supply fuel like that," said Fud. "We'll move you over by the mirror and then you can watch yourself."

Pastor Bob shuffled over to the bureau, his pants and underwear and his two beers keeping him from walking steadily.

"The mirror is too high," he complained. "If I bend over, I won't get to see it."

"We'll stand you on a chair," Fud said. "Boomer, bring the one from Sticks' desk."

I brought the chair and Fud and Sticks lifted a squirming Pastor Jim Bob onto the seat.

"See if you can sustain it a little longer this time," said Fud. "That first one was powerful, but it went out so fast." He lit the flame.

~Boomer~

Pastor Jim Bob squatted down on the chair and turned his head toward the mirror. He took a deep breath, pushed his elbows outward and clenched his fists. Color rushed to his face. He looked like he was prepared to bench press about five hundred pounds.

For five seconds there was perfect silence. Then a rumble came forth. Gas caught flame and shot backward in a bolt of blue and yellow. But this time the roar continued and the flame stayed true and even lengthened its reach.

As it died out, we cheered. "Well done, Pastor Bob."

"Jeez, we could roast weenies on that baby," cried Fud.

Suddenly Pastor Jim Bob gasped. We looked up to the mirror where his eyes were focused in horror. In the reflection we saw an open-mouthed Gracie Maculum, standing in the doorway, her eyes fixed on Pastor Jim Bob's rear end. Like the rest of us, Jim Bob had frozen, unable to reach down and cover his embarrassment.

Gracie seemed unable to move or utter, seemed unaware that the horrid sight had again repulsed her stomach, that the remaining food in her system was rushing upward, about to soil Mrs. Skulsky's new carpet.

Fud, too, had frozen, except for his hand, which had flinched slightly to the right, bringing the still burning lighter into contact with Pastor Jim Bob's tender behind.

When the flame finally penetrated the numbness of Pastor Jim Bob's drunken sensory system, he shrieked and leapt from the chair, careening around the room, only with enough control to side-step the weeping Gracie and her pool of vomit.

It is uncertain how much further the disaster would

have reached, had not a stunned Mrs. Skulsky walked into the room after having checked that the cases of beer had been removed from her doorstep.

Our parents tried to be very stern with us and acted most disappointed that we should misbehave in such a way. My mother, however, had trouble keeping a smile from her face that night when she declared the sentence for our crimes. I sensed that Mrs. Skulsky's description had been more humorous than horrified. While my mother tried her best to deliver a harsh scolding, my father sat in the corner behind his newspaper, occasionally peeking over and shaking his head with a look that said, "Oh well, I suppose one of them had to be a dimwit."

We were not allowed to see one another for a week and for a second week could only meet in pairs. It was torturous, for it had been years since we had been apart for more than a day in a summertime.

Near the end of that summer, an implement truck lost control on the north-side curve and took out the last tree in Skulsky's boulevard. With nothing left to protect her home, Mrs. Skulsky raised such a ruckus with the highway department that they reconstructed the curve to make it safer.

*****

That's the way it often went with our group of five. We were always looking for new adventure, and often it led us into disaster. They were generally harmless disasters, and our parents most often just shook their heads at the mishaps.

Fud, who usually supplied our excuses, had the ability to charm adults away from anger. The rest of us just

~Boomer~

sort of merrily stumbled along together.

As it turned out, not being able to see the group for a week was a bigger deal than I ever imagined.

Without my usual gang, I went in search of substitutes. The most convenient was Denny Fritz, a boy a year older than me who lived just two houses away.

Denny and I had bouts of friendship in the past, but the last time we had hung out together, he had talked me into shoplifting at the Ben Franklin, and I, of course, had been the one to get caught. With some sort of stupid kid loyalty, I had protected Denny and not explained his role in our exploit to my parents as they drove me home from the police station.

My father would have just as soon left me there to strengthen the lesson I was learning, but again with her quiet power, my mother insisted I be sprung.

I resented Denny's getting off scot-free enough to steer clear of him for a few weeks.

On Sundays my family often headed north of Chandler to Benton, where my Aunt Amanda and Uncle Jack lived on a farm. For many years it was understood that these were family outings, which all members would attend. My father controlled them right down to the polka music blaring on the radio in the car.

But gradually my brother and sister joined forces to test the rules and soften my father's discipline in such matters.

Sometimes these trips excited me, particularly during pheasant hunting season, because my uncle's farm was rich with birds.

This Sunday there was no special attraction.

~1956~

Tom and Elizabeth had begged out of the trip to do something with friends, and I really wanted to stay behind as well.

I had not impressed my parents with my behavior in the last week, so they were inclined to take me along where they could keep a closer eye. With my reputation already soiled, I knew whining would only weaken my position, so I tried bribery instead. Washing my dad's truck and weeding the flower garden were impressive offers, since the only chores I ever did were those assigned by my father.

Just when I was feeling very good about my chances to stay behind, my dad reminded me that I still had several days before I could go near my good friends, and that I had better not even think about violating that restriction.

As their car pulled out of sight, I decided that if I were to ever get out of the doghouse, I had better play things straight with my parents on this occasion. Besides, if I scrubbed and weeded quickly, I could still have most of the day to find something worthwhile to do. I turned on the hose and aimed it at my dad's Standard Oil truck parked in the driveway.

When I was about halfway through my mother's weeds, Denny Fritz wandered by with a cane fishing pole over his shoulder. "Hey, Eugene. Hate to pull you away from anything so obviously entertaining, but would you want to do some river fishin'."

It took me about two seconds to decide. After all, I had been a model child for almost two straight hours, and I was really ready for some fun. "Yeah. Just let me get a pole of some kind."

~Boomer~

In the garage, I quickly traded my weeding tools for one of my dad's old fishing poles. I knew better than to take the one he had just gotten himself for Father's Day.

With my tackle box clanging, I hurried down Morse Street to catch Denny. "Where we gonna fish from?"

"Thought I'd go down by the Cedar St. Bridge. You can crawl up under it and get right over the water. I've had some good luck there."

The Fox River ran through the downtown area of Chandler, a block east and parallel to Main Street. Cedar Bridge was about seven blocks from our house. Along the way I practiced casting into people's front yards.

Denny dominated the conversation along the way. While only a year older, he was much taller and bigger than I was. His shoulders were slightly stooped and his walk somewhat plodding.

"That was cool that you didn't squeal on me for that shoplifting thing. Once you got nailed, I got the hell out of there. There wasn't nothin' I could do but get caught or get away, and I figured getting away was better. I been nailed a couple other times in old Ben Franklin. The cops told me if I got caught again, I might get sent up."

"Sent up where?"

"Beacon Lake. Reform school. You know, the Big House. My dad says they're just bluffing. Were your folks really ticked off?"

"My dad yelled at me a bunch, and I got grounded for a couple weeks, but it wasn't so bad. Jeez, reform school, huh."

"Just for lifting a few things from Ben Franklin? I doubt it. Anyway, I been staying out of there. Coast to

Coast is an easier target anyway. With all the piles of stuff in there, no one sees you doing anything."

Denny wiped the shock of red hair out of his eyes with his free hand, coughed and spit a gob into the grass at our side. I thought about following suit, but decided that I should perhaps practice on my own before spitting in public.

A little more chatter brought us to the river bank near Cedar Bridge. The Fox had flooded that spring, and was still filled to the brim. Two hundred yards down stream, water rushed over the dam at the power plant. It was below the dam that we had fished the summer before.

That summer had followed a dry spring, so that no water came over the dam. In the quiet water below, large fish of all kinds lazily floated. That is, lazily, until we got there.

One of the older kids in town got the idea of spearing them, so for several afternoons, a bunch of us had shown up with a variety of weapons. Some had actual ice fishing spears, but others came with pitchforks or even knives taped to broom handles.

Later we learned that it was against the law, but below the dam was pretty much out of sight, and for a few days, no one discovered us.

The water was about waist deep on me, (thigh deep on most of the participants), and clear enough that you could see the bottom. About ten of us wandered quietly, staring downward, weapons poised for attack. When we spotted a northern or a catfish or a carp, we would slide closer to within arms distance, slowly raise our spears above our heads, and thrust downward.

~Boomer~

The fish seemed to believe that this was safe territory, and to be enjoying the sunshine. Anyway, they were lethargic and easy to hit, even for me, the smallest of the group.

For several days, we hauled dozens of whoppers out of the river. We buried most of them on the bank, but each took one home that we thought our parents would believe we caught through legitimate means.

This might have gone on throughout the summer, had it not been for the unfortunate act of Arnold (Bull) Westersie. Bull was one of Chandler's best football players, a tight end whose pass catching records have yet to be eclipsed. Sadly, Bull's hand-eye coordination was not matched by his hand-brain counterpart.

On the fourth morning of our expedition, Bull was fishing with his father's pitchfork. He spotted a small northern, which made a rather aggressive attempt at escape by swimming toward him. As Bull raised his spear, the frightened fish swam between his legs.

Forgetting that his feet were buried in the mud at the ends of his legs, Bull plunged downward with the pitchfork. His aim was true, and he pierced the fish squarely in the middle. Unfortunately, the pitchfork continued downward and stabbed his foot as well.

Had he not been named Bull before, the howl he let out would have earned him the title, and it brought the rest of us quickly wading toward him.

"God, I speared myself. Help me to shore. Help me to shore," he screamed. That process was made difficult, not only because Bull was the largest of the fishermen, but also by the fact that the pitchfork was not only firmly stuck,

~1956~

but had pinned the wriggling fish to the top of his foot.

In an attempt to quiet Bull's howling, one of the other high school boys jerked the pitchfork loose, freeing Bull, but not the fish. Bull fell over into the river, as a pool of red began to surround his feet.

At the hospital Bull blurted out the whole story of our fishing escapades, named names, and estimated dead fish counts. It became somewhat of a community scandal, long before environmental protection entered our vocabulary. Needless to say, all Chandler children were forbidden from ever approaching an unfrozen river with anything but a fishing pole.

But this summer the spring rains had swollen the river, and there was no danger that anyone would be foolhardy enough to wade into the rushing water. In fact, earlier in the spring I thought I remembered my parents warning me to stay way clear of the river because of its flooded state, but those warnings were so long ago, had I thought about them at all, I would have decided that they no longer counted.

By this time Denny had climbed one of the bridge abutments. Its graduated construction was like a staircase, almost inviting us to climb. I followed, and we ascended about eight feet.

A few feet below the surface of the road, a huge cement beam reached out across to another abutment in the middle of the river, and from there to the third on the far bank. The beam was about three feet wide, and if you stooped, you could walk out above the river and sit just below the roadway.

This Denny did without a moment's pause. I

~Boomer~

hesitated and looked down into the swirling river, keeping my left hand firmly on the abutment. I was not a swimmer and had never been especially comfortable around water.

"Come on, Eugene," Denny called to me as he sat on the beam, swinging his legs out over the river. "Get your butt and your pole out here. You can't fish over dry land."

I cautiously released the abutment, ducked my head the necessary twelve inches to clear the upper surface, and started out toward Denny. The walkway was plenty wide, little different from walking down any of Chandler's sidewalks, but having to walk stooped over, and seeing the eight-foot drop to the river, made me take very short, careful steps. I eventually reached the middle and sat next to Denny, but was not yet ready to hang my legs over the edge.

Just then a car drove over the bridge. The whirring of the rubber tires on the pavement was amplified by the cavity in which we sat. I started to put both hands up to my ears, but before I could get them there, the sound softened, and the car left the other side of the bridge. It was an oddly pleasing sound, and made my teeth vibrate just a little. From then on, I looked forward to more cars crossing.

Denny had brought all the necessities for our expedition, a Folgers coffee can filled with worms and a bucket to put the fish in when we caught them. He had filled the bucket with ice and inserted two bottles of Coke.

From the can we each drew a wriggling worm and baited our hooks. This I could do as well as Denny, having fished often on Clear Lake with my father, who even insisted that the squeamish Elizabeth bait her own hook.

We threw our lines into the river. The swift current

grabbed our bobbers and pulled them downstream until our lines became taut. Denny reached into the bucket and pulled out a bottle opener. He handed me his fishing pole, flipped off the cap of one of the Cokes, and traded it for the return of his pole.

"Hey, thanks," I said. It suddenly felt very good to be doing something slightly daring, and to be accepted by someone older than myself. I wished that I had brought something to eat to share with Denny in return for the coke.

We fished without much luck that afternoon. Denny caught a couple of little crappies, and I got one fairly large bullhead, but after an hour and a half of little action, we decided to give up and look for other excitement.

Denny stood up, crouched beneath the roadway, and began reeling in his line. When I tried to do the same, I discovered mine firmly stuck on something.

"Oh, crap," I said. "My line is hung up."

"You're probably in some weeds. Give it a tug and it should come loose."

Keeping my left hand at the bottom of my pole, I grabbed just above the reel with my right. I leaned backward and tugged firmly. I could feel the far end of my line move slightly, as if it were dragging some heavy object. I put both hands to the left side of my head and pulled harder.

Suddenly the line broke, and my pole snapped backward. Unfortunately, it snapped right into Denny's face. It didn't hit him hard, but hard enough to surprise him and make him flinch upward. There wasn't room for his entire height, and his head cracked against the above roadway. The blow robbed him of his balance, and before

~Boomer~

I could reach out, he plunged forward, knocking the bucket of fish over the edge and carrying his fishing pole with him into the swirling river.

"Denny," I yelled.

When he hit the water, he submerged immediately, and to my horror, did not resurface. Denny was a good swimmer, but the blow must have knocked him unconscious, or stunned him enough to keep him from struggling. My breathing doubled its rate, and I started to feel dizzy.

I knelt on my hands and knees and peered into the river, trying to gauge how far the current might have carried him and where he might come up. Nothing. Only the whirling currents of the river.

Afraid of joining Denny in the river, I left my pole behind and frantically crawled along the beam to the south abutment. I was gasping and crying as I scrambled to the ground and ran along the river bank.

I kept my eyes on the water, praying that Denny would bob to the surface and start swimming to shore. I knew that I could be of little help. I was probably the only one in my class at school who couldn't swim, and knew that the current would quickly sweep me away. Still nothing broke the swirling surface of the river.

"Denny!" I yelled. "Denny!" over and over. I knew he couldn't hear me, but I had to do something.

I was approaching the dam a few hundred yards beyond Cedar Bridge. I ran faster hoping I might see Denny wash over the dam and into the shallower water below. The dam was only a five-foot drop, and the water below it far less turbulent. Maybe there Denny could regain control and make his way to shore. Out of breath, I flopped in the grass just below the dam and kept my eyes fixed on its top rim. Nothing.

My hysteria increased. My gasps were deeper and I moaned as if I were beaten. "How could he not have come over the dam by this time? The river is moving so fast." Then I saw that the rim of the dam had captured numerous tree branches and pieces of brush. "Could his body have gotten hung up in one of those branches?" The thought of Denny as a body sent a chill through me.

For a long time I stared at the top of the dam and sobbed. Something kept me from moving, from going to seek help. Probably it was my own part in the incident.

It had happened so quickly, but the image that was stuck in my mind was of my fishing pole striking Denny's face just before he plunged from our perch and into the river. If I hadn't pulled so hard, or in his direction, Denny would still have been with me, fishing from under the bridge. Exhausted, I let my head sag between my knees. I don't know if I fainted or dozed off or what, but suddenly I came to with a start.

I got up, climbed the grassy hill by the bridge and started running toward Main Street. As usual, Sunday afternoon Chandler was vacant. Not a single person or car was between me and my father's gas station at the far end of town. Almost relieved to not encounter another person, I once again began to run, this time toward home. Perhaps my brother would be there and could help me. I ran the eight blocks at full speed, and reached home totally winded.

I exploded through the front door and into an

~Boomer~

empty house. "Tom?" I called. "Is anybody here?" There wasn't.

I went to my bedroom, flopped on the bed and was overcome by another fit of crying. This was the worst day of my life. How could something like this happen? It was my fault that Denny was somewhere in the river. And what was I going to do about it now?

It had taken me a long time to get to that question, but now I realized that I did, in fact, need to do something. I was the only one who knew where Denny was, and I needed to let someone else know.

I ran out the door and back down toward the river. This time when I reached the stop sign on Main Street, two cars were waiting for each other to cross.

Completely out of breath, I ran up to a car with an open window and shouted, "You've got to help me. Please. My friend fell in the river, and I'm afraid he's drowned. Please. Help me!"

The driver of the car jumped out and grabbed me by the arm. "Where did he fall in?" he said urgently.

"Cedar Bridge." I pointed.

The man shouted to the woman to bring the police, and then turned back to me. "Show me where he fell in."

The rest of that afternoon was a blur of unhappy activity. I returned with the stranger to the river, pointed to where we had been, where Denny had fallen. Almost immediately a police car arrived, but it was fifteen minutes or more before a rescue fire truck followed.

All anyone could do is walk back and forth along the riverbank, looking helplessly to where Denny's body might be. Finally, divers were brought in, and they quickly

~1956~

located the body caught up in the tree branches hung up above the dam.

I was hysterical most of time, and the kind stranger to whom I had first blurted my story stayed with me. And when they dragged Denny's body out of the water, he walked me further up the shoreline, so I wouldn't have to see. I did look back and see them performing artificial respiration, but it was no use. They soon stopped and zipped the body into a plastic liner. The police then talked with me. Among the questions was the one I feared, "How had Denny fallen into the river?" I told them part of the truth, that he had hit his head on the cement above us and lost his balance. I didn't tell them or anyone else that my pole had struck him immediately before. All of their other questions I was able to answer truthfully and accurately.

Amazingly, the question that never came up was, "How long was it between the time he fell and the time I found help on Main Street?" It seemed assumed that I had directly sought help. The couple I had stopped, strangers in town, seemed not to notice that I had come at them from the other direction, away from the river. I was so emotional the whole time, that everyone treated me gently. The fact that I had caused Denny to fall, and had not immediately sought help, never came out.

*****

Those facts bothered me tremendously in the weeks that followed. It was not a happy summer. I spent lots of time by myself and found enjoyment in nothing. There was an extra tension around our household, and I knew that I was the reason.

It was like I was suddenly afraid of my parents, at

~Boomer~

least afraid that they would discover the part I had played in Denny's death. I began to withdraw. As soon as I finished eating, I would leave the dinner table for my room, and I seldom spent the evening with them watching television, something I had done regularly for years. They seemed a bit frightened of me as well, or at least uncertain as to how they could bring me back.

My older brother and sister rose to the occasion. We had always gotten along fairly well, and I genuinely liked Elizabeth and Tom. That summer I treasured them. They knew that I was hurting and were unbelievably patient with me.

Tom was a Chandler treasure. He had everything going for him. He was handsome and dashing with thick black hair. He was smart, far and away the best in his class. But beyond all that, he was incredibly kind and thoughtful, someone everybody liked. That summer he took me along on outings for which a normal brother would have begged to leave me behind.

Elizabeth, too, was a paragon of strengths, musically, academically. On top of that she was beautiful, someone whom I would have added to my list of desirable mates had she not been related. Every so often, Elizabeth would just grab and hug me. Normally I would have squirmed to get away and complained bitterly that she was embarrassing me, but that summer I just let her hold me and welcomed the warmth.

At first, my four best friends were uncomfortable with me and mostly stayed away, probably on instructions from their parents. The fact that we had been forbidden to play together was totally forgotten, but a new barrier

~1956~

seemed to keep us apart for a time after Denny drowned.

Oddly, it was my mother, rather than the police, who seemed to suspect that I wasn't telling the whole story. Several times at dinner and around the house I would glance up to find her looking at me. There seemed to be questions in her eyes, and I was afraid of what those questions might be and hoped they would continue unasked. My avoidance of her must have raised her concern.

One night she stopped by my bedroom. My brother, Tom, was on a date, so I was alone in the dark.

"Is everything all right, Gene?" I couldn't see her face, but only her outline in the light of the doorway.

"Yes. I'm just kind of tired tonight, so I thought I'd turn in early."

"Don't want to watch *Gunsmoke*? Have some popcorn with your dad?"

"No thanks. I'd just as soon stay here."

"You've been really quiet." She moved closer and sat on the edge of my bed. "Is it Denny? Is that what's bothering you?"

I was thankful it was dark, or I'm sure the blush on my face would have further given me away.

"You know, it sometimes helps to talk about things. What happened to Denny was a terrible thing, and your father and I are so sorry that you had to go through that."

I couldn't find my voice. Thoughts were rushing around in my head, but it was like the path to my mouth was blocked.

"Is there anything you want to tell us about that day?" There it was. She knew I was keeping something

~Boomer~

back.
    I knew if I tried to speak I would burst into tears and blurt out the story. And who knew what would happen after that. Finally, I managed to utter a breathy "No."
    If she had pressed me, I surely would have crumbled and revealed my terrible guilt, but she somewhat grudgingly accepted my "no" and got up from the bed.
    "Well, if you ever want to talk more about it, you just come to me or your father." She leaned over and kissed me on the forehead. "We love you, Gene, and we are just so thankful that nothing happened to you as well that awful day."
    Nothing happened to me. I wanted to cry out, "Maybe something should have happened to me." But I lay perfectly still and held my breath.
    My mother squeezed my shoulder and walked into the lighted hallway. It was then that I realized something had happened to me that day at the river, and it would be with me for the rest of my life.
    I hardly slept at all that night. I lay awake wondering if I should tell her the whole story of that afternoon by the river. I asked myself, "What would it help?" "What would it hurt?" And the answers were never clear enough to drive me to action.
    Finally, I decided that I was never going to tell the story, that somehow luck had spared me on the day it had taken Denny. But on that same night, I also decided that I am not an honest person, something I would need to remember and be careful about myself.
*****
    What with the shoplifting and the beer drinking and

~1956~

Denny's accident, I think my father was really starting to wonder about me. It's not like he thought I was going to turn into a serial killer or anything. He was just mightily frustrated at how much trouble I had gotten into in such a short time.

I fully understood his frustration. In fact, I was starting to wonder about myself. It was like I was bicycling through life, and my bicycle had suddenly shifted into a higher gear. I was helpless to slow it down. I was speeding faster and more dangerously through the streets of Chandler.

Elizabeth and Tom had been such dutiful children my father had little practice in the skills my deviant behavior required, not to mention that for a good portion of their childhood he had been away in the service, and my mother had raised them alone.

Father's frustration turned to anger rather quickly. Oddly, he aimed that anger at other members of the family rather than me. He would snap at Tom or Elizabeth for leaving a light on or arriving five minutes late for dinner.

Some nights I would hear him growling behind my parents' bedroom door. There was a lot of banging dresser drawers, and I could make out enough words to be sure that I was the real cause of his explosion. I started to feel like he somehow held me responsible for what had happened to Denny. It wasn't ever anything he said, but just the way he wouldn't look right at me or the slight discomfort that entered our conversation, what little we had.

Then one evening at dinner, out of the blue, my father put forth the theory that perhaps I had "entirely too much time on my hands." My mother agreed and suggested some of that time might be well spent in gainful employment. They had obviously discussed this ahead of time and had agreed to present a unified front. What happened next, however, proved my conclusion wrong.

My mother proposed that I spend time after school each day helping out at my dad's gas station. This, along with a renewed focus on my homework, would relieve my hands of this excessive time burden and hopefully keep them from the police station ink blotter, although she didn't really say that last part.

I could tell from the look on my dad's face that when he put forth the "too much time on my hands" theory, he didn't anticipate that my time was going to end up in his hands; however, since the assessment had been his, he saw no way to reject my mother's implementation.

As with many family affairs, my mother quietly got her way. I think it was her voice. She never raised it. It had a warm, musical lilt that seemed to defy contradiction. And as with most things, it turned out that her decision to assign me to my father's care at the gas station was exactly right.

*****

If my father was unhappy with this turn of events, I was really distraught. Right after school was prime friend time. Once we were paroled from our isolation, and the shock of Denny's death began to wear off, our quintet began to plan regular afternoon outings and innings. I was upset that my two hour shifts at the gas station would interfere with these plans, but I didn't feel in any position to object to this prescription of gainful employment.

~1956~

My dad set up a work schedule for me. On the first day I was scheduled, I was invited to an after-school birthday party for Gracie Maculum.

"Well, maybe he could start work on Tuesday," suggested my mother.

"Not a chance," said my father, putting his foot down to show he could be pushed only so far. "If he is going to have this job, then he's going to learn it is his responsibility and that other things will have to take a back seat." It was the first of many lessons I learned that fall as an employee of Boomer Oil Company.

The second lesson came on my first day of work. My dad had just taught me to operate the gas pumps, and I was filling my first car. "$5.00 worth," Mr. Skulsky, Sticks father, requested. My father was close behind me to oversee my maiden pump, so I proceeded slowly and carefully. When I reached $4.90, I stopped and squeezed the handle in little spurts until the pump read exactly $5.00.

I smiled up at my father, who reached down and took the nozzle from my hand; before withdrawing it from Mr. Skulsky's Buick, he shot $.35 more worth of gas into the tank.

"He said $5.00, Dad," I said.

Without responding, he placed the hose back on the pump, and accepted the five-dollar bill from Mr. Skulsky's hand. "That Kent sure did hit the baseball this summer," my dad said. "Doesn't get that from his old man."

"Oh, I don't know. I could sure hit anything you threw up there way back when," Mr. Skulsky said, giving my dad a soft punch in the arm. "Looks like the Yankees and the Dodgers again this fall, doesn't it. You don't be

~Boomer~

skipping any school to watch any of the Series this year, Eugene."

My face got hot and I'm sure turned a bright red. I wondered if it was just a lucky guess, or if he really knew that I had a habit of not feeling well during the World Series. He grinned at me as he climbed into the Buick and left.

The jovial exchange between my dad and Mr. Skulsky surprised me. I didn't see my dad as a kidder. That extra $.35 went unexplained. So I watched. My dad always pumped more gas than the customer asked for. And if they asked for a fill, my dad always rounded downward the amount he asked them to pay.

If he was busy with another customer, he just let them go to the cash register and make change for themselves. No customer ever mentioned that extra gallon of gas, but I'm sure they all noticed it, and in the small town of Chandler with lots of gas stations, my father's customers were always loyal.

So I started running over the asked-for amount as well. $.35, $.40, sometimes I went as high as $.50 if it was somebody I knew. It was a good feeling. And usually the customer gave me a smile or a thanks, even when I slipped and let a little gas run down the side of the car. Somewhere along the line, my dad had figured out that there was a small price to pay for friendliness and loyalty.

Watching my dad interact this way gave me a mixed feeling. On one hand, I saw him in a new light, a warmer, friendlier light. Here he was generously giving a little extra to people just to be nice. On the other hand, it made me a little jealous. It seemed he was never willing to show that

~1956~

same generosity to me. If I did something well, it seemed what he expected of me. I longed for a squeeze to my pump and an extra 35 cents into my tank.

Generally, when I was around my dad, I felt a little on edge. He was a veteran who had served and was wounded in World War II. The details of that experience remained untold. Somehow I had learned that his war story was forbidden territory. The taboo was so strong, in fact, that I was afraid to ask my brother and sister what they knew.

An obvious reminder was the crooked way he carried his left arm. He had a powerful, athletic build, but sometimes he had to twist the entire rest of his body to get that arm in position to do something. At times he would explode with frustration when it caused him to struggle with the gas cap on the lawn mower or even his fork at meal time.

He imposed a military efficiency on many aspects of our household. More than my mother, he insisted that we dress neatly. His eyes would shoot daggers at some of the boys who wore their jeans at half mast, their cracks peaking out above their belts. He would have hung me with my belt if I had tried that.

We had weekly chores around the house. Mine was to mow the grass, and when I finished, he conducted inspection, not just to see that I had shortened every blade, but also that I had steered straight lines in doing so.

My mother referred to me sometimes as "Daddy's little soldier." And that's what I felt like.

Most every car in town stopped by Boomer Oil at least once a week, some once a day. Indeed there seemed

~Boomer~

to be some cars permanently parked there.

The station itself was a small cube of white stucco. Blue trim flaked around two square windows at the front. It was the only building in town that didn't face north, south, east or west. It straddled a corner at the end of Main Street, facing northeast. A one-car canopy stuck out from the roof over the cement slab that housed two old-fashioned gas pumps.

Women who drove in for gas never left their cars. Greetings and payment were exchanged through partially opened windows; feminine shoes seldom touched Boomer cement. The station looked kind of dirty and oily, and there was always a group of dirty, oily men inside or out. They were totally harmless, but it wasn't the kind of place that even a hearty farm wife wanted to frequent.

The exception was Mrs. Maculum, Gracie's lovely mother, who worked as my father's bookkeeper. Her office was a separate room at the back of the station. In contrast to grubbiness of the rest of the place, Mrs. Mac's domain was bright and spotless.

While women shunned the place, men always got out of their vehicles and entered the station. Most remained there for the next hour. Some stayed for the rest of the day. They greeted each other, shared cigarettes and chewing tobacco, gossiped about whose farm was for sale or whose appendix was being removed. For Chandler men, Boomer Oil was the social and political center of the community, and my father was unofficial mayor.

Much of the time, my role around the station was that of a pet. I was a lot like an old dog that each customer would scratch behind the ear and make a joke about as he

~1956~

entered.

"Hey, kid. Weren't you taller the last time I was here?" It was not a bad role. If someone had some candy in his pocket, I always got a piece or two, and I knew more juicy gossip about Chandler than any kid my age had a right to know.

My dad delivered gas and diesel fuel to farms throughout the countryside. My daily presence gave him the chance to make deliveries without closing down the station. After a couple weeks of internship, he decided I was capable enough to leave alone. If trouble arose, there were always several experienced customers hanging around to give me a hand.

That fall there were always several hunched-over men sitting outside the station on blocks of cement. On a nice day the butts on those blocks represented the entire social strata of Chandler. There were Catholics and Lutherans, bankers and farmers, rich men and poor. Differences between Chandler men were forgotten once seated on a Boomer cement block.

They talked by the hour, and while I never felt worthy to sit with them, as I walked by I caught snatches of political and agricultural and economic wisdom.

The only thing that stopped their talk was the arrival or departure of Mrs. Maculum. She was the town beauty and by far its most stylish dresser. She worked only part of each day, so arrived mid-morning and left mid-afternoon when her movements were carefully watched by the block sitters.

She dressed in bright-colored and extremely short skirts, trim, shapely sweaters and the highest heeled shoes

I had ever seen.

As she passed, the men struggled with where they should look. Some, heads bowed, surreptitiously eyed her long, shapely legs. Others boldly looked up, to take in her bosom and her deeply red lips.

Without a hint of discomfort, she spoke to each. She never looked right at them, and the occupants were never the same group, but she never failed to greet.

"Henry."

"Mornin' Cherry."

"Walt."

"Cherry."

"Willard."

"Cherry."

When she had passed into the station, there was always a reverential minute or two of silence as each contemplated the vision. Faces held subdued smiles and on occasion a soft sigh escaped from Walt or Willard.

Only once did I hear anyone comment. Ed Hanson, who was not a regular block sitter, watched Mrs. Maculum leave one afternoon, and when she was beyond earshot gave a low whistle and said, "I sure wouldn't kick her out of bed."

My dad was standing in the door of the station and overheard him. "Come on, Ed. This isn't junior high," he said. It wasn't said jokingly, and a moment of discomfort descended upon the usually relaxed group.

It surprised me that my dad spoke to a friend in a voice that he usually reserved for me, but I figured he was just defending an employee. I had noticed that he didn't look at Mrs. Maculum the same way as the other men, and

~1956~

didn't get all gooey like they did when she talked to him.

Of all the males at the station, I think I was Mrs. Maculum's favorite. She'd send me to the Bluebird Café across Main Street for coffee, and when I brought it to her, she'd talk about how handsome or big I was getting.

She would pour a little of her coffee into a paper cup, add an equal portion of milk and give it to me. Awful as it tasted, I always drank it with a smile, as if she had given me sweetest chocolate. She squeezed the muscles in my arms and sometimes gave me a hug. She always wore the same perfume and smelled like meadow flowers. Sometimes I wished that she wasn't married, because I would have asked her in a minute.

Not that her husband would have cared. Grace's dad had left Chandler and his family about the time Grace was born. Mrs. Maculum had told me that one time when she was explaining how lucky I was to have such a great dad. Grace never talked about her father.

I was glad that Gracie was never around to see her mother fawn over me, because she would have told the others and I never would have heard the end of it.

Grace never came to the station, she said, because her mom didn't want her hanging around where she worked. Occasionally, Fud or Sticks or Pastor Jim Bob would stop by to set up a later activity. My dad always made it clear to me and them without saying a word that I had a job to do, and until it was done, there was no time for play.

That's the way it often was between me and my dad that fall at the gas station. He seldom actually told me what he expected of me or wanted for me. He never told me when he was pleased with me or disappointed in me. Still, I knew those things, and I felt good when I thought I had pleased him and guilty when I was sure I had disappointed him.

It was years later, when I began to disappoint him frequently, that the cautious respect I had for him soured to disdain.

As a boy I never remember having a conversation with my dad that contained more than a dozen words. We just did things. We didn't talk about them. When there was a pause in the traffic, one of us would grab the two baseball gloves from behind the safe and the two of us would adjourn to the lot behind the station where he would squat as catcher for my pitches. Even his bad arm didn't disguise his athletic skill.

He never instructed me, but just caught as many pitches as I could throw, until a car would drive into the station. He would nod his head, and without one last pitch, I would move to the pumps to resume my job.

It was station policy to check the oil on any car that passed through, and at first, that was for me a frustrating task. Every single car had a different kind of hood latch. Some were high up above the grill. Some were low down below the grill. Some had single latches, some double. Some slid to the left, some to the right. And the car owners seemed to take some delight in letting me fumble around at the fronts of their vehicles before revealing the well-hidden contraption.

Those old cars had heavy hoods, too, and despite Mrs. Maculum's claims, my strength was badly underdeveloped for such work. A really low point in my

~1956~

first career was the day I snapped the hood ornament off Hank Radcliff's Buick Roadmaster, while using it to get some lifting leverage. For some reason my dad chose to forgive that blunder, leaving me to wonder exactly what triggered his anger at other times.

Life after Denny Fritz's death seemed fragile and uncertain for me. The regularity of my two-hour shift and the monotony of my gas station chores helped to stabilize it for me. Dad was my drill sergeant, and I was his little soldier.

*****

In kindergarten we became a male quartet: James Roberts, Fred Untiedt, Kent Skulsky, Eugene Boomer. On our very first day of school we were placed around a tiny table on four tiny chairs. Two of us cried at the point of our mothers' abandonment. The others, who were only slightly less frightened, provided comfort.

It was odd that in such a little town we hadn't known each other before. I suppose that we had all seen each other, but paid little attention. We lived in different neighborhoods, our parents belonged to different churches, and our mothers moved in different social circles.

Until school started, all of the children I played with were either the sons and daughters of my mother's close friends or of members at Chandler Methodist.

Over the next years we actually drew our four families together. As we became inseparable, our families became acquainted. As they dropped us off at or picked us up from one another's houses, our parents began to cross whatever barriers had before separated them.

The other three fathers began buying gasoline at my

dad's station. On occasion we would forsake Chandler Methodist to attend First Baptist, where James Robert's father preached. When Sticks' father was hospitalized, my mother took an apple pie to his house and offered to have Sticks stay with us for the week.

Eventually, it was as if we each had four different homes. We wandered in and out of each other's houses freely. We ate at one another's supper table regularly. I was as likely to get helpful advice from the older siblings of my three friends as from my own.

The truth is that each of us might have been more comfortable had we been born into a different household. Sticks Skulsky was the most disciplined and serious-minded of our group. Perhaps this, in part, accounted for his being the best athlete. He had the focus to practice and perfect things while the rest of us were pointlessly playing. Sticks would have fit nicely into the Roberts family in place of James. Mr. Roberts, the stern head of the household, was a Baptist minister. Weekly he exhorted his congregation to walk the straight and narrow, a path it was very easy for Sticks Skulsky to tread. Sticks would have made an exemplary preacher's kid, a perfect bookend with Esther Roberts, Pastor Jim Bob's saintly sister.

James, Pastor Jim Bob, however, was as unlike his sister as he could possibly be. He landed briefly on the straight and narrow as he serpentined wildly across it. The elder Pastor Roberts became more acquainted with school principals, police officers and doctors than he would have liked. Pastor Jim Bob was not a bad person. His curiosity for the unusual just landed him in trouble more than his dour father and straight-laced mother would have

~1956~

preferred.

Pastor Jim Bob would have better fit into the Untiedt family, replacing Fud. They were a fun-loving bunch, the Untiedts. Their house always won the award for most elaborate Christmas display, although most residents of Chandler would have described it as gaudy. They drove the streets of Chandler in brightly colored cars, yellows and purples, at a time when ninety-five percent of the population rode in black or dark green.

Mr. Untiedt shared Pastor Jim Bob's enthusiasm for explosions. They would meet in Ashcroft Park on Sunday afternoons to ignite model rockets. It became a contest to see who could build the largest rocket with the most dramatic liftoff to streak the highest into the Chandler sky.

For the 4th of July, Fud's father brought a truckload of illegal fireworks from South Dakota into town. Pastor Jim Bob was secretly given a priority pick.

Fud would have blended nicely into my family. Like my brother and sister, he was exceptionally smart. Unlike me, Fud would have continued the Boomer tradition of flawless report cards. Fud also shared Tom and Elizabeth's talents in drama and music. Those arts pretty much died in our house when my brother Tom graduated and went off to college. My mother arm-twisted me into joining choir, but I'm afraid that my greatest contribution was to help provide a balance of boys and girls; the scale always tipped toward the girls. But it was Fud who sang the solo at the yearly Christmas Concert.

That means I would have lived in the Skulsky residence, something I could have easily done. I loved Sticks' mother and father. I never felt more comfortable than when I entered their home. Sticks' mother catered to my sweet tooth. She would put her arm around me and lead me into her fragrant kitchen, where she would delight me with her latest cookies or fudge. It seemed that no matter when I arrived, something had just been taken from the oven. Sticks' two older sisters treated me like a young prince, smothering me with hugs and caresses. Both were so beautiful that I couldn't decide which I wanted to marry, that is if I couldn't have Mrs. Maculum. In their presence, I became tongue-tied and shy, which emboldened their teasing. I would have been a happy Skulsky child.

Yes, on the surface it appeared that we had come into this world wrongly assigned.

On second thought, it was probably best that we were christened as we were. Fud's practical jokes would have driven my father crazy. If Mr. Untiedt and Pastor Jim Bob had lived in the same household, they probably would have developed some concoction that would have exploded, leveling the neighborhood. Instead of developing into Chandler's finest athlete, as a Roberts, Sticks would have instead become a saint, and I most certainly would have developed a stutter in the presence of Stick's gorgeous sisters.

*****

1957

It was odd that Grace Maculum became the fifth member of our group. We four boys had no particular interest in girls yet. Grace wasn't a tomboy. She was several months younger than the rest of us. She had little interest in playing sports and dressed like a girl.

~1957~

A tiny person, with a pixie haircut and three freckles on her nose, quiet and self-conscious, she simply joined our group whenever the occasion arose.

She'd sit at our cafeteria table for lunch. She'd join us for a classroom project. She'd walk downtown with us after school. We never objected, because she was genuinely nice. She never chose what the group would do, but whatever we decided, she quietly took part. Before long she was on equal status with the four of us.

She lived on the far side of the river, the wrong side of the tracks in Chandler, so to speak. Those from the hills on the east side were thought of as a rough lot, not entirely suitable for social contact, in the minds of most westerners.

It was a really silly distinction, given how alike we all were. Miss Mac, with her pretty, freckled face and quiet manner, slipped across the river and entered our group, and no one seemed to notice or care that she was a girl and from the East.

Quite often when we were gathering, she would ask me to ride over and pick her up. She said that her mother was often unwilling to let her leave, and it was easier for her to get away with someone standing at the door waiting for her. I didn't ask why Mrs. Maculum was so inclined, assuming Gracie would have told me if it was any of my business.

So one winter Saturday, I pried my hands from my frozen bicycle and dropped it onto a bank of snow in her yard. When I rapped at the door, no one appeared, but I heard voices inside, angry voices.

I couldn't understand what they were saying until I heard Grace's voice cry out, "Don't! Please stop! Oh,

~Boomer~

please!"

The terror in her voice drew me in. I took off my gloves, opened the screen door and entered the kitchen. Their house was not well-kept. The sink was covered with dishes and the table was littered with rags and rolls of wallpaper. The mess always struck me as odd, given how neat Mrs. Maculum kept her office at the gas station.

From another room I heard a smack and another cry from Grace. I stepped around the corner and into the living room. Grace was lying on the couch with her mother hunched over her.

Before I could speak, Grace's mother raised her arm into the air and brought her fist down into Grace's stomach. Grace hugged herself and curled tightly into a ball, tears running down her face.

Suddenly her eyes caught me standing across the room. "Boomer," she cried out. "What are you doing? Why didn't you wait outside? Get out of here!" She leapt off the couch, ran down the hall to her room and slammed the door behind her.

I stood seemingly planted to my spot. More than anything, I was baffled by Grace's anger with me.

Mrs. Maculum slumped onto the couch and patted her hair. She was not the same woman that flowed gracefully into my father's gas station each day. Her skirt and blouse were rumpled and mismatched. Her hair stuck out in all directions.

"Eugene." Mrs. Maculum had always been rather formal with me, and never used my nickname. She rubbed her hands nervously together. "Please come in." She bent over to straighten some knickknacks on the coffee table, as

~1957~

if I might be upset to see it in such disarray.

"I'm sorry you had to see that, Eugene. Grace and I were having a disagreement over household chores. I'm afraid we let it get a little out of hand. Come in. Sit down, Eugene. I'm sure Grace will be ready to go out with you shortly."

She gazed around the room, looking for something to do to cover her embarrassment. Suddenly, she sank to the couch and burst into tears.

"Oh, Eugene, I'm so miserable. I can't stand it anymore." She sat with her face in her hands, sobbing.

I really liked Grace's mom, but I was thoroughly flustered and confused. I walked toward her and sat on the edge of the couch.

"Gosh, Mrs. Maculum. Is there anything I can do?"

She wiped her eyes with the sides of her hands and then looked up with a faint smile.

"Oh, Eugene. You're sweet. No. I'm afraid my situation is far beyond your help." I was close enough to her that when she talked, I could smell alcohol on her breath. Her eyes were droopy and bloodshot. At nine o'clock in the morning, she was drunk.

"The world stinks, Eugene. And Chandler smells worse than most places I've been." Her sobbing renewed.

I wanted to say something to make her feel better, but could think of nothing very helpful. I bent a little closer to her, reached up and put my hand on her head. I stroked her hair softly.

"Gee, Mrs. Maculum, things can't be as bad as all that." I felt really odd touching a grown person in that way.

Rather suddenly, she straightened up and put both

~Boomer~

of her arms around my neck. She pulled my head to her chest and squeezed so tightly that I let out a little gasp.

"You just don't know, Eugene. You just don't know." My face started to feel like it was on fire, and I was having trouble getting my breath back. She continued to hold me and stroked the back of my head with one of her hands. I slid downward and managed to squeeze my head between her breasts and free myself.

"Mrs. Maculum, I gotta be going," I said, getting up from the couch. "Just tell Gracie I'll see her another time," I stammered.

She closed her eyes and put her hands to her cheeks. "I understand, Eugene. I'm so sorry. Please forget you saw this. I'm just not myself."

I could think of nothing to say, so I turned to leave. The door to Grace's bedroom opened, and Grace came walking quickly down the hall, pulling on a jacket. She said nothing to her mother, grabbed me and pulled me toward the door.

"Come on, Boomer," she said. "Let's find something to do."

Her mother didn't try to stop her, but just sat on the couch and tearfully watched us close the door.

Grace rolled her bicycle off the front porch, climbed on and wobbled down the narrow shoveled sidewalk and into the street.

I grabbed my bicycle and followed, but by the time I reached the street, she was already a block ahead. I followed quickly, but she was pedaling so hard that I couldn't catch her. She sailed over the crest of Beacon Hill and went flying down the steep slope.

~1957~

Trying to keep up, I began the downhill stretch much too fast. I skidded across icy patches and felt out of control. At the bottom of the hill, Gracie made a right turn and started off across River Park on a plowed path. By the time I reached her, she was sitting on a mountain of snow that had been dumped by the street crew, staring across to the other side of the river. I climbed the hill and sat beside her.

I was so confused that I decided to wait for her to speak whenever she felt like it. That created a rather long silent spell. Grace sat perfectly still. I started getting fidgety and cold. I packed together a snowball and tossed it out onto the ice of the river.

Finally, I couldn't stand it any longer. "Does she do that to you very often?" I said.

"She used to do it all the time when I was a little kid," she said, "but this is the first time in quite a while. I think she broke up with her boyfriend last night."

"Gosh, are you ok? She was hitting you awfully hard."

"She's not so strong."

I packed another snowball and gave it a harder toss. I was feeling somewhat betrayed. How could the Mrs. Maculum I loved at the gas station be so awful at home?

"She shouldn't be able to do that to you, Gracie. My folks would never hit me. Do you want me to talk to them about this, see if they can talk to your mom or do something to help?"

She turned and looked at me for the first time. Her upper lip was a little puffy from the blows. She spoke softly but firmly.

"Boomer, you have to promise me that you will

~Boomer~

never tell anyone about what you saw today. Not your folks or Sticks or James or Fud or anyone. Just forget about it. I don't want anyone to know my mom does that."

"But Mac, don't you want someone to stop her from doing it again?"

"Boomer, I'm telling you that if you say anything about this to anyone, I won't be your friend anymore. I won't speak to you again. I don't want anyone to know this about my mom. Promise me that you'll never say a word to anyone?"

"All right. I won't say anything to anyone."

"Do you swear on your grandmother's grave?"

"Both of my grandmothers are alive, but I promise. I won't say a word."

"Thanks." She looked back out over the river.

We sat there in silence. I was really starting to get cold, and wondered how long Gracie was going to sit there. I couldn't just leave her.

Suddenly it jumped out of my mouth. "I killed Denny Fritz." Her head turned toward me, but she didn't say anything. Tears started to silently roll down my cheeks. I said it again, "I killed Denny Fritz."

"Boomer, what do you mean? Denny Fritz fell in the river and drowned."

"But he fell because my fishing rod hit him in the face." She stared at me, while I stumbled through that other afternoon on the river. When I finished, she turned back to the river, and we sat again in silence.

Finally she said, "It was an accident, Boomer. You didn't mean to do it. You didn't kill Denny. He fell into the river and drowned."

~1957~

I wiped my damp face with my fingers. I could feel the tears starting to freeze. I felt better having someone else know my secret, but at the same time it was a little scary.

Suddenly Grace leaned over and unzipped my jacket. She put her arms inside around my waist and snuggled her face firmly up against my chest. She looked up and gave me a quick kiss on the cheek.

"I'll never tell anyone," she said looking up into my face.

The morning's happenings had made me dizzy. It was a feeling that I had experienced often since Denny's accident. I wondered if the rest of my life was going to come at me with such speed and confusion. And freshest in my mind was a picture of the distraught Mrs. Maculum clinging wildly to me. Grace seemed intent on not hating her mother for the beatings she received.

So we had shared secrets that day. I felt a strong bond between us, something that would keep us slightly closer than we got to the others. The warmth of her face penetrated my shirt, and the chill I had earlier felt disappeared. From that moment on, we watched out for each other. For a long time, whenever I saw Gracie, I checked her pretty face for any marks of violence. If I were in the dumps, it was always Gracie who quietly pulled me aside and asked if I was all right.

I tried to forget the Mrs. Maculum I had seen that day. I much preferred that lovely scented woman who organized my father's office, but from that day on, I stayed just far enough from her so that she couldn't touch me.

*****

Through the rest of that winter and spring our lives

seemed to mellow. The stability of our school schedule led the five of us forward without a further catastrophe.

One early summer Friday night we made our way home after watching Audie Murphy beat up on the Germans in *To Hell and Back*. With such a title, it had taken a persuasive argument to get all of our parents to agree to our evening out. Fud supplied the patriotic explanation that sprung us free.

Murphy's bravado sent the five of us into the night ripe for adventure. We hid in the shadow of a huge elm, listening as a car chugged over the top of Morris Hill. It was Jim Bob's turn. He waited until the engine noise moved closer, then dashed into the street and stopped in the middle. The headlights, still a block down the street, brightly lit up his white T-shirt.

"Gotcha, Jim Bob," yelled Fud. "Get out of there."

The Pastor bolted to the other side of the street, dove over a hedge and lay on his stomach up close against the bushes. The rest of us couldn't actually see him, but that's what we always did when we played "Illumination." The object was to appear in the headlights of an oncoming car, and then disappear in a flash, or as close to a flash as we could muster.

The car drove between us slowly, the driver squinting into the darkness where Jim Bob had vanished. The four of us ran behind the car, somersaulted over the hedge with a variety of acrobatic ease, and crawled up beside Jim Bob.

"Good job," I said, slapping him on the back. "He spotted you sure." Illumination was just one of our many summer-night games, more dangerous than some, not as

~1957~

dangerous as others. "Your turn, Gracie. Let's see that chartreuse shirt glow."

We peered over the hedge into the darkness, no cars in eye or earshot. Suddenly I spotted a shadowy figure moving along the sidewalk across the street.

"Duck," I hissed. Our five heads dipped below bush level. Slowly we came back up until we could all see the dark intruder making its way through our night.

"It's Ed Swayler," said Sticks. "Let's sit tight until he's gone."

"Right," said Gracie. "I don't want anything to do with him."

If it had been anyone else in Chandler, we would have been hatching a plan to scare the bejeezes out of him, but none of us was bold enough to even suggest that we move closer to this man. Well, most of us, anyway.

Ed Swayler was the local grave digger, and his appearance perfectly fit his occupation. He was a huge man with a severely hunched back which directed his eyes about ten inches in front of his enormous feet.

"He must bump into things a lot," I thought out loud.

I saw him quite frequently at the gas station, and in the daylight he didn't seem so ferocious, but in the night his huge figure and accompanying shadow, cast by a nearby street lamp, kept us at a distance.

While we didn't like to get close to him, one of our favorite activities during sleepovers was to swap Ed Swayler stories, passing on the latest tales we had heard from other sources.

One that always came up was that he ate some of the

~Boomer~

parts before burying a body. I doubted that one, but he was such a fearsome looking figure that it wouldn't have taken much to convince me.

"Let's follow him," said Pastor Jim Bob.

"Are you nuts?" said Grace. "I'm not going near him. I heard he lives in a cave out in the gravel pit and that he tries to lure little kids like us into it."

"He does not," I said. "He lives in an old shack down on River Street. He hangs around my dad's station once in a while, but I've never heard him say a word."

"That's because he can't," said Fud. "I heard he was in an accident of some kind and they had to cut out his tongue. Have you ever noticed how that big head of his doesn't quite fit straight on his shoulders?"

"I'm with Gracie," said Sticks. "I'm not following him anywhere."

Fud chimed in, "*Twenty-One* is on TV tonight and that Van Doren guy is winning a load of moola. We just got a new antenna, so we can actually see a picture now. I'll see you guys tomorrow."

"It's getting late anyway," said Sticks. "My folks want me in early tonight. We're going to Sheldon to watch a ball game tomorrow."

"All right, you party-poopers," chided Pastor Jim Bob. "Then it is just Boomer and me stepping into The Twilight Zone. You lot will be sorry on Monday when we recount our adventures."

I longed to tell him that I wanted less to do with his adventure than any of our three pals. Following people into trouble was becoming a way of life for me, one that would continue for years to come. But the way he had

~1957~

included me in his plan had been flattering and made it hard to back down.

It was a little uncharacteristic of Jim Bob to take the lead. I should have suspected he had something up his sleeve. In addition, I completely forgot that my parents had told me to be in early, as our family had a funeral to attend the next day.

"We'd better get started," said Jim Bob, whacking me on the back and trotting after the now tiny figure of Ed Swayler as he turned a corner and disappeared far down the block. I looked helplessly to the others, threw up my hands and ran off after the preacher's kid.

From behind, Fud yelled, "He eats little kids, you know." Jim Bob led the way as we left the street and cut between houses to shorten the distance of our pursuit. Away from the street lamps of Morris Avenue, I became aware of a bright, summer moon.

I followed closely as Jim Bob darted around trees and hurtled over shrubbery. Suddenly he stopped, slid to one side and stuck out his foot. It caught me ankle-high, and helplessly I lunged forward, my hands, chest and chin skidding across the grass which was just beginning to take on the cool dew. With a laugh, he dropped his rear end firmly on my back.

"Thanks a lot," I grunted. "My mother will really appreciate the grass stains on every single item of my clothing."

With a sly move of my own, I grabbed Jim Bob's left leg, which stuck out in front of my face, and rolled, toppling him onto his side. With a twist and a grunt I righted myself and sat astride his chest. Knowing well his weakness for tickling, I dug my thumb firmly between his ribs and jiggled it violently. He howled with laughter.

"Stop! Please!" he cried. "We've got to get after Swayler, or we will lose him."

I released the good Pastor, stood up and bent over to brush the dirt and grass from my pants. Quickly spotting my vulnerability, he brought his hands to my shoulders and shoved me backward onto my rear end. Then he ran off laughing in the direction we had last seen Ed Swayler.

Suddenly my hesitance to be on this adventure was gone. The joy of my condition swept over me. School had let out for the summer two days before. Ahead of us lay nearly three months of gentle days and nights. My four friends and I had plans to stretch the boundaries of childhood and Chandler. We would romp and wrestle in timeless glee.

I breathed in a gulp of the fresh black air, threw my fists to the sky and gazed at Orion on guard above me. Then I leapt to my feet and streaked after Pastor Jim Bob.

We quickly overtook the stooped and lumbering Ed Swayler. Pastor Jim Bob's asthma threatened to expose our presence. He periodically had to halt and bury a sneeze into his right shoulder.

Dodging from towering elm to towering elm, crouching behind hedges and stifling giggles, we let Ed Swayler lead us to the edge of town and then beyond. We quickly discerned his and our destination, the Chandler cemetery, a few hundred yards outside the southern most row of houses.

Excitement turned to fever as we followed him into the graveyard, using the largest of the stones to hide our

~1957~

pursuit. We were now close enough to Ed Swayler that we could hear him grunt slightly as he plodded along.

Jim Bob put his index finger to his lips to ensure my silence. Swayler might mistake a rustling of grass for a cat or a squirrel, but a voice would surely doom us to his wrath.

The moonlight was so bright that we could easily read the names inscribed on the tombstones, a fact I shockingly discovered when I looked up to find myself squatting on the mound of grass covering my own grandfather. Had I any sense, I should have been mortified or worshipful or scared to death, but with childish fervor, I whispered a quick, "Sorry, Gramp," and moved on to the next tombstone.

Jim Bob crept up beside me. Excitement coupled with his asthma caused him to wheeze. He sounded a bit like Frankenstein's monster, which only added to my worry that Ed Swayler would discover us.

Swayler stopped near a mound of dirt. He picked up a ladder from behind it and stood it upright. We watched as first the bottom and then the entire thing dropped into the earth. Then the monster awkwardly stooped to his hands and knees and disappeared.

"He's digging a grave," whispered Jim Bob.

"No!" I hissed. "I thought he was gathering worms." Jim Bob elbowed me firmly in the ribs, and I returned the favor.

"Come on," said Jim Bob, and I followed as he crossed into a stand of short pine trees that was to our right and about the same distance from the hole in which the object of our adventure now toiled. We watched as

~Boomer~

shovelfuls of soil began to exit the hole and fall onto the dirt pile.

Jim Bob nudged me and I turned his way. He reached into a pocket and withdrew a handful of objects. In the moonlight their shiny, silver coating glowed. I recognized them immediately. M-80s. The most powerful firecrackers any of us kids had ever had the pleasure to explode. It was then I realized why Jim Bob had been enthusiastic to set out on this expedition. Pyrotechnics.

I didn't have to ask where he had gotten them. They were obviously leftovers from Fud's father's stash. M-80s were Jim Bob's favorites, simply because they made by far the loudest noise. Such was their force that not throwing one fast enough was sure to leave fewer than five fingers on the tardy hand.

"This should make the old boy move a little faster, don't you think?" said Jim Bob.

"Jeez, I don't know, Jim Bob. That's liable to scare him to death," I warned.

"Well, at least they won't have to dig another hole to bury him in. I'll toss one over by the grave and let's get out of here."

Always prepared to set fire to things, Jim Bob pulled matches from his other pocket. He lit one and held it to the stiff fuse. Soon the familiar hiss filled Jim Bob's hand. He knew it was unwise to tempt fate by holding an M-80, so immediately wound up and threw it toward the open grave and its occupant. Unfortunately, its flight was interrupted by a pine branch just to our front. The tree caught the bomb, held it aloft for a moment, and dropped it at our feet.

~1957~

"Oh, shit," yelled Jim Bob, committing the sin that his father would have condemned beyond all the others committed during this fiasco.

I turned to escape the imminent blast, but had taken no more than a step when the branch of a tree behind us hit me squarely in the face. The force of the blow knocked me backward to the ground, and before I could begin to recover, the M-80 exploded within an arms-length of my head.

I'd never realized how painful sound could be. It felt like the firework had gone off inside my head. My temples throbbed. I could hear nothing but a high continuous whine. I felt like I was going to throw up. I lay stunned and then finally groped my way to my knees, my hands still covering my ears.

I felt another hand on my shoulder. I wheeled around, prepared to scream at Jim Bob for his stupidity, and stared up into the face of Ed Swayler.

His grip tightened on my shirt, and he yanked me to my feet. He began dragging me out of the trees toward the open grave.

My fear erupted into a steady stream of blabber. "I think my folks are expecting me at home," I pleaded. "Where are you taking me? I think I may have dropped my wallet back in the woods there." I could tell that I was speaking much louder than normal, but my ears were still ringing and I couldn't hear myself.

When he got me near the open grave, he pointed to it and grunted, "Dig." I didn't really hear what he said, but his face was about four inches from mine and I could read his lips.

~Boomer~

"I'm sorry," I shouted. "My mom would kill me if I got all dirty out here." We looked down at my pants streaked with dirt and grass stains from the several falls I had taken earlier.

"Dig!" he repeated. This time I heard him.

"He does to have a tongue," I thought.

He handed me a bucket with a rope tied to it and gave me a shove toward the hole. I could do nothing but step onto the ladder and descend into the earth. The moonlight failed to penetrate this abyss, and I backed into utter blackness.

Five steps. Six. Seven. "How deep do they have to make graves?" I thought.

I reached the bottom and stepped off the ladder onto the ground. I took a step and stumbled over the shovel that Swayler had left. As I bent over to pick it up, something in front of me whispered, "Boo."

It startled me, but was a decidedly friendly "Boo."

"Jim Bob?" I said in a hushed voice. "What are you doing down here?"

"I ran the wrong way. I think I twisted my ankle when I landed."

At any moment I expected Ed Swayler to start shoveling the dirt back into the hole to be finished with us stupid, bothersome kids.

In desperation I moved to the bottom of the ladder and called up, "Mr. Swayler. There are two of us down here. My friend fell in the hole. I think maybe he broke his ankle. Could you come down and help him get out of here?"

I elbowed Jim Bob and he yelled, "Help! I think I

~1957~

broke my ankle."

I was on the verge of hysteria. Here I was, in a cemetery, in a grave, in the pitch dark, and I had just asked the scariest man I had ever seen to come down and join us.

We heard only a grunt from above. Then his legs appeared on the ladder and his huge butt entered the cavity above us. Jim Bob, seeming to think that some dramatics would help our situation, flopped onto the ground and gave out a groan.

"I don't think I can put any weight on my foot," he said as the grave digger reached the bottom of the ladder. "Maybe you could help boost me up on the ladder so I could crawl out, Mr. Swayler. Gene, why don't you go up on top and help pull me up."

I didn't know what he was up to, but I needed no other invitation to get out of that grave. Quickly, I scrambled up the ladder. I peered back into the blackness. Then Jim Bob's head appeared on the ladder.

"Here, Boomer," he said. "Grab my hand and pull. He's got me from below." The Pastor gave a convincing lame act. He moaned. I pulled. Ed Swayler pushed, and awkwardly we hoisted him out of the grave.

Jim Bob was no sooner above ground than he grabbed the ladder, jerked it out of the grave and said, "Let's amscra," and hobbled off between two gravestones.

I hesitated for a moment, turned back to the grave, feeling that some sort of apology was in order. Grabbing the ladder, I pushed one end back into the hole, hoping that as it fell it didn't clobber poor Ed on his skull, and then dashed off to catch Pastor Jim Bob.

My parents were not happy with either the tardiness

~Boomer~

of my arrival, or the condition of my clothing. If they had known where I spent the last hour, I would likely have been grounded until I left home for college. As it was, they sent me directly to my room. That was not a big disappointment, and after my evening's activities, I was happy to go immediately to bed and hoping to still be there at noon the next day.

It took me a while to get to sleep, as my ears were still ringing. When my mother awoke me at 9:00, I was not chipper.

I had forgotten my uncle's funeral. My dad's brother had died the week before. Uncle Walt had lived on a farm south of Chandler. He had been a loner with little time for family, so his death had not affected my parents as a death of any other uncle would have. I had scarcely known Uncle Walt, but had been told I was going to the funeral. It was to be my first.

At breakfast I decided to make one last effort to avoid going.

"No," my dad said, "You're old enough to start learning the facts of life."

I wanted to ask what someone dying had to do with the facts of life, but I could tell he was still mad about the night before, and I didn't want to press my luck.

The funeral was at Beech's Funeral Parlor. My friends and I walked by it every day on our way to school. We'd kid about peeking in the windows to see dead people, but were never brave enough to try. I didn't usually like to walk past there at night, but after last night's escapade in the cemetery, it would be a piece of cake from now on.

Mr. Beech greeted me and my parents at the door.

~1957~

He smiled and shook my hand. It gave me the creeps. I could almost feel the blood and junk that he must touch every day.

A lot of my relatives were standing around just inside the door. They all smiled at us and some came over to pat me on the head. Sometimes I wish I were big enough to look down and pat them on the head. But mostly I wished that I was at home or biking or something.

My mom took my hand and led me across the room. Before I was quite ready for it, there was my Uncle Walt lying in this box.

I wasn't sure it was really him. I mean it kind of looked like him, but I had never seen him in a suit and his face looked sort of plastic. He reminded me of the wax people we had seen in the Hall of Presidents at Disneyland. His casket was covered with flowers, and I could only see the top half of him. I wondered if his legs were still there.

Without thinking I blurted out, "Can I touch him?"

A bit surprised, my mom said, "Well, sure Eugene. That would be all right."

With one finger I touched his hand like I was afraid of getting burned. His skin was cold and rubbery. I knew one thing for sure. Uncle Walt wasn't in there anymore.

We sat in a chapel for the funeral. Everyone was quiet, and nobody smiled, but nobody was crying and feeling too bad either.

In the middle of it I had to go to the bathroom. My mom whispered for me to go back in the lobby. I peeked through a doorway, and there was Mr. Beech and another man standing over Uncle Walt's casket. I could just barely see his face between them. Slowly they brought the cover

~Boomer~

of the casket down until it shut Uncle Walt in completely. Not sure I was supposed to be watching, I shut the door. In the bathroom it hit me. Whether I liked Uncle Walt or not, I was never ever going to see him again. I didn't like that.

As I walked out of the funeral parlor with my family, I thought, "Thank goodness that's over."

Just then my dad said, "It's going to be a little breezy out at the cemetery this morning."

"Good grief," I thought, "I'm headed back to the cemetery." I hadn't been there twice in ten years, and here I was returning for the second time in half a day.

Then a thought struck me that actually stopped me from walking. "You don't suppose that it was Uncle Walt's grave I was in last night?"

It was. We followed a short line of cars, led by the Beech hearse, directly to the site of the previous night's fiasco. My father actually parked our family car not ten feet from the grove of trees in which Jim Bob's M-80 had mistakenly exploded, an event, I might add, which was still faintly ringing in my ears. I think it probably did some permanent damage.

We exited the car and walked together toward the open grave. Since last night, a contraption had been placed above the hole, and a group of men were now placing Uncle Walt's casket on it. Very few of the people from the funeral home had followed out to the cemetery. Not many in town knew or liked Uncle Walt, and it was as though they had thought, "Well, that's enough of that," and gone home.

We barely were enough to entirely circle the grave, and at first there was a space to my right, and then

~1957~

suddenly there was somebody filling it. I looked up to greet them, but quickly snapped my eyes back to the ground in front of my feet. It was Ed Swayler. He hadn't been at the funeral home, so it hadn't occurred to me that he would be here.

I was sure that everyone in the little group of people could see me shaking. I don't remember a single thing that was said or done during the little graveside service. Mr. Beech talked, but his words seemed filtered through jell-O or something.

I half expected that at some point he would stop and say. "As long as we're out here, there's something else that needs taking care of." And then my whole awful story would be told, and I would be disgraced in the eyes of my family for the rest of my life for defiling the grave of a fellow Boomer.

Mr. Beech said his final words, and people began to move away from the grave. I stood frozen, aware that the huge man to my right had not moved. Then Ed Swayler's mammoth hand reached across in front of my face and grasped my father's arm.

My father turned to him. "Ed. Good to see you. Thanks for coming." They shook hands. Then to my surprise, Ed Swayler offered his hand to me. My tiny right hand disappeared into his. I looked up into his grizzled face.

"Sorry about your uncle," he said in his low, gravelly voice. Then he released me and turned to walk away, his head down and shoulders stooped as always.

"Thank you, Mr. Swayler," I said to his back. I stared at him as he lumbered away.

~Boomer~

It was not so much a thank you for his kind thought. It was more like, "Thank you for understanding that I am just a thoughtless, idiot kid and for not telling my father."

I knew he was never going to say anything about the night before, and from that moment on, I never let a mean word be said about Ed Swayler without coming to his defense.

*****

Of my four friends, Kent Skulsky, Sticks, was the most normal. He was kind of a gangly, odd-looking kid, but his shy humility along with his athletic skill made him every adult's favorite.

Whenever I was looking for someone to play with and I mentioned Fud or Pastor Jim Bob, my mother would say, "Maybe Kent isn't busy." She liked all my friends, but felt I was least likely to get into trouble with Sticks.

Sticks excelled in every sport. He could swim faster, jump higher, hit a baseball further, catch a football better, bowl down more pins, make a longer putt, sink a basket from farther out, and score more points at almost any sport than kids much older.

He had neither the build nor the killer instinct that high school coaches might look for in a budding star, but they were already licking their lips as they watched Sticks run circles around the rest of us in playground games.

It was a problem for our little group of five, because Sticks was involved in so many athletic events that it often drew him away from us. I was an all right athlete and often enjoyed watching Sticks and occasionally playing on this team or that with him, but Pastor Jim Bob, Fud and Gracie were hopeless athletes and would rather have

~1957~

watched jell-O congeal than a baseball game.

Sticks was always trying to get us involved in sports so that he could do the things he loved and still spend time with his good buddies. He once convinced us all to join him on a softball team. Jim Bob, Fud and Gracie consented only because Oak, the little town in which the games were played, had a school with a spiral, slippery-slide type fire escape that we could climb up and slide down when our team was up to bat. And, they showed movies on the side of a shed as soon as it became too dark to play ball.

We slid down the slide feet first, head first, sitting, lying, and we saw a couple of good movies, but at the end of our second game, the coach requested Sticks ask three of the four of us not to come the following week. I never went back either.

The answer to our dilemma seemed to arrive in the spring of sixth grade. Mr. McKee, or Mr. Magoo as we lovingly called him because of his google-eyed glasses, was our teacher. He also coached track at the high school, and had decided that, after coaching unsuccessfully for twenty years, he might do well to start with us kids early on.

Thus, in the spring he formed the sixth grade track team and strongly urged all to take part. It seemed like a good idea. Sticks would be the star, but there were enough different events that we might all find our niche. Tryouts were not held. Desire was all we needed, and that we possessed to varying degrees.

Gracie would join only if she didn't have to run, which restricted her choice of events considerably. She said that she had always liked to throw things, so the discus and shot-put appealed to her, even though she wasn't very big.

~Boomer~

Fud had the body of a shot-putter, but not the strength. In phy ed it took several of us pushing from below to get him to do one pull-up. And when Gracie out-threw him in both the discus and shot in the first trial, he slunk off to look for another event. In the end, the choice was made for him.

Fud's father always seemed a bit embarrassed by Fud's inability to score points at anything other than a math test, and saw this new activity as a means through which Fud might lose some pounds and generally shape up. I'm not sure if it came from his playful sense of humor or from a genuine concern for Fud's health, but Mr. Untiedt convinced Mr. Magoo that Fud should train for the mile run.

Pastor Jim Bob was to be our high-jumper. He could actually jump quite high, but his form was that of a pouncing cat. Try as he might, Mr. Magoo could not change this.

I became a sprinter. I wasn't that fast, but I also liked to play basketball, and Sticks thought that sprint training might improve my movement up the court. Sticks moved from event to event beating each of us soundly.

Mostly we just competed against each other. We had practices twice a week after school. Mr. Magoo set as our goal that we beat him in our event. That was all except Sticks, who could beat him in any event, except the high jump, which was his specialty in college.

For Pastor Jim Bob he set a lesser goal, as it was obvious that he would never come within three feet of Mr. Magoo in the high jump. Besides, Mr. Magoo was getting on in years, and the once or twice he actually did a high

~1957~

jump for us, he rose rather slowly and painfully.

The highlight of our season was the Saturday on which Mr. Magoo had arranged an actual track meet for us to compete against the two schools he could find in our area that were willing to form something akin to a track squad.

We practiced three times that week and arrived at school the morning of the meet filled with team spirit and the donuts that Mrs. Untiedt had sent along with Fud. The meet was to be held at Spicer, a thirty-minute bus ride from Chandler, which allowed us time to take ninety-nine bottles of beer from the wall twice over. Rather than listen to it a third time, Mr. Magoo quieted us for a pep talk. He spoke of stretching ourselves to limits beyond. He urged us to bring honor to old Chandler Elementary. He reminded us to go to the bathroom before our event started. He asked us if we had any questions.

Pastor Jim Bob raised his hand and asked if Mr. Magoo thought Russia's launching the Sputnik satellite into space yesterday would put us in any danger.

His response? "Not before the end of the track meet."

Our entrance into the stadium was designed to frightened the other two teams. Mr. Magoo had borrowed uniforms for us from the junior high, and while the other competitors stood in street clothes, we moved as a wave of blue and gold.

Our intimidation continued into the first event, the 100-yard dash, in which Sticks crossed the finish line about 30 yards ahead of me, who just managed to edge out a Spicer boy for second place.

Our dominance then began to crumble. Gracie

~Boomer~

became disoriented while spinning in the discus ring on her first attempt, and launched the disk into a gathering of Bickford athletes who fortunately were able to scramble to safety.

I stumbled at the start and finished a disappointing fourth in the 200-yard dash.

Perhaps the low point of our day took place in the high jump area. Because our uniforms came from the junior high, some of them were rather loose-fitting, Pastor Jim Bob's in particular. He was a little more excited about competing than the rest of us, and as he prepared for his first jump, he quickly stripped off the long warm-up pants of his uniform. Unfortunately, in his haste, he also pealed off his running shorts, and stepped to the starting line wearing a jockstrap and a shirt which was not quite long enough to cover his butt.

Gracie, who had seen this same body part in Sticks' bedroom some months earlier, was first to recognize it. While Pastor Jim Bob crouched into his best approach stance, Gracie dashed to the sideline, retrieved his shorts from inside his warm-up, and delivered them to the good Pastor, who was just about to break for the bar. Word had spread quickly, and two-thirds of the competitors watched as Jim Bob set a world record for donning shorts.

The morning climaxed with the running of the mile. Mr. Magoo had made this one of Sticks two events, so that if the meet were close, we would have our strength in reserve. Our other entry, of course, did not bring high hopes. Fud. The meet was close. We were actually tied with Spicer, but a first place from Sticks in the mile would assure us our victory.

~1957~

The gun sounded. Off bounded the six contestants, although "bounded" was not exactly the verb to describe Fud's running.

Sticks did not disappoint. By the end of the first lap of the quarter-mile track, he was well ahead of the other five. Fud was well behind them.

By the time Sticks crossed the finish line, ending the race and winning the meet, Fud was not far into his third lap. Rather than slowing, Sticks continued running at his smooth, even pace, and it was not long before he once again passed Fud.

As he came in front of the grandstand, I yelled to him, "Sticks. The race is over. What are you doing?"

He yelled back, "I think I can do two miles faster than Fud's one."

Onward he strode. As Fud finished his third lap, Sticks passed him again. He now had two laps left to Fud's one. The other four runners had finished, and Fud was assured of last place.

"Eat my dust, Freddie," said Sticks as he shot by.

"Eat my donuts," yelled Fud back, the strain of the run obviously keeping him from making any sensible reply. But the challenge stirred him and he seemed to hasten his stride slightly.

By the time Sticks passed him again, Fud was very near to the halfway mark of his final lap. Sticks, who had run all out on his first mile, was beginning to flag near the end of this second, spontaneous mile.

By the time Fud reached the final stretch, Sticks had pulled even with him, but was visibly out of gas. Not that Fud had much petrol left. The two staggered evenly

~Boomer~

toward the finish line.

By this time the other competitors had become aware of what was happening, and had gathered near the finish line. For some unknown reason, their allegiance had swung to Fud.

From the group came shouts of encouragement. "Kick it in gear, big guy." "Blister him." "Go, Fud!" Then up came the cry, "Fud, Fud, Fud, Fud." It echoed through the stadium.

Buoyed by this unexpected show of support, Fud reached within himself and pulled ahead of Sticks. But the trim athlete, sensing defeat, lengthened his stride and again pulled even with his bulky competitor.

At the finish line, Fud stretched his chest forward, as Mr. Magoo had taught him, lost his balance and plunged toward the cinders. The top of his head crossed the finish line as he reached out with his hands to brace his fall. Sticks crossed an instant later.

The crowd erupted into cheers. "Fud, Fud, Fud, Fud," they chanted. The members of all three teams rushed to the tubby figure stretched out face first on the track. They swept him to his feet, hoisted him onto their shoulders, and began a victory lap around the track shouting, "Fud, Fud, Fud, Fud."

I stayed behind and crouched by the side of Sticks, who had sunk to the cinders in exhaustion.

"I thought I could do it," he said dejectedly. "I really gave it all I had."

"Look at it this way," I comforted. "You must be the first man in the history of track to finish both first and last in the same race."

~1957~

I helped him to his feet and put my arm around his shoulder. We headed toward the bus.

Ahead of us rolled the triumphant throng shouting, "Fud, Fud, Fud, Fud."

2004

The honk of a car's horn brought me out of my reverie. I suddenly realized that I was standing in the driveway staring at my boyhood home. I had no idea how long I had been there. A woman in a car to my front was gently waving me to one side so that she might pass. I stepped to the driver's side and gave her a sheepish smile. She stopped beside me and rolled down her window.

"May I help you find something?" she asked.

I laughed. "My youth," I said. "I seem to have lost my carefree boyhood."

She played along. "You might try Sverdrup Street over two blocks. There are always lots of boyhoods out playing over there." She paused and leaned closer to her window. "Do I know you from somewhere?"

"Oh, I don't think so," I said. "My name is Eugene Boomer. My parents used to own this house. I grew up in it. Do you live here now?"

"Yes. We moved here about six years ago. Boomer? Was it your dad that just died this week?"

"Yes. I'm here for the funeral tomorrow."

"I'm sorry. I didn't really know him. I didn't even

realize that he had lived in our house. We moved here from Lakeland in '98. We don't know many of the older people in town, unless they go to our church. Would you like to have a look inside the house?"

"Oh, no," I said. "I can't bother you. You're just leaving. No, I don't need to do that."

"Oh, come on. It's no bother. I'm just going for groceries, and I've got all afternoon. It'll be fun for you."

Before I could protest further, she backed the car off the sidewalk, turned off the ignition, and got out. She reached out her hand to me and said, "I'm Joyce Hemseth, and I'll be your tour guide for the day."

Her smiling good nature put me entirely at ease, and whether or not I cared a lick to see the old house, I had no doubt that the next few minutes would be pleasant ones. Her fiery red hair and trim figure caught my eye as she turned away.

She led me up the front steps and held the door open for me. "Let's see if that boyhood is hiding in here somewhere. I enclosed the porch a couple of years ago to give us more space in the living room. That must look really different to you."

I couldn't tell this charming woman that I thought the renovation had ruined the look of the house and possibly crippled my search for boyhood memories. I simply said, "Yes, I spent lots of hours hanging out in that porch."

But as I walked through the door and past the new construction, I felt my breath catch. Had I been asked outside to describe the place, I doubt that I could have remembered a thing, but here before me was the totally familiar.

The living room, into which I stepped, and dining

~2004~

room were separated by an archway. As a boy, I had often fixed a miniature hoop on that arch, through which my brother and I had scored thousands of miniature baskets. The rugs were different, but the hardwood flooring which surrounded them was unchanged.

Mrs. Hemseth respected my musings and walked silently behind me. We passed into the tiny awkward kitchen which held a rectangular table in the exact spot where I had eaten for eighteen years.

The cupboards had been refinished, but they were the same cupboards with the same hardware. I reached out and opened one, almost expecting to see my mother's choice of groceries on the other side.

On the wall to my right was a black heating grate, about two feet square. Below it was a rug, on which lounged a golden retriever who was eyeing me suspiciously. I stooped down and offered it my hand. When he sniffed it harmlessly, I scratched between his ears.

"Cozy spot there, Sport." I said.

"It's Turk," said Mrs. Hemseth. "He loves to sit there in the winter time and absorb all the heat."

I continued petting Turk. "I used to do the same," I said. "On snowy mornings my sister and I would huddle together in front of this vent and listen to the radio, hoping that Chandler would be announced as one of the schools closed for the day." The image was so strong with me that I could feel heat coming out of the grate.

I bent lower and snuggled my head into Turk's neck. He yawned and squirmed a bit in my tightened grasp.

I swallowed the lump in my throat and sighed rather deeply. Standing, I turned back into the room.

~Boomer~

"Mrs. Hemseth," I said, "I've taken too much of your time."

"It's Joyce," she said, "and today all I got is time. Is there something else you'd like to see?"

I looked around the kitchen, and then out of nowhere a thought struck me. I stepped over to a row of cabinets. I reached under the counter top which was waist-high. My index finger found a little wooden latch which I remembered revolved clockwise. This allowed me to lower a portion of the counter's facing. In the resulting opening was a little drawer which I slid outward.

"Good heavens!" cried Mrs. Hemseth. "I didn't know that was there. Six years in this house and I didn't even know about that."

"Neither did my mother for a long time," I said. "I was fiddling around one day and just accidentally triggered it. My mother was the only one in the kitchen when it happened. She told me that from now on it was my secret drawer. She was always hiding candy and little presents in it, knowing that eventually, when I was alone in the kitchen, I would open the drawer and find the prize."

"Oh, you were her favorite."

"No, I don't think so. I'm sure she had other secrets that she shared with my brother and sister. And with my friends and my cousins. No matter who you were, my mother convinced you that you were the most important person in the world. My friends used to love to stay over night at my house, because by morning they felt like royalty. My mother had an endless capacity for kindness."

"You said 'had'. She's not alive then."

"No. She died a year ago, just a year before my father."

~2004~

"I'm sorry. It must have been very hard to lose someone that warm and loving. She sounds like an incredible person."

Suddenly I felt like I had let the conversation slip too far into my personal life. I immediately liked Mrs. Hemseth, but I had only just met her, and I certainly wasn't going to reveal to her that I had virtually abandoned my mother years before her death. I just smiled and shook my head to acknowledge my mother's quality.

Perhaps to keep me from bursting into tears, Mrs. Hemseth moved on. "Where did you sleep as a boy? Surely you want to revisit your old bedroom."

"Oh, if you wouldn't mind. I can't believe I'm taking up your whole day."

She dismissed the thought with a wave of her hand. "Lead on," she said. "It's got to be one of the two rooms down that hall."

I walked past what had been my sister's bedroom and turned left into the room that my brother and I had shared until Elizabeth had left for college, and Tom took over her room.

It was and had always been a dark and rather dreary room, with only one small window. Part of that window was still covered over by a large bush growing up that side of the house. I could remember being really spooked some nights by the scratching of its branches on the window. Twin beds were in the identical position that ours had been.

"I've got two boys that sleep here," Joyce said. "One in sixth grade and one in fourth."

"Two years apart," I said. "My brother and I were four. Being that much older, he kind of resented having to share a room with little brother. It was always his room more than mine, until he moved to the other bedroom. What does Mr. Hemseth do?"

"Usually whatever he pleases. We're divorced. Actually, that's why I moved to Chandler with the boys. To escape."

"I'm sorry. I didn't mean to pry."

"Oh, that's all right. Now we have both shared a bit of our past." Her smile was lovely. I found myself wondering how any man could let what appeared to me a jewel get away.

I realized that I had been starring at her and looked away. I picked up a baseball glove from the dresser and slapped the ball into the mitt.

"Funny. The times I remember most were the times when I was sick and had to stay in here all day. My mom would bring my meals on a tray. When I was in seventh grade, I was sick every day there was a World Series game. My dad actually moved our great big television set in here so that I could watch. I don't believe they let me get away with that." Tears welled into my eyes, and my chin dropped to my chest.

Mrs. Hemseth stepped to my side and gently rubbed my shoulder. It was an incredibly intimate thing for a stranger, particularly a younger stranger to do. I reached up and put my hand on top of hers.

"I guess I found more of my boyhood than I bargained for. Thank you so much for letting me do this."

"You're entirely welcome," she said. "Is the rest of your family here for the funeral?"

"Yes. My older sister just lives over in Shelton. My

~2004~

brother is coming from Baton Rouge. It is going to be very good to see them this week, despite the sad occasion."

"This has been very emotional for you. You must have many happy memories from your years here. Please stop by again sometime. Bring your brother and sister, if you like. I'm sure they would enjoy seeing the old home as well."

I reached my hand toward her. She took it and softly drew me into a hug. The warmth of the gesture took my breath away, and I felt my face blush as it rested on her shoulder. I felt myself enormously drawn to this woman. When we stepped back, I smiled and took another close look at her lovely face, wondering how much younger than I she really was. She followed me as I moved toward the front door.

"It's all kind of awkward, " I said. " I've sort of cut myself off from the rest of the family the last years. I'm afraid we're not as closely knit as we used to be in this house."

As Joyce Hemseth bid me goodbye in front of the house, I was struck by the sad truth of what I had just said. We had been a happy family in this house, and when I left it, somehow the happiness remained behind; indeed, it seemed I left behind any sense of family at all.

On Morse Street we had seemed like one of those all American families. Fud sometimes even called us the Cleevers, after Beaver and his model family from television in the 60s. We sat down to supper together each night. We rode in the car together on Sunday afternoons as *The Shadow* played on the radio.

We weren't wealthy by any means, but our parents were dedicated to making our lives comfortable. In truth, even though my father always maintained a stern front, he

~Boomer~

demanded very little of us.

In turn, Elizabeth and Tom never caused even slight disappointments for our parents. Elizabeth's musical talents with her voice and the clarinet, and Tom's academic rise to class valedictorian were sources of tremendous family pride.

I was more of a trial, with an occasional D in biology, or a speeding ticket on a Saturday night. But then I was faced with filling the impossibly large shoes of my siblings. By my senior year I had accepted my artistic and academic inferiority and tried to find some sense of self in other endeavors. In fact, with much help from my four best friends, I was a very happy teen.

Chapter 2

Liberace and Other Teen Tales

1962

Chandler High School was small enough that with a careful plan and a little finagling, friends could end up in classes with one another. Getting five friends into the same class took more than a little finagling, but with a senile chemistry teacher and a gullible guidance counselor, we were off and running. Once we all had the same chemistry class, our favorite English teacher cooperated with the next step. Then gym, American History and math fell nicely into place, and we were set to spend our senior year together.

We all had reputations as cooperative and enthusiastic students, so the idea of having us together in class struck fear into the heart of no teacher. Perhaps it should have.

Most vulnerable was Mr. Baldwick, our chemistry teacher. At four times our age, he had used up the best of his classroom years. A substantial hearing loss left him unfairly at our mercy.

Mr. Baldwick, like several others of my teachers, had been around to teach my brother, Tom, four years ahead of me and my sister, Elizabeth, two years ahead of Tom. As Mr. Baldwick occasionally pointed out, "my mastery of the Periodic Table" did not quite measure up to the level my

~Boomer~

siblings had achieved.

Our resident scientist, Pastor Jim Bob, reveled in the class and hung on each of Mr. Baldwick's words, which to the rest of us seemed excessive.

Fud was bright enough to quickly master the course material and still have enough time to seek mischief. One day he could no longer contain himself.

We had no chemistry room, so the class was held in the biology lab. The room was surrounded by cupboards and shelves, holding a wide variety of biological specimens.

One large cabinet displayed a skeleton which we promptly dubbed Sticks II. Atop the cabinets perched an array of stuffed animal life. One of these became the object of Fud's attention.

One afternoon Mr. Baldwick stepped into the adjoining storage room to get materials he needed for an upcoming demonstration. At his disappearance, Fud leapt from his seat, and with overacted stealth, crept his way to the cupboard just to the right of the storage room doorway. On top of the cupboard rested a lonely, male, mallard duck. Fud climbed aboard Jane Harkins desk, which allowed him to reach the colorful bird. He grasped the base of the display with one hand, and with the other pinched a large bunch of feathers from the duck. He stuffed them into his pocket, mimed a sinister, hysterical laugh, climbed to the floor and returned to his seat.

The chuckles that rippled through the classroom were certainly not loud enough to reach the semi-deaf Mr. Baldwick.

Almost immediately, he re-entered the classroom, failing to notice the small cloud of dust and a couple of odd

~1962~

feathers that floated to the floor as he passed.

Over the next months, Fud found many occasions to repeat his feather theft. He was uncanny in anticipating the movements of Mr. Baldwick.

Only once did Baldwick re-enter when Fud was anywhere but back in his seat. On that occasion Fud was back on the floor, and when Mr. Baldwick said, "Mr. Untiedt?", Fud deftly plucked his pencil from behind his ear, waved it at the teacher and proceeded to the sharpener. By the middle of the school year, the poor, helpless mallard was plucked nearly bald.

To our surprise, one day Fud raised his hand in a pause of our chemistry work and said to Mr. Baldwick, "You know, Mr. Baldwick, that duck up on the counter is really looking bad. The thing hardly has any feathers on it at all."

A few chuckles came from Fud's classmates. Usually Fud's antics got a mixed reaction, if not wide disapproval from his peers, but everyone had watched his feathernapping escapade with amusement.

Mr. Baldwick gazed up at the decimated skeleton. "Why, my goodness, Mr. Untiedt, you're right. The poor thing is practically naked." This brought a rousing laugh from the class.

When it ceased, Fud said. "You know, I've been doing some work with taxidermy, and if you'd like, I could take him home and see if I can fix him up a little." As far as any of us knew, Fud knew nothing at all about taxidermy.

"If you'd like, Mr. Untiedt," said Mr. Baldwick. "I'll tell Mr. Peterson that you have him, so that he won't be missed."

So this time, with the blessing of the unsuspecting chemistry teacher, Fud once again climbed upon Jane

Harkins' desk to grasp the violated duck.

The next day Fud was a little late to class. When he walked through the door, the students gasped. In his hands he held the stuffed mallard duck, more beautifully arrayed than the original. Fud had apparently saved every feather and had replaced them with surprising expertise.

Mr. Baldwick received the duck as if he were getting the Stanley Cup. He walked around the room with it, giving each student a close look at Fud's artistry.

From that moment on, Fud was Mr. Baldwick's prized student. He beamed whenever Fud gave a correct answer. He patted his back when he returned Fud's perfect or near perfect tests.

To Fud's credit, he returned Mr. Baldwick's generosity in kind. He didn't take further advantage of the old man, but rather became somewhat protective of him. Fud and Pastor Jim Bob became Mr. Baldwick's lab assistants and were invaluable in that role.

At the end of the year Mr. Baldwick retired. At his retirement party, Fud got permission to present the elderly teacher with a beautifully wrapped box.

Upon opening the gift, Mr. Baldwick found the stuffed mallard duck, with the names of Fud and all of his classmates signed upon the wooden base. Mr. Anderson, the biology teacher, had given his blessing to the project, although he must have wondered why this duck had acquired such fame.

*****

Throughout our high school years, our group of five was a brash bunch. We were constantly doing things that we shouldn't, many of them more bold and outrageous than Fud's duck caper. Fortunately, we were growing up in naive

~1962~

times of Eisenhower and Kennedy's Camelot. Our pranks, while mischievous, were seldom hurtful. Had we been growing up ten years later, some of us might have done drugs or done sex, or in the case of Fud, perhaps even done time, but we were blessed with a world whose innocence we could violate with pranks that satisfied our teenage need to rebel, but didn't scar our victims or ourselves too badly. School brought us together daily. We loved it; it was our friend. For Sticks and me, no one personified love more than our English teacher, Miss Naegle.

She was young. She was beautiful. Sticks and I had actually paid two girls ten dollars each for their front row seats so that we could be closer to those absolutely perfect breasts.

Of course, Sticks never would have admitted that he had paid for her breasts. But he had. When she came close to him, he literally couldn't speak. His ears turned red and he couldn't take his eyes off his desk. She thought he was just shy. She thought it was adorable and that she could tease and charm him out of it. The more she teased and the more she charmed, the more tormented he became.

My adoration of Miss Naegle, on the other hand, was entirely sophomoric and sexual. My only torment was hiding the erection I got in English class whenever Miss Naegle wore a tight sweater.

"God, did you see her today when she bent over to pick up that chalk," I said as we left English and headed for gym. "Those babies must measure in at least three Henrys." A Henry was a term some crass boys in our class had devised for the measurement of breasts. It was defined as a cubic handful.

~Boomer~

"Come on, Boomer," objected Sticks. "Clean it up. Miss Naegle has enough goons staring at her. She doesn't need you too."

"You two are smitten," said Fud. "Why doesn't one of you ask her out on a date?"

"Oh right," I said. "Maybe we could double with Pastor Jim Bob and Miss Hawkins." Miss Hawkins was the Latin teacher with a reputation for eating students alive.

"Or Fud and Mr. Baldwick," chimed in Gracie.

"Cram it, Gracie," said Fud and shoved her firmly into a row of lockers.

We walked away in silence, the image of the bent over Miss Naegle still warm in my head.

"Speaking of impending dates," said Grace. "Has everybody got their props gathered for their drama scenes tomorrow?"

Miss Naegle had placed us in pairs and had rehearsed each pair in a scene from a play. Grace and I were playing Professor Higgins and Eliza in *Pygmalion*. Fud and Pastor Jim Bob were doing a scene from Eugene O'Neill's *Ah, Wilderness*. Sticks had been the odd man out, so Miss Naegle had given him a scene from *The Rainmaker* and said she would do the part opposite him.

He was terrified at the prospect. He had rehearsed the scene mostly by himself, because Miss Naegle had been busy with the other groups. He wasn't sure he could remember any lines, much less say them, in her presence.

"I've got the smoking jacket and the pipe and the slippers, Gracie," I said. "Don't forget to bring the jewelry."

"My mom won't let me bring it until the day we do it," she said. "I'll remember."

~1962~

"How about you, Sticks," said Pastor Jim Bob. "Are you all ready for your big scene with the teach?"

"I don't know. I guess," Sticks mumbled. "I don't know why we have to do stuff in front of the class anyway."

"Come on, Stick Man," said Jim Bob. "It's your big chance to win your true love."

"Aw drop it man," said Sticks. "I may not even come tomorrow."

We reached phy ed and finished our day with a game of volleyball.

The next day Miss Naegle's English room was littered with stuff students had dragged in for their scenes. Sticks had arrived, but he looked none too happy about it. I walked over to his desk.

"Hey, Sticks. You decided to come. You don't look so great."

"I didn't sleep all night," he said. "This scene thing has me spooked. I'm not sure I can do it."

"Oh, come on," I said. "You can shoot free throws with hundreds of people screaming at you. This little thing should be a piece of cake."

"I just wish I was doing it with someone other than Miss Naegle. I just get so nervous."

I tried to be encouraging. "Some actor once said that if you are nervous on stage, you should imagine the audience is naked."

"Then I would throw up. God, I just want to get this done. I'm shaking all over and it hasn't even started."

"You'll be all right," I said. "Did you bring your props?"

"Oh, no." He sank his head into his hands on his desk.

~Boomer~

"I forgot those too. Maybe she will let me do it some other time."

"Not likely. She said that we have to do it on our scheduled day or lose all the credit. Just substitute some stuff for your props and do it. You'll be all right."

Class began and our scenes played. Their quality varied greatly. Grace and I were first. I set the scene of Pygmalion by reading a little description Miss Naegle had written for us.

I had tried to memorize it, but lost my confidence when I got before the class and mostly read it. Our scene began with me (Higgins) on stage, and Grace (Eliza Doolittle) entering in a fury.

We began with Eliza's line, "Here are your slippers. Take them. And may you never have another day's luck with them." Her recitation was accompanied by her hurling a pair of my father's slippers in my direction.

I struck an arrogant, Higgins pose. Enter Grace. "Here are your slippers. Take them," she shrieked. She hurled the first slipper.

In rehearsals she had always thrown them at my feet. I have heard that in big games, quarterbacks sometimes throw passes too high at first because of excess adrenaline. Grace evidently suffered a like surge. The first slipper struck me with a thump right in the forehead between my eyes.

"Oh, shit, Boomer," Gracie shouted as she rushed to my side. "Are you all right?"

"Grace!" gasped Miss Naegle as she rushed from her seat in the back of the room.

I wasn't entirely all right. The heel of the slipper had struck me solidly and had set my ears to ringing.

~1962~

"God, you've got a big welt on your forehead. I'm sorry. I'm sorry." Grace burst into tears.

It was later decided that Grace's tears and my expressions of pain were far superior to most of the acting in the scenes which followed.

When it was determined that I had received no lasting damage, Miss Naegle agreed that we should take a rest and give our scene another try later in the hour or the next day, if need be.

Fud and Pastor Jim Bob's scene was without doubt the best of the day. Fud was an accomplished actor who had been in several school plays, and their scene heavily depended upon his character for its power.

At the end of their scene the class sat silently for a long moment and then erupted into applause. It was a nice moment for both Fud and Jim Bob.

The last scene of the day was to be *The Rainmaker*, with Sticks as Starbuck and Miss Naegle as Lizzie. It was cruel to make Sticks wait until the end. By the time the other scenes had finished, his stomach had firmly tied itself into knots, and he looked as if he might pass out. He slumped to the front of the room.

Miss Naegle came forward and found her spot. Sticks stiffly struck his opening pose. There was silence. Miss Naegle cupped her hand to her mouth and said in a loud whisper, "Your introduction, Kent."

Sticks grimaced. "Oh, yeah." He fished into his pocket and pulled out a wrinkled piece of paper. He turned to the front. "Our play is called *The Rainmaker*. I'm Starbuck and Miss Naegle is Lizzie." Sticks was shaking like a leaf, but unlike me, he looked up at us and started to tell us his

~Boomer~

introduction instead of just reading it.

"The play is during the dust bowl days of the thirties when there isn't any rain on the farms. Starbuck comes to town and tells the people that he can make it rain, and they pay him a bunch of money to do it. Lizzie is this young woman about Starbuck's age. She thinks he is a fraud, but she is kind of attracted to him at the same time."

Sticks returned to his starting pose, but then remembered. "Oh, yeah. Starbuck always carries this big stick with him, and throughout the play it becomes a symbol of his manhood." Sticks reached into his pocket. "I forgot my big stick at home, so I'm going to use this pencil instead."

A faint smile crossed Miss Naegle's face, and then with a slight intake of breath, she snapped it back to the stern glare of her character. I knew by the way those perfect breasts were quivering, that was she in the teachers' lounge, she would have been doubled up in hysterical laughter on one of the ugly vinyl couches. But she was determined not to embarrass this shy boy, who was so agitated about performing before the class, that he neither recognized the Freudian implications of his prop substitution, nor that his friends in the class were squirming through all sorts of gyrations to keep from exploding into laughter.

Such was our respect for Miss Naegle that we took our cue from her and maintained our composure, even at the risk of rupturing internal organs.

She was about to do the acting job of a lifetime, and twenty-four pairs of eyes were riveted upon her to see if she could pull it off.

Quickly, she slipped into the raging character of Lizzie, raising her lovely chin into the air and turning away from

~1962~

Sticks.

She snapped, "You're not satisfied to steal our money! You have to make jackasses out of us!"

Hearing Miss Naegle, who never lost her temper, saying the word jackasses in that tone of voice, brought a slight gasp from members of the class.

"Why'd you send them out on those fool errands?" she continued, turning back to him. "What for?"

The force of her performance momentarily stunned Sticks. He stared at her with his mouth slightly open. I think he was genuinely hurt that his beloved would attack him so harshly.

After an awkward pause, Sticks gained his voice and croaked, "Maybe I sent them out so's I could talk to you alone."

Lizzie took a slight step backward, surprised that Starbuck wanted to be with her alone.

"Alone?" she questioned. "Then why didn't you just say it straight out: Lizzie, I want to talk to you alone - man to man."

Sticks was beginning to settle a little, enough to hazard a gesture. He said with a little bit of sarcasm, "Man to man, Lizzie," and he wagged his pencil at her playfully.

The corners of Miss Naegle's mouth again turned up and quivered. She swallowed deeply.

"Excuse me," she said. It came out breathy, almost as a giggle. She swallowed again and steeled herself. If this went on too long, she was in danger of apoplexy.

She again recovered and snapped, "I made a mistake - you're not a man!"

That the unusually coordinated Sticks should at that

moment drop his pencil, was a fluke. Miss Naegle's hand flew to her mouth and her eyes closed. Her face turned red and tears began to leak from her eyes. If the next line had been hers, she could not have spoken.

Sticks seemed momentarily thrown off, but then delivered his next line, "Why are you fussin' at the buttons on your dress?"

In her distraction, Miss Naegle had forgotten that she should be "fussin with her buttons," so to recover, quickly dropped her hand from her mouth to her chest.

Starbuck continued, "Let 'em alone. They're all buttoned up fine - as tight as they'll ever get." Sticks was most uncomfortable delivering this line. I think he thought the "they" referred to Miss Naegle's supple breasts, and gesturing toward them and talking about them made his face turn bright red and his voice crack.

To cover his discomfort, he unfortunately chose to stoop down and retrieve the troublesome pencil, the last thing Miss Naegle wanted re-entered into the scene.

Bravely she fought on. "Mr. Starbuck, you've got more gall."

"A woman gets all decked out in a pretty dress, she must be expectin' her beau. Where is he? It's getting kinda late."

"I'm not expecting anybody."

"Oh, I see. You were- but now you ain't. Stand you up?" On this last, Sticks spontaneously decided upon one final dramatic gesture. With his left thumb and forefinger he made a circle, and on the word "up," he poked the pencil through.

A clatter resounded from the back of the room. I

~1962~

turned to discover that Fud had fallen out of his chair and was clutching his stomach, still struggling to make noises which did not sound like laughter.

Mercifully, the bell rang. We noisily stood to make our exit. Miss Naegle had collapsed into a chair, both hands now covering her mouth, a stunned look in her eyes.

Again, she regrouped. She stepped to Sticks side and put her hand on his arm. "You were very good, Kent. I'm sorry I forgot to do the buttons. Oh, my!" She fanned herself with her hand. "Goodness, I don't know why I was so nervous. Well, that's over now, isn't it?"

Sticks returned to his desk and collected his books and made his way toward the door. All the while she followed him along babbling nonsense. I had never before seen her flustered.

The next day one of the guys in the class tipped off Sticks as to why we had all reacted so strangely to his performance. Sticks' only reaction was to retrieve his ten dollars and move to the back of the room with Fud and Gracie and Pastor Jim Bob. I, however, held fast and retained my proximity to those perfect breasts.

It was only later that I realized Miss Naegle had shamelessly used them against me. Over the course of the year, she turned me from a reluctant reader to a literary enthusiast.

Each night I religiously read her assignments so that the next day I could call her over and ask about a favorite passage. She would bend over my shoulder and point to the words as she explained. She was about the only person in town to call me Gene. It was like she didn't want to be so casual as to call me Boomer, but didn't want to be so formal as to call me Eugene. I loved that and everything else about her.

I would listen intently, breathing in her fragrance, forming my next question to hold her above me. The more wisely I spoke, the longer she stayed and the closer she bent. I racked my brain to discover a unique thought. She glowed when I succeeded.

By the end of the year she had lured me through Dickens and Shakespeare and even T. S. Eliot. Miss Naegle would stoop to anything to foist her favorite masterpieces onto us. I still love her for it. But oh, those breasts.

*****

For a few days Sticks received a good deal of ribbing about the symbol of his manhood. Often he would meet a fellow classmate in the hallway who would smile and tuck his, or even more embarrassing, her pencil behind an ear. But since Sticks was well liked, the teasing died out quickly.

While Sticks seldom did anything to raise the level of school gossip, Pastor Jim Bob punctuated his high school career with a number of legendary faux pax, some of them accidental and others misguidedly planned.

Pastor Jim Bob was the youngest child of Pastor Roberts, the minister of the Chandler Baptist Church. Pastor Roberts' religious philosophy was just to the right of the famous evangelist with whom he shared his last name, and he strove mightily, and with general success, to keep both his congregation and his family on the straight and narrow.

Pastor Roberts oldest daughter, Esther, was well on her way to becoming a saint, or at least marrying a minister in whose church she could be secretary or choir director or both. Pastor Jim Bob's older brother, Paul, was safely away

~1962~

at seminary by the time Jim Bob reached high school.

Jim Bob himself gives credence to the maxim, if you keep having children, eventually your luck is likely to run out. Reverend Roberts must have thought from time to time that after two, he perhaps should have given up his insistence on naming his children for biblical characters, or at least have chosen a different namesake for his third-born than the dutiful, mild-mannered James. Certainly Judas wouldn't have come into father's reconsideration, but perhaps someone prone to occasional straying, such as Thomas or David.

His neighbors would have suggested that Dennis might have been a more appropriate name, after the well-known cartoon character who plagues all those around him with innocent, but none-the-less annoying foibles.

Jim Bob was an odd looking kid. It had something to do with his homemade haircut. His father always managed to make Jim Bob's hair look like it belonged on someone else. His smile, too, seemed just a little large for his face.

This strange appearance was paired with an intense, but somewhat unbalanced, curiosity. If dropping the cat from the roof of the garage resulted in no harm to the animal, would the same thing be true of one of the neighbor's white rabbits? If you built a steep ramp and generated enough speed, how many neighborhood children could you sail over on your bicycle? That sort of thing.

Hospital records confirm that by the time he was ten, Jim Bob had set a Chandler town record for broken bones, most of them his own. By high school, Pastor Jim Bob's classmates were about evenly split between those who admired his "I'll try anything once" approach to life, and those who would cross to the other side of the street when they saw him approaching.

Often it was Fud, the prankster, who lured Pastor Jim Bob into some wayward trap. Looking back, someone should have made a movie about Abbott and Costello with Pastor Jim Bob and Fud as the title characters. They looked the part, and their lives were only marginally less ridiculous than their movie counterparts.

Fud was always saying things like, "I wonder what would happen if you mixed those two together and shook them?"

On one occasion Fud was the innocent cause of Jim Bob's downfall. Fud had the physique of Costello, and he dressed like a nerd more times than not. One day when Pastor Jim Bob came around the corner and saw Mr. Northrup, our world history teacher, stooped over the fountain getting a drink, it is not impossible to imagine how he mistook him for Fud.

Now others might have made the same mistake and said something inappropriate. But when Pastor Jim Bob erred, he did so in a big way.

To the astonishment of the several students hanging around their lockers, poor James slapped a hand on Mr. Northrup's right buttock and shouted, "Fud, you worthless sack of dung."

Mr. Northrup's hand jerked on the fountain's handle, sending a stream of water spouting into his face, so that when he rose and turned to face Pastor Jim Bob, his glasses were dripping profusely.

Happily, it was the lighthearted Mr. Northrop, whom Jim Bob violated, and not our American History teacher, Mr.

~1962~

Preston, who was renown for slamming large boys up against lockers for offenses as slight as littering.

As Mr. Northrop drew out his handkerchief and dried his glasses, he smiled and said to the stunned Jim Bob, "Your water fountain etiquette leaves something to be desired, Roberts. In the future, when you are thirsty, please be a bit less aggressive." He then walked past Jim Bob and returned a hearty slap to the frozen student's butt.

The small group fortunate enough to witness the exchange exploded with laughter. For days butt slapping became a favorite greeting in the halls of Chandler High.

*****

Pastor Jim Bob's unusual exchange with Mr. Northrup did nothing to improve his helplessness and nearly failing grade in history. On the other hand, his facility in the field of science continued to be remarkable.

Ever since his father gave him a chemistry set, with which he, assisted by the rest of us, had twice set the parsonage on fire, Jim Bob had reveled in the mystery of experimentation.

He experimented with every aspect of science. He built extravagant model airplanes with which he dabbled in the science of flight. He probed the mysteries of life by dissecting all manner of road kill.

Unfortunately, when he was with Fud, his main endeavors to advance science were in the area of concoction. He and Fud would mix almost any elements in an effort to create a new color or reaction.

Oddly, it was the creation of new smells that attracted Fud. That fascination led them, and unfortunately me, to one of Chandler's most embarrassing incidents.

~Boomer~

It happened at one of the oddest performances in the history of entertainment, the night that Liberace played a concert in the Chandler High School Gymnasium.

Liberace happened to be the owner of a horse farm outside of Chandler, and one winter while he was visiting, he struck a bargain with a neighboring farmer. Jeb Hitchcock made the deal with the flamboyant pianist. If he would play a concert in Chandler, Jeb would clear his lane of snow every winter for an indeterminate amount of time.

I don't know if Liberace thought that this hick would just forget about the deal or what, but if he did, he badly misjudged Jeb Hitchcock, one of Chandler's most stubborn citizens. After numerous calls to Liberace's agent, Jeb announced one day in the Cardinal Café that Liberace would be playing a concert on April 3, and that tickets would be on sale at the high school the following Monday.

Now Jeb had been promising this concert for quite some time and had become the butt of endless jokes due to his insistence; so, when he made his latest announcement, few took him seriously, and only a handful showed up at the high school the following Monday to purchase tickets. When news got out that there actually were tickets to purchase, the entire town went somewhat insane.

The next morning at 9:00 A.M., Irene Beck, whose greatest challenge had previously been peddling tickets for the district basketball championship, opened her window to a line that nearly circled the school and contained a representative from nearly every family in the four county area.

My dad, who was mildly allergic to crowds, was fourth in line, having arrived at 6:30.

~1962~

When my mom announced that this was "the chance of a lifetime," I didn't realize that she meant my lifetime as well, and that my dad was purchasing tickets for the entire family. I had watched Liberace on television Sunday nights several times with my parents, and I was certain that I could die happy without witnessing him live.

When my father proudly announced that he had gotten "great seats" that night at the supper table, I said without much consideration, "I don't think he is somebody I really want to see. Maybe I'll do something else that night."

For the next ten minutes it was a contest to see who could jump up and down on me the longest. "I stood in line for three hours getting this ticket for you," shouted my father. "You're sure as hell going to use it, and you will enjoy it."

"How could you not want to see Liberace," my mother said, looking at me as if I had just announced that I had eaten the family cat. "That's like saying you wouldn't want to see Frank Sinatra. Eugene, these chances don't come along every day."

I wanted to say that I wouldn't want to see Frank Sinatra either, but the intensity of their rebukes let me know that this time there was no sense trying to squeeze out of it.

For the next month the town was nutty. All anyone could talk about was the upcoming Liberace concert. My mother and two of her friends drove all the way to Minneapolis to purchase the gowns they would wear that night. And while there they picked up frilly shirts and bow ties and other accessories to spruce up the male population of Chandler.

Jeb Hitchcock was elevated immediately to the role of most important citizen. Some years before he had lost his

~Boomer~

wife to cancer, and now suddenly every woman in Chandler was stopping by the farm with a hot dish to be sure he was adequately fed.

Mercifully, the night of the gala arrived before the entire town exploded from the energy of anticipation. Unfortunately, Chandler had no hall remotely appropriate for such an event, and the only place that could seat the ticket holders was the high school auditorium. Because it was simply two levels of seats overlooking the basketball court, it was not as elegant as the deep blue gown my mother had purchased at Daytons for the affair.

In an effort to achieve grandeur, an enormous search light was secured to wave across the Chandler sky from the school parking lot. It had been rented by Tupperman Ford, and was so bright that nearly every uninformed driver happening through Chandler that night made a detour up the hill to see what the heck was going on.

Through a very complicated ticket swapping plan devised by Fud, he, Pastor Jim Bob and I ended up sitting together. Our parents had allowed this in the hope it would stop our whining about having to attend at all.

My brother, who had come all the way home from college, and I relinquished the "best seats in the house" to Pastor Jim Bob's parents, and we retreated to the balcony. From there, brother Tom further swapped this seat with Fud, which landed him beside Fud's older sister, a calculated outcome that made selling the plan to him a cinch.

I'll have to admit that I had never seen my neighbors looking so fine. Men who never wore anything but overalls, appeared in shiny tuxedos with flowers in their lapels. Some of the women were downright daring in their attire. Mrs.

~1962~

Gillespie who lived at the end of our block wore a dress of gold, the top portion of which seemed to float. It had no straps, little front, no back, and had she wore it to any other event that had ever happened in Chandler, her neighbors would have clucked that she would burn in hell for this. But that night she was met with "Oh, Dolores, it's stunning."

My father had intended to walk the four blocks to avoid the traffic snarl he was certain would develop at the school, but my mother was wearing shoes with four inch heels, and demanded delivery as close to the entrance as possible.

My father was right. Everybody in town arrived at the high school at the same moment, and had that moment not been forty-five minutes prior to the start of the concert, Liberace might have played his first two numbers to people groping their way into the dark auditorium. The early arrival allowed everyone to park and to do a fair amount of ogling and admiring.

I met Fud and Jim Bob outside and we stood for a while admiring the rhythmic search light before entering and finding our seats.

The hall actually looked a lot better than I thought it would. Curtains had been pulled to hide all vestiges of the basketball court. The front of the stage had been outlined with rather large baskets of flowers.

Any original identifying markings had long worn off the wooden chairs, so on the arm of each was a piece of masking tape with handwritten seat numbers to match our tickets. Fud sat between Jim Bob and me. The woman to my right wore this pink, puffy dress that sort of spilled out of her seat and into my lap. She didn't seem to notice, and I

~Boomer~

found no graceful way to stuff it back into her territory, so I leaned as far as I could to the left and talked to the guys.

"Did you guys know how to tie your own ties?" asked Fud. He tugged at it and mocked coughing, as if the thing were choking off all air.

"I didn't even have a tie," I said. "This is one of my dad's."

Fud leaned toward Jim Bob, and I heard him say, "Did you bring the stuff?"

Pastor Jim Bob shook his head in the affirmative.

"What stuff?" I asked. "What are you guys doing?"

"Shh!" said Jim Bob sharply, drawing his index finger across his throat.

"We've just got a little surprise for intermission," Fud whispered to me. "Something to spice up the concert." He and Jim Bob grinned at each other.

"Come on," I said out of the side of my mouth. "What gives?"

Just then the lights in the auditorium began to fade, and the anticipation which had bubbled in the town for a month came to a boil.

Once total darkness had been achieved, a follow spot cast a circle of white light onto the stage. Into that circle, to uncertain applause, walked Mr. Peterson, the high school speech teacher.

Usually Mr. Peterson was the announcer at basketball games, and I half-expected him to say, "Starting at piano for Chandler at six feet three inches...."

Before he could begin, from the darkened auditorium echoed a wolf whistle, no doubt from some high schooler not yet aware of proper concert etiquette. A chorus of shhs

~1962~

followed, and I'm sure that my father leaned over to my mother and said, "If that was Eugene, I'll cut off his nuts." And my mother almost certainly said, "Oh, hush, Glen. That wasn't Eugene."

"Good evening, ladies and gentlemen," began Mr. Peterson. "This is the moment we have all been anxiously awaiting. Please join me in welcoming to Chandler, one of the great entertainers of our time, Liberace."

One of the great entertainers of our time. Who was he kidding? On Ed Sullivan he wasn't even as good as that crazy woman and her stupid little sheep.

At that moment something astounding happened. It was as if the entire gymnasium in Chandler Minnesota was transformed into Carnegie Hall.

A host of spotlights focused on the center of the outer golden curtain. It didn't look at all shabby like it usually did with the light shining on it that way. Then suddenly, to the roll of a kettledrum, the whole thing magically folded upward and outward and disappeared revealing a second deep blue curtain, which began crawling up from the bottom until it revealed the most enormous piano I had ever seen. It was white and looked huge from where we were, so it must have looked the size of a semi-trailer from where my folks were.

On top of the piano was this big metal candle thing that had about twenty flaming candles in it. And seated on the piano bench, already pounding out a tune was the most unusual individual any of us had ever seen.

He was dressed from top to bottom in a sparkly sky-blue suit. The lights caught it from every direction and little bursts of light continuously leapt from him. His shoes were white with very large heels, and the right one pumped the pedal of the piano as if he were playing by foot. His silver hair swept to the back of his head and had to be standing up a good five inches at its apex.

But his most striking feature was his smile. His mouth was spread wide, and in it he had to have eighty-five teeth. So accomplished was he at playing that he never looked down, but kept that enormous grin focused right on us.

He was playing Chopin. I recognized it from Music Appreciation class, but he was playing it with more gusto than the guy we had listened to on Mr. Segwick's scratchy old record player.

When he finished the piece, the auditorium exploded with applause. The people of Chandler forgot that they were dressed for Carnegie Hall and cheered and hooted like a Grand Old Opry crowd.

Liberace didn't seem to mind the whistles and shouts and carrying on. He just kept bowing his head practically to the floor and coming back up with that huge grin plastered on his face.

Even when we quieted and he started to talk, he somehow kept that smile firmly in place. That stretching of his cheeks seemed to send his voice up through his nose, and I remember thinking that when he was on Ed Sullivan he sounded like a dork. But the audience loved it and applauded everything he said.

"How do you like the suit?" he asked, and the crowd whistled and roared.

"It was handmade by ten of Italy's finest glass blowers." We howled.

"If I don't sit up straight, the warrantee is voided."

~1962~

We were beside ourselves.

"Do you like the candles?" We did.

"I brought a larger one, but the Chandler fire marshal didn't think it was a good idea."

I could just see Bud Thompson shaking his head and saying without a hint of humor in his voice, "Nope, if you use that one, we're going to have to keep a hose on stage during your performance."

And back to the piano he went, head turned over his shoulder so that we never lost sight of that smile.

He played jazz. He played classical. He even played the newest rage, a Beatles' song, and he did it with such energy that it made performances by the Beatles seem tame.

He used no printed music. He hardly ever looked at the keyboard. His hands and feet pounded so vigorously that at times he seemed to levitate above the piano bench. After a few numbers he took a short break, but almost immediately reappeared on stage in a bright red leather suit that got a standing ovation all by itself.

By the time we reached intermission, people were so hyped up that the level of noise in the lobby was deafening. Little clumps of neighbors recounted Liberace's jokes and re-laughed at his stories and further admired one another's fine attire. I can't think of a happier moment in Chandler history.

Fud, Pastor Jim Bob and I had made our way to the lobby with the rest of the bubbling crowd. We stood in line at concessions and finally managed to get a Coke.

Then Fud led us to the side and ducked into a small area behind the stairway leading to the balcony. I looked over my shoulder to see if anyone was paying attention to us, and when I found everyone engaged in excited conversation, followed Jim Bob into this gap. The area was so narrow that we had to stand side by side and couldn't even turn around. It was long enough so that we could shuffle into the semidarkness, the only light coming from the narrow slot we had entered. I felt kind of stupid, standing in this dark alley sipping my Coke.

"What's going on?" I asked Jim Bob next to me. The echoing noise level in the lobby made it necessary for me to almost shout.

Jim Bob handed his Coke to Fud, reached into his coat pocket, and pulled out a little bottle.

"Ho, ho, ho," chortled Fud as Jim Bob waved the vial in front of his eyes.

"What is it?" I said, just beginning to get the uncomfortable sensation in my stomach that came whenever Fud and Jim Bob had a good idea.

"Hydrogen sulfide," said Jim Bob. "Rotten egg smell."

"Wait a minute, guys," I said. "You're not thinking of opening that in here are you?"

Vivid in my mind was the suffocating smell that had risen when somebody released rotten egg smell in the third floor study hall some months earlier. Rather than punish the innocent, the teacher had moved us all to the cafeteria while they aired out the study hall. For weeks a hint of that sickening odor remained.

I quickly tried to imagine the scene if Pastor Jim Bob removed the cork from that seemingly innocent little bottle. I could imagine screaming, stampeding, trampling. Well, maybe not that dramatic, but it would not have a pleasant result.

"Listen, guys," I said. "I don't think this is such a good

idea. If we get caught, they're liable to hang us."

"We won't overdo it," said Fud. "Jim Bob, just let out a little bit and then we'll slip back into the crowd before anyone smells it."

"I don't know," I said. "I don't know if there is such a thing as a little bit of that stuff."

"Oh, come on," said Fud. "Intermission will be over in a couple minutes. Hurry up, Jim Bob."

I gritted my teeth as Pastor Jim Bob twisted the cork from the little bottle. It was evidently really tight, as he had to pull with his full strength.

Whenever Pastor Jim Bob created one of these concoctions, part of his joy seemed to be the uncertainty of the result.

He wasn't exactly destructive. I mean it's not like he wouldn't have done something different had he known that one of his earlier concoctions would set the parsonage garage on fire. But at that moment when he poured the volatile elements together, he seemed to get this incredible rush. Would it smoke? Would it gurgle? Would it go boom?

"Just a little bit now," I reminded him. I was already starting to edge my way toward our escape hatch wanting to distance myself from this quickly.

While Jim Bob and Fud remembered the awful smell that resulted from mixing hydrogen and sulfur, they did not anticipate the energy created when the two were mixed and confined for some time to a little bottle. When Jim Bob finally loosened the cork, the scent exited the bottle with such force that it literally exploded in his hand. Glass fragments fell to the floor and the smelly liquid dripped from the good Pastor's hands.

~Boomer~

There was no cleaning up after this mess. Our only chance was to vacate as quickly as possible. I slid to my left and tried to re-enter the lobby as unobtrusively as I could.

The crowd was still chattering, so no one paid any attention to me as I shouldered my way through them. Jim Bob's escape was more difficult. Although his hands were plunged into his pockets, the stench was beginning to surround him. He headed straight for the exit and quickly disappeared into the night.

Fud, giggling hysterically, caught up with me, and we hurried to our balcony seats in an effort to distance ourselves from the crime scene.

The odor had begun to escape from behind the staircase. People near it had begun to cough and move away. It didn't take long for the lobby to be engulfed in a truly repulsive stench. The crowd quickly moved into the auditorium to escape the gas.

As Fud and I dropped into our seats, my heart was pounding. I noticed Fud was wearing the silly smirk that always appeared when he was skirting trouble.

I sat in Jim Bob's seat to escape the puffy dress. I was afraid to say anything to Fud, lest it be overheard and the terrible smell be linked to us.

Since the bottle had broken behind the stairwell, and since the air in the lobby had become heated by the crowd, and since hot air rises, the odor quickly made its way up the staircase and into the balcony. It was the second floor audience that suffered through the remainder of Liberace with their handkerchiefs held to their mouths. Liberace played on, and my parents laughed and applauded and cheered, unaware that for some of their neighbors, a full

~1963~

tournament.

I had always been a fairly good athlete, but of the sandlot variety. I played lots of baseball and football on Sunday afternoons in Ashcroft Park. I loved ice skating on the river in the winter and golfing and playing tennis during the summers. I had played hundreds of pickup basketball games on the driveway behind Sticks Skulsky's house, but I had never gone out for any high school teams. I claimed that I didn't want to commit to the long season, but in truth, I never had enough confidence to display my skills in a public arena.

My senior year was the exception. Sticks arm-twisted me into going out for basketball. It was a year when Chandler had some very good basketball players, but not a lot of them. Sticks maintained that I was as good as most, and that I was a shoo-in to make the team. I didn't really believe him, but decided to give it a try, and was surprised that when the final cuts were made, I was still standing.

Part of the reason the coach decided to keep me, he later told me, was that I liked to practice, and at practices I played as hard as when I was in the game, which didn't happen all that often. The eleven other varsity players were better than I, and our team was seldom so dominant that we could afford to play our weak links. Thus, while during the week I contributed as a ferocious practicer, on game nights the coach's eyesight seemed shorter than the length of the bench.

Initially, I feared that being on the basketball team would take away time from my friends in my senior year. I actually had mixed feelings when I wasn't cut. But in the end, the friendships within our fivesome were strengthened.

~Boomer~

I spent more time with Sticks, being on the team with him, but to my surprise, Fud, Pastor Jim Bob and Gracie overnight turned into the team's most devoted fans. They attended all of our games and many of our practices. Their loud cheering bordered on obnoxious. No, it truly was obnoxious. They refused to be guided by the cheerleaders. They made up their own cheers which were rather tasteless. "Lakeland High School, hallowed halls, but their team has got no balls," they would shout.

Sticks was usually on the floor and so into the game that I don't think he ever heard them. But with ample bench time, and with them usually sitting right behind me, I heard it all.

It got so bad that twice after games they were called into the principal's office and asked to tone down their enthusiasm.

Their newly ordered decorum lasted for about a quarter or until the game got exciting, whichever came first. Or they lamely disguised their cheers with, "Sloppy shots and errant passes. Bruton plays like silly people."

Sometimes we traveled as far as ninety miles from Chandler to play; so, when the rest of the town decided the road conditions made it too treacherous to venture out, Fud, Pastor Jim Bob and Grace would be about the only fans on the visitors' side. But that didn't stop them from trying to outshout the home crowd. There were some nights when I feared they might actually be in danger, leaving an unfriendly gym.

I understood Fud and Jim Bob's enthusiasm. Vicarious experience, testosterone and all of that. But what really surprised me was the ferocity with which Miss Mac

~1963~

became involved. Normally a quiet, subdued girl, she became the most boisterous of the threesome. Prior to my participation, she had seldom shown the least interest in sports, and tended to shy away from things competitive. Now she suddenly took unfettered joy in our victories and suffered deep pain in our few losses. Had the team gone into a tailspin, I fear she might have required hospitalization.

Gracie's fervor came to an unfortunate climax late in the season. We were playing at Preston. Preston's gym was a cracker-box affair with bleachers squeezed in on both sides. The fans were very close to the floor, and the cheering during exciting moments was thunderous. We had gotten off to a bad start and trailed the entire first half. In the second half Sticks caught fire, and we pulled even.

The faithful threesome had again stationed themselves in the row right behind me and had, by the middle of the fourth quarter, almost lost their voices from screaming at the referees.

With Preston in the lead by one, Sticks brought the ball up the court toward our basket. Under pressure from two Preston players, Sticks tried to pass the ball into the right corner to John Maynard. A Preston forward stepped in front of John, intercepted the ball and broke free down the court.

"No," shrieked Gracie behind me, thumping both of her fists on my back. And then she made Chandler basketball history.

In a move of uncharacteristic agility, she rose, stepped on the bench next to me, swung her other leg over my head and leapt onto the floor. Before the shocked Preston player could react, Gracie slapped the ball away from him. It rolled to the middle of the court, where a Chandler player grabbed

~Boomer~

it.

Before he could decide if he could legally do anything with it, the whistles of both referees sounded sharply.

There was a momentary silence in the gym, as Gracie stood frozen, both hands covering her nose and mouth. Then all hell broke loose.

The Preston coach jumped all over the referee nearest him. The Preston crowd broke into a chorus of boos, cat calling and fist shaking. The Chandler players formed a loose huddle to talk, unsure of whether they should laugh, apologize or just quietly leave town. All the while an isolated Gracie stood froze to her spot.

Both referees reached Gracie at the same time, took her by her arms, and led her from the court amid a chorus of derisive shouts from the home crowd.

I felt helpless. I wanted to comfort Grace and tell her that everything would be all right, but I didn't think Coach Arnold would take kindly to my exit. Fud and Jim Bob had left their seats to see if they could post bail.

Chandler was assessed a technical foul. A Preston player missed the free-throw. The ball was given to Preston, but the game had lost its momentum.

All anyone would ever remember about it was the girl who had jumped onto the floor and stolen the ball.

Sticks continued his hot shooting and eventually Chandler pulled away and won.

In a rare moment of good judgment, Fud and Pastor Jim Bob quickly drove Gracie out of town as soon as she was released. Otherwise, the following week's county newspaper would no doubt have read, "Three unruly fans found lynched behind Preston High School."

~1963~

Grace was elevated to something nearing celebrity status at Chandler High School.

Shouts of "Good hands, Maculum," echoed through the halls.

She and Fud and Pastor Jim Bob had to make another trip to the principal's office for a third reprimand, but even Principal Riley smiled when he told Grace that she wouldn't likely be lettering in basketball.

The crowning touch was when Gary Compton, one of the best players, and about the nicest and shyest boy at Chandler High School, thanked Gracie for being a true fan. She remained Chandler's number one basketball fan, right through the state tournament.

In some ways, Grace Maculum's wild act got us to State. Rather than becoming an embarrassing miscue, her exuberant charge onto the court demonstrated how badly everyone in Chandler wanted their basketball team to win. Attendance picked up considerably at the games. Other cheering voices began to drown out my trio of boisterous friends. A team which started the season thinking it was pretty good, began to believe it was very good.

For the final home game of the regular season, Coach Peterson started all of the seniors. It was my one and only start. On my first turn down the court, figuring I might not get many chances, I ventured a jump shot.

It missed everything, but Grace and Fud and Pastor Jim Bob gave me a standing ovation and chanted, "Boomer, Boomer, Boomer," as I retreated red-faced up the floor. I wished that I could give them the finger.

Chandler waltzed through the district championship, and in the final game of the regional tournament, the red-hot shooting of Sticks Skulsky led them to a delicious victory over a team thought to be far their superior, Mankato.

Chandler even won its first game in the state tournament, but then was soundly defeated in the semifinal game. The score was lopsided enough that I got to play much of the fourth quarter.

In many ways this was the highlight of our high school careers. We had done what no other Chandler basketball team could achieve. The ghosts of the 1951 team, the boys who should have won, had finally been chased. We gave Chandler's basketball critics at the Legion Club a new year upon which to dwell.

Sometime during those conversations, someone was sure to say, "Remember the game at Preston when that Maculum girl jumped out onto the floor? I'd sure never seen anything like that before."

*****

The senior prom was to be a culminating event in our five-way stroll through high school. In the spring of 1963, we enjoyed the blissful existence that growing up in a small town allowed us. Prom didn't turn out as we had planned, however. By the end of the evening, the first crack appeared in the fortress of our friendship.

Most of our classmates had paired up for the festivities, but we were an odd number as well as an odd group.

In the spirit of the occasion, each of us four guys separately asked Gracie if she would be our prom date. She accepted all four invitations.

Pastor Roberts, Jim Bob's father, offered to be our chauffeur, as he had the biggest car. He gathered us four

~1963~

tuxedo-sporting boys, and dutifully waited as we all went to the door to pick up our date.

Gracie stunned us when she appeared in a gorgeous red gown. We had wisely coordinated our floral gifts so that we didn't obliterate the top of Gracie's dress with corsages. Fud had gotten the flowers for Miss Mac, and the rest brought boutonnieres for each other.

Our entrance into the gym was roughly modeled after the Miss America Pageant. Each couple was announced, after which they attempted a graceful walk up and down a runway, so that parents could get one last high school picture before being banished from the gym.

Our promenade prompted hoots and catcalls from a number of our classmates.

Paul Tilson, who we later discovered had been drinking most of the day, yelled out, "Ain't that cute. Three guys and two girls." It didn't make any sense to me at the time.

With two of us flanking Gracie on each side, the runway was just wide enough for us to parade forward side by side, our arms around one another's waist. At the end we did an about face, reconnected and made the walk back to more jibes and applause.

The Prom Committee had outdone itself. They had selected a forty's theme and decorated the gym like an airport hanger. Underclassmen, who served as waiters and waitresses, were dressed in uniforms from the various branches of the service.

They even hired a big band from Minneapolis, which filled the evening with danceable tunes of Jimmy Dorsey and Glen Miller. A few students complained about having to give up their rock and roll for the evening, but the atmosphere was so infectious, that soon all were dancing cheek to cheek.

Grace paid for the luxury of having four dates. Each of us could sit out three of every four dances, while she was passed from one partner to the next. Anticipating the situation, she had packed a pair of matching red tennies, which she donned after the first dance.

Not being a great dancer, when my turn came, I often pretended to feel sorry for her and took her to the refreshment table or outside for a breath of fresh air, instead of to the dance floor.

Once when we were outside, we sat on one of the benches along the walkway leading to the main entrance. We sat silently. We had spent a dozen years talking. We knew most everything about each other, where we were headed the following year, what we liked in the way of music, cars, vegetables, how we felt about the end of high school. For the moment, there didn't seem to be anything that needed saying. Gracie sat with her head bowed, rubbing the tips of her shoes together and softly humming *Moonlight Serenade*.

Finally, I said something that I had been thinking all evening. "You really are beautiful." I almost added "tonight," but Grace was always beautiful. I just hadn't paid very good attention.

"I kind of wish you were just my date tonight." As soon as I said it, I felt traitorous to our group, so I held back saying some other warm thoughts I was thinking.

At first Gracie didn't seem to hear what I had said. She just continued rubbing her shoes together. Then she looked up at me and smiled. She bent toward me, and kissed me gently on the lips. Then she stood and headed back into

~1963~

the school.

I sat there stunned I licked my lips and tasted a faint sweetness. Did that kiss mean that she also wished she were my date alone? Or had she silently signaled me that she was more comfortable the way things were, as an equal in our group of five.

I rose and walked back into the school, but by the time I entered, Gracie was back into her sequence and dancing with Fud.

Many couples drifted away as the night unfolded, but we had nowhere we would rather be. Chandler High School had been the center of our lives for the past four years, and we weren't prepared to leave it until someone gently pushed us out the door and locked it behind us.

We didn't know what the future held for us. We did know that it would separate us, and frankly, none of us could imagine lives happier than the ones we were sharing.

The next dance belonged to Sticks, but was announced as a Snowball. Other dancers were allowed to cut in on couples throughout the song. Sticks and Gracie swayed to *In the Mood*. Sticks' athletic prowess couldn't conquer his shyness, and their movements were tentative and stiff. I hadn't noticed that before.

I got up and moved out onto the gym floor. Grace saw me coming, and when I tapped Sticks on the shoulder, she slid into my arms.

I held her closer than I had in our dances before the kiss. She responded by lowering her head onto my shoulder. I pressed my cheek against the softness of her hair. It felt wonderful, and my dancing was less awkward.

Fud's tap on my back surprised me. I had quickly

~Boomer~

settled into Grace's embrace, and longed to finish the dance there. I momentarily thought of squeezing Grace and ignoring Fud's interference. But the kiss was little reason to believe that Grace preferred my arms, so I gave her the squeeze, but handed her over to Fud.

Next to us a girl cut in on Jane Petrie's date, Art, leaving her partnerless. Before I could head off the floor Jane said, "Would you like to dance, Boomer?"

I really would have preferred to sit down and ponder my new feelings for Gracie, but Jane and I had always been friendly, and I couldn't turn her down. "Sure." We started off in an awkward shuffle. "Are you having fun tonight, Janie?"

"Oh, kind of." She stared away over my shoulder. "Art and some of the guys brought a keg in somebody's pickup, and he keeps sneaking off to have a drink. Some of them are getting really loaded." She looked about ready to burst into tears.

"That's too bad. He should be in here with you. You look great tonight, Jane."

"Thanks Boomer. You're sweet." We were dancing near Fud and Gracie, and as we passed she looked over and smiled.

Just then Paul Tilson and his date danced up to the other side of Fud and Grace. It became obvious that he was one that was pretty loaded.

Paul was a Chandler football star and had a reputation as a bully. He staggered a bit as he danced, and when he spoke, his words were slurred.

"Hey Maculum, can't you find a man to dance with?" He said it loud enough that everyone in the vicinity heard

~1963~

him. Grace turned her face away. Fud tried to steer them away, but Paul clumsily maneuvered after them.

"Don't you get tired of dragging that faggot around the floor?" he taunted. "Hey, Untiedt, why didn't you wear a dress tonight instead of pants?"

Fud stopped dancing and turned to Tilson. "Why don't you leave us alone, Paul? We're just trying to have a good time."

"Wouldn't you have a better time dancing with Boomer or Roberts, you fuckin' queer?" He reached out and gave Fud a shove. Everyone in the area had stopped dancing to watch.

I stepped between Fud and Paul. "Come on Paul. What are you doing? You need to get some fresh air. Linda, why don't you take him outside for a bit?" I said to his girl friend.

"Why don't you let him fight his own battles, Boomer?" Paul said, reaching up to push me as well. I grabbed his wrist before it reached me. "Or are you as queer as he is?" I hoped that this wouldn't go any further, since even drunk, Paul could no doubt beat me to a pulp.

Just then the music stopped and Jane Petrie's boyfriend, Art James, came up behind Paul and grabbed him by his shoulders.

"Hey, easy Paul," Art said softly to him. "Let's not spoil the party. Sorry, Boomer. I'll take him out for a bit." I released Paul's wrist and Art led him away.

"Jerks," Paul snarled as he let Art guide him.

When I turned around, Grace and Fud were gone. The band had struck up the next song and people were resuming their dances. I looked across the gym and caught a glimpse

~Boomer~

of my friends exiting. I made my way between the dancers and followed them out.

By the time I passed through the front door, they were seated on a bench. Fud was leaning forward staring at a spot between his feet. Grace was gently rubbing his back. When I got closer, I realized that Fud was crying. I stepped around the bench and stood behind them.

Finally, I said, "Don't let that jerk bother you Fud. He's drunk and just likes to act tough. That crap he was spouting. It doesn't mean anything."

Fud took a deep breath and sighed. "Yes it does," he said. " It means more than you can imagine." He paused and took another breath. "Paul seems to know something that I don't think you do."

I gave a nervous laugh, "Huh. Not likely. I know you better than I know my own brother."

"Maybe you don't Boomer. Maybe there are some things that you just don't understand." Grace said nothing, just kept gently rubbing Fud's back.

"What do you mean?" I said. "What is this stuff that I don't know about you?"

"Well, I didn't especially like Paul's terminology, but basically he's got the idea right." Grace put her arms around Fud and laid her head softly on his back.

"Fud, he called you a queer," I said.

He looked up at me. "Like I said, he seems to have gotten it right."

"Are you saying that you're a homo?" Fud slowly nodded his head up and down. "When did you decide that?" I said with more anger in my voice than I intended.

"Boomer, don't," said Grace.

~1963~

I moved around to Gracie's end of the bench and sat with my back to them. We sat in silence for a minute, or maybe it was five minutes. I was stunned and having trouble focusing my thoughts.

It was Grace who finally broke the silence. "I'm not finished dancing," she said. We both pivoted to look at her. "I mean it. This is a good night tonight, and I'm not ready to have it over. This is going to be all right, Fud. It doesn't change anything. You're still our friend. We still love you. We've got all summer to deal with this. Right now I want to dance."

She stood up and held out her hand to Fud. He took it and rose to her side. Then she held out her other hand to me. I sat still. Part of me wanted to sit there and review the past and my friendship with Fud to discover how I could have ever missed this. But Gracie wouldn't let me.

"Come on, Boomer. It's all right. It's your turn to dance with me." She seemed to have accepted this news about Fud without pause. I wondered if she had known all along.

"Boomer?" She leaned over, put her hands firmly on my shoulders and shook me gently. "It's ok."

I bit my lower lip to help keep back tears. It felt so good to have her touching me. Suddenly the new feelings I was having for her overpowered any new feelings I had about Fud, although I hadn't begun to sort out what those feelings were. I took Gracie's hand and the three of us headed back into the school.

About five feet from the door Gracie stopped and turned to Fud. "Now I know why your feet are so light on the dance floor."

~Boomer~

Fud stopped, dropped her hand and looked at her. "You little shit," he said. Then they both exploded in laughter and fell into one another's arms.

I stood apart, overwhelmed by the intensity of the new feelings I had for these two people I had known all of my life. We entered the gym and joined Sticks and Pastor Jim Bob at the punch table.

*****

Despite that night, it had been a peaceful voyage, and we had made it together. From our first days of kindergarten to our last days of high school we were inseparable. And except for an occasional disease or fracture or miscue by one of us, we had moved smoothly through childhood.

Life for most people had been reasonably quiet for our decade and a half. We had been led war free by fatherly presidents. Our stable parents had nurtured and directed us beside the still waters of the idyllic Fox River. Chandler schools had instilled us with strong, Midwestern values and prepared us to fly.

But already there were signs that our next flight was not going to be the gentle floating of our childhood years. The autumn before graduation the Cuban missile crisis momentarily shook our security. In the South the civil rights movement sprang to life as James Meredith was escorted by police to his classes at the University of Mississippi.

But our Midwest, was far from Cuba or Mississippi. As we walked across the stage for graduation, we preferred to dwell on the good things in life.

Our graduation speaker focused on John Glen orbiting the earth, without mention of Nikita Kruschev's hand poised over the button that could destroy that earth. We didn't

~1963~

know that our beloved president would be assassinated in a matter of months. None of us were even aware of the 15,000 advisory troops stationed in Vietnam. We certainly didn't suspect that far-off place would play the central role in our lives.

By the time we would regroup, we would have each changed so that fifteen years of friendship would be sorely tested.

2004

The visit to my boyhood home and the warmth of Joyce Hemseth raised a nostalgia for Chandler that I wouldn't have thought I held. I actually found myself wondering what it would be like to settle back into the Midwest and pursue the attentions of this lovely Mrs. Hemseth, of whom I knew almost nothing.

For the next hour I drove up one street and down the next conjuring memories. The cruising strengthened the experience, for as teens we had spent hours in our parents' Fords and Chevrolets aimlessly meandering back and forth up and down Main Street. When I had driven, I always turned a block earlier than my friends to avoid passing my father's gas station. I didn't want him knowing how much of his thirty-five cent gas I was wasting.

Again, I was amazed at how many houses were familiar to me, how many times I could recall the name of the family that had lived there in the 50's, how often I could picture the former residents.

I drove past the old high school. Chandler had built a new high school on the outskirts of town, but the old

~Boomer~

building still occupied its square block. It was fairly well-kept, but a broken window here, a scrawl of graffiti there, signaled its disuse. I ignored those flaws and imagined that it was Saturday, and come Monday, a flood of students would be inside tormenting their teachers as we had. As always, I smiled at the memory of Liberace pounding away in the gymnasium.

I might have spent the rest of the day wandering memory lane had I not made an arrangement to meet my sister, Elizabeth, for lunch in her hometown, Shelton. I turned onto Highway 17, noticing that Chandler had two traffic lights, doubling the one whose installation had created such an uproar in my teen years. Twenty miles later I parked in front of Judy's Café and scrambled out of my car and into the arms of my oldest sibling.

For the umteenth time that day I was surprised at the strength of the emotions that grabbed me. Elizabeth sobbed into my shoulder, and I squeezed her tighter and tighter, trying to keep from bursting into tears myself. After a long embrace that must have raised whispers from the passing Shelton residents, we entered the café and found a quiet booth near the back.

"You look great, Elizabeth," I said. "How is it that the oldest of us keeps looking the youngest?"

"Oh right, Gene. Haven't you noticed that my skin seems to have outgrown me, and that the excess is sagging in some rather unattractive spots."

"It's just not true, Sis. I had forgotten how really beautiful you are."

"Would you mind sharing that thought with Ray a few times this week? Sometimes I think that he has forgotten."

"What? Are you and Ray having troubles?"

"Oh, no. We're fine. It's just that we are old and we've been married so long. That you're so beautiful talk doesn't come up so often anymore. Thanks for being a convincing liar." The waitress stopped at our booth and took our order.

"Are Tom and Marge staying with you this week?"

"Yes. A whole plane-load of Boomers gets in this afternoon and they will drive down from the cities in some sort of caravan. It took them a while to get all of the kids and grandkids organized to come. There won't be an empty floor space in our entire house. It's a good thing that you are staying at Mom and Dad's."

The mention of Mom and Dad froze the conversation. In the pause Elizabeth reached across the table and softly took my hands in hers. "I can't believe that they are both gone." The tears returned to her eyes.

"I know. I've been thinking the same thing all afternoon. For the very first time in our lives we don't have a parent. I know that I've been a awful son. A week ago I wouldn't have thought that Dad's death would make very much difference to me. I haven't said five words to him in years, and all day I've had this ache to talk with him, to ask him what he thinks the rumble is in my car engine, to find out how he thinks the Twins will do next season."

Elizabeth shook her head, as tears returned. I continued talking. "I thought I was finished with this when Mom died. For months I beat myself up. How could I have been so selfish to desert her? She was the best. And I just walked away and let her live and die without me. And now

~Boomer~

Dad. I didn't think that with Dad it would matter so much. But it does. How could I have been so damned stupid?"

Elizabeth reached across the booth and took my face in her hands. I closed my eyes. Her fingers softly massaged my face. Suddenly these hands felt like my mother's hands and the sensation was so strong that I expected to hear her voice saying, "Now watch your language, Eugene." My eyes snapped open to be sure she wasn't there.

"Don't do this to yourself, Gene. It doesn't serve any purpose now. You had a lot of good times with the folks. They were good parents and you were a source of pride and joy. Things don't always turn out the way we want them to, but the good things are still there. The rest can't be changed."

"How many times did you try to get me to patch things up with Dad? I just never could get the point. He had you and Tom and the grandkids. All I ever seemed to offer was aggravation. I was pig-headed enough to think that I could get along without him, and I certainly didn't think he wanted me around. I guess that I always thought he favored you and Tom anyway. And why wouldn't he? You two were perfect."

"Oh, Gene. Isn't it funny. Growing up, I always thought you were his favorite. He'd spend hours with you throwing that darn baseball back and forth. Do you remember one day in Ashcroft Park? You had taken your kite over and gotten it flying all by yourself. You had a huge ball of string on it, must have been thousands of feet, and you just kept letting it out. That kite got so high that it was only a dot in the sky, and when you went to pull it back in, the pressure was so strong you could hardly budge it. You tied

~2004~

it to a tree and came home to ask Dad if he would help you get it down. At first he just said, 'Oh just cut it loose. The damned thing only cost a quarter. You can get another one tomorrow.' Elizabeth's accurate imitation of my father sent a chill through me. "But you begged. This was your favorite kite, and you couldn't just let it go without trying to bring it down. So he grumbled and trudged over to the park and spent the next hour hauling that stupid kite back to earth. And with his bad arm, that was no easy job. If that would have been mine or Tom's he would've said, 'You got it up there. You get it down,' and not budged from behind his newspaper."

The warmth of the memory brought a smile to both of our faces. "For a long time I used to try to figure out what went wrong between us. I'd try to pinpoint an exact moment when the love I felt for him turned to anger or hatred or whatever it turned into." I stopped as the waitress moved toward us with our food. We adjusted plates and things around the table and took our first bites.

After a sip of her Coke Elizabeth said, "And?"

"And?"

"And what did you decide was the moment that you stopped - that your feelings changed for Dad?"

"Of course it wasn't a particular moment. It started in the summer after high school. We started to argue. From then on it seemed like a big boulder rolling downhill. We couldn't ever seem to agree about anything. Admittedly, I did some really stupid things during that time, but it seemed like he was just waiting for me to screw up so he could criticize. And then there were things that really shouldn't have mattered, but all we could do was argue about them."

~Boomer~

"What kind of things?"

"We'd argue about my friends, about Fud being gay, about this girl I was dating. I could never figure out why he cared about it."

"Oh, a boyhood romance. Why didn't I know about this? Was it anybody I would know?"

"Sure. She was practically like a sister. Grace Maculum. We were friends our whole lives, and the summer after high school we started to date some."

"Oh I loved Grace. Her mom used to work at Dad's station didn't she? She was a cutie. Whatever happened to her?"

"I don't know. She is someone else that I deserted long ago. The thing is that Dad just had so much trouble with us dating. I guess I could have understood if she has been some sort of freak or something, but my God, Gracie was about as pleasant as girls come. Dad and I used to actually have shouting matches over it. And after that it seemed like all we could do is fight about everything. Vietnam. The divorce. Pick an event and we fought over it."

"Well, the fight is over now, Gene. Tomorrow, when you say goodbye, just remember him as that wonderful guy with the bad knees and crooked arm who crouched in the back yard trying to flag down your wild pitches. The rest of it just doesn't matter."

Chapter 3

The Poetry of Protest

1963

In the summer of 1963, the inevitable separation that the group of five had only talked of began. Sticks had been in Civil Air Patrol for several years, but this was the first summer it would take him away from Chandler for training. Immediately after that he would leave for the University of Minnesota for preliminary basketball practices. That was probably fortunate.

Of the four of us, Sticks had the hardest time adjusting to Fud's coming out. A tension developed between them that immediately affected the dynamics of our fivesome. I was never quite sure if my own discomfort signaled a change in my relationship with Fud, or if I was only bothered by the more obvious discomfort that Sticks was having. Probably it was both.

For Fud, the negative signals he received from Sticks started coming from other Chandlerites as well. As a nerd he had always been shunned by members of certain school groups. As a gay nerd he started to experience belligerence.

For this and other reasons, he decided to get an early start on college. Half way through the summer, he moved to Iowa City for some preliminary work to his engineering studies. He made no attempt to re-enter his closet, and became involved in campus gay rights activities. He lived in a house with a group of politically active upperclassmen, and Fud quickly got involved.

In August he was in Washington, D.C. when Martin Luther King laid out his dream, and that dream captured Fud and would forever change him and the rest of us.

Pastor Jim Bob would be starting community college in the fall while living at home in Chandler. Much of the summer, however, he spent in Iowa City with Fud. Much to his father's dismay, he worked in a pizza joint to pay for a room, and spent his nights carousing, or at political meetings with Fud.

August found me and Gracie alone in Chandler. Grace, despite encouragement from both me and her mother, had decided that more school was not for her.

She took a job waitressing at Dale's Road House Restaurant on the outskirts of town, and settled into the world of work. That summer I worked for an agricultural company in town doing a variety of jobs, mostly involving driving trucks or other pieces of agricultural equipment over which I had marginal control.

Since Gracie worked most nights, our schedules didn't match very well, but sometimes I would drive out and pick her up when her shift at the restaurant ended. We didn't exactly date, but rather tried to replace as a twosome, the friendship we had nurtured for years as a fivesome. We knew that at the end of the summer I would be off to the University of Wisconsin in Madison.

Late night entertainment was rather limited in Chandler. Sometimes we would take in a movie at the Alton

~1963~

drive-in, or we'd just drive to Crystal Lake, borrow a rowboat from a workmate of Gracie who had offered it any time, and row out into the middle under the stars.

The boat was sort of a homemade job. It was more of a duck boat than a row boat, with a bench at either end, and a flat bottom. That made it very stable, but cumbersome to row. Gracie sat opposite me, as I rather tediously ploughed the boat through the water.

The end result was worth the effort, however. The cool breeze kept the bugs away from us, and the soft waves lapping against the side of the boat lulled us into a trance. Away from the rest of the world, we began to see each other in a pleasant new way. I wouldn't have thought that there was anything new to learn after spending nearly our whole lives together, but I was wrong.

Without the other three in the mix, we began to discover that we hadn't shared very much of what we really thought and felt. Oddly, at the age of eighteen I had hardly ever been alone with a girl. Gracie always left it to me to lead the conversation. And not being very good at it, I usually began awkwardly.

"Gracie, don't you ever want to do anything but be a waitress in this one-horse town?"

"Well gee, Tex, maybe someday," she teased. "But right now my mom still sort of needs me, and I don't feel a particularly strong urge to move on."

"How is she doing these days? I don't see her very often now that she doesn't work for my dad."

"It's funny. She's so beautiful and so bright and so friendly, and yet somehow she just can't seem to get her life in order."

~Boomer~

"Is she still drinking a lot?"

"Yes." She was silent for a bit. The darkness made it difficult to see her face, to read how she was feeling beyond what she was saying.

"Just after she quit working at the gas station it got really bad. She always made sure she was sober when she went off to work, but without work to go to, she had no reason to stop drinking. I still don't understand why she quit working."

"Does she still get violent with you when she's drunk?" I thought back to long ago when I had seen Mac's mother strike her.

"No. We sort of worked that out. She still throws things sometimes. Just not at me. I think if she could just find a good friend. She's been in and out of so many relationships with men in town. And the women all avoid her as if she has the plague. I'm just about all she's got right now. It must be nice having regular parents that you get along with."

"Well, we have our moments. My dad really wanted me to go to the University of Minnesota with Sticks. I don't know why it matters to him so much, but we have had some pretty tense moments lately." I swatted a bug that was circling around my face. "Do you ever hear from your dad?"

"Not a thing. I guess that if he had wanted anything to do with me, he would have stayed in the first place, so I'm not surprised that he hasn't tried to re-enter my life."

"Do you and your mom ever talk about him? I mean, do you know much about him? Does she tell you things?"

"All the time. I think she really misses him even yet. She blames herself more than him for their breakup. I guess

~1963~

I'll never really understand what made him leave."

I felt the boat wobble as Gracie got up from the front and moved back to me. She sat in the bottom of the boat between my legs and leaned her head against my chest. I leaned over and put my arms on top of hers and my face up against her cheek. She turned her head and softly kissed me on the chin.

The feeling of her prom night kiss had stayed with me for weeks, and this one renewed the surge of warmth and excitement. I bent my head and very softly touched my lips to hers. We sat holding each other without saying a word for the next half hour or so.

I had seldom felt restricted by our group of five, but suddenly I much preferred being alone with Grace. Had I not been leaving for college in a week, romance would surely have entered my life for the first time. The warmth of her body against mine kept me cozy, but I could feel her starting to shiver in the night breeze. With mixed feelings I rowed her back to shore.

*****

The other thing that tempered romance was my father's reaction. Long after my college decision had been irreversible, he had kept pressing the issue; there was a noticeable chill at the supper table. One evening he had just finished his latest pronouncement about Madison being on the outer edge of the universe, both geographically and politically, when in desperation I tried to change the subject.

"In a way," I said, "I wish I weren't going anyplace at all. Just when I have to leave I've got a relationship going that would be really fun to pursue."

This was news to both of my parents. They looked up

at me. It obviously pleased my mother. "A relationship?" she said with a sly gleam in her eye. "What's this about now? Are you seeing someone from school that we don't know about?"

"No." I blushed. "Grace Maculum. We've been going off by ourselves a bit more and it's just been going really well. I mean, we've always been really close as friends, and now it just seems like we may be ready to be more than friends."

My mother's smile continued as she took another bite and chewed. The announcement had a rather strange effect on my father. Frankly, I wouldn't have thought that my romantic life would have any interest for him at all, but it seemed to.

"How far has this relationship with Grace gone?" He showed the discomfort that discussing such matters with a son might give a father. He didn't look at me and had a bit of a shake to his voice. I remembered that once before he had cautioned me about seeing too much of Gracie.

I tried again to lighten the mood. "Dad, if you are going to give me the birds and the bees routine, I have to tell you, you're a little late. While I haven't exactly been around the block, I'm aware of how the process works."

We quietly continued eating. I thought the subject was closed, but it wasn't.

"I just don't think it's a good idea. You'll be leaving here in a couple of weeks."

My mother stepped in at that point. "Oh, for heaven sakes, Glen. Gene and Gracie have been friends forever. If they want to have some fun this summer, why shouldn't they. I think that is just wonderful, Gene."

"Being friends is one thing. But when you start

~1963~

talking about having a relationship.... I think it's a bad idea and I think you should back up."

I was tired from the day's boring work and I flared, more sharply than I intended. "Jesus Christ, Dad. What's the problem? You'd think that I had announced I was dating Fud."

"Well, from what I understand, he would probably enjoy that, but that's a whole different issue. And I'll ask you to watch your language. You're still living in this house for another week, so we'd appreciate it if you wouldn't pollute it."

"Oh, so now Fud isn't good enough for you either. Gracie and Fud. Any of my other friends you want to pick on?"

"I didn't say she's not good enough..."

"Well, why don't you just butt out. I'm eighteen years old. I guess I can handle picking my own friends."

"You haven't always done so well in that department. One of them is a queer. So maybe you could still stand to listen to some helpful advice." By this time we were yelling at each other and my mother had left the table.

"Your advice has never been very helpful, and when it comes to my personal life I'd just as soon you keep it to yourself."

"As long as you are living under my roof and eating my food, I'll give you as much of my advice as I choose. And don't forget who's paying your way to Madison, stupid as he thinks it is."

"Oh, God, I knew it would come to that eventually. Are you going to hold that choice over my head forever? I'll do the best that I can to pay for my own college, and if you

~Boomer~

want I'll even pay room and board until I leave." I slammed my napkin onto my plate and stormed to my room.

I sat at my desk shaking. In all of our disagreements over college I had never spoken to my father that way. I moved to my bed, laid down and tried to get a grip on myself.

Suddenly, life felt kind of fragile. Much of it was no doubt the uncertainty of leaving home and entering college. Another part of it was watching friends disappear. Fud, Jim Bob and Sticks had always been just a phone call away, and now I didn't even know their numbers.

What was left of my old life seemed wrapped up in Gracie. With her I felt the familiarity of the past. Perhaps my father was right. Perhaps I was being unfair to her and to myself in changing our relationship just as I was leaving.

After my surge of anger, I couldn't admit our argument had been entirely my fault, but I did mumble an apology the next day. Dad accepted it without much conviction.

Gracie and I saw each other once more before I left town. We didn't mention our night in the boat, and I tried to move our relationship back to the chummy tone it had always had. We hugged and said goodbye, and as I walked away I thought that of all the things in my past, Gracie would be the one I missed most. I should have remembered that thought and acted upon it in the months and years ahead.

*****

I suppose that one of the things for which I have always resented my father is how right he was about my college choice. Neither of us had any understanding of why he was right when he and my mother dropped me off in

~1963~

Madison in the fall of '63. It just turned out that he was right.

Dad gave me a very chilly handshake and got into the car, leaving my mother to apply the hugs and the tears and the "I can't believe the last of you has already left the nest."

Dad had always been a die-hard University of Minnesota fan, traveling often from Chandler to Minneapolis for Gopher football and basketball games. It was almost like he had attended Minnesota himself, although his schooling had ended with high school. It was natural that he would have preferred his son to attend the home state University rather than its arch-rival in Wisconsin.

In the next four years, however, I gave him many more reasons to despise the University of Wisconsin than a few lost football games. If I had followed his advice and accompanied Sticks to the University of Minnesota, those four years, and perhaps the rest of my life, would have taken a different route. Looking back, it is scarey how quickly my life's direction changed.

During my freshman and sophomore years in Madison, I found myself gravitating toward the social, rather than the academic. I had declared architecture as my academic area, but I was as yet not prepared for its rigors.

I was a perfect example of the small-town boy who got lost in the big university and ended up making a lot of bad decisions. I had always been a follower. In high school Fud or Jim Bob or Sticks had always determined our direction.

Now I was simply following a new crowd. And while Fud and company had led me into some childish misdemeanors, my new friends led me into more dangerous territory. Floating along in a nightly cloud of pot was more pleasant than sweating over a calculus textbook.

By the end of my second year I had a less than average record, and a degree in architecture was looking unlikely. The following summer I worked on the college building and grounds crew and moved into a house on Mifflin Street, a neighborhood which housed an assortment of dissidents.

Our summer nights were a fuzzy mix of booze and drugs and political argumentation. On one occasion this resulted in police involvement, which resulted in parental involvement.

For my parents, my behavior was foreign territory. Tom and Elizabeth had been such good kids that parenting them had brought only joy and pride. The only time my parents had been to the police station with them was the day Tom was awarded a Policemen's Scholarship as Chandler's Model Teen Citizen.

Bailing me out of the Madison Police Station was an event my folks were ill prepared to handle; however, nothing could shake my mother's love, and she pretended that if she prayed and wished hard enough, everything would be fine. My dad began his withdrawal from me that would accelerate with each of my future indiscretions.

By the time the next school year started, I had become really attached to substances detrimental to study. My junior year continued my academic disaster. In the first semester I was well on my way to failing anything that had to do with architecture. The only course I was passing was "The Poetry of Protest."

When my midterm grade report reached Chandler, I was summoned home for consultation. One look at my gaunt, unshaven state, and my father diagnosed the problem.

~1963~

He fancied himself a man of action, and this time that action was to cut off his financial support.

As he put it, "I'm not paying so some pothead can sit around on the floor reading commie crap." At equal volume I yelled that I didn't need his money, that I could take care of myself.

With nothing other than economics determined, I returned to Madison and "The Poetry of Protest." Little did I know that an internship in that very field awaited me. The Vietnam War was heating up, as was the protest movement, which in Madison was centered in Mifflin Street. In the final semester of my junior year, my most noteworthy activities were becoming a member of the Students for a Democratic Society, and joining my neighbors seated on the ground in front of Bascom Hall yelling anti-war slogans. I got an A in "The Poetry of Protest."

That summer I once again stayed in Madison to work. Along with my campus job, I took a night job waiting tables at a nearby restaurant. I would show my dad that I could pay my own way.

Unfortunately, what I didn't show him was that I could accomplish much of anything academically. As I started what should have been my senior year at Madison, academically I had not yet achieved the level of junior. But at least it was my money going down a rat hole, not his.

*****

1966

By the end of those three years I had completely lost track of my four high school friends. I had spent all of my summers and many school holidays in Madison working.

~Boomer~

When I visited Chandler during the school year, I always found that Sticks and Fud were at their Universities of Minnesota and Iowa.

I did spend a warm evening with Pastor Jim Bob during one of my stops in Chandler. It was great to catch up, but not as much fun as it had been in our boyhood when Jim Bob was creating concoctions and setting them on fire. Things had changed. We had grown apart.

On one visit home my mother asked, "Why don't you look up Grace? I see her around town every so often." I noticed that my father lowered his newspaper and shot her a cold scowl. I offered some lame explanation, but for the rest of the evening I rolled my mother's question around in my head.

Why didn't I call Gracie? I didn't have an answer. We had gotten so close the summer after high school. The first time I was back in Chandler was the following November. I had thought about calling her but hadn't. With each successive visit after that, I felt less inclined to call, until I didn't even consider it.

In retrospect, I can guess why. More than losing my friends, in those three years I had lost myself. The confidence with which I battled my father was not deeply rooted. In those moments when I actually considered my future, the road was unbelievably blurred. I wasn't sure what I wanted to be. I wasn't sure what I believed. Frankly, I wasn't sure that I was anyone that Gracie would want to know.

*****

Left to me, that might have been the end of our fivesome. It was Fud who renewed the contact. In January I got a surprise letter from him. He had written my mother

~1966~

for my address.

In February there was to be a demonstration on the Madison campus attempting to block recruiting interviews by the Dow Chemical Company, producers of the chemical agent napalm that was being used for a variety of destructive ends in Vietnam. Fud was joining a bus-load of students who were riding up from Iowa City to join the protest. He asked if we could get together.

I responded that the best place we could meet would be at the demonstration, and that he would find me under the flagpole at Bascom Hall.

A political demonstration was about the only thing that could get me up before noon those days. By 10:00 A.M. I was seated underneath the flagpole just in case the Iowa City group arrived early.

Around me were about six thousand of my fellow students. The word had definitely gotten out. The temperature was near freezing, so little knots of students where building bonfires and warming their hands.

From the steps of Bascom Hall, speakers vividly described the effects of napalm on its victims, be they animal, vegetable or human. Beside the speakers was a huge reproduction of a photo picturing Vietnamese women and children running from their village which had just been sprayed with napalm. At the center of the photo was a naked girl whose clothing had been burned from her body by the chemical.

A rock band then played a couple of protest songs, the crowd singing along with "We Shall Overcome," a tune that had made its way over from the civil rights demonstrations that were also heating up.

~Boomer~

The next event was the burning of draft cards. Male students were invited to mount the steps and together set fire to their "tickets to the war." I was tempted to join them, but didn't want to lose my place and miss Fud.

The crowd leapt to its feet and roared as the tiny flames and smoke drifted off the hands of the participants. Dozens of policemen stood throughout the crowd. Outnumbered a hundred to one, their faces were grim with the tension of uncertainty. While some no doubt would have liked to "bust some heads," the unfavorable ratio demanded caution.

As I was sitting down, I spotted Fud moving through the crowd toward me. Playfully, I let him try to find me. He came right to the flagpole and peered into the sea of faces.

His appearance hadn't changed from our days in high school. That round head sat firmly atop that round body with hardly a neck separating them. His eyes momentarily caught mine but then continued on. I smiled. After circling the pole he returned to my side and once again looked at me.

"You new in town, stranger?" I said.

He smiled. "Boomer?" he said. "Boomer? Good God man, are you auditioning for *Hair*?"

While his appearance hadn't changed, I was barely recognizable. My black hair was now shoulder-length and my face held a scruffy beard.

I stood up into a firm bear hug.

"Your mom seemed a little uneasy talking about you when I phoned," said Fud. "Now I see why. My God, Boomer, you're a hippie."

"And apparently you're not. I thought that maybe your hair would be as long as mine, Fud. You look like an

~1966~

accountant." I sat and pulled him down beside me so that we wouldn't be blocking anyone's views.

"I'm a closet hippie, Boomer. You know, you come out of some closets and you step right into others. Right now I'm finding I can be a more effective demonstrator with a clean-cut appearance. The people I need to talk with listen to me better this way. But I can't get over you. Man, I would have looked at you all day and never recognized you if you hadn't spoken up. What's going on with you, man?"

"The times they are a changing, my friend. Listen, Fud. It's kind of awkward talking here. You want to go somewhere a little quieter and get some coffee?"

Before Fud could answer, the crowd rose to its feet and cheered something the current speaker said. I hadn't heard what it was. Just then a kid about my age pushed past me and walked to the flag pole. To the cheers of those around him, he began lowering the American Flag which had been flapping at the top.

As the flag came closer to him, so did a number of policemen from different directions, but the crowd was so enormous their progress was slow. There was no effort to make a path for them, so they had to push people aside.

The demonstrator at my side opened a knife with which he evidently planned to cut the cords holding the flag. But when the flag reached the bottom it was still about 10 feet off the ground. Whoever regularly put it up and took it down evidently used a ladder. The prospective flagnapper leapt into the air but fell well short of his goal. With little time before the policemen arrived, action needed to be taken quickly.

"Here," I said, "I'll give you a boost. Climb on my

~Boomer~

shoulders." I crouched on the ground with one hand on the flag pole. My new partner didn't pause, but put one of his feet on each of my shoulders.

"I don't know, Boomer. This may not be such a good idea," said Fud at my side.

Others yelled support. Several pushed past Fud and helped me get to my feet and hoist this guy, who was about my size, up the flagpole. I looked up to see him sawing away at the cords which held the flag. They were tougher than he had anticipated, and before he could severe them, three of the policemen had reached us.

One of them reached up toward the boy on my shoulders and said, "All right, guys. That's enough. Climb down and leave the flag there." Again I glanced up to see my new friend continuing to hack away with his knife at the cords.

The atmosphere around us was volatile. Some demonstrators started shouting encouragement to us and others began abusing the policemen, who had now become a group of about a dozen.

Fud had been pushed away from the scene. I was pretty much stuck there. I couldn't just step away and let my compatriot fall. Suddenly the demonstration on the steps had halted and the focus was our scene at the flagpole.

"Get down from there, kid, or I'll pull you down," yelled one of the policemen. There was a chorus of boos from the crowd. The guy above me continued to cut away.

The policeman next to me grabbed his ankle from my right shoulder and yanked. He came plummeting toward me. Two of the other policemen reached out to break his fall. I ducked, and while the policemen did slow his descent, he

~1966~

landed squarely on my shoulders. Two policemen, the flag cutter and I landed in a heap.

"Damn. He cut me," yelled one of the policemen.

I sat up and saw him clutching his bloody hand. The other policemen acted quickly. They circled us, isolating us from the crowd. Two had drawn pistols, and I was dismayed to see that one of them was aimed at me.

The shouting and chaos around us was eclipsed by a policeman's voice screaming, "Drop the knife."

The frightened young man quickly tossed the knife to his side, just as the flag above him finally gave way and floated down on top of his head. A policeman rushed forward to rescue the flag, as others jerked us to our feet. In no time we were handcuffed.

While other demonstrators shouted support, none resisted as we were quickly pushed through the masses to awaiting squad cars. I tried to spot Fud in the crowd, but couldn't find his face before the car door was slammed in mine. The other demonstrator had already been loaded into the other side.

Two policemen got into the front seat, one of them the man who had been cut. He now had his hand wrapped tightly in a towel, and didn't appear overly concerned about his wound.

My partner in crime turned to me. "I'm Peter Baker," he said, offering me his hand. I shook it. "Man, I'm sorry about this. I didn't mean to get you involved." I gave him an uncomfortable smile and shook my head.

"Hey, man." He turned forward to address the policemen. "I didn't mean to cut you, man. It was an accident. I mean, you just dragged me down. It's not like I

~Boomer~

was trying to hurt you, man."

The policeman neither turned nor responded. The other officer said, "I'll drop you at St. Mary's on the way to the station. You might need some stitches in that thing and some shots. Who knows where the hell that knife might have been."

"I didn't mean to cut you, man. It was an accident. I mean, what are we going to be charged with anyway?"

The injured policeman's head snapped to the rear. "Just shut up, kid. You've got the right to remain silent, and damn it, you better exercise that right. You'll get a chance to tell you side at the station."

The following two hours are not among my favorite memories. There were lots of questions, some pictures and fingerprints taken. We were given a more formal reading of our rights, and I used my one phone call to contact my parents. I knew that they would become involved in this, and I felt that perhaps it was best for me to contact them first. I knew that my mother would answer the phone. My father would only if she were not there.

I could hear the disappointment in her voice, but as always, she assured me that everything would be all right, and that they would get to Madison as quickly as they could. I started to give her directions to the police station, but she cut me off.

"We know where it is dear," she said. "Remember. We've been there before." I had hardly ever heard sarcasm from her, and that tone let me know how deeply I was hurting her once again.

"I'm sorry, Mom."

"We'll get there as soon as we can. Goodbye Gene."

~1966~

She hung up before I could say anything further. I could picture the next half hour at home. My father would follow her around the house shouting, as my mother silently packed their bags and wondered how she could have kept this from happening.

It must not have been a busy day at Madison Jail, for Peter Baker and I were each given our own cell. I settled onto my cot, looked at my watch and made a guess that my parents would arrive that evening. That is unless my father convinced my mother that it might be good for me to spend a night in jail. Before I could begin feeling sorry for myself, a familiar face pressed itself between two of my bars.

"Fud. What are you doing here?" I felt a surge of hope having a friendly body in the building with me.

"Don't get excited. I'm not here to spring you or spend the night." A policeman came to his side, unlocked my cell door and let Fud in.

"I'll be back in thirty minutes," said the officer, as he locked the door. Fud came across the cell and joined me on the cot.

"Well, this is certainly an unfortunate turn of events," he said. "Is there anything that you want me to do for you? Anybody I can call?"

"I already called my folks. I guess I'll just wait for them and see what's to be done. It's not a huge crime. I can't imagine they will keep me in here for very long. Aren't you headed back to Iowa pretty soon?"

"I've got about an hour. I'll take a cab back to catch the bus in a little while." We sat in silence for some time.

Finally Fud spoke. "Are you ok, Boomer? I gotta say that I'm a little surprised to see you looking this way, and I'm really surprised to see you in here."

"Oh come on, Fud. You saw what happened. It's not like I've turned into an ax murderer. Besides, you're into the protest movements. You know how these things go. You look cross-eyed at a pig and you get arrested. I'm surprised you haven't spent some time in the slammer."

Fud laughed. "Maybe I've been lucky so far. So, how's everything else? How's school going? Will you graduate in May?"

It was my turn to laugh. "No, I don't think that graduation is in my near future. Maybe not even my distant future. The truth is, Fud, I've gotten a little side-tracked."

For the next twenty minutes we shared our recent lives. I recounted my disintegrating relationship with my parents and my dismal academic achievements.

Fud, too, had pulled away from his family since high school. Mr. and Mrs. Untiedt had struggled with the discovery that their youngest was gay. So far they had not found a way past it, and family gatherings were awkward.

Academically, Fud was, as always, a star. He was set to graduate with highest honors and had already enrolled in the graduate engineering program at Iowa City.

We talked briefly about politics and our involvement in the anti-war movement. While I was the one who looked the role of protester, it was Fud who held the passion.

When he talked of the movement, there was fire in his eyes and voice. He seemed to have an understanding of the issues far beyond me. The leadership roles he had taken, the places he had spoken, the people he had met and worked with dwarfed my pitiful involvement. It felt like he was really protesting, while I was only playing at it. As usual, I

~1966~

was just following the crowd without much sacrifice or conviction. It seemed ironic that it was me sitting in the jail cell and not him. Maybe he was just lucky, or smarter, or maybe just a better person. I felt a stab of envy.

"Listen Boomer, I'm out of here in a minute, but one thing I wanted to find out this weekend is about your plans for this summer."

"Well, I hope that I'm out of jail by then," I joked.

"I decided that I would take a break before graduate school and spend the summer in Chandler. Maybe work on some of the family stuff. Anyway, Jim Bob and Gracie are still living there, and it turns out Sticks will be home until the end of August as well. Wouldn't it be great if we could reunite the Fab Five. What will you be doing?"

"I don't know. I haven't been back for a summer since high school. I guess that I was just planning to get a job here. Maybe take some summer classes and see if I can catch up a bit."

"You really look like you could use a break from all of this, Boomer. Why don't you think about coming home with the rest of us? It will probably be our last chance ever."

The policemen appeared and without saying anything unlocked the cell door.

Fud stood up. "Think about it, will you? The group just wouldn't be the same without you there to screw things up." He stuck out his hand.

"I'll think about it," I said, taking his hand. He pulled me into a hug. "I gotta get out of this mess first."

"You'll be fine, Boom. But think about Chandler this summer, huh?"

"I will." And then he was gone and I had nothing to

do but sit behind bars and think of Chandler. Part of me was excited at the prospect of reliving the old times with the old group. Certainly nothing since then had brought me the joy of those days. On the other hand, I wasn't excited about living with my parents, or about having to explain my dismal college failures.

I needn't have spent much time trying to decide. Events did that for me, and more quickly than I could possibly have imagined.

My parents arrived about 8:00 P.M. that evening to bail me out. The police really didn't have any charges on which to hold me. One piece of great fortune was that I had no marijuana on me at the demonstration. It would not have been unusual if I had.

My folks hadn't eaten, and the jailhouse fare hadn't filled me, so we went to a restaurant. They had decided they would spend the night in Madison and return to Chandler the next day. My mother wanted me to return with them, but I insisted that I had to stay at school, that I had work to do.

"What work?" my father questioned. "By the looks of your last grade report there is not a lot of work happening." That began a series of angry accusations lobbed back and forth through gritted teeth.

"What are you doing at this demonstration anyway? Why don't you start paying more attention to what we sent you here to do?"

"Dad, I thought you sent me here to learn how to think. And what I am thinking is that this Vietnam War is wrong. That it has got to be stopped."

"So you think that you know better than our President, than our leaders, what is right for this country?"

~1966~

"We've got the right to question our leaders in this country when we think they are headed in the wrong direction." Our voices were getting louder, and others in the restaurant were beginning to look our way.

"So this is what I fought for twenty-five years ago, gave up my right arm for, to save a country so that a bunch of radical cowards could just give it back?"

"Nobody in Vietnam is trying to take our country, Dad."

"But they are in Russia. Look what they tried to do in Cuba."

It was my mother who put a stop to it. "Honey. We're exhausted from the drive and still need to find a hotel. Can we talk in the morning?"

We did talk the next morning, but of course, resolved nothing.

I could just as well have gone with them to Chandler. Two days later I was called into the Dean's Office and informed that I was being expelled from school. The police had informed the school of my arrest and incarceration. But the Dean insisted that this latest incident had little to do with my being dropped. He plunked my transcript in front of me and quietly pointed out my unacceptably slow progress toward a degree. He said that he was sorry, that he hoped I could find another school or a job where I could be more successful.

After dropping this latest bomb on my parents, I decided to spend a little time in Madison working and tying up loose ends. I hoped that my dad would lose his voice from yelling before I arrived in May. Then I would fulfill Fud's wish by joining him and the others for the summer.

~Boomer~

It surprised me that the University had acted so quickly to drop me after the demonstration. My experience had been that the huge, complicated administration plodded toward action. Perhaps they had been watching me for some time.

I received a bigger surprise the day I pulled into Chandler with my worldly belongings in two duffle bags. Tucked amidst my parents' mail was a draft notice informing me that, since I was no longer an active student qualified for deferment, I was hereby invited to the Minneapolis Armory for a physical and induction into the military. Who said the wheels of bureaucracy grind slowly?

*****

I spent my first weeks at home wishing that my parents still lived on Morse Street in my childhood house. I felt like an intruder in their new one. Those first weeks were enormously uncomfortable.

The tension doubled when I carelessly missed a stop sign, but did not miss the other car that had entered the intersection, and mangled the front ends of both vehicles, one of them my parent's new car.

The presence of my draft notice made the already tense atmosphere completely explosive. We took turns detonating. Sometimes one of us lit the fuse, and sometimes it was just spontaneous combustion.

My father was livid about my college meltdown. He brought it up at least once each day to beat me over the head. The draft notice was actually balm for his wounds. Since he had no idea what to do with me, he seemed to think that if anyone could save me, it might be the army. I've often wondered if my father helped the local draft board find me.

~1966~

As always, my mother was just the opposite. I think that she would have left me in Madison Jailhouse if she thought it would keep me from the military. That prospect brought her daily to tears. Perhaps my mother's only flaw was being too loving. She should have grabbed me by the scruff of the neck and slapped me until I shaped up. Her unshakeable support and sympathy allowed me to think that I was reasonable and right.

I was simply ticked off at the world. At the end of the approaching summer I would head to basic training, and as much as I hated the idea, there seemed to be little I could do to change it.

If it had only affected me, I would have strongly considered bolting to Canada. But that would have left my father living a nightmare in Chandler. His service in World War II was a thing of enormous personal pride, even though he wouldn't talk about it with his family. At his gas station he faced just about everyone in town on a daily basis, and I couldn't imagine torturing him with a "cowardly" son. As angry as I was with him, I couldn't hurt him that way. It seemed odd that in this I would consider my father's feelings more than my mother's. I think that my mother would have preferred me to desert.

And thus it began. Soon the others would join me and we five high school friends would spend one last summer together in Chandler.

Chapter 4

Roy Orbison and Other Reunion Tales

1967

    I arrived in Chandler about a month before Fud and Sticks. I was really embarrassed that in four years I had made no effort to contact Gracie but did nothing to bridge the gap. I was sure that I would bump into her on Main Street at any moment, but it just never happened.

    With few entertainment options, I did contact Pastor Jim Bob, and we met twice for movies or drinks. On our first outing we ended up at Lee's Bar on Main Street, where Jim Bob filled me in on his life and the lives of our three friends. Having lived in Chandler since birth, Jim Bob had the small town gossip on every resident, past and present. What he hadn't heard directly from Fud, Sticks and Gracie, he had picked up from the many grapevines that twisted around the people of our small town.

    Lee himself served us our beers as we settled into a booth. During high school we had been allowed into the bar to shoot pool on rainy Saturday afternoons, surrounded by old men playing Gin Rummy between their beer glasses. It felt a little odd to be the ones holding the beer glasses now. I also felt considerably uncomfortable at how little I knew about the last years of Jim Bob's life.

    "A banker, Jim Bob?" I laughed. "As I recall, when we

~1967~

played Monopoly you wanted nothing to do with that job."

He laughed with me. "Well, it just kind of happened. My two years at college didn't seem to lead anywhere in particular, so when this job opened up in the bank I just applied. I didn't really expect to get it. I wasn't very qualified, but Mr. Bernard said that if I was willing to take a few classes to get up to speed, he was willing to see what I could do. It probably didn't hurt that Mr. Bernard goes to my dad's church."

"Do you like it?"

"You know, I really do. I've always liked Chandler and it is a very comfortable place to live. There are a whole bunch of old people at the bank. I keep taking more and more classes at Mankato. Mr. Bernard seems to really like me and says that if I stick with it, chances for advancement are going to be plentiful. Besides, it's kind of fun helping the people I've known all my life."

"Good for you. But come on Jim Bob. Still living at home?"

"I know. I know. That was supposed to just be temporary while I settled into my job. I'm just hooked on my mom's cooking. This fall I'll find a place of my own. What's the big deal anyway? You're living at home."

"Just for the summer. That is, if I don't get thrown out before it ends." I tossed it off as a joke, but felt painfully aware of the possibility. I took a drink of beer to cover my embarrassment.

"I saw Fud a few weeks ago. He said things have been a little rocky for you lately."

"I'm afraid that he saw me at my rockiest. Behind bars." I wasn't quite ready for explanations, so changed the subject. "What's new with Fud?"

"Nothing much. He had just failed his draft physical. Evidently all that extra weight was good for something."

"Fud was drafted too. Boy, they're not wasting any time trying to nab us."

"Truth is, they were especially anxious to get Fud. He's written some heavy anti-Vietnam articles for the local newspaper. People in town have been pretty upset by it. I think the local Board thought they had him. He had applied for a deferment to go right into graduate school and they had denied him. Really strange, huh. His opposition to the war almost got him into it and his weight is going to keep him out."

"How about you? Why haven't they shipped you off? Can't they find anyone else to keep track of Chandler's money?"

"4F too. My asthma. Don't you remember me sneezing my way through high school?"

I felt a surge of jealousy at the seeming good fortune of my two friends. "So it seems that I'm the only one of us healthy enough to wage war."

"Not the only one. Sticks will be with you."

"Sticks got drafted too?"

"Not drafted. He enlisted. End of the summer he is off to Officer Candidate Training."

"Sticks, an officer? What's with him?"

"Oh I don't know. Sticks has always been kind of interested in the military. Remember all that Civil Air Patrol stuff he did in high school?"

"I guess. I never thought of him as a leader of men. He's so soft spoken. What happened with his basketball? I kept looking at the Gopher box scores this year, but I never saw his name. He used to get in once in a while."

"He didn't go out this year. I guess he got tired of riding the bench. Things were a bit tougher at the U than at old Chandler High. He got interested in ROTC and just decided that if he wasn't going to play, he might as well spend his time somewhere other than Williams Arena. Anyway, he can fill us in when he gets home."

That left only one person, the one I was dying to hear about. "Do you see much of Gracie?"

"She keeps her money at the bank. I can't tell you how much she has. Customer privacy, you know."

"I don't care about her money, Jim Bob. How is she doing?"

"Fine. She really hasn't changed. Still the same sweet Gracie. She still lives at home too."

"Figures. How is her mother?"

"She hasn't changed either. Still has her ups and downs. Chandler is not a good place to have a drinking problem. Most people in town are really hard on her. She is still the most beautiful woman in town, so people like to look down on her for something."

"How about Gracie? Any big romances in her life?"

"Not that I know of. She still works at the Road House. Of the five of us, I guess she really has changed the least. But when I see her, she seems happy. You know. Same old Mac."

"I really don't know. I probably haven't seen her twice since the summer after high school. It is kind of embarrassing. I really have cut myself off from Chandler these last four years."

~Boomer~

"Yeah. What's going on with you? Flunking out of school. Getting dragged off to jail. I always thought that might happen to Fud or me, but never to you, Boomer. You always seemed to be the orderly one of our group."

Pastor Jim Bob sounded a little too much like my father, which irked me a bit. I sighed. I realized that I was going to have to probably explain myself more than once that summer, so I started to ponder exactly what that explanation was.

"It's weird. Things haven't really gone the way I planned. Well, not that I had much of a plan. But it just seems like I've gotten kinda lost since high school. Then I was always with the right crowd. You guys. We got in our share of trouble, but it was just fun trouble and never hurt anything. Well, unless your dad hasn't been able to get the smell of smoke out of the garage. But now, I don't know, it seems like every thing I do ends up a disaster. And it all seems like fun, just like it did in high school, but the end result always seems to be more trouble. I don't know. I guess I just haven't found out what I want, who I am."

I took a long, slow gulp and emptied another beer. "But now, according to my father, the army will supply me with that needed identity. I'm not so sure. This whole Vietnam thing has me spooked."

"I know. Harland Herne just left for there today. You remember Harland from our class?"

"Sure. They live south of town don't they."

"There were eight guys from around here flying to California for a few days before shipping to Vietnam."

"I can't believe that will be me in a couple months. I've never been more than two hundred miles from Chandler

~1967~

and now they are going to fly me half way round the world."

"Ah, who knows. Maybe it will be done by this fall. They'll probably send you to Georgia."

"Not a whole lot better."

We waved our empty glasses at Lee, who responded with full ones, and our reminiscence continued on into the night. At the end I felt a little better that I now had some knowledge of my friends' recent pasts. Now I wouldn't have to start out as if I had just flown in from some other planet.

Later that night, as I pondered the information Pastor Jim Bob had given me, I wondered how much the last four years had really changed us all. Now for a few weeks in the summer of 1967, before Sticks and I would step into the uncertainties of military life in a country at war, he and I would join Pastor Jim Bob and Gracie and Fud in an attempt to reclaim our carefree Chandler youth. It remained to be seen if the joy of that youthful time could override the changes that had taken place.

*****

Our first outing together seemed to indicate that nothing had changed since high school, including our maturity. Gracie finished work at the Road House by six o'clock, so the rest of us met in the parking lot where we would plan our evening.

The collection of cars in which we arrived clearly established our economic status. Only Jim Bob's Chevy Impala looked like it could carry us outside of the city limits. Sticks and Fud arrived in ancient rattletraps, both having parts held on by duct tape. I had no car at all and had arrived with Fud.

That moment when Gracie walked out of the

restaurant and joined us was one of sheer, unadulterated silliness. She sported that same pixie haircut, and kiddish smile that made her look ten years old.

We compressed into a group hug and spent the next couple of minutes jumping up and down and howling. When we released, we had so much to say to each other that we couldn't get it organized and kept interrupting one another and finally ended up just laughing.

For me, it felt like I had escaped my struggles of the last four years back into the safety and security of my best friends. Judging from the laughter and back-slapping of the others, something similar had happened to them.

If Sticks still had objections to Fud's sexual preference, they only surfaced briefly when Fud had earlier given him an awkward hug.

When we were finally settled down enough to be coherent, Sticks suggested that we adjourn to somewhere more pleasant than a gravel parking lot. None of us had thought beyond that point, so a good deal more confusion ensued.

The only thing that we could establish for sure was that, according to Gracie, a Robert Redford movie, *Barefoot in the Park*, was showing at the Shelton Drive-in Theater. For lack of anything better, this became our destination. Next came our transportation. Sticks and Pastor Jim Bob had the only cars large enough to carry all five of us in any comfort. Unfortunately, Jim Bob wasn't sure his had enough gas to get back into Chandler, much less to Shelton, and he had brought no money to purchase any.

At that point we pooled our resources, only to discover that we not only didn't have enough money to put gas in Jim Bob's car, we didn't even have enough to get us all tickets into the drive-in.

"Not to worry," maintained Fud. "We've got enough for some. We'll just carry the rest through in the trunk. We'll wait until it is dark enough to cover our crime."

"But let's keep enough money for popcorn and drinks," suggested the perpetually hungry Pastor Jim Bob. "As long as we are putting somebody in the trunk, why don't we put in three people. Then we'll have plenty for food. Sticks and Mac can drive through as if they are on a date."

At no point did anyone say, "Look, we're twenty-two years old, some of us college graduates. Do we really want to hatch this sophomoric scheme?" It was obvious that we all did.

Happily, Sticks' car had plenty of gas. Unhappily, it was in the worst condition of any of our cars, in truth, of any car in Chandler, even if you included most of the ones in the salvage yard across the road from the restaurant.

Pastor Jim Bob called "Shotgun." Fud, Gracie and I crawled into the back seat. Sticks taped the door shut and we were off.

We needn't have worried about arriving at the theater before dark. We had to visit a rest stop halfway between Chandler and Shelton to refill the radiator, and if Sticks tried to go more than fifty miles per hour, the '58 Plymouth shook as if it were about to lift off.

A mile before we reached the drive-in entry, we pulled off into a farm lane to rearrange our seating. We passed all of our loose change to Sticks, so that he would have enough to purchase two tickets, and then Fud, Pastor Jim Bob and I climbed into the trunk of Sticks' car.

~Boomer~

For such a big car, it didn't have a very large trunk, and with the rotund Fud taking up more than his share, it was downright crowded in there. Two of us faced one way and Pastor Jim Bob the other, so I had one of his tennis shoes in my face. The trunk wasn't large enough for us to simply lie side by side, so Jim Bob was somewhat on top, propped up half by me and half by Fud.

As Sticks closed the trunk, he said, "Good God, Pastor Jim Bob, you work in a bank. Couldn't you have brought enough money to pay our way into a movie?"

From our dark pit we heard the front doors slam and the engine start. Initially, there were some exhaust fumes that found their way into us, and I had a moment of panic that we might all suffocate without seeing Jane Fonda. Once we were back on the road, the air cleared.

We soon felt the car turn, and assumed we were on the lane leading to the drive-in. The road was a mine field of potholes, no doubt placed by the owner to punish any people stupid enough to traverse it in the trunk of a car. With each bump, Pastor Jim Bob floated upward and flopped down, slamming a knee into my chest or an elbow into my groin.

"This had better be a pretty damn good movie," I muttered to Fud.

We pulled to a stop. I discovered that we could hear the conversation inside the car rather clearly, mostly because of a rather large hole in the rear seat upholstery. My fears of suffocating were further allayed.

"Two, please," I heard Sticks say in his best "I'm a model citizen" voice.

A man's voice gave some muffled directions, and with a "Thanks" from Sticks, we moved forward.

~1967~

Once we were in, Sticks yelled back at us, "I'm going to the back row until we get unloaded. Then we can move closer to the screen."

We circled, rose up over a hump and came to a stop. We heard two car doors open and close and footsteps to our right side, or to our left side in the case of Jim Bob. We heard some metallic scratching on the trunk, and we waited with anxious anticipation for the lid to pop and for fresh air to rush in. But there was no pop, no air.

"Come on, Sticks," yelled Fud. "Get this thing open. Jim Bob is crushing me."

From above us we heard a muffled, "I'm trying," and something that was indistinguishable except for the word "stuck."

More scratching and grunting, but still no popping or air. It was really starting to get stuffy in that trunk.

"Jim Bob, could you move your foot to the right. It's on my nose," I complained.

"Sorry." Still no movement from the trunk lid.

Again we heard a car door open and felt some movement above us. Someone had entered the back seat. A voice came through the hole in the upholstery. It was Gracie.

"Ah, guys. We've got a problem. The lock was kind of frozen, and Sticks tried to force it and... ah... he kind of broke the key off in the lock."

If Gracie said anything else, it was drowned out by the three voices yelling obscenities at her. In a little while, when we had expended all of them that we knew, we fell silent.

"Gracie, are you still there?" I said to the back seat. "Gracie?"

We were quiet again. We heard mumbling from

outside, but couldn't understand what was being said or what was going on. Again, we felt someone in the back seat. Again it was Gracie.

"Ah, guys. The manager was just here. He saw us jerking on the trunk and came down to see what was going on. Sticks fessed up, so he's gone back to the office to get a crow bar to get you out. Are you guys still all right in there?"

"Oh we're just great," shouted Fud. "All we need is for Pastor Jim Bob to let one and we're all goners."

"Oh don't say that," I groaned. "He'll gas us for sure."

Suddenly we heard more vigorous scratching and banging on the lid. For a moment it was quiet, and then the trunk lid flew open so violently that it slammed back down before any of us could move.

Now the lock was broken, however, so we could lift it and crawl out of our torture chamber.

"For crying out loud," scolded the manager. "Aren't you people a little big to be pulling a hair-brained stunt like that?" He continued to chew us out.

I think that if we had just been able to get into the car and drive off, we would still have been home free. "You can't drive with your trunk flapping all over," said the manager.

"It's all right," Sticks assured him. "I've got plenty of duct tape in the car."

It was at this point that Sticks found why he hadn't been able to get the trunk key to turn. By mistake he had inserted the ignition key. So much for driving off scot free.

Now the manager decided that as long as he was going to have to call a tow truck, he might as well make a second call to the police. The policeman, of course, arrived first. It was the same policeman who had picked us up in

~1967~

Shelton on Halloween night of our junior year of high school.

We had driven over with a carload of rotten fruit and vegetables, and had been cruising the streets bombing the cars of our Shelton rivals. Fortunately, we hadn't yet done much damage, serious or otherwise, and this policeman had just kicked us out of town with a warning that if we returned, we would spend the night in jail.

On the way back to Chandler we had dumped our ammunition, but not before it had effused an obnoxious smell into the upholstery of my parent's car.

It was perhaps our good fortune that it was the same policeman on duty this night. With uncanny memory, he recognized and immediately linked us to the other incident. It was like he had been reunited with some long-lost relatives. It actually tickled him that he had twice caught the same five people, four years apart, doing two of the stupidest crimes he could remember in his thirty years of police work.

He gave us the same lecture that the manager had delivered earlier, but it lost some of its power when he kept pausing, going "Heh, heh, heh," and shaking his head.

Still smarting from my last bout with policemen, I stayed to the background and kept still.

Sticks, on the other hand, was so nervous and embarrassed at being caught that he babbled endlessly to the poor policemen. He apologized for what we had done at least five times. He told him how we were best friends and together for the first time in ages. He begged him not to put this on his record, because he was going to be an officer in the military and didn't want anything like this on his record. He said that both he and I would be in the army at the end of the summer.

~Boomer~

The policeman's only response to all of this was, "You are the ones who are going to be defending the country? Oh, I'll sleep better at night now."

He was really very nice about the whole thing, and when the tow truck arrived, he said he couldn't wait to see what we would be up to in four more years, and sent us off. He even laughed when Fud asked him if we could come back to see the second show if it didn't take too long to get the car started.

*****

And so we were off and quickly running on the backward trek to our past lives. We laughed all the way home that first night, recounting all the other scrapes we had gotten ourselves into over the years. For a few hours, it really felt like nothing had changed since high school.

One of the early indicators that our little group had changed, however, happened a few nights later when we actually did get into a movie together.

It was *The Graduate*. Even though it was showing in Chandler, we had to drive forty miles to Emmitsby to see it, because Pastor Jim Bob, at age twenty-two, was still living at home, and his father didn't want anyone in Chandler to see any member of his family attending such a movie.

The five of us had seen dozens and dozens of movies together, but until that night I don't recall us ever discussing any of them, and we certainly didn't disagree about them to any depth beyond whether or not we liked them. That night, however, on the ride back from Emmitsby, we found ourselves actually shouting in disagreement.

Fud had laughed loudly throughout the movie and on the way home couldn't stop talking about how effectively the

~1967~

film had skewered the idea of the American Dream and how really tuned in he had felt with Benjamin throughout.

It was Sticks who most vigorously objected to Fud's glowing review. Evidently, college had not so much changed Stick's rather conservative viewpoint, but it had definitely made him more vocal about it.

"That was the stupidest movie I've ever seen. Who gets a scuba-diving suit or a new sports car for presents? And I don't know a single friend who is having an affair with the wife of their father's business partner. That's just stupid."

"You missed the whole point," argued Fud. "Haven't you ever felt like just dropping out of this whole capitalist rat race that is being shoved down our throats? Wouldn't you like to do things your own way, instead of the way your parents expected you to do them?"

"No. My parents have been really good to me. I couldn't have even started college without their help."

Fud threw up his hands. "I give up. You just don't get it."

I thought maybe I could ease the tension. "I just think that if they are going to show somebody nude in a movie, it should be Katharine Ross and not Anne Bancroft. And if they are going to show anybody nude, they should at least hold the camera still so you can see what's going on."

But my attempt was not taken lightly and was countered by Gracie.

"Oh, is that all you want to go to movies for, to see naked women? If that's it, why don't you just go to Mankato to the X-rated theater."

"I was just joking. And how do you happen to know there is an X-rated theater in Mankato?"

~Boomer~

"I can't concentrate on my driving with all of you yelling at each other," Pastor Jim Bob said. That silenced us for the moment. We all sat quietly smoldering at someone else in the car.

Then Jim Bob piped up. "At least I think they should have gone back for the little red sports car."

"Oh, for crying out loud," shouted Fud. "That car was a symbol of their parents' generation. They couldn't take that with them. They had to leave on the bus." And then we all yelled at each other for another fifteen minutes.

By the time we reached Chandler, tensions had eased and we were laughing about our squabble. It was just a little skirmish, but it was a signal of larger ones to come. In the past we had been so close we had virtually thought as one. Our years after high school had led us down different paths, and some of the philosophical directions we had headed were about to collide.

*****

The following week we set up an outing to an amusement park in Arnolds Park, Iowa, and a favorite high school haunt, The Roof Garden.

The Roof Garden was a dance hall that in the '60s was on a circuit regularly visited by many of the top rock music performers. In the summers between our high school years we had spent many steamy nights listening to the likes of The Everly Brothers, Little Stevie Wonder, Neil Sedaka, Del Shannon. We had seen Buddy Holly, Ritchie Valens and The Big Bopper not long before the plane crash that ended their careers.

For a teenager, The Roof Garden was about as close to heaven as one could get. Or hell if you were a teenager's

~1967~

parent. It was the second floor of an ancient wooden building.

If you missed the entrance by a foot, you ended up in the Funhouse, not entirely a bad mistake. For the girls it was more of a mistake than for the boys, because the first twenty yards of the entrance to the Funhouse was mined with holes in the floor out of which shot air with such force it could blow skirts up over heads.

The Roof Garden was the kind of place that was a hotspot in the sixties, but couldn't even exist today. It had one entrance up a narrow wooden stairway. Everything in it was made of old dried wood. The maze of electrical cords on the floor and ceiling could only have passed the inspection of a mad scientist.

Smoking was allowed - no, encouraged, and with a scarcity of ashtrays, cigarettes were generally snuffed out on the wooden floor. Had a fire started, the place would have vaporized in about five minutes, and the only thing that could have possibly saved anyone was that, because there was no air conditioning, the windows were always wide open, and we probably could have crawled onto an overhang and leapt the ten feet to the ground, spraining an ankle at worst, but escaping immolation.

Dancehall was perhaps the wrong name for The Roof Garden, as few people actually danced to the music. We pressed in as close as we could get to the stage, and stood worshipfully swaying to the rhythm of the band, which was generally a couple of guitars, a keyboard and a trap set.

Fud and I were always fascinated by drummers, so we would always squeeze into one side where we could watch him bang and clang. We actually had our own sets of drum sticks, with which we tried to recreate our idol's rhythms on restaurant tables later in the night.

Today, entertainers of their quality and renown play in city-block-sized auditoriums with tens of thousands of screaming fans, most of whom are so far away that they watch huge television monitors, rather than the actual performers. But at the Roof Garden, we stood ten feet from Chuck Berry. He carried on a conversation with us between numbers.

One of our favorite Roof Garden experiences had always been the performances of Roy Orbison. Orbison was a master of musical climax. He would start each song in a soft, smooth voice. As the words of some sad love tale would unfold, his voice would build. By the end, his powerful voice would tower above the full volume of his backup band, and his audience would be left with ringing ears and throbbing hearts. It was to his show that we headed on yet another hot summer night in 1967.

Once again we would need to nurse Stick's car to our destination. Pastor Jim Bob's was in the shop for brake repair. Gracie, who had been through Arnolds Park most recently, warned us that things had changed since the last time we had heard Orbison croon *Pretty Woman*.

She was right. The rough edges of The Roof Garden had been polished. The wooden exterior had been replaced by shiny aluminum siding. The wall of windows which had overlooked the lake had been covered. The Funhouse was nowhere to be seen.

We purchased tickets and entered the Garden up a wide new staircase. The inside, too, had been cleaned up. The band's area had been enlarged and was now surrounded

~1967~

by a railing which kept the audience from crowding the performers. An opening band, loud and ordinary, was playing when we arrived.

We stood just inside the door and looked on. "Kind of makes you miss the dirty, dingy old Garden, doesn't it?" shouted Fud over the music.

"I brought something along that'll bring it back," said Pastor Jim Bob. He reached into his pocket and pulled out a pack of Tarington cigarettes.

We had all learned to smoke at the Roof Garden. I'm not sure that any of us really wanted to. None of us had gone on to become regular smokers. It was just part of the atmosphere to create a blue haze to encircle the band. It was also that little bit of rebellion that edged us toward adulthood in the '60s. Even Sticks, the athlete, smoked at The Roof Garden, although I'm sure he never lit a cigarette outside those walls.

"Sorry to spoil your fun," said Sticks, "but it looks like that has changed as well." He pointed to a sign on the pillar near us. "No Smoking." We looked around and saw that the regulation was definitely in force. No one in the hall was smoking.

"Jeez," said Pastor Jim Bob, "We can't even be bad anymore. Guess I should have brought some dope instead."

I thought, but didn't say, "I wouldn't have minded."

The crowd was a mixture. There were a few like us, "old timers," back for a trip down memory lane with a favorite. But mostly it was a high school crowd who seemed to care little who was playing. More of them actually danced. They didn't seem to have dance partners, but just gathered into little clumps to twist and shake and shout to each other.

~Boomer~

Roy Orbison didn't disappoint, however. His show was almost unchanged from the ones we remembered. One would have thought that the years of singing in smoky dance halls would have withered his voice to nothing.

But there he stood, his weak eyes shaded by sunglasses, heaps of thick black hair atop his head, declaring to us in song that "he'd had a woman, mean as she could be."

Once again we were transported back into a happier time. At one point we actually put our arms around one another's backs and swayed together to a ballad.

At the second break in the show we made our way to the refreshment booth to get something to help us cool off. The evening was hot and sticky, and while we hadn't noticed it during the hypnotic trance of Orbison's music, our clothing had begun to cling to us in damp, sometimes visually so, places. Had we not been part of the problem, I'm certain we would have wrinkled our noses at the odor of the heavy air.

"What a hoot!" said Jim Bob. "Can you believe the guy can still sing like that?"

"I think he's better," said Gracie. "I can't remember him hitting those high notes that easily in the old days. I wonder how old he is."

"I wonder how much he can see. He always has those dark glasses, and he never really seems to be looking at anything," said Sticks.

"Oh shit," said Fud. "I'll see you guys back at the band stand." He abruptly turned and headed back the opposite direction.

"Fud, What are you doing?" I called after him. As we watched him retreat two larger than average guys pushed past us and followed Fud's course. We watched as they caught up to him. One of them reached out and grabbed Fud by the shoulder and turned him around. Immediately the rest of us scrambled back to our friend to see what this was about.

As we arrived, the bigger of the two lugs was saying to Fud, "Listen, you fat shit. We told you we didn't want to see you ever again. What the hell you think you're doing?"

Fud looked past them to us. "Guys, these are my old college friends, Patrick and Daniel."

"Friends, my ass," said the one Fud had designated Patrick. "Which of you pussies is tubby's girlfriend?"

"Well, we know it's not one of them," said Daniel. "The girl."

We outnumbered them, but none of us were fighters, and Patrick and Daniel probably outweighed four of us.

I tried to be the peacemaker. "Listen. We're just here to have a good time. How about just leaving us alone?"

"We're here for a good time as well," snarled Patrick, "but we don't want to do it with homos and dikes." This last he spit out at Gracie.

"Leave them alone," said Fud. "They're nothing to you, so just deal with me if you want to."

"Oh, we'll deal with you all right, "said Patrick, "just like the last time we saw you, with all of your faggot friends." He reached out and shoved Fud, who would have fallen over backward, but instead crashed into a person just behind him.

Fud turned and apologized to the young man. Patrick spun him around and raised his fist to throw a punch. The ever agile Sticks stepped in and grabbed Patrick's arm at the bicep, so that by the time his fist reached Fud's abdomen, it had almost no force at all.

~Boomer~

Patrick wheeled on Sticks. "You want some of this too, you little prick?"

Fortunately, before anyone gave anything to anyone else, the dance hall security guard stepped into the middle of the scene. Patrick and Daniel backed off immediately, as if police trouble was on the bottom of their list for evening's activities. The police sent us our separate ways with a warning to stay apart.

The conflict left us shaken, and we decided to call it a night. I was pleased to see that Sticks had so quickly come to Fud's defense.

"Jeez, Fud, Does that kind of thing happen to you often?" Sticks asked. "What kind of college you been attending?" I checked behind to be sure that Patrick and Daniel weren't following us toward the exit. They weren't. But as we left the hall and headed for the parking lot, we really did step from the fireplace into the fire.

From up ahead of us in the crowd we heard screams and angry shouts. Screams and shouts were always common in the amusement park, but these weren't the joyous noise of roller coaster riders. People were dashing to the side of the street, tripping over one another and falling to the ground. Suddenly a hail of rocks pelted the crowd around us. One slammed solidly into my shoulder.

"What the hell?"I shouted.

"Get off the street," I heard Fud shout from up ahead. I grabbed Gracie by the arm and pulled her to the side, just as a mob of African American guys stormed past us. They knocked down anyone not quick enough to move to the side, including an elderly man and woman who lay confused and battered in the street.

~1967~

Some of them carried sticks and baseball bats which they thankfully just waved and didn't use on the people in the crowded street. The shouting mob hurtled forward to the end of the street, turning and flinging the last of their stones back into the crowd. Then they raced off yelling into the parking lot.

The stunned crowd began to move cautiously back onto the street. Gracie and I found Fud and Jim Bob.

"Are you guys all right?" asked Fud.

I rubbed my arm where the stone had hit me. "We're fine. What was that all about?"

Just then Sticks joined us. "Let's get out of here," he said. "Everybody is going to be leaving and it's going to be chaos." He started off.

As we followed, we passed through groups of people who were comforting friends and helping them to their feet. Police sirens were screaming, as several squad cars raced into the park area. Sticks was right; it would be best to make a hasty exit.

He reached his car ahead of the rest of us, and when we arrived we found him staring at it in disbelief. Every window in his rattle-trap Plymouth was smashed. The back and some of the side windows were entirely gone. The windshield was still there, but badly cracked. The hood and trunk had new dents, joining those already there.

"Look what they did to my car," he shouted to us as we joined him. "Why me?"

We looked around, and it became obvious that it wasn't just him. Dozens of the vehicles around us had broken windows and broken headlights and dented fenders.

"What in the hell was that all about?" I said to Fud.

~Boomer~

He shook his head and said, "Oh, I've got a good idea."

Before I could ask him what he meant, two policemen barged between us, one of them shouting, "You people are going to have to stay put for a while until we get some statements."

For the next hour we sat on the hood of Stick's beaten car as policemen viewed the damage, collected information and filled out reports.

As they worked, people talked to one another, trying to get some explanation of the rampage. "Well, they're not from around here," a person next to us told a policeman. "There aren't that many black people that live within a hundred miles of here."

"They sure knew what they were up to," said the woman with him. "They weren't here for fifteen minutes, and look at the damage they did." We looked around. Hardly a car had escaped the rampage.

Finally, after a cop had asked us some questions and filled out a report, we were allowed to leave. The windshield in Sticks car was reasonably clear in front of the driver, and neither headlight had been touched. It would be a breezy ride back to Chandler, but with one pause at the rest stop to refill the radiator, we could probably get home.

We were quiet as we drove out of Arnolds Park. It was after midnight, and we were all tired and tense, so what happened next was understandable this time, but it was to become a pattern of the rest of our outings that summer.

It was Fud that opened the can of worms. "You think this was bad, just keep an eye on your TVs, folks."

"What are you talking about?" I asked.

~1967~

"There have been racial incidents around the country for the last few years," he said, "but they haven't really amounted to much. There was a lot of talk on campus this spring that this is the summer when it is going to explode. Martin Luther King has been trying to keep it peaceful, but people are losing their patience, and it won't take much to set them off."

"But why Arnolds Park, Iowa?" I said. "It's not exactly the center of racial oppression in the nation."

"That's a mystery, all right," Fud admitted. "We're kinda far from Newark or Detroit."

"And why my car?" moaned Sticks. "I've never done anything to a black person worse than fouling him on the basketball court."

"Maybe some of us white folks are going to have to take some shots before the country wakes up to what is going on here," Fud said.

Again, the usually mild mannered Sticks jumped on this with a surprising amount of anger. "You mean because you're black, you should have the right to run around the country bashing up other people's property. That's crazy."

"It doesn't give them the right," Fud countered, "but it's not hard to understand why it might happen. The Civil Rights Movement in this country has really stalled. Let's face it, the blacks are the poorest part of our population, and we're not doing a whole hell of a lot to help them."

Hearing Sticks and Fud on opposite sides of this argument was another reminder of our changes. In high school both had been apolitical. Sticks had been into sports, and Fud into goofing around. They hadn't appeared very interested in the larger world, but evidently college had raised their consciousness. It had also led them in different directions.

"Come on, guys," said Gracie, "we're just tired. It was a fun night for a while." She and Pastor Jim Bob were obviously uncomfortable with the friction in the air.

"Isn't that Orbison something?" said Pastor Jim Bob. "The guy just doesn't change."

"I don't care how bad things are," Sticks continued the argument. "People can't go around destroying stuff. Even your hero, Martin Luther King, believes that. You think he'd approve of what they did to my car tonight."

"No." Even Fud was a little taken back by the uncharacteristic emotion with which Sticks was arguing. "But some people in the movement are getting impatient with King's approach. It's not putting food on their tables. Some of their other leaders are planning to take things in a different direction."

I was quietly trying to work out where I stood on the issue and felt awkward entering the argument between my two good friends.

Finally, I offered, "What you are talking about is anarchy, Fud. Is that really the way you think things should be settled?"

"I'm not promoting. I'm just saying that sometimes maybe it is necessary to move things forward when they get stuck."

"You call bashing up my car moving things forward? Sounds backward to me."

"There have been plenty of times when violence has been necessary to get things done. It's the old end-justifying-the-means argument. I mean, what are these people

~1967~

supposed to do, sit in the back of the bus until we decide it's OK to let them come forward."

The back of Stick's neck was beet red. He gave up the argument, but I could tell that he had discovered something else about Fud that he really didn't like. It was the beginning of conflicts which would drive them apart.

Whether or not Fud was right in his justification of violence, his prediction that it would come was right on. In the next months, cities across the country burst into flames. Chicago, Baltimore, Newark, Milwaukee, Detroit, Minneapolis. We watched on our televisions as they burned.

It was jarring that it had started in our midst, and in Arnolds Park, a place that had brought us so much peace and joy. It appeared that our journey forward was going to be more difficult than our journey past had been.

*****

That summer, while we tried to frolic in Chandler, the war in Vietnam had reached its most critical time. The Commander of the forces, General Westmoreland, was asking that 200,000 more US soldiers be sent to bolster the effort. In response, President Johnson had agreed to send another 45,000 troops. I hoped that diminished my chances of going by three quarters..

At first I hadn't paid a great deal of attention to the war. In my first years of college I was too busy with other things, some constructive, some destructive, to worry about the other side of the world. On the Madison campus, however, student involvement in the anti-war movement became more vocal, and eventually drew me into it.

One morning I had stumbled into the middle of the first campus protest against the presence of recruiters from

Dow Chemical Company. The anger and passion of the demonstrators had surprised me.

But what had frightened me was a group of Vietnam veterans, some missing limbs, most in wheelchairs, who were a part of that demonstration. I became aware of more and more things about the war that I didn't understand and didn't like.

Fud, had discovered quite early the significance of Vietnam. His friends, who had been involved in the civil rights movement for much of his first years at school, became more and more associated with Students for a Democratic Society and the anti-Vietnam movement.

Fud had also decided that if he was going to be a part of the protest, he was going to understand the issue; while his major emphasis remained math and science, he kept taking social studies courses, particularly focusing on Southeast Asia.

By the time he returned to Chandler in the summer of '67, he was incredibly knowledgeable on the issues of Vietnam.

Later into the summer he would demonstrate that knowledge by writing more articles for *The Chandler Sentinel*. It was something that would have gone down well in the University of Wisconsin student newspaper, but was generally not well received in rural Minnesota, particularly from someone who would not be serving himself. The articles were exceptionally well-reasoned and written, but in Chandler, Fud might as well have published a picture of himself burning his draft card. The community response would have been about the same.

Sentiment really turned against Fud, when in the

~1967~

week following the second article, the town learned that it had lost its first young man to the war.

The parents of Ronnie Parsons, a high school classmate of ours, were visited by two military men who informed them that their son had been killed in action. Ronnie had gone into the army right out of high school. He was part of the special forces who were the very first combat soldiers to enter Vietnam.

We had not been close to Ronnie in high school. He had been somewhat of a loner and a bully, but the idea that a guy we knew had actually died in the war brought something that had seemed far away right to our doorstep.

In truth, it shook me. I was already certain that I didn't want anything to do with Vietnam, and this reminder that people were actually dying there did nothing to change my mind.

Unlike Fud, I kept my objections to myself, saying little of my fears to my friends, but I found myself thinking about it almost continuously. In a few weeks I would be in the army, and it seemed there was nothing I could do to change that course.

This was an entirely new sensation for me. In our small, Midwestern haven, our lives had, for the most part, made sense to us and remained within our control. Now I suddenly had a huge, dark cloud above me, and I feared that the impending storm would sweep me into a dangerous and unpredictable stream.

Ronnie Parson's death had a different effect on Sticks. It steeled his resolve that the military was the right choice for him. Ronnie's giving his life for his country was the noblest of sacrifices. While Sticks had no desire to share Ronnie's fate, he was passionate to serve his country in whatever way it needed him. Such patriotic sentiments were shared by most of the citizenry of Chandler, but brought him into frequent conflict with Fud and tore our little group apart.

Nearly every time I was with Fud he would plead with me to do something to save myself from this useless war. Sticks would always object, and a new argument would erupt. Once it happened as we were lying on the beach of a nearby lake.

"It's not a war, Fud. It's a police action. Nothing has been declared."

"Do you think Ronnie Parson's parents care what they are calling it?" Fud refused to pull his punches. "He'd be just as dead."

"But what did he die for?"

"My point exactly! What did he die for? Nothing that justifies his loss."

"Don't you think, Fud, that there are times when we have to stand up for ourselves as a nation? You want to talk about history. Take a look at more recent history. Do you think that Castro would have pulled his missiles out of Cuba if we hadn't called his bluff and forced him to?"

"Probably not, and there sure are lots of missiles aimed at us from Vietnam." I knew the sarcasm in Fud's voice wasn't going to sit well with Sticks.

"Do you think this bathing suit makes me look fat?" said Gracie, trying to steer the conversation elsewhere.

"Oh, right," said Jim Bob. "Like anyone is going to tell you that it does. Are you trying to start a fight, Mac?"

Sticks was not deterred. "Look, the Communists are just looking for a chance to push us around, and if they prove they can do it in Vietnam, who knows where they will push next?"

"If we weren't there, they couldn't very well push us now, could they?" Fud countered.

"So you don't think we should help our allies when the bullies of the world are overthrowing them? Hitler would have really appreciated that attitude in the Second World War."

"Ho Chi Minh is no Hitler. Look, the French had no business being in Vietnam. If we'd have let the Vietnamese kick them out without interfering, the whole thing would be over now. Early on, Ho Chi Minh wasn't even inclined toward Communism."

"Well, he sure seems to be now."

"Yes, when they're supplying guns to help get rid of us."

The rest of us sat watching the debate like a tennis match. I wished Fud would stop the argument. I didn't think Sticks could. He had chosen to be in the military and was certainly on his way to Vietnam. In trying to deny Fud, he was trying to justify the whole course that his life would take. For him the argument had really become personal, whereas for Fud, it still seemed philosophical.

I was caught in the middle. I too would probably end up in Vietnam, but I didn't have Sticks' need to see it as a noble mission. On the other hand, if I really agreed with Fud, and thought Vietnam a tragic mistake, why did I still have my draft card in my pocket? Why hadn't I burned it with my buddies in Madison? I had answers to none of this, so I just sat in the back seat and listened to their wrangling.

I had to hand it to both of them. They didn't back

down. The arguments kept getting more frequent and more bitter.

After Ronnie's death, Fud took a great deal of abuse around town. One instance actually ended with his being beaten. But two weeks after Ronnie's death Fud again made his anti-Vietnam feelings known in *The Chandler Sentinel*. It was really hard for Sticks and him to be together after that.

More and more I found myself longing for the days when Sticks raced up the basketball court and Fud conspired with Pastor Jim Bob to create a concoction in the parsonage garage.

*****

As the summer heat settled into Chandler, my family relationship continued to smoulder and boil. I had decided that, since I was being drafted into the army at the end of the summer, for three months I would remain jobless and carefree. Initially, this had not set well with my father. For him, idle hands were the devil's playground, and with me he had evidence of the truth of the maxim.

I assured him that I wouldn't be a financial burden, that I still had a meager amount in my savings account, enough to keep me in hamburgers for the summer. Besides, when I was hanging around the house, he was at work. By the time he got home for dinner, I was usually out with all or part of the group. The fact that I would soon be off his hands and into the military kept him from badgering me more than he did.

My mother and I actually grew closer that summer. It was, in fact, her last chance to mother. Tom and Elizabeth were long gone by that time, and I hadn't been around much in the last four years. For at least a few weeks, she had her

~1967~

baby home to spoil.

She had always loved my four friends, so was happy to see me back with them. She loved to let me sleep in until sinful hours and feed me lavishly huge breakfasts at noon and hearty dinners in the late afternoon before I disappeared for the evening. All along, she knew that I was avoiding my father and it hurt her, but she wanted to keep the peace as well, so served as accomplice.

Unfortunately, the summer wasn't short enough to keep us apart entirely, and one afternoon in August our schedules crossed. I was seeing Gracie that night; the rest were busy with various things. She was working, but the early dinner shift, so I was going to pick her up for a late movie.

My father arrived home from the station earlier than usual, and since I hadn't yet eaten, I decided to tempt fate and have dinner with my parents.

It was a bad idea. My dad had a bad day at work and was itching for a fight. Before we finished our salads, it had begun. It was not long after one of Fud's anti-Vietnam articles, and it became our dinner topic.

"It seems really chicken-hearted for someone who is exempt from the draft to write such crap," was his opening volley.

"Oh, I don't know," I said, trying not to be too confrontational. "Fud has a right to his opinion, even if he's not going to Vietnam."

"What does he know about it? He's just spouting all that pinko nonsense he got from those agitators he hung out with in college. That doesn't make him an expert on foreign policy."

~Boomer~

"Does Fred know what he is doing yet this fall?" asked my mother, trying to steer the conversation into peaceful waters.

"Yeah, he's headed back to Iowa for graduate school."

"So while you and Sticks and the rest of our boys are fighting for this country, I suppose he will be marching around campus giving aid to the enemy."

"Look, Dad, there's no guarantee that I'll be going to Vietnam. And if I do, I'm not going to be happy about it. The truth is, if I can find a way to avoid it, I'm going to take it. Actually, my thoughts about Vietnam are just about the same as Fud's."

Oh, boy, I'd done it again. I looked at my mother, whose jaw set firmly, ready for the onslaught.

"Oh, I might've known. What is wrong with young people these days? You think that all the stuff you have in this country comes to you on a silver platter. Don't you realize that freedom is an expensive commodity, and you just might have to pay something for it along the way? In my day, when we were called to serve, we went. We didn't second-guess our leaders. We didn't tromp on our flag. We had guts."

"Oh, I don't know. You left your wife behind with two small children. Some might say the war wasn't where you were needed most." As soon as I said it, I knew I had gone too far.

He rose up out of his chair. "How dare you?" he shouted.

My mother rose as well, "Gene, Glen, you stop this!" We froze. My father stood above me, the urge to strike making his hands shake.

~1967~

"You are both saying things that you don't mean. Now stop it so that we can finish our dinner in peace." I had seldom seen my mother put her foot down so firmly, and it seemed to surprise her as much as it did the two of us.

After several tense moments, my father sat back down. We each took a bite in silence. My father's face was still flushed, and his jaw was so tense he could hardly chew.

Finally, he gathered himself together enough to say, "If you think that leaving my family behind was easy, was what I wanted to do..."

"I don't. I didn't mean that. I'm sorry I said that." I floundered for a way to reverse the damage.

In trying to decide what I should do about the military, I had wondered why my father chose the course he did in the war, or if he had any choices in the matter, but his firm taboo on the subject kept me from ever addressing it. I couldn't believe that I had just broached the subject in such a harsh and thoughtless way. This wasn't how I wanted to start my evening or end his day. I looked for a way to diffuse him.

"Look, Dad, I know what you are saying, and I'll go where the army decides to send me. I just don't understand what's going on in Vietnam very well, and I'm not sure what we're doing there is defending our freedom. But mostly I just wish this wasn't happening to me right now. I just think I need some time to get things straightened out for myself."

He had been looking right at me. This last seemed to relax him, and he broke his stare and leaned back in his chair. We all took a bite of dinner.

Taking a last swallow of milk, I got up from the table. "I gotta be going. I'm meeting Gracie after work."

~Boomer~

"Just you and her?" The tension was immediately back in my father's voice.

"Yes, just the two of us. I'm old enough to date, you know." I tried to say it jokingly, but it came out sarcastically.

"You're not taking up with her again, are you? You know how I feel about that relationship."

I closed my eyes and took a deep breath to compose myself. "It's not a relationship. We are just going out on a date."

"I just don't think it is right for you to get involved with anyone right now. It wouldn't be fair...."

"Just drop it, Dad. I don't know what your problem is, but it really is none of your business. If I want to date Gracie, I will date Gracie. If I want to marry, Gracie I'll do that too. It is none of your business. And in a few weeks I'll probably be on the other side of the world, so none of it will make much difference. So, let's just forget it."

He waved his hand at me as if in agreement of the last and went back to his dinner. I shook my head and turned for the door. "Bye, Mom."

For the moment, the war, both our personal one and the one in Southeast Asia, went back to hanging ominously over our heads.

*****

I was noticeably quiet that evening out with Gracie. We said very little on the way to the theater. We had been out alone several times throughout the summer, but had never gotten entirely comfortable and had never talked about why I had disappeared from her life for four years after high school. My silence continued as we drove away after the movie.

~1967~

Gracie moved us forward. "It's kind of hot. Want to go out to Sunny Lake?"

"I guess. You don't suppose that old row boat is still out there, do you?"

"I know it is. I've actually taken it out by myself a time or two. Vern doesn't care."

"All right. Maybe we can catch a breeze out there."

At the lake I took the blanket from the back seat of my folk's car and we made our way to the shore. I rowed us to the middle, tossed the anchor overboard and reseated myself on the back bench. Gracie stretched the blanket across the bottom of the boat, sat on it and leaned back between my legs, her head resting against my stomach.

It was exactly the position she had taken on the night four years earlier, the last night before I deserted her. For a moment I felt wonderful and awful at the same time. Then those four years seemed to vanish and in their place came the same warmth and excitement I had felt that night. "Comfortable down there?" I asked her softly.

"Do you remember the movie *High Society*?"

"Kind of. It was Bing Crosby wasn't it?"

"And Grace Kelly. Remember when they took the boat *True Love* out on the bay. Grace sat just like this in Bing's lap. Let's watch that movie sometime, shall we?"

"Sure." We sat in silence for several minutes.

"Hey Bing, why so quiet tonight."

"Well, Grace..." I would play along. It was the only time I could remember calling her Grace. "I don't know. I'm starting to dread the end of summer. It is starting to sink in that this army thing is really going to happen. God, Gracie, I'm no soldier."

~Boomer~

"Well, not yet, but maybe you will be."

"That's just it. I don't think that I want to be. This Vietnam thing is starting to spook me. I think Fud is right. We haven't got any business over there. We're not going to stop Communism by beating up a bunch of peasants on the other side of the world."

"Maybe you won't have to go. Some broadcasters seem to think that it will be over soon. Maybe it will end before you're out of basic. Or even so, maybe you won't get sent there. There are a lot of places we have soldiers stationed. Maybe you'll end up in Germany or England. Join the army. See the world. Maybe I'll even come visit you in Germany. You always told me I should get out of Chandler. Would that be far enough for you?"

More silence. "You getting along any better with your parents?"

I blew out a long breath. "We had another blow up at dinner tonight. My dad is still really bitter that I botched college and ended up with a rap sheet instead of a diploma. He seems to be waiting for me to screw up again. He's a 'the army will make a man out of you' kind of guy, so I think he believes it will probably happen to me in these next two years. Who knows? Maybe it will. He's usually right."

I moved down with Gracie on the bottom of the boat so that I could put my arms around her. The boat gently rocked back and forth. I held her close.

"I don't know. I just have a bad feeling about this. So many guys seem to be ending up in Vietnam these days, and some of the things going on over there really sound ugly. I just don't want any part of it."

She leaned forward and turned around. On her knees

~1967~

she held my head hard against her chest. "You want to take me to Canada?"

Her tone of voice didn't let me know if she was kidding or not. I pulled my face back and looked up into hers. "Can we row there?"

She laughed, "We can try." She sat up, grabbed one of the oars, dipped it to the water and rowed us in a circle.

"At this rate the war will be over before we get there." I grabbed her and pulled her back into my lap. "You know I've really thought about going to Canada. If I did go, would you come with me?" There was a long pause without an answer. "You don't have to decide. I'm not going."

She buried her head in my shoulder. "Oh, Boomer," she sobbed. She pulled away and wiped her eyes with her hand. I fished in my pocket for my handkerchief and handed it to her. She wiped her face and returned to her Grace Kelly position.

"You want to know the silly reason I could never go to Canada?" I could feel her head shake in the affirmative. "My dad. He and I haven't said four civil words to each other in two years, and yet he's the reason I won't burn my draft card."

"It's natural to want to please your parents."

"I don't think it's that. I think he has given up the idea of being pleased with me. I just don't want to make life miserable for him and Mom. I've done some stupid things in the last years that I'm not very proud of. I just don't want to do that again. That crummy gas station is his life, and he sees just about everybody in town there. I don't want him to have to answer embarrassing questions about me over and over again."

~Boomer~

Gracie sat quietly rubbing the calf of my right leg. "Funny. Here I am coming to his support, and I'm so mad at him I could wring his neck. Tonight at dinner he was jumping up and down about Fud's article in *The Sentinel*. I took Fud's side and we ended up yelling at each other again." We sat quietly listening to the little waves lapping up against the boat. I didn't tell her that she had been part of the argument as well.

"Bing?"
"Yes, Grace?"
"I would have gone to Canada with you."
"Really?"
"Sure. What have I got to leave behind?"

Without speaking we stood. The boat rocked back and forth. We staggered a bit to gain our balance. I took the blanket and centered it across the bottom of the boat. Grace slipped her shirt over her head and pealed off her shorts. As I undressed, she unclipped her bra and lay down on the blanket. It all happened so quickly, and my emotions ranged from embarrassment to excitement.

I sat beside her on the blanket. I had been with girls in my college years, but nothing that meant much to me. This meant everything, and it was brand new and wonderful. I had no idea what Gracie's encounters had been, but I wanted ours to be just right.

She ran her hand over my chest. I closed my eyes, as it took my breath away. I bent down to kiss her, moving slowly to find her lips in the darkness. She opened her mouth and softly massaged my lips with hers. My hand found her breast, and her back arched as I gently rubbed it.

"God, Boomer, this really feels good," she whispered

~1967~

and then caressed my ear with her lips.
    She turned on her side, and I lay beside her and held her tightly. The breeze blowing off the lake heightened my sensitivity. I felt like my body was about to explode.
    I brought my fingertips down the center of her back and across her buttocks. She shivered. Her hand slipped between our hips and found my erection. "Oh wow, Gracie," I gasped, "I think you hit my jackpot."
    She giggled. We held still, except for our heavy breathing. Then she giggled again.
    "What?" I gasped.
    "Nothing Boomer. I'm just so happy." Her mouth found mine and pressed hard against me. When she finally came up for air, she sighed and said, "This is so strange." More silence.
    "Bing, do you remember four years ago after high school, that night we ended up out here?"
    "Like it was yesterday. Gracie, I'm sorry that I disappeared from your life. I've been so stupid, wasted so much time. Gracie..."
    She put her fingers to my lips. "Shh. It doesn't matter Boomer."
    "Yes it matters. I should've stayed in touch. I'm just starting to realize how much I've missed you and now, I'm leaving again. What's to become of us, Gracie?"
    "Maybe something. We'll just have to see. I'll still be here when you get back again."
    "You'll probably be married with two kids by that time."
    "I doubt it. There has never really been anyone quite as interesting as you, Boomer."

~Boomer~

"You're kidding." I would never have believed that Gracie, that anyone, would say that of me. I turned her face toward me and tried to see her expression in the dark. "When was the first time you thought so?"

"I think I always felt it. But Prom night was the first I ever admitted it to myself."

"Really?"

"I mean we all had fun that night, but what really made it special was every fourth dance with you. I couldn't wait until it was your turn, even though you couldn't dance."

"Oh come on. Who was better?" I pretended to be wounded.

"Fud. He may not be athletic, but he can be smooth and graceful."

"I bet his mother made him take dance lessons." We held each other in silence.

"You're going to think I'm making this up, but now that you mention it, there were times that night I remember wishing you were just my date," I said. "Wow, if you were feeling that, how could I have missed it?"

"Oh, I don't imagine that I showed it much. We were still a fivesome, and I knew that you were going away at the end of the summer. It was something I felt, but I didn't have expectations anything would come of it. Not for plain, old Gracie."

"Oh God, Gracie, don't always sell yourself short. You're anything but plain. You're bright and beautiful." I paused and tightened my grip on her. "But you're right. We've always been a package deal. Until this summer I wouldn't have thought about you romantically any more than I would Fud. God, it was like we were all married."

~1967~

"I know. I felt it too. And it was great. I wouldn't have given up those times for the world. It was just that when high school ended, I could feel us all splitting apart, and I realized that you were going to be the one I missed most."

"And I just went away and let you miss me."

This time I started the kiss. When we separated, she whispered, "And now you're leaving me again."

I held her as tightly as I could. "Oh God, Gracie, I don't want to go. Maybe we should go to Canada."

"No, you'll bring pride to your father and I'll bring comfort to my mother, and what we want will just have to wait a bit."

"But two more years? You're not going to sit around and wait for me for two more years."

"Yes I will. I'll wait for you, Boomer."

"I can't ask you to, Gracie. It's just so long." I sat up on the seat of the boat. I was near tears. "Aw Gracie. It is going to be hard enough to leave you at all now, but to leave you for something I'll probably despise is really crummy."

She slipped back into her Grace Kelly position. Her naked back against me felt wonderful. "We've got a few days here, so let's just see what comes of them."

We sat perfectly still for so long that I thought perhaps she had gone to sleep. I thought about how heated we had gotten, how exciting it felt. But we had stopped before actually having sex, and I wasn't sure why. I wasn't even sure who had stopped.

Sex had been the farthest thing from my mind when the evening started. I wondered if she was disappointed that we hadn't gone further.

~Boomer~

Then something my father had said at dinner flashed into my head. When he had told me I should back off my relationship with Gracie he had said, "It wouldn't be fair." Was it possible that he had been trying to protect my friend instead of condemning her?

It wouldn't have been fair to Gracie if we had made love. The second to the last thing I wanted to do was leave for the army. The first would have been to leave Gracie behind pregnant. Had I over-reacted to my father's advice, and in doing so, built another wall between us?

It seemed that we had grown so far apart, whatever one said, the other took as criticism. If I was wrong tonight, I doubted that I could find the voice to apologize. But right now all I wanted to feel was the warmth of Gracie next to me.

Gracie stirred between my legs. "Bing," she said, "could you be a gentleman and row me back to shore?"

"Sure, Grace. I'll row you to the moon if you want."

*****

While the rest of us might have let the group go at that point, it was Pastor Jim Bob who kept trying to hold it together. He kept arranging things for the five of us and trying to soothe hurt feelings.

The night after Gracie and I had our romantic boat excursion, Jim Bob planned for us all to go to the county fair. Still on cloud nine from the previous night's outing, I would have preferred to do something alone with Gracie. At least at the fair I could probably sneak in a private ride on the Ferris Wheel away from the others.

I was crushed when, with four of us in Jim Bob's car, Sticks announced that Gracie wasn't feeling well and wouldn't be going along. I was also most confused as to why

~1967~

she would call Sticks and not me. I did my best to not be a wet blanket for the rest of the evening, and at moments even got into the spirit of the fair.

We actually acquired a fifth member for the group. At the very first booth, Fud threw a wooden ring (his first toss) onto the neck of a coke bottle and won a bear that was nearly as big, and exactly the same shape, as he was.

For the rest of the evening, we took turns lugging it around. It was actually the bear and I who got a private ride on the Ferris Wheel. The others hooted and howled as I pretended to make out with my new, fuzzy date.

The tension between Sticks and Fud was still there, but Pastor Jim Bob refused to let that dampen the evening. He conned them onto the Tilt-a-Whirl together.

They were the only two on the ride. Just before they took off, he shouted to them that he was going to pay the operator to keep the ride going until they made up and hugged. It took about fifteen minutes and seven of Pastor Jim Bob's dollars, but finally they relented and did a lap in one another's arms. Jim Bob and I applauded as they rolled to a stop, still hugging.

It turned out they hugged again sooner than they might have desired. As they came down the runway to exit the ride, Fud was so dizzy that he staggered a few steps, stumbled, turned and lunged into the arms of an almost equally dizzy Sticks.

Happily, when Fud threw up, it was with such force that it landed some yards away, rather than dribbling down Sticks' back. The two of them spent the next half hour sitting very quietly on a bench with the bear between them. Meanwhile, Jim Bob and I spent another seven dollars failing to tip over milk bottles.

~Boomer~

I had to hand it to Pastor Jim Bob. He masterfully orchestrated the whole night with one purpose in mind, to hold us together. I had started the evening wishing desperately that I were with Gracie instead of them. I'm sure Fud and Sticks weren't excited to be in one another's company. But by the end of the night, we left the fair arm in arm. From there we adjourned to Lee's Bar in downtown Chandler and toasted each other's health until closing.

By the time I got home, it was much too late to phone Gracie, so I showered to clear my head a bit and fell into bed.

The next day I phoned her house twice. Both times I got her mother, who assured me that she would let Grace know I had called when she returned. She didn't seem inclined to tell me from where she would be returning. I hung around the house reading most of the day, but no call came.

I knew that Gracie had to work, so I decided to pick her up after. Maybe we could make a return trip to the lake. Condoms crossed my mind, but I didn't know where I could get them. I was shy enough that I couldn't just waltz into the Chandler Drugstore, even at my age. The town grapevine was amazing, and I could just imagine the next day when half the town was trying to figure out who Boomer was bonking.

Besides, I wasn't even sure that I wanted to have sex with Gracie. I mean, I wanted to have sex with Gracie. But our relationship was shifting, and I didn't want to fumble that in any way. When I thought of the other night, I couldn't keep myself from smiling. If we had another one just like it, I doubted if even orgasm could top it.

As I wasn't exactly sure when she finished, I parked and went into the restaurant. Her boss said she wasn't there, that she had asked to take off an hour early, and that

~1967~

her mother had picked her up.

All right. Something was going on here. I felt like I was being avoided, but I couldn't imagine why. Maybe she wasn't feeling so well yet. But then she had been out much of the day and she had come to work. I had gotten such a boost from the warm connection Gracie and I had made in the last days. I wasn't going to feel right until I was sure that connection was secure. I drove toward her house to get an explanation.

Her mother answered the door. "Hi, Eugene." She didn't invite me in as she usually would have.

"Hi, Mrs. M. Is Gracie all right?"

"She's in bed. You won't be able to see her just now." The way she said it made me uncomfortable. Something strange was definitely happening.

"Did you tell her that I called today?"

"Yes." No explanation.

"She didn't call back. I was just wondering... Is there something wrong with Gracie, Mrs. Maculum?"

"No, she's fine. She's just tired."

If I left without seeing Gracie or some explanation, it was going to drive me nuts.

"Mrs. M., couldn't you just see if Gracie is awake and if I could see her for just a bit? It's kind of important."

Mrs. Maculum sighed and looked over my head. "Eugene, Grace isn't going to want to see you for a while now. I'd appreciate it if you would not try to see her the next couple of weeks."

"The next couple of weeks? I'll be in the army in the next couple of weeks. I'm not going to leave without seeing her."

"I really wish you would."

My frustration was turning to anger. In fact, it would have turned some time ago had I not been somewhat in awe of Gracie's mom.

"I'm sorry, Mrs. M., but I really think that this is something between me and Gracie, and, forgive me for saying it, but I don't think it is up to you to decide if we see each other."

"This is Gracie's decision, Eugene. She doesn't want to see you."

"That's crazy. The other night we.."

"Grace told me what happened the other night, and that's really what this is all about. She's not ready for that kind of relationship with you. You've been such good friends for so long. She doesn't want to lose that with you leaving."

My mind was spinning. "I didn't think we were losing anything. I thought we were gaining something, and that's the way she seemed to feel too. But listen, this is something that I shouldn't be talking to you about. It's between me and Gracie. Couldn't you just wake her up so we could straighten it out?"

I looked up and there were tears streaming down Mrs. Maculum's face.

"I'm sorry, Eugene. You're just going to have to understand." She started to close the door.

"Understand what? I don't even know what's happening here."

"I'm sorry." And she closed the door on me.

*****

I didn't even try to sleep that night. So many things were rolling around in my head that it hurt. I drove to Sunny Lake and rowed myself out into the middle. I sat for hours reliving the last night I had spent there with Gracie and

~1967~

trying to make some sense of what had happened since. I tried to imagine her back with me, to feel her there between my legs in the boat. My emotions boiled over in every direction.

"They can't keep her from me until I leave," I thought. "I won't let that happen." But then if it was really Gracie who didn't want to see me again, what was the point in my resolve?

My body was exhausted. I could scarcely row back to shore. I drove back to Chandler and got home just as the sun was peeking out.

Luckily, my father had already left for work. All I would have needed was another exchange with him. In all of our fights we had never touched one another, but had he been there to cross-examine me, I think that I would have punched him.

Instead, it was my mother who knocked at the door just after I had fallen into bed.

She stepped into my room. "Are you all right, honey?" she asked.

"I'm fine," I lied.

"You don't look so fine. Where were you all night?"

"I went to the fair with the guys again," I lied. "I don't know..." I didn't have the energy to explain it to her.

She came over and sat on the bed beside me. "Is it what happened with your father at dinner the other night? Is that what's bothering you?"

I didn't answer.

"I wish you two could get together on things. He really loves you, Gene. It's just that...."

"Why can't he just get off my case. Accept me as I am?" She didn't answer. "Mom, do you think he loves me as much as he does Tom and Elizabeth?"

"Oh, Gene, of course he does. Why would you ask that?"

"I've never felt that he does. I've never heard him say anything negative about either one of them. I know I've done some stupid things and maybe don't measure up to them. But even when I've done something good, he doesn't seem as proud as when Elizabeth sang or Tom came home with another perfect report card. I've always felt that I was maybe just one too many kids for him, that by the time he had fathered Tom and Elizabeth, he didn't quite have enough energy to deal with me."

"Oh, Gene." She pulled me into her arms. I waited for her to deny what I had said, or defend my father, but she just held me.

Finally, she pushed away from me but hung onto my shoulders.

"I've always been honest with you children, and I'm going to be now." She sighed. "It shocks me to hear you say that you felt like an extra child. But in some ways, that's what you were." Even though I had just suggested it, my mother's confirmation sent a chill through me.

"When your father was away in the military, we planned the rest of our lives through the mail. It was our way of escaping our loneliness and seeing past the fears of the present. One of the things we decided was that we would have only two children. Your practical father maintained that two was all that someone in his business could hope to afford. So we had settled into being a family of four."

I lay back on my bed and just let her talk.

"When your father was wounded, I had a surprising mix of feelings. Of course, I was devastated that he had been

~1967~

hurt, but it meant that he would be coming home. After all of the lonely nights, suddenly he was here. I'm absolutely certain that you were conceived on the very first night of his return."

Something between a gasp and a laugh escaped from my mouth. Had the light not been so dim, I'm sure my mother could have seen me blushing. Never in our lives had we shared such intimate moments, and for me, the warm excitement let me forget the agony of the day.

"When I discovered that I was pregnant, my first reaction was terror. I was still adjusting to having your father back, and there were adjustments to be made. The war had changed him greatly and not just his wounded arm. I was getting to know a new person.

" But I had made this agreement with the old person to have no more children, and we hadn't had time to talk about or modify that agreement when I discovered it would be broken. So I kept the surprise of you from your dad for nearly three months.

"And in that time I decided that you were a very happy surprise for me. I don't think I had really convinced myself that my childbearing days ended with Tom. I was overjoyed to be pregnant again. That lasted until I could no longer hide it and had to break the news to your father.

"The idea of another mouth to feed shook him up. It really was the hardest time in our marriage, the only time that I felt we weren't working together. Throughout the pregnancy I felt utterly abandoned. He seemed more distant from me than he had while in Europe. It was as if he held me entirely responsible and had no intention of raising a third child. I wasn't sure our marriage would survive it, and I was scared to death."

~Boomer~

I stared at my mother. It was as if I had never really known her. How could I have lived my whole life with her and never talked this way? I reached out and took her hand. She looked up into my eyes and smiled.

"And then you were born and we were back together. You were a beautiful baby, who needed a mother and a father. Your father felt that as strongly as I did. And from that time on, he felt the same about you as Tom or Elizabeth.

"You were a different child, and presented different challenges, so I won't deny that we treated you differently than the others, but it wasn't for a lack of love. And if that's what's bothering you, Gene, don't let it.

"You and your father just need to find some way to accept one another's differences without seeing them as weaknesses." She rubbed my forearm softly. "Please believe me, Gene. You've always been as important in this family as Tom or Elizabeth."

"All right." I'm not sure I was totally convinced, but I did believe that, at least, I was of equal importance to her. "Anyway, that's not all that's bothering me, Mom."

"Then what is it?"

I rolled onto my side so that I faced away from her. "You know I mentioned at dinner that me and Gracie are.. were... starting to get close. Well, I must have missed something somewhere. Dad doesn't have to worry about that anymore. I guess that she doesn't feel the same way about it as I do. Suddenly she won't even see me."

"Oh, Gene." She climbed onto the bed beside me and put her shoulder up against my head. "I'm so sorry. What a thing to happen just before you have to go. I'm sure that it's just a misunderstanding of some kind."

~1967~

I felt like a ten-year old. I had this big kid problem, and it was only my mother who understood me, who felt bad for me. I was torn between feeling grateful toward her for it and feeling ridiculous that I was burying my head into her soft shoulder. I fell asleep there. I don't know how long she stayed with me.

*****

I awoke mid-afternoon. I hadn't eaten in almost twenty-four hours and was famished. My mother, of course, took care of that and then asked me if I would pick some things up for her downtown.

As I drove away from the grocery store, I saw Gracie walking along Main Street. I thought she saw me too, but then she ducked into the Ben Franklin on the corner. She was obviously avoiding me.

I re-parked the car. I didn't exactly know what I should do. I didn't really want an uncomfortable confrontation in the dime store. I spotted her mom's car further up the street, so decided to wait for her there.

In a few minutes she came out and headed in my direction. When she finally saw me, she stopped, stared at me for a bit, and then began walking more quickly toward the car. I was standing beside the driver door, and she walked right up to me.

"Boomer, I know this is hard for you to understand, but I can't see you anymore before you leave." I reached down to take her hand, but she pulled it away and turned to the side.

"I don't understand. I thought you felt like I did, that what we had going was really good. I mean, the other night..."

"That's just it. The other night we got carried away.

~Boomer~

Boomer, what am I supposed to do? Fall in love with you for four days and then just have you leave again for two years?"

Hearing her say "fall in love" calmed me. It wasn't that she had mistaken her feelings for me. She was perhaps just frightened by those feelings.

"Listen Gracie. I don't want to rush you. You said the other night that we had a few days to see what develops. That's all I'm asking for. Can we walk and talk a little bit?"

"No, we can't. I can't let this go any further. I just need to stay away from you now, and maybe someday things can go back to the way they were. That's what I really want, Boomer."

"I don't know if they can. Something really nice happened between us the last few weeks, and I don't want to give that up, even if it never goes any further." I wasn't being entirely honest. I knew in my heart that I desperately wanted this to go further, but I didn't want to frighten her more than she already was.

She leaned back against the car. She bit her lip and looked to the sky, struggling not to cry.

"Boomer, this is so hard. I don't know how I can explain it to make you understand."

"We were so close in the boat the other night, so open to each other. What changed, Gracie?"

I watched her tortured face as she tried to shape the thoughts. Whatever was happening to her, the pain of it showed clearly in her sad eyes and twisted mouth.

"You've got to believe that I care for you very, very much. That hasn't changed. The only thing that has changed is me." Again, she seemed unable to go on.

"Can't we just get together later on tonight and talk this thing through? I just need to understand what has

~1967~

happened, where we're at. I don't want to leave with this empty feeling I've got now. Leaving is going to be crummy enough without that."

"The other night we started something that can never happen, and we've got to stop it now. I can't be with you and do that."

My frustration boiled over. "But why can't it happen," I said more angrily than I had intended. "You said that ever since prom night you have known that you cared for me. How can you so suddenly just turn that off? It doesn't make any sense."

She burst into tears. "I can't. It's just too hard." She yanked open the car door and fell inside. Frantically, she tore through her bag, looking for her keys. She jammed them into the ignition and started the car. She sat gripping the wheel and staring forward.

Finally she rolled down the window. She looked up at me and said, "Please don't hate me, Boomer." Then she rolled up the window and sped down the street.

I stood watching until her car disappeared into the distance. As I walked back to my car, I remembered my mother's milk and butter left sitting in the heat.

*****

The next two days were only marginally better. One order of business was packing together those belongings that would be of some use to me in the army. I had eight weeks of basic training ahead at Ft. Leonard Wood, Missouri. Instructions sent with my orders said that less would be better when packing. For the most part, the army would give me what I needed.

Trusting their generosity, I packed a few of my favorite clothes, my baseball glove and three books that I had bought for the summer, but never touched.

My sister, Elizabeth, came to town to see me before I left. I hadn't seen her for quite some time, and her being there was a blessing. The hours I spent with her were about the only happy ones I had in those days.

We hugged a very long time when she left. Then she held me at arms' length and said, "My baby brother is going off to war." And then she hugged me again and cried.

"God," I thought, "there's a lot of crying going on these last days." I could have done without the "going off to war" part, but it was really nice of her to take the time to see me off.

My dad and I kept a civil distance from one another those last days. He was content that I was going into the army. He knew that I wasn't happy about it, and he wisely let me be disgruntled in silence. If he had given me a "be brave and make your nation proud" kind of talk, I might have beaten him to a pulp.

My mother was right on the edge. Every time I looked at her, she was nearly in tears. She couldn't fit enough of my favorite foods into the few meals she had left to make for me.

My second to the last night, I awoke and felt someone in the room with me. I lay still but heard nothing.

"Mom?" I said.

"I'm sorry, Gene. Just go back to sleep."

"Come sit by me, Mom."

I felt the bed softly depress. She reached out and rubbed her hand along my arm.

"When you went away to college, I thought I knew where you were going, so I didn't worry about you very much. And then when things started going badly, I realized

~1967~

that I should have worried more, but it was too late. This time I really don't know where you are going, but wherever it is, please know that I am worrying about you."

I tried to lighten things. "I'm going to Missouri, Mom. What can happen to me there?" She didn't laugh. "I'm going to let you worry a little about me, because then I know you are thinking about me. It will be good to know that somebody is thinking about me."

"Then I'll not stop worrying until you are back with me again."

We sat still and listened to crickets chirping outside of my window. Finally I said, "Mom, are you happy?"

"Of course I am. Why do you ask?"

"It just seems like you've spent your life going along with everything Dad wants, and I just wondered if you ever get tired of that. Don't you have some dreams, some places to go, some things to do that have been pushed away because of the rest of us?"

"The answer to the last part is yes. But I suppose we all have dreams that we give up for this or that reason. I don't know that makes us necessarily less happy. What do we know? Maybe those dream things would bring us sadness instead. We have to be happy with what comes to us in life."

"I know. You have to live life to love life. You always say that, but isn't part of living that life grabbing hold of your dreams and running with them, Mom. I think that you should start sorting out some of those things you really want to do and drag Dad off to them. And if he won't go, then maybe sometimes you've got to leave him behind. Until you do, I'm going to be worrying about you too."

"That will be nice. Thank you. You go back to sleep

now." She got up and left, but I'm sure that I felt her in the room again later that night.

Anytime I was alone in those two days I tried to work out what had happened with Gracie. She was so distraught that she couldn't make sense. She had been unable to put into words how she felt, so over and over, I tried to do it for her. She had said several times that she cared for me. She had been equally resolute that she could not be with me again. If she really cared, how could it hurt to be with me?

Our relationship had changed so quickly. Our night in the boat had been like an emotional explosion. Was she afraid that any more of those explosions would make my leaving unbearable? Was that it? Was she afraid she was losing me?

Elizabeth had said, "My baby brother going off to war," and then she had cried. Were people really afraid that I wouldn't come back? Should I be afraid that I won't come back?

And then I would ponder what I should do about it all. I felt like I was really falling in love with Gracie. If she was feeling that too, and it was frightening her, should I just walk away and let it be? That's what she had begged me to do. And where would that leave us? Probably the same place we had been the last four years. Nowhere.

Maybe I was naive to think that those years of separation could just disappear. But what about the fifteen years of friendship we had before that? Was this summer really the end of all of that? Had the friendship among the five of us served its purpose, and now was it to be sacrificed to Vietnam and the harsher, more complicated world into which we had grown?

I had so many questions, and the person with whom

I most wanted to share them was keeping me away.

*****

For my final night of freedom, Fud and Pastor Jim Bob demanded to take me out for one last toot. I didn't have to leave for Minneapolis until afternoon of the following day, so I was comfortable staying out until the wee hours.

Sticks wasn't along. That didn't surprise me. I didn't ask if he hadn't been invited or if he had declined. I assumed that Gracie had been asked and, of course, declined. I didn't ask Fud and Jim Bob what they made of that. I decided to relax and just enjoy what was left of our little company.

The boys had decided that we would spend the night touring the bars and clubs of Mankato, the only reachable town large enough to have a varied selection of bars and clubs.

For several hours we hopped between pubs on the main drag. After two or three, we landed in one filled with college students that had a fair rock group playing. We settled in, danced, drank and enjoyed my last night of freedom.

With quite a few drinks in me, and some attractive young girls dancing in front of me, I almost forgot the frustrations I had been having with Gracie, and where I was headed the next day, until Fud shouted across the table.

"You know. Boomer, if we were to just saw off your right index finger, you wouldn't be able to fire a rifle, thus rendering you useless to the army. What do you say?" I assumed he was joking, but the idea didn't seem entirely without merit.

"Not a bad plan," agreed Pastor Jim Bob. "Maybe we should just start a bar brawl and get him thrown in jail."

But we did neither, and before long we realized that

~Boomer~

we had to head back to Chandler and my next day's appointment with Uncle Sam. Pastor Jim Bob had not been drinking as heavily as Fud and me, and was still in fairly good condition to pilot his car. He did take the precaution, however, of staying beneath the speed limit.

On the long drive home Fud continued his game of "How will we keep Boomer out of the Army?" The object became devising the most ingenious scheme to get me rejected by Uncle Sam. The closer we got to Chandler, the more outlandish the schemes became.

Pastor Jim Bob, who had never outgrown his fascination with concoctions, offered to create a thick purple substance which I could inject up my nose with a syringe. Then as they were shaving my head at the basic training induction center, I could ask them to pause momentarily, as I had the sniffles. With great energy I could then blow my nose, exploding a purple mass into my army issue handkerchief. Upon seeing my violet discharge, I would promptly fall out of the chair onto the hair-covered floor, and lie twitching uncontrollably.

Midway into the game, Fud paused to make a serious plea. "Really, Boomer," he said, "you've got to find a way to stay out of Vietnam. That place is screwed up."

Over the summer I had listened to Fud wrangle with Sticks over the issue, debating patriotism and foreign policy and politics. Oddly, I generally agreed with what they were both saying. Fud's arguments centered on the details of Vietnam, on the history, on the statistics, on the questionable goals and strategies we were pursuing in the war. Sticks didn't have the knowledge or understanding to refute his contentions, so he stayed to the issues of patriotism and protecting the world from communism.

~1967~

It was no wonder the country was so divided on the issue. Both sides seemed right. And so while a battle raged on this side of the Pacific, I was headed toward the one on the other side.

In final desperation Fud devised the winning plan to keep me from danger. I would fake a disease which I would call numerical reversicosis. The only symptom would be my uncontrollable tendency to reverse the numbers 2 and 5. Wherever 2 appeared in my military identification, I would write 5 and vice versa. If a drill sergeant screamed at me to "give him five," I would drop down to the ground and do 2 pushups.. His contention was that, since the Army runs by the numbers, my numerical defect would get me discharged in no time.

He would draft me a letter as Dr. Heinz Fudwick documenting my long struggle with the disease beginning in elementary school, when at age 5, I had consistently shown up in a 2nd grade classroom. The plan would begin with my showing up 3 days late for my September 2 flight.

As we entered Chandler and negotiated the dark streets toward Fud's house, we were surprised to pass Sticks' car parked curbside. We couldn't tell if there was anyone in the car, but the temptation was too great for us. In Fud's drunken state, he was ready to drop his animosity toward Sticks in hopes of a new adventure.

"What do you suppose the Stick man is doing over here?" asked Pastor Jim Bob. "He doesn't know anybody on Tyler Street does he?"

"There's probably nobody in it," said Fud from the back seat. "He was probably just driving down the street and that pile of junk died for good." He gave out a heehaw and slapped me on the back.

~Boomer~

I had reached a point somewhere between passing out and falling asleep, so my responses were fairly fuzzy and incoherent.

"It's worth a try," said Jim Bob. "Let's see if we can scare the pants off him."

"Speaking of which," I slurred. "You don't suppose that Sticks has been sneaking out on the sly and dating some young Chandlerette? Maybe his pants are already off?"

"Ho, ho, ho," laughed Fud, rubbing his hands together at the prospect. "What a way to end the summer, catching Sticks with his jeans on the floorboards."

As Pastor Jim Bob circled back, we hatched a plan. As he was the only one within striking distance of sobriety, he would have to do the quiet work. Fud and I would stagger along as best we could.

We parked around a corner, two blocks from where we had spotted Sticks' car. Trying to keep from uncontrolled giggling, we moved closer, keeping houses between us and our target. Finally, we were behind the house directly across the street from the car. We still couldn't tell if there was anyone in it.

While Fud and I crept to two boulevard trees, Pastor Jim Bob circled and came up behind the car in a low and silent crouch. We watched as he reached the rear bumper, lay on his back and disappeared under the car.

We suppressed our excitement and waited for some action. First, we heard a scratching on the underside of the car. I was laughing so hard on the inside I was about to rupture an organ.

We waited. Nothing moved. Suddenly a clanging sound came from beneath the car. Pastor Jim Bob was banging on the muffler, which was, no doubt, not too well

~1967~

attached in the first place.

    The door to Sticks car flew open and out climbed our friend, pants still on, I noted with some disappointment. He stepped to the middle of the street and gawked back at his car. This was our cue.

    As quickly as our drunken legs would carry us, we raced into the street and grabbed the stunned Sticks, who barely had time to stand straight up and turn toward his howling attackers.

    Fud grabbed him high and I grabbed him low. We hoisted him into the air, lugged him to the side of the street, and fell upon him on the grassy boulevard.

    At first he seemed too surprised to move, but once he hit the turf, knees and elbows and fists flew every which way. A fist hit me squarely below the eye, and a howl went up from Fud, who was apparently tagged as well.

    I rolled away before receiving any more damage and yelled, "Cease fire, cease fire, Sticks. It's Boomer. It's Fud. We give up."

    "You jerks!" Sticks yelled. "What are you doing out here?"

    I was laughing hysterically and holding my cheek, trying to ease the sting. Fud was rolling around on the grass, rubbing his hands up and down his shin, howling in pain and laughing at the same time.

    As I sat up, I looked directly at Sticks' car, where a second person was just ducking back inside and closing the passenger door. I got enough of a view to see that it was Gracie. My laughter stopped immediately. A rush of emotions surged through my spinning head.

    "What the hell is this?" I said, staggering to my feet. Fud still lay on the ground moaning, and Pastor Jim Bob was brushing the remainder of the loose tar off his pants.

I staggered to Sticks' car and pulled open the door. "Gracie, what the hell is going on?"

She looked up at me with something akin to fear in her face. "It's nothing, Boomer. Nothing's going on."

I came unglued. The alcohol fed my anger so that I could scarcely focus my eyes. "So this is why you couldn't see me anymore? This is how much you care about me?"

"It's not what you think, Boomer. There's nothing going on."

I was of no mind for explanations. I'd seen all I wanted to. I stuck my head into the car next to Gracie's face.

"I always thought you were an honest person. At least I won't make that mistake again."

Two hands grabbed my shoulders from behind. I was yanked from the car and dumped back on the grass. Sticks stood above me.

"Leave her alone. Nothing is going on, Boomer. And what does it matter to you anyway? We were just out here talking."

"Right, and I just spent the evening at the convent." I stood up. Suddenly, with my head lowered I rushed at Sticks. My head caught him in the stomach and I jammed him up against the back fender of the car. He grabbed me around the neck and we struggled with each other.

Fud and Pastor Jim Bob stood by gaping, not understanding what was transpiring. Finally they went into action and each grabbed one of my shoulders and pulled me away from Sticks.

"You're nuts," he yelled after me. "You don't know what you're doing."

Gracie had gotten back out of the car. "Boomer,

~1967~

please stop. I just needed someone to talk with."

"I thought I offered you that a couple days ago. God, what an idiot I am." I staggered away from the rest toward Jim Bob's car. My face felt like it was swelling. My head hurt where it had collided with Sticks' ribs. Suddenly, I lurched to the side of the street and vomited in the grass.

Fud and Jim Bob caught up with me. They helped me back to my feet and supported me as we wobbled back to Jim Bob's car. They didn't ask me for explanations as we drove the few blocks to my house. Maybe they knew more about the situation than I did. Suddenly I didn't know if there was anyone in the group I could trust.

"You need help getting inside?" asked Fud.

"No, I'll make it."

"Hey, man, are you OK?"

"Yes. Listen, thanks for tonight, you guys. It was almost all a really good time."

"We'll be up tomorrow before you leave," said Jim Bob.

"See you then. If I'm up yet." I slammed the door and held onto the top of the car to steady myself. Pastor Jim Bob got out and tried to help me, but I awkwardly pushed him away and staggered toward the house. When I reached the door, I turned and waved. Jim Bob circled his car, got back in and they drove away.

Instead of going inside, I sat down on the front steps. My head was still spinning. I didn't know if the alcohol or the events of the last days had me more disoriented.

I rubbed my temples, trying to clear my thoughts, trying to make sense of some kind. The last times I had been with Gracie whirled through my head. I tried to fit each thing that she had said into the discovery I had just made.

~Boomer~

Some of them fit perfectly. Some of them didn't. I was still too drunk to make my mind work efficiently.

Suddenly I was on my feet, half walking, half running toward Gracie's. I had nothing in mind. It was as if my feet had simply taken over.

I made my way quickly across town, ducking off the street and behind houses in her neighborhood. I hid behind her neighbor's house and peered out toward hers. Sticks' car was parked in the driveway. No one was in sight.

I slipped out into the front yard and flopped down beside a huge tree. The faint glow from the street lamp shown on each side of my legs, but in the shadow, I was invisible. I waited without any plan, without anything at all on my mind. I was totally exhausted. My eyes had adjusted to the darkness, so I could see things around me clearly in the dim light.

I don't know how long I sat there. I was on the verge of sleep, when the passenger door of Sticks' car opened. Gracie climbed out. She circled around to the driver's side and disappeared from view. I couldn't tell if they were talking, or sharing one last kiss. That's what I pictured them doing.

The car started and backed away, leaving Gracie waving by the side of the driveway. The headlights cast other shadows from my tree and probably brought me into view, but no one was looking my way.

I sat there watching Gracie. Part of me wanted to race across the yard and grab her, and part of me wanted to just walk away. Before I could do either, she walked out of her yard and headed down the sidewalk. I let her get more than a block away, and then followed in the shadows of the front yards.

~1967~

She walked quickly, like she knew where she was headed. I stayed well back from her. There was no one else out, and she was easy to keep in sight. She walked down Beacon Hill and into River Park. She crossed the park to the edge of the river and sat down, burying her head in her hands. I moved from tree to tree, and when I got about ten yards from her, stopped and watched.

We stayed that way for quite some time. The only other time I could remember us together in this park was the day when we were kids and I walked in on her mother striking her. She had run here to feel bad that day as well. That seemed from another lifetime.

I didn't think that I moved, but she suddenly seemed to sense me there. She turned her head back toward me.

"Who's there?" she said, her voice cracking slightly. She waited. "Is there someone out there?"

I waited for a few seconds longer and then stepped out from behind the tree. I walked toward her.

"Boomer." She said it in a dejected voice.

"Aren't you at least a little happy that I'm not the Boston Strangler?"

She turned her face back to the river. "You shouldn't be here. I don't want you here."

"Well, hang in there. Tomorrow I will be out of your life forever."

"I don't want that either, Boomer."

"Well, what is it you do want, Gracie. I've been wracking my brain for about three days trying to figure that out, and I'll be damned if I can."

For a while she didn't answer. "I want things to be the way they were. I want to be back at the prom. I want to look my most beautiful, and I want to dance the night away with my four best friends. And after, I want a limousine to pick us up and drive us to the moon."

"But you said I was the one you had a special feeling for that night. I was the one whose arms you wanted to dance in. Is that still true, Gracie? Am I still the special one? Or is it Sticks?"

She didn't answer. I sat down on the grass behind her and brought my face up close to her neck. "Don't Boomer," she whispered.

I put my hand on her arm and softly kissed the back of her neck. "Stop it." She pulled away but I grabbed her arm and held her down.

"What happened to us in the boat was real, Gracie. You can't tell me that you didn't feel it." She struggled to free herself, but I held firmly to her wrist.

"But I don't feel it now. And I never will again. You've got to leave tomorrow and forget about that night. It will never happen again."

My frustration boiled over. I shoved her flat to the ground, reached over and grabbed her other wrist, pinning her to the grass.

"You can't do this to me. You can't make me believe you love me one night and then toss me off the next. Are you going to do the same thing with Sticks the night before he leaves? I don't understand you."

She was fighting to free herself and the more she thrashed, the tighter I held on and the more angry I got. The alcohol was still fuzzy in my head and fueling my aggression. I put one of my legs over hers and pushed down on top of her, pressing my lips to hers.

She swung her face to the side. "Please, Boomer. Please stop." She gasped and struggled violently, but made

~1967~

no attempt to call for help.

I worked my other leg between hers and pried her knees apart. I let go with one hand and reach down to grab her skirt. She beat my chest with her free hand as I jerked it up to her waist. I grabbed the bottom of her blouse and pulled it out of her skirt, tearing it in the process.

Then she brought her knee up into my crotch with more strength than I would have believed she had. My breath exploded out of me, and the pain rolled me off her and into a ball at her side, where, for the second time that night, I threw up.

I lay perfectly still. I was afraid that if I moved, some body part would fall off, probably something that I would need later in life. Gradually, my breathing slowed, and the pain, which had radiated through my whole body, returned to my crotch.

I was certain that Gracie had run for her life once she had freed herself. Would she run to her mother? Would she run to the police? I had this sickening feeling that I could be in serious trouble. But more awful than that was the realization of what I had just done. I had attacked a lifelong friend. I deserved to be in trouble.

I rolled over slowly and painfully. There was Gracie sitting beside me, looking down into my face. It was a very calm look, without a trace of anger or fear in it.

"Gracie, I...." My voice hadn't recovered from her blow.

"Boomer," she interrupted, "I want you to be very, very careful these next two years." She bent over and kissed me on the forehead. "And then I want you to come back to me." Then she got up and walked out of my life just as I had walked out of hers four years before.

~Boomer~

*****

    The next day I boarded a bus and headed toward Ft. Leonard Wood, Missouri, the first leg on my trip to Vietnam. My life is filled with great ironies, but this is my favorite. Had I stuck to my convictions and returned to Madison, I would have entered combat more quickly.

    In the fall of '67, the demonstrations against Dow Chemical continued on the University of Wisconsin campus. In October they turned ugly. Policemen in riot gear and swinging billy clubs stormed into crowds of students. It may well have been that while I was pretending to do battle in basic training, my friends were engaged in a real battle on a college campus. And here I was, believing in that real battle, but forsaking it to enter the war.

Chapter 5

It Don't Mean Nothin'

1967, Winter

  I always say that '67 was the year without Thanksgiving. I boarded a plane in Oakland the day before Thanksgiving. Mid-flight we crossed the International Date Line, and before we could land, it was the day after Thanksgiving. Fitting. I thought I had nothing for which to be particularly thankful.

  I stared out into the blackness, broken by mysterious bursts of yellow from the ground. I wondered what dangers these flames signaled. Were they exploding bombs? What part of the war was below us? I felt like I needed to be afraid, but had no idea what I should fear.

  On the ground I felt entirely disjointed, disconnected from everybody else on the planet. The last four months I had been floating, moving from army base to army base, training in this, training in that.

  I had been in units with boys, eighteen and nineteen year olds, with whom I had little in common and to whom I formed little attachment. My college education and the fact that I could type like the wind (by army standards) had earmarked me for clerical training. I had been told I might still end up in a combat job when I got to Vietnam, something that would probably make my father proud, but would terrify my mother. She was so distraught the day that I left for

~Boomer~

Vietnam that she nearly followed me onto the airplane.

During my stateside training, I had gradually resigned myself to whatever was ahead in the next two years. The constant summer battles with my father made it almost a relief to be away from home. The mess that had developed with Gracie and Sticks left me assured that our friendship was finished. We had all changed too much to ever again be the old gang of our school days.

Sticks would be arriving in Vietnam in the next months, but after our turbulent parting, I didn't anticipate making contact with him. So, as I stepped into Vietnam and prepared to wage war, there was no one that I was desperately missing, and no where else I particularly wanted to be. Maybe my father was right again. Perhaps in the army that I could regain my foothold and find some direction for my life.

*****

"Welcome to the 73rd Replacement Company," read the sign. It signaled a hospitality which did not follow. I had been on airplanes and buses and trucks for more than thirty hours. All I wanted was a place to lie down. But since entering the army, I had learned that what I wanted and what I got seldom corresponded.

Each time I moved to a new base, I began by doing the same thing, and this would be true, even in a war zone. I learned to brush my teeth. Our new keepers marched us into a vacant lot, passed out olive green toothbrushes, and yet again, gave us the army's by-the-numbers training in oral hygiene.

"Do not brush up and down," commanded the sergeant. "Once you have stroked upward, lift your toothbrush and return it to the bottom of your gums. You

~1967~

will now brush with fifteen repetitions on the lower right-hand side of your face. Ready. Begin. One, two, three, four...." And on we brushed through the night.

In a way it was comforting. If they stood us in a field with no other weapon than a toothbrush, in how much danger could we be?

In the barracks, just as I was about to fall asleep, my eyes caught something moving in the aisle. Waddling across the floor was the largest bug I had ever seen. It was the size of a baseball, and appeared to be a cross between a June bug and an armadillo. Then a frightening thing happened. It spread wings and flew. I knew I was far from home.

I knew that this creature would have held great fascination for Fud and Pastor Jim Bob, but had none for me. The prehistoric-looking thing wobbled down the center of the barracks, circled and returned, landing on the back of the GI dozing across from me.

"Aaahhh, god dammit!" the poor man shrieked, shaking his body violently. Later I was to learn that the unscientific name of this bug was, indeed, the Flying-God dammit, christened for the screams of nearly sleeping GIs whose naked backs it violated.

*****

Purgatory. That's what the 73rd Replacement Company was. You knew it was only temporary, and that you were on your way to some place, but in the meantime were being unexplainably punished. And part of the punishment was the sense that beyond purgatory might be hell.

The main activity of each day was to stand in a dusty field, while a sergeant bellowed the names of those who would ship out. Beside me, in a single duffel bag, rested all of my worldly belongings, at least all that I would need in this new world. As soon as my name was called, I would board a bus, be transported to the airport and on my way to my assignment.

I longed to have my name called. I knew nothing of these places, Xuan Loc, Ka Tum, so one would be as good or bad as the next. I just wanted to replace someone and find out what that meant.

For three days I stood. When the list had been read, I picked up my belongings and returned to the barracks for another night in Purgatory.

On the fourth day my name was called. Cu Chi was my destination. I asked others if they knew anything of this place, but they were preoccupied asking the same of Tay Ninh or Duc Tou. Another man who was being sent to the same place said that Cu Chi was the headquarters for the 25th Infantry Division. Infantry was not a word I wished to hear.

Our huge C-130 cargo plane lumbered down the runway. Just as I anticipated leaving the ground, the plane began to slow. The engines sputtered and we rolled to a halt.

After a few confused minutes, one of the pilots turned to us and said, "Gentlemen, your plane is broken." The hatch opened. We boarded buses and returned to our barracks.

Welcome to this man's army. I wondered how many men had spent their entire year in Vietnam trying to escape the 73rd Replacement Company. Whoever said that in the Army you hurry up and wait, certainly had the waiting part pegged anyway.

With nothing to do, I sat on my bunk and sulked. Finally, I decided that writing a letter would be better than nothing. I thought about starting a letter to Gracie.

I opened my pad of paper, wrote the date in the upper

left corner and paused. I sat for the next fifteen minutes staring at the empty page. The only picture of her that would come into my head was the frightened one of her struggling against me that last night in the park. I sat for another fifteen minutes.

Finally, beneath "Dear Gracie," I wrote only "I'm sorry. Boomer." I folded the paper, put it in an envelope and wrote her address on the front.

The other person I wanted to write was my mother, so I dated another sheet. "Dear Mom." Again the words stuck on my pen. What would I share with her? My fears I would keep to myself. I was scared enough for both of us. I didn't know where I was going or what I would be doing. I had nothing to tell. I slammed the pad to the floor and turned my face to the wall.

The next day my plane left the ground. Not easily. It took three good bounces to send it airborne.

Seating in a C-130 is on benches along each side of the fuselage. Above and behind me were masses of wires, the guts of the plane that I really didn't want to see. All through the flight, a technician with a flashlight walked back and forth, examining the wiring and shaking his head. I had not really minded that my plane had failed the day before on the runway, but I was prepared to object if this one shut down in mid-flight. Before I could fret, the plane dipped sharply. Thirty sets of young eyeballs widened.

"We have to go straight down," the technician shouted. "We don't want to get shot at." I cringed. Somehow I had hoped that being shot at would not be a part of my Vietnam experience, and here, five days into my visit, I was already taking evasive action. The plane quickly leveled off. Three more healthy bounces and we rolled to a

~Boomer~

stop.

The back of another truck. More temporary barracks. More forms to complete. More lines to stand in. Cu Chi had all of the same features that had made the 73rd Replacement Company so endearing: Heat, dust, rotten food.

To increase my chances of lasting the year, I needed to complete a jungle survival course, a three-day review of basic training with emphasis on particular snakes, diseases and enemies I should either kill or avoid.

We reviewed old army strategies, like those in reaction to an ambush. Proper procedure was to open fire, and with guns ablazin' advance toward the ambush. Even in basic training, this advice had seemed questionable to me, and I was quite sure that as long as there were objects to hide behind, my advancement would be retarded. I figured that if ever ambushed, I would die cowering behind a jeep.

By the middle of the second day I was firmly convinced that facing a snake or the Viet Cong could not possibly be worse than another day of this training.

*****

My third night in Cu Chi I was assigned to guard duty. It was an internship, culminating my in-country training.

Sitting nervously in the back of a steamy deuce-and-a-half (a large, noisy truck) on the way to the perimeter, I realized that parts of my body were going to be damp for the next year. The air was heavy with moisture, as were my underarms.

A huge, black man at the front of the truck leaned forward and shouted above the noise of the engine, "Which one of you guys is Boomer?" I waved in his direction.

He moved back and sat beside me. "I'm Perkins, your

date for the evening. By the looks of that uniform, you ain't been in country long."

"Three days," I confessed.

"Oh, shit! Just my luck. I hope we don't get attacked tonight. Me, stuck out in the dark with a new guy named Boomer." He laughed. That, and the smiles of the others, tempered my panic at the thought.

The camp was circled by a mound of earth, interrupted every four hundred yards or so by a wooden tower. I climbed the ten-foot ladder and crawled into one of those perches. Perkins handed up the machine gun. For the first time, I looked out into Vietnam beyond a military camp. The front of the tower extended forward and was buried in sandbags. At the base were dozens of Claymore mines, explosives that were aimed outward toward the enemy. A wire ran from each of these to a mass of detonators within my arm's reach.

The first hundred yards beyond was a wasteland of wire. Slinkys of concertina wire, some tightly wound and others with high loops had been placed at five foot intervals.

Earlier in the week, Vietnamese trainers had shown us how easily they could slither through the razor-sharp loops. More explosives dotted the gaps between the wire. In the light I couldn't imagine anyone getting through this maze. After dark I wasn't so sure.

Beyond the wire were two tiny villages, one of them Cu Chi, the other Phuoc Vinh, Perkins informed me. They were filled with trees of an emerald green that made other colors nearly invisible. Cu Chi village looked clean and inviting against the brown, dusty, military camp.

As the villages disappeared into the darkness, we set up our machine gun. My partner was to alternate two hour

~Boomer~

shifts with me. I took the first shift, but he stayed atop the bunker, perhaps sensing my tension. Perkins was a heavy equipment operator from Georgia. He was about my age, but we had almost nothing else in common.

About an hour into my shift, I heard someone approaching from behind and to our right. Picking up his M-16, Perkins stepped to the back of the bunker.

"Halt, who goes there?" The response was the sharp bark of a dog. Perkins raised his rifle and snapped a shell into the chamber.

From the dark came an angry, "What the hell are you doing, man? You lock and load on my dog, and I'll lock and load on you." A metallic click followed. Suddenly the war threatened to erupt behind me. I sprawled to the floor of the bunker.

"What the hell you doin' out here with a dog?"

"I'm the roving guard. Keepin' you bastards awake. What's your problem, man?"

"Next time around keep that damn dog quiet, or I'll quiet him for you."

"Easy, Perkins," I offered from the floor. "He's on our side, isn't he?"

"Well, he damn well better shut that mutt up."

"Fuckin' hothead," the patrol shouted as he moved past our bunker and headed up the line. "Let's be stayin' awake up there."

Perkins put down his gun, perched on the sandbag wall of the bunker and lit a cigarette. My first shift done, I sat and talked with him for a while, but then decided I had better get some sleep to keep me alert in my next turn.

I climbed down from the bunker, blew up my air mattress and laid it on a level spot. I lay uncovered, letting

~1967~

the breeze cool me. I looked into the sky for Orion. The Big Dipper. Nothing was familiar. It was not a Minnesota sky. I felt so far from Chandler. I might as well have been on the moon.

I wondered what my friends were doing. I wondered which of them I could even call friends anymore. I regretted that we had parted on such bad terms.

I wondered if Sticks was on his way to Vietnam yet. Was Fud off protesting this war somewhere? And Gracie. Most of all, I wondered what Gracie was doing.

I awoke with rain pelting my face. I grabbed my mattress, now flat as a piece of paper, and scrambled into the bunker. Perkins was relaxed and smoking, staring across the bunker line.

"I really slept," I said. "Why don't you get some? I'll be O.K. this time."

"Think I will," he said. "There's a culvert across the road. Think I'll pull up in there. It's nice and dry, and if I'm lucky, nothing else will join me. Keep your shit together man, and yell if you need me."

Alone in the bunker, I looked out into the blackness. The rain had cooled the air, and I shivered in my wet clothes.

I raised the starlight scope to my eye and aimed it into the night. Magically, the instrument supplied light to the scene before me. It was like a very bright, green moon had risen. I watched a rat paw his way between sections of barbed wire.

I peered into lifeless Cu Chi. I wondered what I would do if something happened on my guard. If something started toward me, could I fire the machine gun? Would I detonate a mine? Would I kill someone?

Before I could answer, shots were fired in Cu Chi

village. They were tracer bullets, so I watched them enter Phuoc Vinh. There was a moment's silence, and then the red streaks went in reverse.

Suddenly, I had a front row seat for the war. A web of red strands connected the two villages. It was impossible to tell which strands were traveling which direction. Yellow flashes erupted in Cu Chi. Each flash was followed by a loud report.

I crouched behind the machine gun, hoping that the fire would not at some point turn in my direction. A flare burst above Phuoc Vinh, brightly illuminating the entire area.

Perkins scrambled into the bunker. "You start this?" he shouted over the noise. Seeing my confusion, he laughed. "Don't worry. It happens all the time. Gooks shootin' at gooks."

"Which side is the enemy?" I yelled.

"Who knows? Maybe both sides. Maybe neither. They don't know who they're shooting at."

Suddenly, on the runway parallel to the bunker line about a hundred yards behind us, there was a massive explosion.

"Holy Shit!" yelled Perkins. "We're under attack." Before he could utter another "Holy Shit," another explosion erupted and another tower of flame shot into the sky. Machine gun fire peppered the night from the same direction. Perkins crouched near the back of the bunker, and I crawled over beside him.

On the runway we could see the skeletons of two Chinook helicopters engulfed in flame. More gunfire sounded and a series of sharp cracks rattled just below us.

"Jesus Christ, they're firing this way," shouted Perkins. "Get the sixty over here."

~1967~

     I low-crawled across the floor of the tower. Terrified that I might not last a week in Cu Chi, I raised myself to a crouch and lifted the M-60 machine gun off of its stand. I scrambled back to Perkins, who grabbed it from me, hoisted it to his shoulder and perched the barrel on the pile of sandbags at the back of our bunker. Sirens were wailing across the camp. We stared at the two huge balls of flame that were quickly reducing the helicopters to rubble. Perkins head swivelled back and forth.

     "You see anything out there?" he barked. "I don't see anybody. Where are the bastards?" He wheeled around. "Get back to the front. Maybe they're coming from that way too. Get on the Claymores. You see anything move out front you start pushing buttons. Shit, I would get the new guy tonight." He shoved me toward the perimeter side of the bunker and wheeled back to guard our rear.

     I crouched behind the sandbag wall, raising my head just high enough to see over the edge of the bunker. I could hear more gunfire behind me and vehicles racing through the night.

     I heard flares pop from that direction. I turned my head to see the bright green light bathing the airstrip and the two burning choppers. When I looked back into the blackness to my front, everything looked like it was moving. Then it was still. I couldn't tell if my eyes or my nerves were playing games with me.

     "Perkins, I think I see something. Maybe not. I can't tell if there is anything out there or not. God almighty!" My whole body was shaking, particularly my hands, which were resting on the tangled mass of detonators.

     I'm not sure if I again thought I saw something and actually pushed a detonator, or if I was shaking so badly that

~Boomer~

I inadvertently pressed the button. There was a bright flash out front of me. Then suddenly our bunker was peppered with a blast of dirt clods and metal. Before I could move, something raked across the side of my face. I screamed and dropped to the floor of the bunker.

"God, I'm hit!" I screamed. I put my hand to my face. In the darkness I couldn't tell if it came down covered with sweat or blood, but a sharp burning sensation made me think it was blood.

Perkins rushed across to my side. "Where are you hit? You all right?"

I was pretty much hysterical at this point. "My face. My face. What the hell happened? I just pushed one button and all hell broke loose."

"Gooks must have turned around some of our Claymores. For God's sake, don't blow any more. I gotta watch out front. Somebody sure as hell has been out there. You be okay?"

"I don't know. Can you see my face? How bad is it?"

Perkins reached into his pocket and pulled out a cigarette lighter which he lit. He held it up to our faces. "You're okay. It's just a scratch. Not much blood. It is already drying. Come on. Let's get back on watch. They may still be out there. We'll clean you up later."

He helped me onto my feet, then grabbed the M-60 machine gun and humped it to the front of the bunker where he peered out toward our jungle of barbed wire.

I felt my face, which was still stinging. I picked up my M-16 and moved to the back of the bunker to watch. There would be no more sleeping this night.

On the runway the two helicopters continued to burn. Dozens of our vehicles had now surrounded them. Some

~1967~

men stood helplessly by, unable to save the huge choppers. Others rushed in and out of the darkness, unable to find any enemy to capture or kill.

For the next hour we had little idea what was happening, but kept a careful watch in all directions.

Perkins called in a report to headquarters. He stressed that some of our Claymores had been reversed. That message needed to be gotten to the other bunkers, so that none of them would fire on themselves as we had.

With my handkerchief and water from my canteen, Perkins helped me clean up my face. He confirmed that my wound was little more than a scratch. "Probably not Purple Heart material," as he put it.

Finally, the roving patrol returned to our bunker on their regular rounds. They were different men than had approached us with the dog earlier.

"Halt. Who goes there?" shouted Perkins.

"Roving Patrol. Perkins, that you? You guys okay in there?"

"Yes, we're all right. Boomer took a little shrapnel to the face. Blew a Claymore that was aimed our way. VC must be up to the same old tricks. Tell the guys along the line not to blow any until they're checked out."

One of the two roving patrol guards reached the top of our ladder and climbed onto our bunker. "We won't be telling the guys to your south anything. They're wasted," he said.

"What are you talking about?" asked Perkins.

"The guards next to you are dead. Whoever blew those helicopters went out through their bunker and managed to slit their throats on the way. God, it's a mess over there."

~Boomer~

"Who were the guards?" asked Perkins.

"Didn't know them. From Charlie Company though. I don't know how those sneaky bastards could get in and out without somebody seeing or hearing them. What a hell hole. You guys be alert tonight. We don't know where they are, and this whole thing may not be done yet."

We wished him well as he climbed back to the ground and headed with his partner toward the next bunker. He needn't have worried about me staying alert throughout the rest of the night. I was so frightened that I couldn't have closed my eyes on a bet.

I sat staring into the darkness, wondered if this was what my next year would be, moving in a constant state of fear, knots firmly clutching my throat and stomach. I wondered if I would ever see my family again. For the first time, the possibility that I might not survive Vietnam pressed down on me like a huge stone. It seemed like I couldn't completely catch my breath.

Perkins talked me through the night and tried to comfort me. He insisted that what we had just experienced was unusual, that the base camp had not been attacked or penetrated in months.

He pulled a thermos out of his bag. " Want a coffee?" He handed me the cup and poured out a black steaming stream. He took a drink from the thermos. I had never been a coffee drinker, but at that moment I permanently became one. Suddenly it didn't matter that Perkins and I had little in common. I was very glad to have him there.

By the end of that night I counted him a close friend, and even though I would never see him again, I wouldn't forget his name, his face, his laugh.

*****

~1967~

The next day I was transferred to my unit. I was brought in from guard duty on the back of one deuce-and-a half truck. I loaded my belongings onto a second deuce-and-a-half and was carted to the other side of the base.

I was exhausted. The events of the night before felt like a dream from which I had just awakened.

I was assigned to the 65th Engineering Brigade, which sounded better than infantry. A brigade of engineers. If Fud had been fit for active duty, maybe this is where he would have ended up as well. Probably not. If he had been fit for active duty, he more than likely would have ended up in Canada.

My orders said that I was to be the company clerk for Bravo Company. I climbed off the back of my taxi at a gate proclaiming, "65th Engineering Brigade - First in, Last Out."

At first I assumed this was a noble statement declaring the persistence of my new unit, but when I noticed that our neighboring unit, the 588th, boasted, "We drop our rocks anywhere," I supposed that ours had sexual overtones as well. A passing sergeant directed me to the Bravo Company Headquarters.

Like all of the Quonset huts in Cu Chi, Bravo Company's headquarters was buried in sandbags. I had been told that rocket and mortar shellings were a common thing on these base camps, and the bunker architecture was designed to take up shrapnel and protect the occupants. Somehow I wasn't entirely comforted. I preferred an unbunkered house somewhere away from such threats.

The inside of the headquarters looked just like every other army office. There was nothing distinctive about a Vietnam day room. A counter divided it in half, and on the other side of the counter were desks covered with paperwork and radio equipment. A sergeant behind the counter greeted me.

"Yes, I'm Corporal Boomer. I believe that I have been assigned to this unit." I fished into the top of my duffel bag for a copy of my orders.

"Hey, you're me," said the sergeant, who appeared to be a year or two younger than I.

"I beg your pardon?" I said.

"You're my replacement. I'm Sergeant Browning. Welcome to Bravo Company. I'm the company clerk, and I am short."

"You appear to be about as tall as I am," I replied. "Do they fill this position according to height or something?"

He laughed. "No, short means you don't have much time left in this hell hole. I am going to train you in for the next two weeks, and then I am off on the big bird, back to my honey, stateside."

Two weeks left. That sounded a lot better than a year. "Congratulations. Where are you from stateside?"

"Iowa. Ames, Iowa. Gonna be back there shoveling snow and manure in fifteen days."

"I'm from Minnesota," I said, "so I just left that. The snow, not the manure. I live in town."

"It's kind of chaotic around here this morning. Most of our available guys are out on the bunker line cleaning up from last night's attack. VC blew up a couple choppers and wasted two guards on the way out. I hear one of them only had three days left in country. You hear the racket?"

"I had guard duty. I was in the bunker next to where they were killed. The explosions were about a hundred yards from our bunker."

"No shit! Hell of a way to start your tour. Well, you

~1967~

should have a better day today. Things are usually very quiet around here, and as Company Clerk, you won't be pulling much guard duty. Spending too many nights in this luxurious chamber."

After a few minutes of sharing Midwestern memorabilia, Browning checked me into the company and told me where I would find things, the mess hall, the enlisted men's club and so forth. Then he sent me off to my new residence. "Fourth hooch on the left," he pointed.

A hooch, I gathered as I walked, was a large pile of sandbags with translucent plastic windows in it. The fourth one on the left was in considerable disarray.

What appeared to be its contents were sitting outside on the dirt. Beds, footlockers, stereo speakers, a strange maroon, overstuffed chair. I opened the front door and peered inside. The dim room was completely empty. At the other end was a man with a rag tied around his face, pouring liquid from a can and spreading it around the floor with a broom. From my time at the gas station, I recognized the smell of kerosene. The room reeked. He saw me, but kept sweeping.

"Hello," I called. "My name is Boomer. I'm new in."

"Well, if you don't want to live up to your name, don't do anything stupid like light a cigarette," he yelled through his rag. He poured more liquid and went on sweeping. My eyes started to burn.

"The company clerk said that I'm supposed to move in here."

"Oh, Boomer, the new clerk. We expected you yesterday. Come on outside." He opened the door and followed me out. "This shit will eat your lungs." He stuck out his hand and I shook it.

~Boomer~

"I had to pull guard duty last night," I said, "so they kept me an extra day."

"Guard duty? Jeez, they didn't waste any time with you. I'm Macelroy, Mac." My mind flashed back to my other Mac, Gracie. I felt another instant of loneliness.

"Do you mind if I ask what you're doing in there?" I said.

"Dieseling the floor. It's the only cure for cockroaches. We were overdue. We hadn't dieseled for a month. Holmes got some cookies from home day before yesterday. He put them in his locker and the cockroaches ate 'um before we got a taste. The smell will go down so we can move back in tonight. You met anyone else?"

"Just the company clerk." I looked at the beds strewn across the area, wishing I could lie down for a nap on one of them. "How many guys live in a hooch?"

"With you, nine. Eight in the main, and Moon lives out in the back porch. Moon's getting short." Another lucky one. "After today he's got only ninety-nine days left. A two-digit-midget. Big party tonight to celebrate. If you help me spread this crap, I'll invite you."

I suspected that I would have been invited anyway, but took the broom Mac offered and prepared to diesel. I threw my bag onto the overstuffed chair.

"I'd leave your bag somewhere else," Mac said. "The chair is Moon's. He ordered it from Sears, and he won't let anyone touch it. It's the only thing on the base that's not olive drab."

*****

Moon, it turned out, was the mail clerk. That role enabled him to get a chair from Sears to Vietnam. Virtually every Specialist 4 or lower not on guard duty showed up to celebrate his "shortness."

The starting time of the party was announced when "Purple Haze" blared from the hootch across the path. Past an already growing pile of beer cans, I stepped into a world somehow beyond Vietnam.

The room was lit by swirling, colored lamps. The beds were standing against the walls, surrounding nearly a hundred men, pressed together in a single mass. The only way to move was to slip sideways past other steaming bodies. A real purple haze of smoke and pot thickened the air. Eight enormous pulsating speakers threatened to blow the walls apart.

Somehow in the noise and chaos, others became aware that I was the new guy in camp, so my hand was never left without a beer. Hands slapped my back. Drunken, smiling faces pushed in front of my own.

"You from Minnesota? No shit. I'm from Hibbing. What the hell are you doing way over here?"

And suddenly I let go and became a part of this hysterical mayhem. It was reminiscent of parties I had attended in my out-of-control college days, and yet it was different as well.

Those bashes had always seemed filled with anger and rebellion, with people divided into little snobbish knots. This was a real celebration, with loud laughter and camaraderie.

The tension from my terrifying night on guard duty was sucked into the music, and what was left of me felt wonderful. I knew no one in the room, and yet I had never felt closer to people in my life. Suddenly my loss of Fud and Gracie and the others didn't seem to matter. Maybe it was my lack of sleep or the warm buzz of the beer, but I decided

~Boomer~

that since I had nowhere to go, and no one to meet, Vietnam was probably as good as anywhere else. Whatever was to happen in the days to come, these were the men who would face it with me; as we yelled and swore and sweated there together, it felt like we could probably handle it.

A pause in the music. "Mooooon," roared a group in the far corner. A rotund specialist four with a bright smile and a Fu Manchu mustache threw his arms into the air and roared, "I'm so short."

"Baby, take another little piece of my heart," screamed Janis Joplin. I pressed my way across the room toward Moon. I hadn't yet met him.

"I'm Boomer. I just moved into your hootch this afternoon. Congratulations."

"Oh, you're the new company clerk. I got a letter in the mail room already waiting for you. Damned if I know how it found you here. Your boss, the First Sergeant, is a prince. You're lucky there, but watch out for the Sergeant Major. He pisses olive drab."

"Thanks," I shouted as someone pulled Moon away, and someone else slapped another beer into my hand.

"No sweat GI," Moon yelled back to me. "In 265 days they'll be giving one of these for you."

That thought sent a momentary chill through me, but then the no where to go and nothing to do sensation and another swallow of beer smoothed me out.

"All is loneliness," crooned Joplin in the background. A letter in the mail room? For an instant I wondered if Gracie had written even before there was time to get my "I'm sorry" to her.

*****

The next morning our unit's contribution to the war

effort was considerably impeded. Browning, the man I was to replace, ran through our hootch with a wake-up call long before the sun would rise. No one in our hootch moved. He stopped at the foot of my bed.

"Boomer." He lifted the end of my bunk and let it slam to the floor.

I managed to open my eyes, but could not bear to move. "Uh huh."

"Formation in five minutes. First day on the job. Chop-chop. Better be on time."

"I hear you. Do I have time to shower?"

"After formation. Come on, girls. Holmes. Mac. Up and at 'em. Moooon," he yelled as he went through the porch and out the back door.

I struggled to a sitting position. I had that familiar sensation from my college days of my head being detached from my body. Not knowing how formal morning formations were, I pulled on my pants, shirt and boots from the night before. They reeked of smoke and dope.

Assuming formations must take place near HQ, I staggered through the darkness. I spotted Browning standing in an opening, a clipboard under his arm. I took my place beside him and turned to face the troops.

"Tent hut," barked Browning.

I looked out into the darkness. There was only one man in front of us. At Browning's command he shifted into something between at ease and still being asleep.

"Roll call," barked Browning, raising his clipboard and poising his pen.

Without opening his eyes, the only man in formation drawled, "Bravo Company all present or accounted for."

The declaration so shocked me that I turned to

Browning and said, "What? There are eight guys asleep in my hootch."

With a wry smile Browning looked over at me and said, "Well, then they're all accounted for, aren't they?"

"Right." It was my first lesson on how the army in Vietnam was different from stateside duty.

"At ease," commanded Browning. Our one soldier's posture went unchanged.

"There will be a practice red alert today at nineteen hundred hours. Dismissed." The company broke formation, and he headed off into the darkness.

"You can shower now," said Browning, "and you probably want to change that uniform. The first sergeant is in Tay Ninh today, so the sergeant major will probably be around to harass us. The guy thinks he's in Ft. Dix, not Vietnam. He'll have you polishing your boots if he can't see his ugly reflection in them."

Back at the hootch, I undressed, strapped on a towel and headed for the shower. My hootchmates had not yet stirred. I stumbled through the porch where Moon slept in his hammock and painfully picked my way across the rocky yard. The next day I would remember to wear a towel and combat boots.

The deserted shower room was a box with four pipes protruding from one wall. Turning the knobs below the first two pipes got no response. The third, however, sent a solid stream of frigid water glancing off my shoulder. Painful and primitive as it was, the icy stream was just what I needed to clear my head for the first day of duty. Taking a deep breath, I plunged into it.

*****

The euphoria of being short made Browning a really

~1967~

relaxed supervisor, and with my real boss, the first sergeant, off for the day, work began casually.

That lasted a few minutes until I was sent to get the mail and literally bumped into the sergeant major. He was a solid, bowling-ball of a man with only fuzz for hair, and when we turned the same corner at the same time and collided, I fell backward while he continued forward, coming to rest above me.

"Excuse me, sir," I bumbled, picking myself off the ground.

"I'm not sir, soldier," he growled. "I'm an enlisted man. I'm Sergeant Major Hickcock. Who the hell are you, and do you know anything about Moon? It is past 7:30 and the mail room isn't open."

I fumbled, unsure which question I should answer first. "Ah, I'm Boomer, sir. This is my first day here."

"Boomer? That your name or your job description? Heh, heh," he chuckled at himself.

"Ah, name. I'm the new Bravo Company Clerk. Um, ah, the mail room may not be open for a while. Maybe Moon had to do guard duty or something." It was a pathetic attempt to cover my new mate, but the only lie I could muster at the moment.

"Moon doesn't do guard duty. Come to think of it I haven't seen any of the enlisted men this morning. Something's up. Boomer, huh. What the hell do you do around here?"

"As I said, sir, I'm the new Bravo Company Clerk."

"If you call me sir again, Boomer, I'll have you down doing pushups. We expected you day before yesterday. What happened?"

"Division HQ had me on guard duty night before last,

so they didn't bring me over until late yesterday. I was out on the bunker line when that attack happened."

"Well then you need to tighten up your shit, soldier. Two choppers lost and no body count to show for it. Not a great job of guarding if you ask me. Let's see if you can keep up the 1st Sergeant's jeep better. The thing's a disgrace. Browning has turned lazy since he's gotten short. Carry on."

"Yes, sir," I blundered and followed with an awkward salute, something I had never mastered.

"I'm not a sir, soldier," he bellowed. "And save your salutes for the officers. I work for a living. Jesus Christ," he mumbled as he pushed past me and rolled on, shaking his head.

Back in the day room I reported my encounter to Browning who laughed uproariously at my misfortune.

"Don't worry about it," he comforted. "You won't have much to do with Hickcock. He's pretty short himself and doesn't leave battalion HQ very often. He'll be gone before you know it, unless somebody decides to frag him again in the meantime."

"Frag him?"

"When some of the grunts come back from the boonies, they don't appreciate the stateside bullshit that lifers like Hickcock put them through. A couple months ago one of them rolled a grenade into his hootch. If the good sergeant major hadn't been on a late night drunk at the NCO club, he would have been blown away. Nam's dangerous for different people for different reasons."

I wondered what my own dangers were to be.

Browning put me to work. My first duty was to re-type a letter of sympathy written by the first sergeant to the family of a B company man who had been killed the week

~1967~

before. It shook me a bit that this would be my first duty. I wondered how often I should have to do it. The letter was rather vague, but comforting, stating what a fine young man the deceased had been, and how he had died a credit to his unit. I began typing.

"How did this guy die?" I asked Browning.

"Not a happy story. Some sergeant had just gotten a promotion and went to the NCO club to celebrate. He didn't have his stripes yet and they kicked him out. He came back with his M-16, climbed on the stage and opened fire. Sixteen guys wounded, but Baker here was the only one to die."

"This letter doesn't really explain....."

"What do you want to write, Boomer, that some wacko went berserk and gunned down your son while he had a cocktail in his hand?"

"I don't know... I just... I don't know."

"It's not your job, Boomer. Just type the letter and forget it. It don't mean nothin."

For a long time I just sat staring at the letter. I tried to rationalize what I was doing. The first sergeant was trying to make a cruel circumstance somewhat less painful for a family. That had to be the right thing to do. And yet if he did it, a family would never know the truth of how their son, or father, or brother had died.

No matter what, Browning was right. It was a decision way beyond me. I typed the letter exactly as it had been written. As I typed, I wondered how many other families recount the real, tragic story of their lost loved ones and how many find comfort in a lie. And I wondered if Browning really felt that "it don't mean nothin." I didn't feel that and I wondered if I ever would.

*****

~Boomer~

The letter Moon had told me about the night before turned out to be from my father. Somehow he had found out my duty station, even before I had. It was an unexpected letter in which my father told me how proud he was that I had finally accepted my patriotic duty and decided to serve my country as he had. He said that he realized we had some difficult times the last few years and that he hoped that was behind us. There was no hint of an apology in his tone for things he had said to me, and I didn't feel this letter put it all behind us.

It did not help that my being a soldier seemed the only thing in my life in which he could find pride. I didn't want my father's pride for being a soldier, and rather than healing wounds, that declaration of new respect left me cold. I decided that I would not answer that letter, but would let Chandler slip further from me and see if in my new surrounding I could find something to put in its place.

*****

1968

We raced across the countryside in the jeep, me driving and the first sergeant sitting on his "donut," a pad to soften the blows to his hemorrhoids. I was driving much faster than I cared to, but there was a deuce-and-a-half about thirty feet behind me that showed no inclination to slow down.

"Shit, Boomer, can't you miss a bump once in a while?" the first sergeant shouted.

"Sorry." I swerved, but hit the next pothole dead center. The First Sergeant's rear-end left the donut, and his head hit the canvas above him.

~1968~

"Holy shit!"

We came up over a hill, and suddenly in front of us was a Vietnamese in his water buffalo cart, traveling about 350 yards an hour. The modern and ancient worlds were about to collide.

Having no time to brake, I swung into the passing lane. Fortunately (for us, unfortunately for him) its only occupant was a motorcyclist who missed us by heading for the ditch.

Back in my own lane, I slowed down and began to breathe again. As the deuce-and-a-half raced by us, the soldier in the passenger seat looked down at us doubled up in laughter.

"I wish they'd keep those things off the road," roared the first sergeant. "We damn near made buffalo burger out of that one."

On the straight stretches I glanced to the side where fields of rice lined the road. In one, a woman stood before a contraption resembling a high-backed wicker chair. Beside her stood her pair of water buffalo. She had an armful of the grain and was beating it into the wicker mechanism, evidently to separate the grain from the straw.

"They hate us, you know," said the first sergeant.

"I'm not surprised, after what we've done to their country," I replied.

"No! The water buffalo. It's our smell. Drives 'em nuts. Don't ever get close to one. They can rear up like a horse."

The road widened and we entered a village, Trang Bang by my map. It was notorious for Viet Cong activity. Holmes had told me to watch my back in Trang Bang. The center of the village was mobbed with people. They shopped at open markets along both sides of the street. We could only crawl forward in our jeep.

Vietnamese surrounded us. I wondered which of them were the enemy and would have killed us in a different setting. Small children climbed onto the running boards of the jeep. The first sergeant tousled the hair of a small boy and gently pushed him away.

On my side, another boy, perhaps ten years old, pulled at the sleeve of my shirt. "Hey Joe. You give money, I take you home my sister."

"Careful," I said, pushing him away. "Don't get your feet under the tires."

"Come on, G.I. Sister number one girl." I looked straight ahead and tried to will the jeep through the mass of bodies in front.

The midday heat and the congestion pressed in on me, and at the first break in the crowd, I raced forward. On the outskirts of Trang Bang I accelerated abruptly, trying to raise a breeze to dry me out and clear my head of a small child's offer.

Suddenly another jeep was beside me. In the passenger's seat was a sergeant with a black and white MP band at his bicep. He motioned me to pull over. I looked at the first sergeant, who just shrugged.

The MP walked to my side the jeep. "You were speeding coming out of Trang Bang there," he said to me.

"I was... I didn't know... I was afraid that... It seemed." I blubbered for some response. The idea that I was about to get a speeding ticket in a war zone suddenly seemed perfectly consistent with everything else I had experienced in Vietnam, and it suddenly seemed very funny.

"You were going about forty-five, and you were still

~1968~

in the twenty mile an hour zone."

"Right. There's no telling how many VC I might have run over." As soon as I said it, I regretted it.

"Listen, smart ass.." He tapped me on the shoulder with his night stick. "If you want to keep driving this thing, you best watch both your foot and your mouth."

The first sergeant rescued me. "Sergeant. We have a meeting in Tay Ninh and we're running a little late. I've been pushing the boy to hurry it up."

"All right, sergeant, we'll let it go this time, but you better get him on a tighter leash." He gave me one more tap with the stick and headed back toward his jeep.

I pulled back onto the road. We drove a distance in silence. "You know, Boomer," the first sergeant said, "there are a lot worse jobs over here than the one you've got."

That was true, and I got the message very clearly. I was going to have to keep many of my thoughts to myself in the year to come. "Sorry. Thanks for bailing me out." I swerved and missed a large hole in the road.

*****

I gradually settled into my life in Cu Chi. My job as company clerk brought me in contact with loads of people. Although some wouldn't have been on my list of prospective best friends, they were an interesting lot and generally pretty friendly.

Cu Chi was a large enough base camp that it was equipped with all of the luxuries a prosperous nation could supply its men in combat. We at the 65th Engineers had our own tennis and basketball courts. My hootchmates and I used the latter almost nightly.

I sometimes wished that Sticks had been assigned to our unit, so that he and I could have pulled off some of the trick plays we had perfected on his driveway. In Cu Chi basketball allowed us to get some exercise and relieve the boredom of having little else to do, no where to go, and no way to get there if we had somewhere to go.

Well, that was except for the night that Macelroy got drunk, broke into the motor pool, stole a tank, and drove us to the swimming pool at 25th Infantry Division Headquarters. Stateside, we probably would have all been court-martialed for the stunt, but in Vietnam, all it got us was a little extra KP.

Every so often a live stage show would appear at the enlisted men's club. The performers were from Korea or Taipei or Japan. Usually it was a band behind a parade of singers.

The singers were mostly female and wore costumes that aroused the attention of hundreds of sex-starved GIs. There was something a little bit cruel about those entertainments. Some of the singers were wonderful. Or at least we thought so with a handful of drinks behind us. There was one who imitated Janis Joplin. She screamed out into the smoky darkness and we went wild.

Many of the Asian singers spoke little English, but were amazing in their mastery of the songs. They would recreate the originals without a clue as to what they were singing.

"Rollink, Rollink, Rollink down the Reever," the not so look-a-like Tina Turner would chant. But she had the costume and the moves, so that if Tina herself had been there, we couldn't have been more excited.

The favorite song was "I Wanna Go Home." It was in every show and was saved until everyone in the room was sufficiently drunk. The singer would croon the verse, and we would join on the chorus. "I wanna go home," we would howl on the first line. "I wanna go home." We always felt it more on the second line. And by "Oh Lord, I wanna go home," most meant it with all their hearts.

I sang as boisterously as any, but occasionally I pondered if, in fact, I did want to go home. I even sometimes wondered if I had a home to go back to. When I failed to answer my father's first letter, he hadn't attempted a second. Gracie never answered my pathetic apology. My mother wrote faithfully, but as the year went on, the letters became almost mechanical, each nearly identical to the one from the day before. I wrote to or heard from no one else.

Our evening entertainment often ended the same way. A black GI would decide to get more involved in the show. He would mount the stage and engage the singer in dance. After a few moments of this, a totally inebriated white man would decide to stand up for his race by matching the antics of the first.

Immediately the group would divide, blacks on one side, and whites on the other. It didn't matter that moments before they had all been celebrating together. At that point I always left. Usually I had come with my black friend, Tuck, and I couldn't stand to see him on one side and be on the other.

Many of my best friends were black. It was a big change from Chandler where half the population had never spoken to a black person.

The next day I would get a full report on the brawl from Macelroy. Normally, everyone had been too drunk to establish any lasting grudge or land any serious blow.

Tuck and I talked a lot about the racial tension in Vietnam. He was always different when he was with the brothers than he was with me. "Why is that, Tuck?" I once asked him. I guess I expected him to deny it.

"Because what I got with them is different from what I got with you," he said.

"Does that mean our friendship can't be as close?"

"It doesn't have anything to do with close. It has to do with different. Bloods just have some things in common because of who we are. And you can't understand those things because you're not a brother. When we slip skin and jive one another, we are just getting strength from something we share."

Tuck was one of the nicest people I've ever met in any color. And then one day his father died in the states, and the following day he went home as a sole surviving son. And then it really didn't matter if he was black or white. He was just gone.

That's the way relationships were in Vietnam. They could be very, very strong, and then suddenly they were very, very over. But in Tuck's case, at least he wasn't very, very dead.

For a while after he left, I found myself desperately missing my four Chandler friends.

*****

Along with the obvious negative of being in a war zone, Vietnam was filled with numerous minor frustrations.

For example, the "b" on my typewriter in the day room was broken. Each time I confronted the letter, I would have to dip my hand into the top of the machine, grasp the arm of the "b" key, and jam it onto the paper. It gave new meaning to the term "manual" typewriter.

I became an expert at writing letters containing synonyms for "b" words. While I loved my boss, the first sergeant's vocabulary seemed to contain an inordinate

~1968~

number of "b" words, and I was never quite sure that he wasn't doing it to needle me a bit. He sprinkled every letter generously with "battalion," and "battle" and "barracks." Of course, it didn't help any that we were Bravo Company.

The last straw was when the first sergeant composed a letter listing conditions under which enlisted men could attend the upcoming Bob Hope Christmas Show, in which he referred to "Bob" ten times in eight sentences. After finishing the letter I stormed into his office demanding that I be transferred to a Vietnamese Unit where the men's names would be Nguyen and Dong instead of Bobby and Ben.

Sergeant Boyd rejected my request for transfer and promised to do his best to get a replacement typewriter, which arrived long after he was gone and twenty days before I left Vietnam.

*****

Danger in Vietnam came in unexpected places. One evening an explosion shook the tin roof over our hootch.

"Incoming," shouted Holmes as he rolled off his bunk, SOP, standard operating procedure, for such circumstances. Following his lead, I rolled to my left, whacking my forehead on my footlocker just before reaching the floor. I slid against the sandbag wall of our home, hoping it would take up any shrapnel headed in my direction.

My foot hit one of the many mousetraps we had set for midnight visitors. The thing snapped shut, scaring the hell out of me.

"I'm too short for this shit," bellowed Moon from the porch.

"What happened to the red alert sirens?" I yelled.

"They only work when it's practice," Holmes returned.

Suddenly a dripping, naked Macelroy was standing in the middle of the hootch. "Hell's bells, I just about got wasted."

Holmes shouted, "Well get down, or the next one will frag your ass."

"Next what?"

"Incoming."

"What incoming? The water tower just fell on the shower building."

It took a few moments for this news to register. I got to my knees, pulled back one of the translucent plastic windows and peered out into the compound.

Already a scraggly, half-dressed group of GIs was beginning to gather around what used to be our shower room. We filed outside to join them.

Two of the legs supporting the multi-ton water tank had collapsed, sending it crashing onto the rather fragile building in which we showered at least twice daily.

"My God, Macelroy," Holmes said. "How the hell did you get out alive? Was anybody else in there?"

"Me and Reinquist were at the far end. Those were the only two showers that worked. God, if we'd a been down here, it'd be all over. Greased by a water tower."

"I'm too short for this shit," grumbled Moon, and headed back toward the hootch. Others started to walk away, but Macelroy just stood there shaking, still naked.

"You O.K. Mac," I said.

"No shit, I'm O.K. How do you think the lifers would have reported my death to my folks if that thing had gotten me?"

"Probably say you died in glorious combat in the bush, single-handedly attacking a battalion of Charlie."

~1968~

Macelroy crouched on the ground and vomited.

*****

I now scarcely thought of Chandler and had completely traded in my old group of friends for a new one. A quirk of fate reversed that course.

I had dropped the first sergeant at Division Headquarters and taken the jeep to the PX to shop for cheap stereo equipment, when a familiar face crossed my aisle. I ran to catch up with it.

"Sticks?"

And who should turn to face me but my old friend. "Boomer. Hey, man, how are you?" We fell into a clumsy embrace.

Because of the bad terms on which we had left each other in Chandler, this was really an awkward moment. I was ecstatic to see him, but aware that the last time I had been yelling and calling him names.

"What are you doing here? How long have you been here? How long will you be here? God, this is weird." I couldn't clear my head enough to make sense.

"I've been here about three weeks. I'm doing some training with my unit, and then we are off to the bush."

"Who are you with? What's your unit?"

He turned his shoulder and flashed me his yellow lightning bolt, the insignia of the 25th Infantry Division. Then he lifted his lapel and showed me his second lieutenant bar.

"Oh shit. I'm sorry, Sticks." I came to attention and snapped off my best salute. "Good morning, sir," I barked.

"Oh, cut it, Boomer. Good Morning, Sticks, sir will be good enough. I'm still not used to this officer stuff. How are things with you? You're over at 65th Engineers aren't you?"

~Boomer~

"You knew I was here, and you didn't try to get in touch? Jeez, Sticks."

"Well, you might remember that we didn't part on the best of terms, and frankly, I wasn't sure you'd want to hear from me."

For a moment I couldn't say anything. If you had asked me ten minutes earlier, I probably would have said that I never wanted to see him again. But here he was, and whatever conflict had interrupted our friendship was washed away by a flood of good memories.

"Oh God. I'm sorry, Sticks. I was such a jerk. I just don't know what got into me that night."

"That's O.K. I've never quite understood what happened. It's like things just took over, and before I knew it, I'd lost control, and we were all at each other's throats."

"Are you and Gracie still in touch?" I asked uncomfortably, not quite sure I wanted to hear his answer, but evidently not as ready to put it all behind us as I had just said.

"Boomer, there was never anything going on between Gracie and me, and I had no idea that it would have mattered to you if there was. I've never understood what happened with her last summer. After you and I fought, she seemed to want to be left alone. I actually didn't see much of her."

"Have you heard from her since you got here?"

"I wrote to her once, but I never got anything back." Sticks looked genuinely hurt by Gracie's rejection. I knew how he felt. "I just wish the whole thing had never happened."

"Done. It never happened. The hell with it. What the hell we gonna do with a girlfriend ten thousand miles away anyhow. Hey, are you going to be around for a while? Could

~1968~

we get together sometime and celebrate?"

"Man, I wish we could, but I'm just here to pick up some stuff, and then we're off to Tay Ninh. Tomorrow we head to a firebase near the Cambodian border. Things are really heating up over there."

"Yeah, I know. Some of our guys are over there building a bridge into Cambodia. It's supposed to be some big secret project. I read in this mornings *Stars and Stripes* that Johnson says the war won't be escalating into Cambodia. What bullshit! Why do they need a secret bridge going in there then."

"Listen, Boomer, I gotta run. It was really good to see you. I guess when my guys stand down, they come back here for R & R. When we do, I'll look you up. Relive some old times. All right?"

"That'd be great, Sticks. Hey man, you take care of yourself. I hear that some of that crap out in the bush is number ten. You keep your head down and your shit together. Hear? -- Sir?" I added with a smile.

"I hear. Thanks, Boomer. We'll see you in a couple months." He turned and walked away.

As I watched him disappear, a huge lump formed in my throat. Would I really see him in a couple months? Our unit alone had lost ten men since the start of the Cambodian operation.

I had never really seen Sticks in the military, much less as an officer. He was such a gentle, kind soul. Did he really have what it takes to lead a squad of men into a loaded jungle? And more important, could he bring them back out?

Along with those feelings came a wave of guilt for how easily I had cast off my years of friendship with Sticks over a vague, confusing disagreement.

~Boomer~

For the next few days I spent a good deal of time thinking about my old life and friends. I wondered how the rest were doing, and I longed to laugh and play with them again.

*****

From the day I arrived in Vietnam I had heard rumors about an impending end to the war. Browning, the guy I replaced, had told me before he left that I probably wouldn't be in Vietnam my full year.

There were stories about the 25th Infantry Division, to whom we were attached, moving back to Hawaii, its base of operations. Daily, *Stars and Stripes* told of our victories, of how we were gradually wearing down the enemy and capturing the allegiance of the population through a program called Vietnamization.

Things around Cu Chi had been quiet since my first night of turbulent guard duty, so I suspected that the rumors were probably true, although I wasn't as desperate to catch that big freedom bird as some around me.

Some of the married men were beginning to count on those rumors, were sure that it wouldn't be long before they were back in the arms of wives and children.

*****

And then the war exploded for all of us. Near the end of January, just two months after I had arrived, the Viet Cong launched a major offensive throughout South Vietnam on the first day of Tet, the new year holiday.

We had also heard rumors of this offensive. It was supposedly targeted far north of us, the Khe San area. Reinforcements had already been moved there to squash the action before it got started.

To everyone's surprise, the fighting not only

~1968~

intensified in the North, but everywhere else in the country. Virtually every provincial capital came under attack. Thirty-five miles to our south, the city of Saigon burst into flames. The Viet Cong attacked the Presidential Palace and succeeded in overthrowing the U. S. embassy.

To our north, Tay Ninh, our unit's other base, was under heavy rocket and mortar attack. Most of our men and equipment were moved there, although our main headquarters remained in Cu Chi. For me this meant frequent trips back and forth between the two camps. Usually I drove for the first sergeant, but sometimes we were able to catch a helicopter lift. Often we stayed a day or two in Tay Ninh.

The sense of security that I had begun to develop in Cu Chi was blown to hell by the rocket explosions that nightly shook our compound in Tay Ninh.

One evening, as we were stupidly standing outside in formation, a rocket exploded so close that it knocked us all to the ground and killed three of our men. It was days before my ears stopped ringing, weeks before my hands stopped shaking, and my idea that maybe it was all right for me to be in Vietnam was dashed forever.

It was also in Tay Ninh that I began to observe the futility of our war effort. Just outside of Tay Ninh stood a mountain, Nui Ba Din, the black virgin mountain. The U. S. controlled the bottom of the mountain, surrounding it with fire bases. We also had a communications station at the top of the mountain. But the Viet Cong controlled the middle of the mountain, where they had burrowed a maze of tunnels.

Every once in a while, some colonel would get a wild hair to drive the VC off the mountain. Helicopters would circle the peak. They would bomb so furiously that soon Nui

~Boomer~

Ba Din would disappear into the smoke and fire.

The Viet Cong, of course, would simply pull back into the heart of the hill and have lunch while the noise continued. Five minutes after the bombing stopped, they would resurface and reclaim control.

Such was the nature of this war. Tons and tons of ammunition were expended to no avail. It was not a war to be won by power and force. The enemy was not powerful. But they were wily and patient, and they were playing on their home field. By the time we would begin to understand the rules of the battle, we would have lost the will to fight.

We controlled the top and the bottom, but right in the middle of us sat the enemy, and we were helpless to eliminate or defeat them.

Meanwhile, our men in the bush were getting massacred. Hardly a day went by without casualties. Death, which had only lurked on the periphery of our daily lives, now staged its offensive.

I still worked in relative safety. It was not like I was out in the boonies stalking or being stalked by Charlie, but death became more and more a part of my job. I accompanied the first sergeant to the hospital to comfort men whose wounds were so severe we knew they wouldn't live.

I typed more and more letters of condolence to parents of dead soldiers. The first sergeant discovered that I had a facility for writing, and soon turned the composing, as well as the typing, over to me. It was a job I didn't relish, and sometimes I sat for hours trying to find the right words. I refused to fall into a formula which I could reproduce quickly, only changing the names.

One day I sat staring at my typewriter, trying to draft the first of three letters to the families of our men who had died when the rocket had interrupted our evening formation. As always, I had my radio turned to the Armed Forces Station, the only one we could get.

The announcer was reminiscing that a year ago, three astronauts, Gus Grissom, Edward White and Roger Chaffee, had burned to death when fire swept through their space craft during a launch simulation.

As I sat struggling to compose my letters, the entire world was mourning the death of the astronauts. A year later their names and sacrifices were still fresh in our national memory.

And who would remember the loss of three soldiers from the 65th Engineering Brigade? Certainly their parents and families, who were not yet aware of their deaths. Certainly we men who stood beside them moments before their lives were abruptly stopped. But in comparison to the attention drawn by the deaths of the astronauts, our three men would die in relative obscurity. Three deaths were not equal to three deaths.

I redoubled my effort to compose my letters, driven by a need to capture a significance in the lives and deaths of our soldiers.

I worried greatly about Sticks during this time. I had heard nothing from or about him since our encounter in the PX. After Tet, I had tried to get information about his unit, but I could find neither their location nor their status. It was as if they had disappeared from the earth.

The only encouraging thing was that Sticks' name had never appeared on the frequent and long lists of 25th Infantry dead and wounded. I hoped that this meant he was alive and safe somewhere.

*****

~Boomer~

At one point I should have feared for my life, but by the time I realized the danger, it was past. At a time of particularly heavy casualties, the first sergeant decided that he wanted to drive to the Cambodian borders where our engineers were building the secret bridge. Normally, we would have taken a helicopter to such a remote outpost, but none were available, so we set off in our jeep.

It was a torturous drive, over unsecured roads, through deserted territory. By the time we got there, we had to quickly turn back to avoid being caught in the darkness. Most of our men were far out on the bridge and unavailable to us.

My driving on the way out had been too slow, too tentative for the first sergeant. He took over the wheel, and we raced back toward Tay Ninh. About half way back, we came upon a small convoy that we had met on the way in. The lead truck lay on its side, smoldering. It had hit a mine, which had tossed it from the road, killing the driver and two other men. By the time we reached the scene, the dead and wounded had been medevaced, leaving the rest of the dazed men starring at the smoldering rubble, once a two and a half ton truck.

As we drove on, I wondered where that mine had been when we had passed going the other way. Had it been planted later? Did we inadvertently miss it? Given what the mine had done to that huge truck, if we had hit it, would there have been any of our jeep left to be found? I felt reasonably secure much of the time I was in Vietnam. But I suppose so did a lot of those who didn't return.

That night I again spent thinking of home. Lots of questions bounced around in my head. Would I really survive another two hundred days and get back to

Chandler? What had happened to Sticks, and would he ever escape the jungle? What was the rest of our merry group doing in the states? Would we ever be a group again?

    I decided to break my self-imposed isolation. Fud was the person with whom I felt I might still connect. Since I had no idea where he was, I would send it to his parents' address with a "please forward."

    I found it a relief to honestly describe my new life to someone from my past. I told him about the Tet offensive and the dangers and fears of my situation. I could never have written to my mother about such things.

    I wrote about Sticks and my concern for him. Again, I could be honest, because I knew Fud would understand and share my fears, even though he and Sticks had argued bitterly about Vietnam.

    I asked him about Pastor Jim Bob and Gracie. I had hurt Gracie so badly the night before I left that I was unsure we could ever be friends again. When I asked about her, I discovered I still had strong feelings and really wanted to know how she was doing.

    And finally, I asked Fud about himself. Where was he and what was he doing? Was he actively marching against the war I was waging? I told him that I hoped he was, and that if I were on his side of the ocean, I would be marching beside him.

    It was almost three months before I got an answer. An outsider reading his letter would have thought that he was the person writing from the war zone. He wrote it on April 5, the night after the assassination of Martin Luther King. The event had devastated him and set him to pondering the turbulence of the times in comparison to the stability of our teen years. A good half of the letter described the battles he had fought in the streets of American cities.

He had passed up several engineering offers and returned to a college campus to be involved in both the civil rights and anti-war movements.

Ironically, it was to Madison, my old campus, that he had returned. Centered there, he had been traveling to cities around the country for marches and demonstrations on both issues. Just a week before the assassination, he had actually marched beside Dr. King in Memphis. Fud wrote about how powerful and charismatic King had been. He didn't know how the movement could proceed without him at its head.

Fud said that he was heartsick about Sticks, that every life lost in Vietnam was a wasted life; he couldn't bear the thought of losing a close friend to that war, even a friend with whom he had fallen out.

He had lost track of Gracie. She had quit her job and left Chandler soon after I had left for the army. Someone had said that she moved to the Twin Cities, but he didn't know if that was true.

He and Pastor Jim Bob had remained connected. The good Pastor was still working at the bank in Chandler, but came to Madison on weekends when Fud was there.

Fud was glad that I still shared his view of the war, and begged me to do everything I could to return from it unchanged. He said that he would give anything if the five of us could once again hatch one of our stupid stunts together.

I didn't reply to Fud right away. I wanted to wait a bit in the hope that I could send him some good news about Sticks. That news didn't come, and it didn't seem that I had much to tell him.

Then I received a second letter from him. He had

~1968~

written it on June 6, the night after Robert Kennedy had been assassinated. The letter was hollow and haunting. It was hard to believe that it had been written by Fud, the practical joker who had seemingly taken nothing seriously in the first twenty years of his life. He was emotionally empty. He said that he had run out of hope and money.

He was heading home to Chandler for the rest of the summer to renew his job search and figure out where he wanted to be and what he wanted to do, now that he had grown up.

It struck me how Fud's experience in the last eight months had been so like Sticks'. Both had believed in a cause. Both had thrown themselves into the battle with naive faith. Both were at the mercy of elements far beyond their control.

Fud would now retreat to recover and redirect his energy. I could only hope that Sticks would have the same chance.

*****

One hot July night the first sergeant let me use our jeep to take our group to the 25th Infantry Division enlisted men's club for a night out. There was an Australian group singing, and word had it that a shipment of quality beer had made its appearance in Cu Chi. Usually the clubs had plenty of generic looking beer with uninspiring names like Brown Label, but on occasion a supply of Budweiser or Blatz or Old Milwaukee would appear, and rumors spread quickly throughout the units.

By the time Holmes, Moon, Macelroy and I arrived, the festivities were under way. At one end of the hall, the band performed from a small stage. They had two attractive female singers who were drawing a fairly large crowd. Other bunches of men sat around tables, drinking and talking as the noise would allow. We found a table and borrowed enough chairs to seat ourselves around it.

The tables to each side of us were engaged in a favorite GI activity, the pyramid-of-beer-cans challenge. Each table would try to construct a taller stack of beer cans than any other group in the room. To win, you first of all needed to drink more beer than anyone else in the room, and yet keep a clear enough head and a steady enough hand to construct the aluminum mountain.

We decided that we would enter, although the tables to both sides had a good head start. We would have to drink fast to catch up. But then we had Moon on our side, a man who could pour down more beer without any visible effect than anyone I had ever met.

We each emptied our first can in two swallows and lined them up to create a portion of our base. A firm code of honor was adhered to in the challenge. No cans could be used that weren't emptied at the table. Nothing could be done to disturb the pyramid at a neighboring table. Once the pyramid was started, it could not be dismantled and reassembled, although it was permissible to add layers to the outside edges, if a group happened to out-drink the width of its initial base. We decided to start with a base of ten cans and lined up the empties from our second round next to those of our first.

From that point on, the pyramid was not the object of much attention. It merely grew as cards were played, food was eaten and conversations held. When the band took a break, we were able to converse without screaming.

Holmes, who clerked at Battalion Headquarters, always had a wealth of stories calling into question the effectiveness, if not sanity, of our superiors. Tonight was no exception.

"You're not going to believe this one," he began, his standard opening. "The colonel is on a rampage over our appearance again."

"What does he care what we look like over here? We're not going to the prom," Macelroy said.

Holmes went into his best impersonation of his boss. "It's discipline. We can't perform like a disciplined unit if we don't look like a disciplined unit."

"Oh, God," I said. "What is he going to do to us this time?"

Holmes explained, "It seems that facial hair may now be the key to discipline. He feels some of us are becoming too hairy. He had me drawing pictures of men with mustaches all afternoon. Tomorrow he is going to pick one to become the battalion mustache. The sergeant major is going to tack up this picture all over the compound, and anybody with a stache that's longer or bushier than the one in the picture is going to be forcibly trimmed."

Macelroy slapped Moon on the back. "Moon. Your hairy lip is history."

"The colonel touches my lip," threatened Moon, "and his next week's mail goes up in smoke. I am too short for this shit." By this time we had reached the row of five on our pyramid. It appeared we had started our base too narrow.

I noticed a group of five men enter across the hall from us and stand near the doorway. One of them caught my attention. He was wearing a second lieutenant's bar, something you didn't often see in the enlisted men's club. His face was shadowed from the light, but the rest of him looked familiar. His body looked dejected. His shoulders sagged. His chin was nearly on his chest, and he didn't speak to the other men. None of the group looked like they were out for a good time.

The band came back onto the stage and started their next set. The two female singers had donned even shorter skirts, much to the approval of the men near the stage. The group I had been watching came further into the room and crossed toward the stage.

When they did, I recognized that the lieutenant was none other than Sticks. I got up from our table a bit unsteadily and moved to greet my old companion.

When I reached him, his head was still down. I put my hand on his shoulder, but he didn't respond at all.

"Sticks," I said, close to his ear, as the band was once again at full volume. Very slowly he turned his head and looked at me. It was Stick's face I looked into, but it wasn't his eyes. These eyes were vacant, and there wasn't a hint of recognition in them. We just stared at each other for a moment.

"Sticks," I said again. "It's Boomer. I've been worried about you, man. It's good to see you."

One of the other men in the group saw that I was talking to Sticks and stepped back alongside us. "You know Lt. Skulsky?" he asked.

"Yeah, sure," I said. "We're good friends. We were high school classmates, weren't we, Sticks?" I looked to him for confirmation.

For a moment he just looked back at me. Then his lip started to quiver and then his head. "Boomer," he said softly, and then his eyes closed and his chin returned to his chest. He was crying, but no sound was coming out.

"We just got in from the bush," said the other man. "I'm Andrews. We were in some really deep shit out there.

~1968~

The Lieutenant is taking it pretty hard. We thought we'd bring him along to get his mind off it, but it ain't going so well. Maybe you want to take him outside and talk old times. We're going to be here for a while."

"Sure, thanks," I said. "Hey, Sticks, let's get out of the noise and jaw a little bit."

He just shook his head up and down slowly. I took his arm and led him toward the exit. As we left, I caught Moon's eye and motioned that I would be outside. He waved back.

The cooler air outside helped to clear my head which had been fuzzied by four quick beers. Sticks walked beside me like a zombie.

"Let's go sit out back on the movie benches," I suggested. The back wall of the EM club was painted white, and on other evenings we sat on benches to watch films. Tonight we had the place to ourselves as we sat side by side. For a while I just looked at him, his hands in his lap and his chin down.

After a bit he turned his face toward me and gave a sad smile. "Boomer," he said again, softly.

"Do you want to talk about it, Sticks? Would it help if you told me what happened out there?" He didn't answer. "Where were you guys? I tried to find out something about your unit, and it was like you had dropped off the face of the earth. Where were you?"

"Cambodia. We were in Cambodia." He said it as if he had announced to me that he had just returned from Hell.

"Figures," I said. "The war's not in Cambodia. President Johnson still maintains that the war will not be spreading to Cambodia." I said it ironically, but Sticks took it literally.

"Well, President Johnson is a liar," he said forcefully. It was the first time I had heard Sticks say anything critical of his country or the war effort. In fact, Sticks never said a negative word about anything. The change in him was frightening.

"What happened, man?"

Finally he seemed to gather himself enough to tell the tale.

"The Viet Cong were shipping supplies south through Cambodia. That whole Tet thing. The supplies to pull that off all came down through Cambodia. We were in there to cut off their supply lines. By the time we got there, they were waiting for us. Every trail was booby trapped. Any that weren't, led us right into ambushes. They were in the trees. They came out of the ground. We couldn't see them. We couldn't find them. They'd fire at us from the villages, and when we went into the villages they wouldn't be there. They cut us to pieces. Those four guys inside. They are the only four guys in my platoon that aren't either dead or wounded. Boomer, yesterday I saw my platoon sergeant's legs blown off by a booby trap."

"Oh, God, Sticks. I'm sorry." I put my hand on his shoulder.

"I didn't think it'd be like this, Boomer. It's not a fair fight. We can't find them to fight with them. They know where they are going, and we don't. I don't want to go back out there, Boomer. In a week they're going to make us go back out there." Tears streamed down his face.

"I'm supposed to be leading those guys, Boomer. How can I lead them when I don't even know where I am going or what I am doing? I don't want to lose any more of my men, Boomer."

~1968~

"Oh, Sticks." I wanted to say that he didn't have to go back into the boonies. I wanted to say that we'd do something to keep him safe.

But who was I to say such things. It was only a piece of dumb luck that I wasn't out in the bush like Sticks. I had little control of my own life, and certainly none of his.

"They can't send you back into that. Your commanders must see what is happening to you. They've got to do something to protect you. This current offensive seems to be about over now. Maybe things will quiet down. They've got to see what you guys have been through. They can't send you back to that."

Sticks gave a derisive laugh, something else I had never seen him do before.

"The shots are being called a long way from the bush. Those generals back in Long Binh don't seem too worried about those of us in the boonies. I've got five months left to be here, Boomer, and right now I wouldn't give a plugged nickel for my chances to get back to the world."

"Come on, man. Don't talk like that. You're going to make it back and live until you're ninety-three and have thirty-eight grandchildren."

"That's what the guys in my platoon thought too, and most of them didn't live to see twenty." He got up from his seat. "Listen, Boomer, thanks for the words of encouragement. I hope things go all right for you here. I'm really tired and want to get back to our hootch. Let's go inside and find the guys."

"Sure, Sticks. Listen, can we get together again tomorrow. I think I can spring free and we can go swimming or do something around here." We walked together around the side of the club.

"Could we wait a day? I think that I will sleep most of the day tomorrow. I haven't had much lately, sleeping on the ground. Then I want to get some letters off to my folks. I haven't done much of that either. I'm not sure what I'll say anyway. I sure can't tell them what I've been doing. Dear folks, today I shot three gooks and one of my friends had his head blown off. Don't wish you were here. I'll write again soon, if I still have my right hand."

The knot in my stomach tightened. I thought I might faint or throw up. I couldn't believe that anyone could be changed so drastically by anything. In two months Sticks had literally become a different person. As I held the door for him to enter the club, I felt helpless to bring my old friend back.

We found Stick's platoon seated at the back of the room. Like Sticks, they looked exhausted and dejected. They stared at the stage, but didn't seem to be listening. Their vacant eyes were windows to minds that were somewhere else, somewhere lost.

Sticks told them that he was really tired and wanted to hit the sack. None of the others objected. They finished their drinks, and stood to leave.

Sticks and I agreed to meet at the division swimming pool on Sunday afternoon. He said that he wanted to go to church. I hoped that he would remember our date. I couldn't imagine what was going on in his head.

The five of them headed off like robots toward the door. One of them, the guy who had spoken to me earlier, turned back to me. He was a sergeant and a little older than Sticks or the rest of the group.

"Your friend is Number One, man. He saved my ass, all of our asses, more than once out there. He's not like the

~1968~

other officers. He's one of us. We'll take care of him. Any one of us would take a bullet for him. He's pretty shaky right now, but he'll be O.K. If anyone can get us through this shit, the Lieutenant can." He stuck out his hand. "My name is Woody. You take care now."

I shook his hand. "You too, Woody," I said. "You keep your heads down."

"Right. The Lieutenant calls you Boomer. What do you do around here, Boomer?"

"I'm the Bravo Company clerk over at the 65th Engineers."

"Well, you keep an eye on that typewriter, Boomer. Those sneaky bastards might even slip a booby trap into that."

He said it good-naturedly, with the little humor left in him, but it stung me a bit. It embarrassed me that I was living in such relative safety in Vietnam, while others, my good friend included, faced such turbulence that they would never be the same. I could have as easily been in fire fights. I could have been ambushed. I could have tripped a booby trap. I could have seen my friends and my enemies butchered. But, it was happening to others instead.

As I watched Sticks leave the club, I wondered, "If fate were to put me in battle, how would I react." I was certainly no stronger than Sticks,. and unlike him, I had come to Vietnam not even believing in the cause. After seeing him, I knew for sure that I could never step into battle without being permanently changed, and not for the better.

I walked back to the table where my new group of friends remained. Their pyramid of cans had risen. They had widened its base to twelve cans and were well on the way to a peak. The band had stopped playing and was packing away instruments.

"Boomer," slurred Holmes, "we thought we'd lost you. What's up?"

"That lieutenant I was with is a good buddy. He's just come back from some deep shit. Most of the men in his unit are dead. He's really on the edge. He doesn't want to go back out."

"Nobody should have to go out to something like that," said Moon.

The thought that any of us could be sent into the bush very easily, brought a sober moment to our otherwise drunken state. The bartender came toward us with a fifty-gallon oil drum.

"Closing time, gentlemen," he said. "I applaud your architecture, but the time has come to get your cans into mine."

"I'm too short for this shit," said Moon, and with a savage punch he sent our night's work sprawling to the tabletop.

*****

Most days in Vietnam didn't seem very much like we were at war. That following Sunday was one such day. I donned my swimming suit, and under the always blue Vietnam sky, lay back in a recliner, beer in one hand, book in the other, next to the 25th Infantry Division pool.

Soon after arriving, I was joined by Sticks and three of the men he had been with at the club two nights before. Sticks seemed better than he had that night, but he was nowhere near being his original self. He was more responsive, and able to carry on a very normal conversation. But the sadness was still very much in his eyes, and when no one was talking to him, he would drift off into an almost

~1968~

comatose state.

At one point he got up, walked over to the edge of the pool and dove in. I kept my eyes on him as he effortlessly glided to the other end of the pool, reversed and headed back. That athletic body had certainly not changed. He stayed under the water seemingly forever. I stood up and was on the verge of diving in to bring him up, when he surfaced with a huge gasp for air. We spent the next two hours relaxing in the sun. There wasn't much talking. Sticks' friends spent most of the time in a deep sleep. It was as if they hadn't slept in months. The noise and chaos of the crowded pool failed to faze them.

Sticks lay silently staring at the sky, but he didn't sleep. His eyes seemed incapable of closing. He talked if I said something to him, but his responses were short and vague.

At one point I asked him if he had written his letter to his folks the other night, and he just said, "I couldn't." He didn't explain any further, and I didn't feel I could ask for it.

Soon after noon the sun turned from comfortable to relentless. Sticks' friends began talking of food. A group of GIs near us said that there was a local market in the village of Cu Chi, and that they were driving off base for lunch.

I had generally avoided the local food, which I had been told would likely give me one kind of stomach discomfort or another, but our neighbors of the pool said that they had eaten at the market often and had not gotten sick.

They were leaving shortly in a deuce-and-a-half and invited us to ride out. They did say that from Cu Chi they were driving on to Saigon, and that we would have to walk back. Cu Chi was only a half mile outside the military camp's perimeter, so it wasn't much of a walk. With no other plans for the afternoon, Stick's friends said they wouldn't mind going.

Sticks seemed a bit uncomfortable with the idea but silently acquiesced. I decided that if I were going to be in this place for a year, I could just as well get out into it a little and bump elbows with the locals.

We went back to the hootch where Sticks and his friends were staying during their R & R. I had brought only civilian clothes along, but Sticks and the others donned their uniforms. Two of the men even slung their M-16s over their shoulders. We found our ride, boarded the back of the truck and bounced off toward Cu Chi.

Some days in Vietnam were like a holiday. It was as if we had caught a flight to a paradise island and were touring the exotic sights. Shopping in the primitive village. Bargaining with the friendly natives. We strolled the main street of Cu Chi, a dirt path lined with merchants. Smiling mama and papasans beckoned us to view their wares. Children ran up to us with wooden artifacts, grabbing our hands and drawing us toward their parents.

Each shop, or spot, (there were no structures other than the grass umbrellas which shaded the merchants from the sun), had only a few items, but no two items were exactly the same, and the artistry was striking. Intricately carved wooden plates and lightly woven mats and baskets.

I picked up a wooden statue of a Vietnamese fisherman, complete with pole and dangling fish. It showed the Vietnamese people the way I wanted to think of them, rather than as an enemy not to be trusted at any cost.

"How much?" I said to mamasan, pointing at the statue.

"Ten dollar," she said, picking up the statue and

~1968~

pressing it toward me.

The price seemed more than fair to me, and I was anxious to avoid bargaining with my total helplessness in her language. I drew ten dollars of military payment currency from my wallet.

"No, no," mamasan shouted. "GI have dollar?"

I had no American currency, but only the military's version that resembled Monopoly money. Embarrassed, I floundered on with my pigeon English. "No have dollars. Only have MPC. You take MPC?"

"No dollar?" she repeated, pulling the statue back.

"No dollar."

"Twenty dollar MPC," she said, re-offering the statue.

I understood the reason for her raising the price. I had heard that the black market for American dollars was rampant. She could make a good profit with dollars. The MPC she could only spend in the military camp if she worked there, which she likely did. I had also heard that striking a bargain was part of the culture.

"Fifteen MPC," I offered.

After a momentary look of hurt, she smiled a toothless grin. "O.K. GI. Fifteen." It was a good sale. We both were happy. She handed over the statue which I tucked carefully into my pocket.

We moved down the street in search of lunch. At the next spot sat a beautiful, young girl with what looked to be her grandmother, but was probably her mother. Both were dressed in the attire which virtually all country women wore. The black, silk, loosely fitting pajama pants. The coned straw hat. The white au dai, an overgown which fitted like a tight blouse at the top, but extended in a front and back panel to nearly her ankles.

~Boomer~

I always wondered how they did laundry, for those gowns were always a brighter, cleaner white than ever Mrs. So-and-so achieved with her Clorox on American TV.

The girl must have been in her teens. Her dark-skinned face with its high cheek bones was lit by a shy smile of brilliant teeth. The glossy black hair narrowed her face and fell to her tiny waist. She sat with her hands folded in the lap of her trim body.

It was not hard to see why GIs were overwhelmed with desire for them. I fought that sense and wished that somehow I could make a simple, friendly connection with this glowing person.

Next to her was mamasan, chattering happily. She looked ninety, but was probably not yet fifty. Diet, work and war had etched two years into her face for each one lived. She had the same vibrant smile as her daughter, but it was all but toothless. Her wrinkled hands held out fruit to us. It looked delicious. Mysterious yellow and green and red shapes filled baskets before us.

"You like?" mamasan said. She held out a prickly red ball to us. I held back, so she took a bite from the fruit. Bright red juice streamed down her chin. She cackled and wiped it with her hand.

Her daughter giggled with her and held another out toward me. I later wondered if it was this that gave me the incredible case of diarrhea I had the following week, or if it was the events of the rest of the day. But I couldn't resist the smile of that beautiful girl.

Near the middle of the village I noticed that Sticks was not enjoying our walk. He wouldn't approach any of the Vietnamese merchants, but kept as close to the middle of the path as he could. He had an agitated, uncomfortable look on his face. I walked back to see if I could get him something to eat.

"No. I'll eat back at camp. I shouldn't have come here, Boomer. This wasn't a good idea." He brought his hand up to his mouth, and it was shaking badly.

"Are you all right?" He didn't respond. "Let's go over in the shade and sit for a bit. We've been out in the sun too long." I led him off the main path of the village to a tiny grove of banana palms beside a hut.

The other men continued on through the village. We sat on a mound of dirt beneath one of the trees. Sticks was fighting for air, as if he had just finished a long run. We sat in silence, and gradually he seemed to relax, his breathing returning somewhat to normal.

"O.K.?" I asked. He nodded that he was. "What happened out there?"

"I don't know," he said in a way that made me sure he did. His eyes took on that glazed, far-away look again. "It's just so much shit." It occurred to me that this was the first time I had ever heard Sticks swear. Even in high school, where swearing was a rite of passage, he had resisted. I waited silently as he seemed to be carefully sorting what he wanted to say.

"I've been in a lot of villages like this in the past weeks. Some of them weren't as friendly as they look though. In Cambodia they all looked beautiful and gentle, but some of them weren't. Or maybe they were. I couldn't tell." He put his face in his hands. Again I sat helplessly witnessing this tortured display of emotions I wouldn't have believed were inside my friend.

"One night last week we were out on patrol. We thought we had found Charlie, and we thought we could surprise him. We crept our way right into another ambush. There weren't very many, but by the time we could return fire, they had picked off three of us. They were all out front of us, so we just opened fire. We blasted every square inch, down on the ground, up in the trees. How anything survived it, I'll never know. But they did, and in the light of our flares we saw two or three of them retreat into the village just down the hill from our position." Sticks paused in his story. I just looked at him. I couldn't believe that someone I knew so well could have gone through what he had experienced.

"Some of us stayed on the hill and tried to piece together the wounded. Sergeant Dolby took a patrol and headed into the village. They didn't receive any fire heading in. It was quiet down there for a long time. And then we started hearing short burst of fire. And then some of the huts started going up in flames. More shots. More burning straw huts. Before long it looked like the whole place was on fire." Sticks stared off toward the main street of Cu Chi. By the look on his face, I could tell that he was still seeing this place aflame.

"All of our men came out of that village alive. When I asked Sergeant Dolby what had happened, he just said, 'Fuckin' gooks will think twice before they hide Charlie again.' Then we packed up our three body bags, hauled them back to the LZ and flew back to the fire base."

I was too stunned to say anything. Sticks hugged his knees and started to rock back and forth.

"Afterward I had to write up my report on the patrol. I went to Dolby and asked him what I should put down happened after the ambush. He said, 'Nothin happened. We got ambushed and lost three good men. We returned fire but are not sure if we inflicted any casualties. We returned to the

~1968~

firebase. End of report.'

"I said, 'What about the village?'

"He said, 'There wasn't any village. I don't remember any village, and neither do any of my men.'"

"God, Sticks. What did you do?"

"Dolby's not a bad man, Boomer. I don't like what happened out there, but I don't blame Dolby. It's different in the bush. Nothing makes any sense. None of the rules apply." He started to rock back and forth again.

"I try to forget the village too. But I can't. I wasn't even there, but if I go to sleep at night, I see it as clearly as if I had been. Each time I dream it gets clearer and more awful. I think it will drive me crazy."

"We've got to get you some help, Sticks. When we get back on base, we'll find somebody. I've gotten to know the Division Catholic Chaplain a bit, Father Parsinon. He could help us get to the right place. We'll go to him as soon as we get back."

"I'm afraid if I talk to anyone I'll spill my guts about that village, and I can't do that. I can't get Dolby in trouble or our men. He was just doing what he had to do. Besides, I don't even really know what happened. If I started talking, I'd just be telling them my nightmares. I don't know what really happened."

"It's all right, Sticks. You don't have to tell them everything. But you need to talk with somebody. You need to get some help. You can't go on feeling like you do now. We'll get you back to camp and decide what to do there."

I got up and helped him to his feet. We walked back into the center of the village and spotted the other men up the path having something more to eat. I told them that I thought we should get back to the base. One look at Sticks and they knew he wasn't doing well. They finished their food quickly and followed us as we moved toward the edge of the village.

Just as we exited Cu Chi, we came across a group of ARVN, Vietnamese soldiers, lounging by the side the road. One of them looked to be about twelve. With an M-16 slung over his shoulder, he looked like a kid who had been very well costumed by his parents and sent out for an afternoon of playing war.

Past the soldiers was a line of bundles. I got almost up to them before I realized what they were. They were bodies. I hadn't immediately recognized them because they were incredibly mutilated. Several had no heads, and limbs had been severed and slashed. They were naked but covered with mud.

I think that I would have thrown up, but my body seemed to entirely shut down. I couldn't move. I couldn't turn my eyes away. I even counted them. Ten bodies. The young soldier, sensing my reaction, laughed. He prodded the end body with the barrel of his M-16.

I heard Sticks groan behind me, and the sound released me from my trance. I grabbed him by the arm and quickly walked him past the spectacle and down the road.

When we had walked a way beyond the village, Stick's friend, Woody, said from behind us, "You all right up there?"

I wasn't sure we were, but answered, "Yeah, we're O.K. Who were those bodies?"

Woody said, "Viet Cong. That's Charlie, the enemy."

"But how awful! They were cut to pieces."

Sticks, who had been walking along in a seeming trance, was following our conversation.

He said, "Some Vietnamese believe that in the

afterlife you have the same body that you leave the earth with. By chopping up their enemies, they are punishing them for eternity." After a few more steps he added, "I wonder if you have the same mind in the afterlife, the same dreams? Maybe that's what hell is."

"Naw," said one of the other men behind us. "Hell is in Cambodia. We already been there." We walked along in silence.

About half way back to the camp we passed an open field, which judging from the smell and the mess, was a village garbage dump.

"God, look at the size of that rat," Woody said. We all peered out into the trash heap, where about twenty yards away a rat the size of a small dog was nosing its way through the garbage.

Suddenly a single gunshot popped from just behind and to the left of me. I jumped and turned toward the sound. One of Sticks' men had raised his M-16 and taken a shot at the rat. He fired a second shot which kicked up a spirt of dust just behind the rodent. The confused animal started moving more quickly, but in our direction.

"I wouldn't do that," said Woody. "You don't know what the hell's out there."

The warning was no sooner given than the other man unloaded a fusillade of automatic fire. One or more of the shells hit the rat, stopping it in its tracks. At the same moment there was a ping and something popped from the ground.

Instantly, I heard Woody's voice scream, "Mine!"

Why I reacted so quickly, I'll never know. I had no combat experience. The instant the word was out of Woody's mouth, I hurled myself flat into the shallow ditch between the road and the garbage field.

The explosion that followed shook the ground violently. The sound stayed in my ears long after the concussion passed. Someone behind me was screaming and swearing.

I lay still for a moment, stunned. I felt a sharp pain in my side and reached down to see if I had been hit by flying metal. I knew exactly what had happened. I had paid enough attention to training films to recognize "Bouncing Betty," a land mine that bounces into the air and explodes at waist height, sending a field of shrapnel in all directions.

I discovered that my wound had been inflicted by the wooden Vietnamese fisherman I had purchased in the village. My tumble to the ground had decapitated him and wedged his fishing pole about an inch into my abdomen. The screaming and swearing continued behind me.

I raised to my knees and pulled the wooden sliver from my side. The man who had fired the weapon was sitting on the road, writhing and yelling. One of the other men had rushed to his side. I could see a bloody patch forming on the back of this man's shirt. The man who was screaming was bleeding badly from his face and arms.

I looked to the left and found Woody bent over a prone Sticks. I scrambled to my feet and raced back to them.

I looked down over Woody's shoulder and screamed, "No!"

Sticks' face had been nearly torn off by the blast. His throat had been slit and his uniform slashed from the waist up. I sank to my knees beside the Sergeant. It was obvious to both of us that there was nothing to be done. Nearly all of Sticks' blood was already seeping into the dirt that surrounded him.

~1968~

He had evidently been standing upright when the blast had reached him. It flashed through my mind that the same blast had slashed inches above my back. I would later have periods of enormous guilt that I had gone down so quickly and left my friend unprotected. Of course, had I paused for an instant, I would have shared his fate.

*****

Of all the mistakes that were made in Vietnam, this one seems to me the greatest. I've never been able to understand how we could have let Sticks get away from us. It's like one of those accidents where you hear about a child getting caught in a piece of farm machinery.

You say, "How could they have let him get that close to something that dangerous?"

Sticks was so kind and gentle. How could we have placed him in a situation so cruel and careless?

Sticks was going to make the world a better place. In his own soft way, he was going to touch people wherever he went. He was going to coach kids in baseball. He was going to be someone's most trusted employee. He was going to be the model father and husband. And we let him get too close to the machinery and it chewed him up.

The rest of that day has taken on a surreal quality for me. I remember every single moment in minute detail, but I remember it with a sensation of looking on from the outside, not as having been there at all.

I sometimes wish that some piece of shrapnel had grazed me on the way by, to remind me of the part I did and didn't play that day. But other times I think that the sense of detachment from those events is the only thing that kept them from driving me crazy. Or maybe they have driven me crazy.

A jeep pulled up along the roadside. The driver immediately got on his radio, and within minutes a chopper was landing on the road near us. The soldier who had fired his rifle was placed into the bubble on one side of the helicopter. Sticks body was slipped into a plastic bag and carried to the bubble on the other side. His only role now was to serve as ballast and balance against the weight of the other wounded man.

Woody and I and the other soldier who was not badly wounded scrambled into the chopper with the medics, and we immediately lifted off. Thump-thump-thump-thump.

It is the sound which epitomizes Vietnam for me, and I suspect for most who were there. That thump-thump-thump-thump of a helicopter. Even today, if I am out walking and the Channel five news helicopter unexpectedly flies over, I am instantly transported to Southeast Asia. It is such an unmistakable sound, and it was pulsed into me every day I spent in Vietnam.

Generally, when I flew in helicopters, I sat in a small indentation on the side of the chopper next to the door gunner. The first time I had done this, it had scared the hell out of me. The gunner perched behind his 60-caliber machine-gun, which gave him something solid to hold on to. As we went airborne, however, I quickly noticed that I had nothing in front of me.

Somewhat panicky, I shouted to the door gunner, "Isn't there supposed to be a strap or something to keep me in?"

"Don't worry," he yelled. "You won't fall out. Centripetal force."

I desperately tried to recall my high school physics knowledge to reassure myself. I thought I remembered that centripetal force kept the earth from flying off into space, but wasn't sure how that meant I wasn't going to fall out of this helicopter.

"Oh, well," I reasoned. "If we fly nice and straight, maybe whatever force is supposed to keep me seated won't be tested."

No such luck. Thirty seconds into our flight we banked hard to the left, and I found myself on my back, staring at nothing but blue sky. In another fifteen seconds we banked equally hard to the right. I grabbed the barrel of the machine-gun as I looked straight down into treetops. The door gunner gave out a hearty laugh.

"Is he trying to dump me out?" I screamed.

"We follow the river." He pointed downward. "That way we are less likely to get shot at by a sniper." But by this time we were looking up into the sky again.

"Oh, great. Either we get shot out of the sky, or I plunge to my death." On our next bank downward, I looked ahead at the river. I groaned. There was not a single straight stretch for as far as I could see. I made a mental note to throw up when we were banking right and not left.

I learned to love the door gunner's cubby hole. Over the initial fear of falling, I thrilled to every dip and turn. It was like a carnival ride that had left its framework and operator behind. We skimmed across treetops, circled over villages, and chased rivers and streams. From the air the Vietnam landscape was beautiful. From the sky it seemed to me a land of peace and glory.

But for others, it was from the sky that the war was waged. Some nights, while on guard duty, I would watch Cobra gun ships on attack missions someplace in the distance. Three or four of them would circle an area far enough from me that I could not hear the thump-thump-thump-thump. Pink and white tracers danced in swirling arcs. Rockets, like reverse roman candles, streaked from air to ground. Below them the earth glowed a radiant red.

It was a beautiful vision, unless you realized that ten miles away a village or forest or field was being shredded to bits by the horrific force of exploding metal and flaming heat.

Our ride to Cu Chi that day was a short one. We scarcely were in the air before we started back down, aiming for one of the red crosses outside the base hospital. As we landed, another chopper landed on the pad next to ours. The medics jumped from both aircraft and scrambled to transport their patients quickly inside.

The chopper next to us had brought in a young Vietnamese woman who was about to give birth. She cried out in pain as she was lifted onto a stretcher and rushed into the hospital for delivery.

Our wounded man was also slung onto a stretcher. Woody and the other injured man followed along and disappeared through swinging doors.

The pilot and copilot opened the bubble over Sticks. They lifted the bag out and set it to the side of the helicopter pads. I was grateful that they set it down gently, as if it somehow mattered. The pilot ran over to a ground mechanic nearby. He pointed to Sticks' body and shouted something that I couldn't hear above the din of the whirling blades. Then he and his partner re-boarded their chopper and lifted off.

Thump-thump-thump-thump. The beat pounded in my ears. Helicopters were the pulsing hearts of the Vietnam War. At times they brought life and at times they brought death, and on this afternoon I had seen them bring both.

~1968~

Thump-thump-thump-thump. I can close my eyes at any time and in any place and bring the sound clearly into my head. And with the sound comes the picture of me, weeping over the plastic bag containing the lifeless body of my friend. As I stood there in tears, a surprising phrase came out of my mouth.

"It don't mean nothing, Sticks."

It was more an automatic response than something I really thought. It was a phrase that we GIs used constantly to explain all of the absurd and unexplainable events of the war. We said it to cool our anger at a stupid order from an officer. We said it to explain a falsified body count that we knew was an inaccurate summary of a battle. We even used it to ease the pain of losing a comrade. It don't mean nothing. We said it about things that really didn't mean much of anything, but we also said it about monumental things that would mean something to us for the rest of our lives.

But sadly, when I look back on the Vietnam War, perhaps no phrase so aptly evaluates it as, "It don't mean nothing, man."

*****

After Sticks' death, the rest of my stay in Vietnam was fairly miserable.

I didn't go to the memorial service that was held on base for him. I didn't know who to blame for Sticks' death, so simply blamed the army; I had no desire to hear a bunch of officers who didn't even know him saying what a great soldier he was and how his country treasured his sacrifice.

I was still in Vietnam, so couldn't attend his funeral in Chandler. I wish I had been there. Perhaps something happened there that would have filled the gap left by Sticks' death.

~Boomer~

I later conned a clerk at Division Headquarters and got a look at the letter that was sent to Sticks' parents. As I suspected, it told nothing of how Sticks really died. It praised his valor in the field and even contained a quotation from someone in Stick's platoon thanking Sticks for saving his life. I felt at least that part was honest.

Soon after Stick's death, those few friends I had made in Vietnam left. Mac was last to leave. These men had greeted me warmly and become good substitutes for the friends I had lost just before leaving home. Like my friend Tuck before, when they left, it was final. I have never heard from or contacted them since.

Their replacements weren't the same. They were angry, selfish boys who didn't seem to need me in the same way that I had needed support upon my arrival. I never grew attached to them, and, in fact, I can recall none of their names or faces.

I turned inward. I read voraciously. But sometimes while I sat with a book, I would stop reading and just stare at the page. And during those times, I thought about my life. I decided that the past wasn't where I could or probably even wanted to go. The death of Sticks had further severed my tie to Chandler. Whenever I thought about my past, it eventually led me to Sticks and that was literally a dead end. As I pondered leaving the army, I felt entirely lost. I wanted to think of neither my past nor my future.

*****

I remember the morning I left Vietnam. In the end, I had actually been given a choice. I could have extended my stay in Vietnam by a month and then been entirely done with the army. If I left at the end of my year, I would have several months of duty to serve in the states.

~1968~

For a long time I waffled on the decision. What was an extra month? I had survived twelve and didn't relish the idea of playing stateside soldier at Ft. Whatever. But I had witnessed many who had extended their duty in Vietnam. Their last days and nights were hell. The idea that they could have been gone haunted them. They became paranoid. They became peevish. They became drunken. They counted the minutes.

Also, if I extended for that extra month, I would celebrate another Tet in Vietnam. I decided that I would prefer the rockets of Time Square, viewed peacefully on TV, to the real live ones of Cu Chi.

And so after 365 days, I sat in the back of a deuce-and-a-half waiting to leave Cu Chi. I thought to myself, "Of all the places I may visit in my lifetime, this is certainly the one I will never see again." With that in mind, I tried to look at everything really hard, and suddenly after wanting this day to come for so long, a certain sadness washed over me.

As we drove through the main gate, we met the Vietnamese women coming from Cu Chi village for their day's work. I would miss these smiling, industrious people. I regretted not getting to know them better, not getting to know more of their language. I waved and wished them well. Most of all, I wished them peace.

In a mile or two we came across the point in the road where Sticks had died. We were still driving slowly because of the stream of natives headed toward the base. I stared at the spot in the road where Woody had bent over Sticks.

There were so many things that we could have done differently that day to steer us away from that spot. But what if we had? What would have been in store for Sticks beyond this point? Would he have simply been saved to be destroyed by another senseless moment somewhere in the jungles of Cambodia? It was pointless speculation. I put it aside.

Spirits were high when I took my seat on the plane at Tan Son Nhut Airport just outside of Saigon. "Freedom Birds" we had always called them, and I boarded one with a group of men who instantly bonded. We were leaving Vietnam together. The uniform of the smiling stewardess who greeted us was covered with service medals. Men gladly gave up their purple hearts for a kiss on the cheek.

I expected this to be a rowdy flight home. We rolled down the runway, and at liftoff a rousing cheer seemed to catapult us forward.

But after a few moments of backslapping and handshaking, a strange silence filled the plane. The men had momentarily shared their joy, but then quickly drawn back into themselves. Later, when I went back toward the toilet, I looked at the faces along the aisle. They were quiet faces, some of them tear-stained faces. I couldn't tell if they were on men looking forward or backward, but they were looking somewhere, and for the moment, at peace doing so.

No one was sleeping and no one was talking. I took my seat and joined their contemplation. As we re-crossed the International Date Line, we regained those hours we had lost on the way over. I wondered if it was a blessing to have extra hours. What lay ahead of us in the aftermath of Vietnam? For which of us would this truly be a freedom bird and for which would it merely push us forward into a new kind of prison.

*****

1969, Summer

My return to "the World" might have been better had I been able to walk off the freedom plane and into civilian life. At Fort Dix New Jersey I spent most of my time nurturing my anger toward the military for wasting two years of my life pursuing a cause in Southeast Asia that now, more than ever, seemed to me without a purpose.

And at the core of that waste and my anger was the death of Sticks. On one hand, because it had happened half way round the world, it seemed like it hadn't happened at all. Yet Sticks was on my mind every waking hour. Every soldier in olive drab had Stick's face. In the dark my anguish turned to nightmares, except now the bloody soldier in my arms didn't have Sticks face. It was Denny Fritz. I felt myself going mad. It got so bad that I was afraid to sleep.

Both college and the military had given me great training in how to handle, or mishandle, any negative emotion: Fear, boredom, anxiety. A little pot always did the trick for me. Once again it became my way to relax, to smile, to sleep.

Out of the army, I returned to Chandler. I moved in with my parents and learned that procuring drugs in a small town was easier than in the big city or on a college campus.

The town seemed wounded to me, as if it had lost a limb in the war. Nothing felt familiar. My group of friends was no longer there to comfort and sustain me. Fud was still living in Minnesota, but far away from Chandler. Gracie had disappeared to the Twin Cities. Her mother still lived in town, but somehow Grace had finally made the break and flown. I didn't press anyone for the details.

Pastor Jim Bob still lived in Chandler and worked at

~Boomer~

the local bank. We tried to go out several times, and while the occasions were warm, without the others, a kind of discomfort hung over us, and our outings became infrequent. I became aware that we had little in common, that his friendship was important to me in the context of our group of five, but that without the others, Pastor Jim Bob would probably not have ever been such a close friend. Or maybe I had just changed, so that I didn't recognize his friendship.

Mostly it was the absence of Sticks that soured Chandler. It was like a huge black hole in the middle of Main Street. I avoided driving by his house. I couldn't visit his parents. He was the ghost that rode with me as I cruised the streets alone.

The townspeople were mostly uncomfortable with me. A small town respect for veterans of any ilk kept them from spitting on me, as was happening to other vets in other places throughout the country.

A kind of aura was growing up around Vietnam Veterans. The war had obviously done something strange to us. No one was quite sure in what awful atrocities we might have taken part.

I did nothing to dispel the image, letting my hair grow to my shoulders and remaining cool and aloof. Sticks became a symbol of patriotism, a local hero who gave his life for country. I was an awkward reminder of an uncomfortable war that had been mishandled and had turned ugly.

Things were even more uncomfortable at home. My parents simply didn't know what to make of me. I was sour and detached much of the time. My father tried to be proud of my service, but when I met his pride with scorn, our common military service became a point of conflict rather than unity. Our separation that had begun in my college years only widened.

My mother desperately tried to slip back into mother mode. She seemed sure that whatever my condition, she could feed me out of it. She also believed that Vietnam should be placed firmly behind me, and that I should get on with life. If my father asked questions about my experience, she promptly changed the subject or left the room. I much preferred her approach, but it also hurt me a little that she didn't seem to want to know what the last two years had done to me. She just wanted to get her old son back and have him be happy.

I tried several jobs around town. The city street department. The Coast to Coast store. People were willing to give me a chance, but when I became dissatisfied for one reason or another, I alienated them by quitting. My reputation as having changed gradually mutated into being shiftless. My father never offered me a job at the gas station. We both knew that would be a disaster.

The only potentially positive development was a relationship with Deanna Westbrook. Deanna's father farmed to the west of Chandler. She had graduated in the high school class after me. Her mother had died of cancer in her junior year, and Deanna had slipped smoothly in as substitute, feeding and caring for her father and two brothers who worked with him.

In a desperate search for something to do around Chandler, I asked Deanna out, and whatever our eventual incompatibilities turned out to be, our immediate need for companionship and/or sex squelched them. Within two months I had asked her to marry me.

My parents received Deanna as a savior. Whatever scars college and the army had left, they prayed that marriage would erase. And at first we really did give them reason for hope. We made an attractive couple. I even cropped my hair for the wedding, which was very small. Just a few family members from each side stood with us in Deanna's tiny, country church.

Later, when we spent evenings with my parents playing cards, we really did appear a happy group. Never was a daughter-in-law received with more open arms.

Things went downhill quickly after the wedding. I became more and more restless in Chandler. The most logical places for me to find employment were with my father or her father, and I refused to consider either. Deanna's allegiance to her father was strong, and it seemed to me that she was spending as much time husbanding him as me.

Finally, I insisted on leaving Chandler and returning to Madison, where I thought I would have a better chance finding a job. Deanna was miserable there without any family or friends. We moved into a tiny apartment, and both set out to find jobs, she being the more successful, finding work at a garden center on the outskirts of Madison. By the end of eight months there, we had begun to hate each other.

I knew that the wreckage was my fault, and I knew that Deanna didn't deserve her unhappiness, so I simply gave up on us. Deanna moved back to Chandler with her family, and I stayed in Madison away from mine.

My parents refused to believe that there wasn't something that I could do to hold us together. They had accepted Deanna as their daughter, and my father blamed me for turning her away.

For them, marriage was a permanent state. The idea of separating would have been as foreign as the idea of moving to China. When I divorced my wife, it was as if I divorced my father as well. Any visits I paid to them in the months after, ended in anger for my father and pain for my mother.

Finally, to save us all, I moved to California, resolved never to set foot in Chandler again.

*****

For twelve years I pretty much kept that resolve, having little contact with my mother and less with my father. My sister, Elizabeth, was heartsick at our separation, and got me information about my parents whether or not I asked. She enticed me back to Minnesota for the graduation of her oldest son. Even that time I avoided my father almost entirely.

In Los Angeles my life became more and more settled. My earlier interest in architecture renewed, and I landed a job with a growing firm. It was run by two brothers who were in the process of taking over the company from their aging father.

The Sherson brothers, both veterans of Vietnam, helped me finish my college degree and get training that allowed me to slip right into a useful role in the firm. I finally hit a stride, and worked very hard to make up for the wasted time I had spent in the last several years. I bought a nice, if over-priced, house, where if I lean far enough to the right on my deck, I can see the ocean. I started to feel like a Californian, and pushed the Midwest further and further from my mind. That might have been the end of it, had not two events transpired to bring me back.

Chapter 6

War Without End

1983

It was the year of my 20th high school class reunion. I had gotten the invitation and filed it away in a pile of interesting, but not to be acted upon, papers. I had never gone back for a reunion and had no intention of going back for this one. There were still people around Chandler about whom I was curious, but things that had happened to me since high school snuffed that curiosity.

A few days prior to the reunion, I got a call from Fud. He was my only remaining link to my high school class, and that was not a strong link. We still sent one another birthday cards, which also served to announce any new events in our lives. For many years Fud's address had remained the same, as had his job as civil engineer. After completing college and graduate school, he had settled in Rochester, on the far side of the state from Chandler. Hearing his voice sent waves of conflicting emotions through me. My hand holding the receiver was visibly shaking.

"God, Fud. It's great to hear from you. What, are you calling to arm-twist me into coming back for our class reunion? Think it's time for me to put in my first reappearance, do you?" I was flustered and struggling for

~1983~

things to say, and the reunion was the first to pop into my head.

"It's been cancelled, Boomer. I'm calling some of the classmates to let them know."

The tension in his voice should have told me that whatever was behind this cancellation was not a happy thing. But I had not yet recovered from the surprise of hearing his voice and I blurted out, "What, did somebody die?"

A sound, something between a gasp and a laugh came over the line. Then there was a pause. "Boomer, the reunion isn't the real reason I called. Something bad has happened back here. In fact, somebody did die. Jim Roberts."

"My God, Fud. Has he been sick?" I had heard almost nothing about Pastor Jim Bob for a decade.

"No, he wasn't ill. Boomer, someone shot him." Fud's voice shuddered on this last phrase.

"What! Shot him? What are you saying?"

"I'm saying that someone shot Jim." The anger in Fud's voice stopped me. He was obviously on the edge. A dozen questions sprang into my head and I fumbled for the right ones.

"Fud, do they know who did it? Was it an accident?" It had to be an accident. No one would intentionally kill the gentle Jim Bob.

"It was a classmate of ours, Boomer. Harland Herne. It had to do with Jim's work at the bank. Harland was losing his family's farm, and Jim was the one who had to tell him. Listen, Boomer, I can't talk about this right now." He sniffled and took a deep breath. "The funeral is this Friday, Boomer. I'd like you to be there."

"Of course I'll be there, Fud." I said it automatically without really deciding that I would be there. My thoughts spun out of control. The rest of our conversation was a blur, with me unable to bring words to the questions that later flooded my mind.

Late into the night I tossed in my bed, playing our conversation over and over in my head.

Next, I recreated my old friend Jim Bob, his bouts of harmless mischief, his vulnerable sensitivity. No quality he possessed could possibly have induced anyone to shoot him.

I pondered Harland Herne as killer. That even made less sense. Harland had been a pleasant, shy farm boy. His involvement in school was secondary to his father's need for help on the farm. It was pretty much understood that the farm was where he would stay after high school. The only interruption to that plan was Vietnam. Harland was drafted and served his two years nearly the same time as I did. I didn't really know anything about his experience there.

I began to realize that I didn't know much of anything about anyone from Chandler, whether they were close friend or slight acquaintance. How badly I had neglected my past. A friend of mine had died, and I hadn't a clue as to how deeply I should mourn. Had Jim Bob died in high school, it would have devastated me. Shouldn't it still? I felt so far away from it, almost like a stranger had died. What did it really have to do with me?

But Fud's voice and his anguish kept coming back into my head. "Boomer, I'd really like you to be there." It wasn't a lot to ask, to say goodbye to a past friend.

And while doing that, perhaps there were others to whom I needed say hello. The last years had tempered my anger with my father, and I still considered Fud a friend. And then there was my mother. I suddenly felt a mountain of guilt for the way I had pushed my mother out of my life.

~1983~

Perhaps it was time for me to re-enter their lives. The next morning I called the airline to make a reservation.

*****

I telephoned my sister, Elizabeth, and announced I was coming to Minnesota.

"Oh, I'm so sorry about James, Gene. Will you stay with us? We have a bedroom just waiting for you. We just lost Brian to the University and his room is crying out for an occupant."

"Thanks, Elizabeth. To be honest, I was really hoping for that invitation. I'll be going to Chandler for the funeral, and it would be really convenient to go back and forth from your place. Anyway, it would be nice to spend some time with you and Ray."

There was a pause and a sniffle. "Thank you for saying that, Gene. It would be really nice. Some of us have missed having you around here a whole lot."

I wasn't quite sure who she was including in her "some of us," but I suspected from our past conversations that she was referring to our parents, at least my mother.

"Elizabeth, could you not tell the folks that I'm coming. I haven't called them because I really don't want to stay there, and I don't want to refuse an invitation from Mom. I haven't worked out yet when and how I will see them, so please just let it go."

"You're not thinking of slipping in and out of town without seeing them, are you Gene?"

"No, it's not that. I'll see them. I just haven't worked out how and when. Have you seen them lately?"

"Of course. I see them every week. They're fine. Mother is as busy as ever keeping the church running, and Dad has coffee every morning with his old cronies. Oh, last week he pulled out into an intersection without looking and the police car that was turning the corner scraped across the front end of his pickup. Do you believe that? The police car." Elizabeth's laugh told me that it wasn't serious.

"Was he all right?" I asked anyway.

"Yes, he was fine. He claimed that the policeman hadn't signaled and he thought he was going straight. The only thing that upset him was that the policeman issued him a ticket. 'First one in sixty years of driving.' Can't you just hear him?"

"Is he having eye troubles or something? Should he still be driving?"

"Oh, he's fine. He just wasn't paying attention. Half the drivers in Chandler are the same way. These old duffers wandering around the streets. It's like riding in the bumper cars at an amusement park."

It felt so good to be sharing a laugh with my older sister. I was thinking that I wanted to keep her on the line as long as I could, when she said, "Listen Gene, I have to pick up Ray at the gas station. I'm really glad you are coming. Save some time for us, will you. It seems like forever since we talked."

"It does, doesn't it. Thanks for the invitation, Elizabeth. I'll call you when I get to Minneapolis. Let you know what my plans are. Say 'hi' to Ray."

"I will. You have a safe trip, Gene. We'll see you soon."

The rest of the week was spent tying loose ends together at work so that I could be gone.

In the midst of my rushing around I would suddenly get a flash from the past and think about what lay ahead in Chandler. Seeing Fud would be wonderful, and I was

~1983~

surprised by how strongly I anticipated seeing Elizabeth. Over the years I had gotten used to being away from family, and the thought of being with her gave me a warm rush.

The prospect of seeing my parents brought me a confused but even stronger reaction. When I thought about it, I actually began to shake. Guilt, excitement, anger. My emotions were on such a roller coaster I couldn't imagine what it would be like when I actually saw them. I decided the best emotion to get me prepared was hope, so I crossed my fingers and said a prayer that going home turned out to be a joy.

My first flight out of LAX was cancelled because of a mechanical, which set me several hours off my plan. When I landed, I called Elizabeth to tell her I was in, but that I was running late and would be driving directly to Chandler for a reunion with Fud. She said that the door would be open and the bed in my room turned back.

"Be noisy on the way in," she said. "I'll get up to greet you."

A three-hour drive from Minneapolis brought me to Chandler at 6:30 P.M., just when I told Fud I would meet him at the bar of the golf club.

Along the way I contemplated how I should work a visit to my parents. After a lot of meandering, I decided that I should have called them from California and kicked myself for procrastinating. From there I swung entirely to the opposite extreme and decided I would just show up and surprise them, hoping that it would be a happy event and that they wouldn't slam the door in my face. By the time I reached the Chandler city limits, I had considered every option and settled on none.

As I entered the drive to the golf club, I wondered

who of my old acquaintances besides Fud might be there. Probably many had made plans to visit for the reunion and had just come on regardless of the cancellation. Others, no doubt, would be in town to attend the funeral.

Whenever the class of '63 had other reunions, it seemed like I was at an unsettled point in my life that would require continuous, awkward explanations. At least now I had a life for which I wouldn't feel I had to apologize. I found myself hoping that the place would be filled with classmates.

I had been a congenial high school student with no real enemies. I had been athletic enough to run with the athletes, smart enough to think with the bookworms, rebellious enough to occasionally have lunch with the outcasts, and insecure enough to need each, in case I failed with the others. But always, it was that same group of five that really made my world go around.

*****

I pulled up to the club house and parked. As close as I had been to Fud in those early years, I still felt like I was going in to see a stranger. It had been more than fifteen years since I had seen him. In each of our birthday exchanges we said that this should be the year that we got together. And each year that resolve was forgotten two days later. At least on my part.

What would Fud the adult be like, for I hadn't really known him beyond his teens? What would we talk about? Of course we'd talk about Pastor Jim Bob. We'd recall how the Pastor had slapped Mr. Northrup on the ass, thinking it was Fud. We'd talk about how Jim Bob pulled off his shorts while preparing for his high jump at the sixth grade track meet. Maybe we'd talk about Sticks and the hundreds of baskets he had made. Maybe. I had never talked with anyone about Sticks after his death in Vietnam.

So much had changed since Fud and I had been real friends. Would the changes be more important than the things we had retained? It gave me a funny feeling to be headed toward reunion, when I had purposely avoided it for so many years.

I entered the square building that had changed little in forty years and always looked to me more like a bomb shelter than a golf club. Above the door was a sign, Chandler Country Club. Evidently the membership had risen above the status of mere golfers.

The room I walked into was dimly lit and filled with smoke and country music. The bar stools were all filled, and several small groups sat at tables. I thought that I recognized the bartender and was about to walk over to him when a man at a corner table across the room caught my attention with a wave. No one else was expecting me, so it had to be Fud. He had gotten up and was moving toward me with arms extended.

"Boomer, you old shit," he said and grabbed me in a hug.

"Fud. God, it's good to see you, man," I said. It was an automatic response. I hadn't yet decided how good it was to see him.

He held me in that hug, much longer than I would have, had I been controlling it.

"Boomer, Boomer, Boomer," he repeated. He pushed me back but held my arms in a tight squeeze. There were tears in his eyes. The speed and intensity of his emotional outpouring caught me off guard. I tried to quickly take inventory of what I was feeling. It still wasn't clear to me.

"Come on. Let's sit down. We've got a lot of talking to do." He turned and headed back toward his table. He had put on a lot of weight. He had always been a chubby kid, and he had turned into a very large man. I followed and sat down across from him.

"It's too bad that things didn't work out for the reunion," I said, trying to start with a mundane topic.

"With the funeral tomorrow, we just didn't think anyone would feel like celebrating tonight, so we contacted everyone and told them we would hold a reunion next summer instead. It was too late to just change weekends. And you are going to come, by the way."

"Fud, I can't believe that Jim Bob is dead. What happened?"

"What happened when? A lot of water has run under the bridge since you left Chandler, Boomer boy."

"But Jim Bob? How could it happen? There can't be a less likely murder victim on the face of the earth."

"Sometimes circumstances don't wait around for what should have been. What about Sticks? Do you think there was ever a less likely war casualty?"

"Christ, Fud, we're not even forty and there are only three of our fivesome left."

"Do you still think of us as a fivesome? We haven't been together for almost twenty years. And the last time, we didn't exactly separate on the best of terms."

A waitress interrupted us for drink orders. When she walked away, we just sat looking at each other. There were so many memories and so much to be said that it was difficult to find a starting place.

"Did Harland Herne just go nuts or what?"

Fud rubbed the wrinkle between his eyes with his

~1983~

index finger.

"Things have been tough around here these last years, for the farmers. The bank had to foreclose on a lot of loans to good people, and Jim Bob always took it upon himself to be the bearer of bad tidings. Boomer, he called me the night before he got shot. He had put off going to the Herne farm for a day. He was really shaken by what he had to do. He was kind of frantic. It was like he'd had some sort of premonition that things weren't going to go well. I actually told him that maybe he shouldn't go out there alone. God, I should have insisted that he not go alone." Fud raked his fingers through his thinning hair.

"Don't do that, Fud. You couldn't have known."

"People in town say that Harland has never been the same since Vietnam. I guess that he was in some very heavy fighting. Then he had some health problems the last few years. Agent Orange stuff."

"He left Chandler just a couple months before Sticks and me. I guess that I never heard what his story was. God, that war is still going, Fud. It's still with me every night, and if Harland Herne was in the worst of it, it was with him every night too."

"Then his dad got killed about five years ago. Some kind of fall out on the farm. Harland tried to keep things together, but you know that he was never very smart. And these days even some of the smart farmers are going under."

"Is he in jail here?"

"Yes. An hour after he shot Jim Bob he drove into town and turned himself in. Brought in his gun. Christ, he shot Jim with an M-16. How the hell did he still have that? Folks say that he hasn't said five words since."

The waitress brought us our drinks. At this point I

~Boomer~

really felt like I needed mine. In one swallow I downed half and said to her, "Don't stay away too long." She smiled and left us to reminisce.

"I just remember Jim Bob as he was, goofy and harmless. None of this sounds like it could happen to him. You said that he always went to do a foreclosing himself. Wasn't there somebody else at the bank to help him with that ugly job?"

"It's a long story. I think he felt it was a kind of penance."

"Penance? For what?"

"A while back Jim made some bad investments, and to bail himself out he took some money from the bank. Not a lot, and he had actually paid it all back before it was discovered. When it came out, he felt like he had let everybody in Chandler down. He lived his whole life in this town, and now he couldn't look anybody here in the face. Not to mention disappointing Pastor Roberts Senior. You probably remember how sympathetic he was to Jim's errors. Shit, this is all so unfair, Boomer." Fud closed his eyes and took a deep breath. I waited until he relaxed.

"You seem to know a lot about this, Fud. You and Jim Bob have really stayed close, haven't you?"

"If he wasn't my very best friend, Boomer, he was very close, and he was certainly my longest friend. People didn't know Jim very well, Boomer. He was so gentle and funny all the time that everyone seemed to think he was just happy-go-lucky. He felt things a lot more deeply than people realized."

"Things like what?"

"You probably didn't even know this, but he took Sticks' death really hard. Sort of an irrational guilt. He said to me once, 'Sticks was too good to die. He did everything right. He didn't deserve it. It should have been me.'"

Fud was looking down when he said this or he might have noticed my lips start to quiver. "I've got to go to the can, Fud. I'll be right back." I quickly rose and stumbled away from the table.

In the bathroom I turned on the cold water and splashed handfuls of it into my face. I looked at myself in the mirror. I thought, "I certainly understand what Jim Bob felt about Sticks. But he was wrong. I was the one who should have died in Vietnam instead of Sticks." That thought had bothered my sleep for the last two decades. But I had a far better reason to believe it than Jim Bob did. I had never said that to anyone, and I certainly wasn't going to say it to Fud tonight, so I splashed more water into my face and tried to settle myself.

Fud had ordered us another drink and seemed to have settled himself as well. "Come on Boomer, let's talk of happier times." He smiled. "Do you remember when I outran Sticks in the mile?"

I laughed warmly, "Yeah, I kinda remember that. Seems like there was something funny about that race though. Wasn't there?"

"I don't recall that. Just a good honest foot race."

"God, we were really something weren't we."

"I guess you could say that." We sat for a while silently pondering what we had left behind.

"We did everything together. I've never felt that way about anybody since."

"Not even Deanna?"

"No." I blushed at my admission. "Deanna was a mistake from the start. I had survived Vietnam. It seemed like marriage was the next thing to do, and I grabbed the first one who came along. She's a really good person, but we were never very happy."

"She's still in Chandler. Did you know that she remarried?" Elizabeth had told me this news long ago. "She and her husband opened a bakery on Main Street a couple years ago. Jim Bob told me about it. I've never been in the place."

Now thoughts of my failed marriage raced through my head. How different my life might have been. I wondered if I could have been happy living in Chandler as an adult. I had always thought not, even though I had been so happy there as a child.

Deanna had desperately wanted us to stay in Chandler, but I refused. It was a continuous point of tension with us. We could never visit Chandler enough to satisfy her. It was one of the many things that drove us apart.

"When was the last time you were in Chandler, Boomer?"

"I don't know. Five, maybe six years. I came back for my sister's oldest boy's graduation."

"They still live in Shelton?"

"Yeah. We still talk on the phone a lot. We get along pretty well."

"You staying with your folks?"

I laughed. "No, I'm staying with my sister. I didn't tell my folks I was coming. I suppose I'll have to see them sometime. I just haven't figured out how."

"Jeez, Boomer, what happened? You always got along with your folks. I mean, my God, you guys were the All American Family."

"I don't know. It happened kind of gradually. I guess

truthfully it was pretty much my fault. Bombing out of college. The drug stuff. The divorce. It seemed like every time I saw my parents after high school, it was to announce some new disaster in my life. My father never took them very well. He always blamed me and threw my upstanding brother, Dr. Tom, in my face. Every visit ended in a row with him. Finally, I just said screw it. This isn't making anybody happy, and I moved far enough away that he couldn't see me mess up, even if I did. And the funny thing is, that's when I stopped messing up. I'm doing fine in California. I'm working for a good firm, and I'm really liking some of the designs I'm doing. I've just never found a way to come back here and mend the fences."

I took a drink and pondered if it was something I wanted to venture on this trip. "I think it really hurt Mom. She'd never say anything against my dad, but I think maybe she blames him for driving me away. She used to phone quite often. I could tell she would wait until he was out of the house, so she could talk. But I think she has given up on me too. I don't hear from her very often anymore."

I sat there silently staring into my beer glass. I could feel Fud's eyes on me. A mixture of feelings was boiling inside me, and they were much stronger than I had anticipated. I had underestimated how much a part of me this place continued to be.

"You've got to see them, Boomer." Fud spoke softly, with long pauses between each thought. "People change. Give him a chance. Remember how my dad and I fought when I was in high school. He was Mr. Jock, and his chubby son just didn't measure up. I wasn't going to put any trophies beside his on the shelf. I wasn't going to pitch any no-hitters. I hated him for a lot of years."

~Boomer~

"Yeah, I remember you spent a lot of nights at Jim Bob's rather than going home."

"Well you know what, Boomer. I love my father now. We get along just fine. He brags about my accomplishments to friends. He and my mom come to visit me in Rochester all the time. He accepts me for who I am, and that includes some things that are a lot harder for him to understand than that I'm unathletic."

"You mean being gay?"

"Yeah. Who'd think my dad would be more accepting of that than that I couldn't play football?"

"Has it been hard, Fud? " He and I had never talked about it very much. Our time spent together since high school had been short and very occasional. Whenever I was with him, it was always the same old Fud.

"At times. It was in high school, once I realized it and decided to hide it. The group I lived with in college was terrific. They really helped me adjust to it. Once I decided that I didn't care if it bothered anybody else, it all became much easier. Then I discovered that the people who didn't care were the people that I wanted to know anyway. I've got no complaints. I've had a good life."

"Anybody special in your life?"

Fud shook his head. "We've been together for about seven years. He owns a gift shop in Rochester. You'd like him, Boomer. He makes me laugh a lot."

"That's great, Fud. How about your folks? Are they still in Chandler?"

"Sure. You'll see them tomorrow. They'll be at the funeral. My dad and Jim Bob were still good friends. It's funny, them being such different ages. But they just seemed to have a lot of things in common. Hardly a week would go by that Jim Bob didn't have dinner with my folks. He was really good to them, Boomer. That's another reason why this is all so hard."

"I know. I just can't make myself believe this is all happening."

"But let's get back to your dad, Boomer. You've got to give him a chance. Don't go back to California this time hating your dad."

"Yeah, well Fud, you don't know some of the things we've said to each other. He's going to have to stop hating me as well." I started to feel that same pressure in my chest, that difficulty breathing that I had felt the last times I had been in the presence of my father. I took a deep gulp and finished my beer. The pretty waitress quickly replaced it with another.

It seemed like wherever our conversation started, it ended up on a road that I didn't want to take. Again I tried to change the subject.

"Do you ever see Gracie?" I asked.

"I haven't for a long time. She's never come back for reunions either. Her mother still lives in the same house. One time, maybe six, seven years ago she was here visiting and Jim Bob and I ran into her at the gas station. She was on her way back to the cities. I suppose she still lives up there. She was doing some kind of receptionist job back then. She looked the same. Still short hair, and that kiddish grin."

"God, I miss you guys, Fud. It's been fifteen years, but it all seems like yesterday. It just seemed like we'd always be friends."

"Well, that last summer we spent together tarnished that a bit."

"I guess you're right. I just like to remember the good

times."

"It's funny, when you started falling for Gracie, I thought maybe you would end up together." It surprised me the way he tossed off the phrase, "you started falling for Gracie."

"How did you know that I had started to fall for Gracie that summer? I didn't think we were that obvious."

"Are you kidding? You guys hooked up every chance you got that summer. Pastor Jim Bob and I used to speculate on whether or not you would end up married. And then by the end of the summer you were yelling at Gracie and pounding on Sticks, and before I ever found out what happened, you guys were off to Vietnam and Gracie was off to the cities and the four winds would never blow us back together."

"I know. It just got really screwed up at the end. Things just fell apart with Gracie. That is if there was anything to fall apart. Maybe she was never interested. Maybe it was all just in my head. Anyway, when I talked with Sticks in Vietnam, he didn't seem to know anything at all about me and Gracie, and yet you say that you guys talked about it all the time."

"With Pastor Jim Bob. You know as well as I do that Sticks and my eyes didn't see the same things at all that summer. Every time I was near him, it ended in a battle. There's some more guilt for me, that Sticks and I parted enemies, and he never came back for me to say that I was sorry."

"You didn't part enemies. You just didn't agree on things, on the war."

"Well, you and Sticks didn't exactly end that summer as bosom buddies either. I never thought I'd see you two beating on each other the way you did that last night."

"You're not the only one. I don't know. It was just stupid. I was drunk. I got carried away, and I guess I misread Gracie's feelings. It just blew up on us somehow. Anyway, Sticks and I put it behind us in Vietnam. We talked about what happened. It was ok. Anyway, shit, like you said, it didn't matter. He never came back."

I felt myself babbling. This evening was taking twists and turns that I really didn't want to follow. The realities of our little group were starting to interfere with my fond memories.

"What a waste. That fuckin' war." Fud drained what was left of his coke.

"Waste. God, if you only knew." I intended to say this last to myself, but then realized I had said it aloud and looked up to see Fud eying me questioningly. I steered him away. "I was there, Fud. A lot of guys besides Sticks didn't come home."

"Jim Bob told me Sticks' dad really took it hard. He was never the same. At the funeral he looked so angry. No tears. He just stared straight ahead. He hardly even responded to people that spoke to him. Sticks' mom just led him around. I've hardly seen them since."

"They're one of the reasons I wouldn't let Deanna talk me into staying in Chandler after we got married. It really bothered me seeing them around town. I guess that I feel a little bit like Jim Bob did. Why did I get to come back alive when Sticks didn't? That's just one of the many things in my life that I ran from."

I took a long swallow of beer and decided to reveal to Fud something I had told no other person. "I was with Sticks when he died."

~Boomer~

"Oh, Jesus, Boomer. I didn't know that."

"Nobody does. I've never told anyone. I've never even been to see his parents, to talk with them about it." I laughed uncomfortably. "God, I had an amazing amount of baggage with me when I flew to California, didn't I?"

"Well, what are reunions good for if its not dredging up a bit of muck from the past. Anyway, it's not too late to unpack some of that baggage, Boomer. Wouldn't it be nice to fly back this time with a little lighter load?"

"Oh, hell. I don't know. I never think about any of this stuff when I'm out there. If I hadn't come home this weekend, I wouldn't be dragging us through all of this."

"The Boomer I used to know hated loose ends. You were always the one that kept the group on track. As long as you've got some time here this weekend, why don't you try to do some mending. Why don't you go up and see your folks tonight? Mine are expecting me in a little bit.

Good old Fud. Always the man of action. Taking the bull by the horns. I knew that he was going to push this as hard as he could, but I also knew that, as usual, he was exactly right. I had spent the last years building a new life to rationalize escaping the old. But a few hours in the old world was beginning to convince me that it was too much a part of me to be denied. Maybe it was time that I started facing the ghosts of my past.

"You know, Fud, I think I'll start with something other than my folks. Sort of build up to that one. I think I'll go see the Skulskys if they are around tonight. Do you know if they live in their same house down on the highway?"

"As far as I know." Fud took the last swallow of his cola. "You know, Boomer, I'm not sure that is going to be easier than your parents. You're going to open up some old, raw wounds if you see the Skulskys."

"I know. But Fud, they've never known the truth about Sticks, and they deserve to. I'm the only one who can tell it to them. Or will."

"The truth?"

"I've never told anyone what happened to Sticks, and I may be about fifteen years late, but they really should be the first ones to hear my story. If it goes well, I'll tell you tomorrow."

"Fair enough. I'm not looking forward to tomorrow. Saying goodbye to a good, old friend." Fud's eyes started to fill.

"Yeah. I'm afraid it's that kind of weekend. Awkward hellos and painful goodbyes." I stuck my hands out across the table and held his wrist.

*****

What I felt as I drove the highway back into Chandler was not unlike what I had felt one night in 1967 as my plane made its final approach into Bien Hoa, Vietnam. That same uneasiness was with me now, as if I were re-entering dangerous territory.

I followed the curve at the edge of town and pulled up in front of Sticks' house. All of the large trees that used to guard the place from runaway vehicles were now gone and replaced with new ones. New - their size indicated that they had probably been there for fifteen years. Probably planted about 1967, the year Sticks and I had left for Vietnam.

I wondered what life had been like for the Skulskys since Sticks' death. Fud had said that his father had taken the news badly. I wavered in my resolve to visit them, to tell them the truth of Stick's death. Perhaps memories buried that deeply needed to be left alone.

~Boomer~

"I've got to see them," I said aloud. As to whether I would tell them the truth, I would leave that decision until I knew for sure it was the right thing to do. I knocked at their door.

A woman I readily recognized as Mrs. Skulsky opened the door a crack and said, "Yes?" She hadn't changed as much as I would have expected. She looked great.

"Mrs. Skulsky, my name is Gene. I was a high school friend of your son, Kent."

Her mouth flew open, as did the door. "Boomer!" she shouted. "My goodness, it is wonderful to see you. It's been so long. Oh, my manners. I haven't even invited you in." She stepped to the side, and as I squeezed in past her, she grabbed and hugged me.

"Earl," she shouted into the house. "You're not going to believe who's out here. It's Boomer, Kent's good friend. Earl, come out here and say hello." She grabbed my arm and led me toward the living room.

The house had changed very little, and I recognized nearly everything in it from the many days and weeks I had spent there in the distant past.

By the time we passed through the doorway, Mr. Skulsky was up and headed our way. He had changed much more than his wife. He had lost a great deal of weight and looked old in a way that Mrs. Skulsky did not. He smiled and reached out toward me with a friendly handshake.

"Please sit down, Boomer. Could you spend a little time with us?" said Mrs. Skulsky.

"Sure, Mrs. Skulsky. That's why I came by." I went farther into the room and sat in a chair to which Stick's father gestured. They took seats as well, the same seats they had sat in when I used to be in the house years ago.

~1983~

The first thing that I saw when I looked out across the room was a picture of Sticks in his dress military uniform on the table between Mr. and Mrs. Skulsky.

"Oh, Boomer, it is so good to have you here," repeated Mrs. Skulsky. "What are you doing these days? Where are you living?"

"I'm living in L. A. I'm an architect for a small firm out there, Sherson Associates. I'm doing just fine."

"Are you remarried? Have you married again since.... Deanna?" It was clear that once she got into the question, she was uncomfortable and unsure she should have started it.

"No. I've only made that mistake once so far," I laughed. "Maybe someday. Right now I'm all right on my own."

"And what brings you back to Chandler?" she rushed forward. "Oh, of course. Jim Roberts' funeral. What an awful thing. We just can't understand what would make him do such a thing?" This, too, was a subject with which she was uncomfortable.

"Well, where are my manners?" She stood. "Can I get you something to drink, or a cookie to nibble on perhaps?"

"No thanks, Mrs. S. I was just out to the golf club with Fud, and we had a drink out there. I'm fine."

She sat again. "Oh, Fud. It would be good to see him too. You kids were such good friends growing up. Where has the time gone?" She looked to her husband, as if he would surely have the answer.

Mr. Skulsky had not said a word since I entered. Now he simply smiled to his wife and nodded his head. For the first time I noticed something strange and vague in his eyes. I suddenly realized that he didn't know who I was. He

341

continued nodding and smiling, no longer remembering what had started him.

Mrs. Skulsky sensed that I had seen the change. "Earl has his good days and his bad days. Don't you, Earl? Today was a good one, wasn't it? We got along pretty well. Some days are about all we can handle, but at least we have managed to stay in the house so far. Haven't we?" More smiles and nods from Sticks' dad.

I didn't know what to say. I didn't know how much he understood and felt, and I didn't want to say anything that might hurt or upset him, so I dodged.

"Well, you two look really good. I would have recognized you walking up Main Street in a crowd. And the house looks just the same too."

"Do you remember..." Mrs. S paused and laughed. "Do you remember the time that the beer truck crashed in our front yard, and you kids dragged a case of beer up to Kent's bedroom?"

I nodded and grinned. "Yeah, I remember. How did you ever get Gracie's vomit stains out of the carpet?"

"Oh, that's not the worst mess I had to clean up after the kids. But they were all good kids. Weren't they Earl?" She talked to him just as she always had, just as if he could understand it all and would be returning a thoughtful answer shortly.

And so the three of us talked on, all of us listening, but only two of us understanding. We talked about growing up in Chandler. We talked about where we had been and what we had done. The Skulskys' lives had been very modest. Most of the places they went and things they did involved one of their three remaining children. Otherwise, they had seldom left Chandler and almost never Minnesota. Mrs.

Skulsky was very interested in everything I had done in the past fifteen years. I actually started feeling like I had come home.

I had convinced myself after leaving Chandler that it was not a great place from which to harken. But between my reminiscences with Fud and Sticks' mother, I was beginning to regain some of the warmth I had felt toward the place during my happier times there.

"How are your folks, Boomer? It's disgraceful in such a little town, but we haven't seen them in such a long time. We just don't get out. How are they?"

"O.K., I guess. To tell you the truth, I haven't been up to see them yet this visit. My dad and I haven't gotten along very well for a long time, and I haven't really spent much time there recently."

"Oh, Boomer. That's too bad." We sat in silence for a bit. "You're going to see them now aren't you?"

"Well... I don't know. It just seems like every time we get together, we end up yelling at each other. We just don't seem to see eye to eye on anything. I know it hurts my mom, but I've just kind of given up trying in the last years."

"Boomer, you've got to mend fences with your father. A family is too precious a thing to let slide." She continued twisting my arm even more tightly than Fud had just an hour before. "Your parents are such good people, Boomer. You maybe don't know it, but they were wonderful to us when we lost Kent. Your mother brought us food for days, and your dad came and took Earl out fishing several times. And my word, what a comfort they were. It was like they had lost their own son." It flashed through my mind that perhaps they felt they had.

Partly to stop her from heaping on the guilt, and

partly because it seemed the natural opening, I switched the conversation to the topic that had brought me there.

"Mrs. S., how much do you know about Sticks death?" I looked to Mr. Skulsky, but he was dozing in his chair and now really not hearing the conversation.

"Oh, not so much." She sighed. After fifteen years, I could see that the pain was still very much with her. "We got several letters from the army. They all said what a fine soldier Kent was and how much his loss was being felt by the men in his unit. They didn't really explain what happened. Sue and David, Kent's brother and sister, wanted to investigate further and find out what happened, but I told them not to, that it wouldn't bring him back or help anything. The letters said that he was a hero, and that was good enough for me. Earl was so miserable after it happened that I didn't want to dwell on it any more than we already had."

"Mrs. S., I was in Sticks' division, so I know some things about him that I think you should know." I wasn't yet sure enough of my direction to tell her that I had been with him when he died.

"I don't want to hurt you any more than you have already been hurt."

She didn't say anything, but the fact that she did not stop me, led me forward. I started gently, not sure where I would proceed.

"Everything those army letters told you about Sticks being a good soldier and a hero was true. I talked with men who served with him, and they had nothing but good things to say about him. Some even told me that Sticks had saved their lives many times over."

I went on. I told her about Sticks job and how difficult it was for him. I told her how dangerous it was in Vietnam, and how bravely her son had faced it all. I even told her the story of the village that the men in Sticks' unit had destroyed, and how badly it bothered him that innocent people had died.

She never once looked down but looked right into my eyes. She listened intently, but never asked me questions. Mr. Skulsky continued to doze in his chair. At one point she got up and covered his lap with a blanket. She lovingly patted him on the shoulder. Disease had clouded his mind to ensure he would never again face the truth of his son's death.

For fifteen years Mrs. Skulsky had created her own cloud, believing that the best way to rebuild her life. When she turned back, I could see the sadness in her face. I began to question what I was doing. I still felt that this gentle woman had the right to know how her son had died, but she seemed reluctant to claim that right. What was I doing forcing it upon her? Was I really doing it for her, or was I still struggling to relieve my own sense of guilt for not helping my friend when he desperately needed me? I couldn't go any further.

"I really should be going, Mrs. S. Thanks for having me in. I hope I haven't upset you with all of this."

"Boomer, there isn't a day that I don't spend some time thinking of Kent. It's good to know that his friends haven't forgotten him either. In a way it felt good to share that thinking time rather than doing it all alone. I'm afraid that Earl has lost track of most of the things we've done." She looked sadly across at the shell of the man with whom she had shared most of her life.

"I'm sorry, Mrs. S." I was sorry about many things, but I was still too cowardly or ashamed to explain them further, so I left it at "I'm sorry."

~Boomer~

We stood together. She moved forward and hugged me. It was a comfortable, warm hug, as if we had spent our whole lives knowing each other. I tried to return the warmth, and held on until I felt tears on my cheek. They were mine. Her eyes were dry.

She followed me outside and down the front step. "It was great to see you Mrs. S. You take care of yourself, will you?"

She smiled and nodded. "You have a safe trip back to California, Boomer."

As I looked at her smile, I realized that taking care of herself meant taking care of her lost husband, just as she had cared for her children and other people all of her life. It was a face of total selflessness and it made me feel really weak and ashamed. I finally turned to go.

I had gone about five steps when she said, "He didn't die in combat, did he?"

I stopped but didn't turn around. "What makes you think that, Mrs. S?"

"A little while after Kent was gone, I received a letter from a boy in his platoon. He sounded distraught. He asked for our forgiveness. He didn't say what he had done. He said that it was an accident, and he held himself responsible for Kent's death. He said that he would never forgive himself, but he hoped that somehow we could. I wrote back to him and said that we did forgive him and that he needed to forgive himself as well. Then I destroyed his letter and never showed it to anyone else, not even Earl. It seemed to me the only way that we could get on with our lives."

I turned back to her, my face now streaming with tears. "I was there when it happened, Mrs. S. I wasn't ten yards from Sticks when he died."

"Oh, Boomer, I'm so sorry," she said. With all of her pain, her first thought was still with mine. I returned to her and we once again hugged.

We sat down on the front step and I finished the story which I had come to tell. This time she asked questions. Who was the man who set off the mine? Did I know anything about what happened to him later? Had Kent been in pain? What was the last thing I remember him saying?

I told her how the night before he had gone to write her a letter, but that he didn't know what to tell her, that he didn't want to worry her about his safety. I told her how sorry I was that I hadn't done anything to save him.

"Boomer," she said, "I'm glad that you came back from Vietnam, and if Kent had to die there, I'm glad for him that his best friend was with him when it happened. I'm sure that you did what you could to comfort him."

I didn't say that I was too late, that, in fact, there was no comfort to be given. Mrs. Skulsky seemed to have adjusted to my news of her son's death, to have incorporated it all into her world of faith and forgiveness. The earlier look of sadness had left her face. I felt better that my sense she should know the truth still seemed right, that it had perhaps eased her burden rather than sharpened it. It was too soon for me to tell if it had done the same for mine.

Another hug and I again moved away from her. Once again she stopped me. "You're going to see your parents now." I couldn't tell if it was a question, a command or merely a statement. I decided maybe a command, and one this strong woman had a perfect right to make.

"Yes, I'm going to see them," I promised. "I think that I've faced as much of my past as I can for one night, and they are probably already in bed, but tomorrow morning after the funeral I'll go to see them."

"Good. You never know when people are going to leave you, so you've got to stay close." I didn't know whether she was talking about my folks or about Sticks who had left her so suddenly or about her husband who was leaving her gradually. Probably about all of them.

"Thank you, Mrs. S." Again words failed me and I left without telling her that I thought she was the most wonderful person alive.

*****

I shouldn't have postponed seeing my parents. Doing so turned out badly.

The next morning Pastor Jim Bob's funeral was another strange walk through my past. I sat with Fud toward the front of the church. The real Pastor Roberts and his wife, James' parents, sat bowed in the pew to our right with their other children and their families. They didn't look up as I entered.

I tried to glance around at the mourners behind me. I wanted to see who from Chandler had come to the funeral. I recognized no one. I'm sure that I must have known some of them, but with only a glance, I couldn't put names to faces. It was another reminder of how far from Chandler I had retreated.

I began to feel uncomfortable sitting next to Fud, as if I were perhaps invading where I no longer belonged. I was mourning a friend I had left years before, and the depth of my sadness was not to be set beside that of his. I had worked so hard to leave Chandler behind, to escape all the problems it held for me.

Fud and Jim Bob had managed to maintain their close relationship through whatever problems they faced. And now those problems had claimed one of them, and Fud was left alone to cope. For me to step back in and offer a shoulder seemed weak.

The service was grim in a way that I suspect most funerals are for murder victims. Some funerals are a celebration of the deceased's life, but it is hard to celebrate when a life is cut short so violently.

It did contain memories of the good person Jim Bob was. It told tales of the deeds he had performed in the community, but it stayed far away from his actual death and who had caused it. In a way it was like one of those army letters that Stick's parents had received. It dispensed a kind of vague comfort. For me there was no comfort, but only guilt. I hadn't been there in time to help Sticks, and I had long ago forsaken Pastor Jim Bob.

When the service ended and I got up to leave, I turned to face my parents, seated several rows directly behind me. I had stupidly overlooked the obvious fact that they would attend the funeral.

The expression on my mother's face was a mixture of joy at seeing me and sadness that it should be a surprise encounter rather than a happy homecoming. The expression on my father's face was not mixed. It was sheer anger. It was the anger of all of our past arguments sharpened by his anger that I had sneaked into town without coming to see them. The night before at Elizabeth's I had spent some time thinking about how to best meet my parents. That rather rosy plan was now out the window.

I again gave my condolences to Fud and told him I would try to see him before I left. It was another appointment I failed to keep. He then got into a car with Jim Bob's parents and headed off to the cemetery. I had planned to go out as well, but now changed course to meet my parents. They came out of the church and greeted several groups standing around the steps. Then they moved across the yard to where I was standing.

Before I could speak, my father went on the attack.

"Well, Eugene, I'm surprised you didn't run off before we were able to get out here."

"Hush, Glen," my mother said softly.

"Mom. Dad." I gave my mother a brief hug but knew better than to even offer a hand to my father at this point. "I got in late last night, and I didn't want to bother you, so I just stayed with Elizabeth. I was planning to see you this afternoon."

"Why couldn't you let us know you were coming? Would that have been too much to ask?"

"I wasn't sure that I was coming," I lied, "and then at the last minute I just flew out. Fud hadn't let me know that our class reunion was canceled, so I went out to the golf course first, expecting to spend the evening there." Why could I never be with my parents without lying and dodging?

"So you got here in the evening. That's not so late. It's not a big place. You could have made it home." He wasn't going to make this easy.

"Dad, I'm sorry. You know the last time I was here, things didn't go so well. Frankly, I didn't know how welcome I would be at home."

"Oh, Gene," my mother said and I realized that I had clumsily hurt her again. Maybe that's why I usually lied.

"I just needed some time here by myself to prepare for the fray." I tried to say it light-heartedly, but it wasn't taken so.

"So that's what visiting home is. A battle. That's a

~1983~

very nice thing to tell the people who raised you."

"Jesus Christ, Dad, that's not what I want it to be. It just seems like that's what it is. Can't we just let up on each other a bit?"

"I see California hasn't improved your language. I don't think I will stay around here to be cursed at. Marion, I'll be in the car when you have finished saying your goodbyes." He turned and marched off to the parking lot.

My mother and I stood silently and watched him retreat.

"I'm sorry, Mother. God, I should have come up last night."

"I don't think that would have helped, Gene. He just would have found some other reason to blow up at you. He's just so bitter about you. He's not like this about anything else in his life. He's just as gentle and loving. We've never gotten along better."

"And I'm the one big disappointment in his life."

"I don't think he's disappointed in you. In fact, I think he is proud of what you have done for yourself."

"Well, he has a funny way of showing it."

"When has he had a chance to show it, Gene? You've cut yourself off from us. You won't call or write. We don't really even know what's going on in your life. We don't really know who you are, Gene. We raised this little boy. And he was a wonderful person. But somewhere along the line for some reason he changed, and we have never been given the chance to become reacquainted." It was the only time in my life that I remember my mother criticizing me, and it stung.

I had no excuse, so I continued the attack. "He just refuses to forget and forgive some of the things I did. O.K.,

I gave up on his daughter-in-law and I didn't give him grandkids. Can't he get over that? He's got other grandkids."

"I'm sorry, Gene. I've tried. I used to think that he was the problem, but I don't anymore. If there is a solution to this terrible warfare, you'll need to find it inside yourself, not with him. You've got to live life to love life, Gene."

"You always say that, Mother, and I'm never quite sure what you mean."

"Life hands us all kinds of things, both good and bad. And the beauty of life is stepping up to those things and dealing with them, not complaining about them or running away from them. If you are going to love your father, Gene, you are going to have to start accepting him as he is and dealing with that, rather than blowing up and slamming the door behind you."

"It seems to me that it was him who just walked off in a huff."

"You were probably right in not coming last night. Until something changes with you, you won't find a warm welcome at home. Gene, you're not a failure in either one of our hearts. You're just a big empty space where a son used to be. It made me sick for a long time, but gradually I have learned to fill that space with other things and your father has helped me to do that. He's not perfect, but he's not the villain you make him out to be, and I won't stand here and have you criticize him."

I wasn't ready to take all the blame, but there was enough truth to what she said that I didn't want to defend myself further. I felt like a little boy who had just been caught shoplifting, which was really strange, because when as a little boy I had been caught shoplifting, my mother had

~1983~

been rather gentle with me.

"Are you leaving for California yet today?"

"Tomorrow. I guess I'll drive over to Shelton now, spend some time with Elizabeth. I haven't decided if I will go back to the cities tonight or stay down another night."

"I'd like to invite you to stay at home, Gene, but it just wouldn't work. You're better with Elizabeth. Maybe she can even help you to find your way back to our family. Goodbye, honey. Drive carefully on the way to Shelton. There is that awkward road construction about half way there."

The incongruity of her last thought actually made me smile. So she hadn't given up on me entirely. She didn't want me dying in a fiery auto crash.

"Goodbye Mother." Another tentative hug. "Take care now."

When she had gotten a few steps away, I followed and said, "Would you and Dad ever consider coming to California for a visit? Maybe things would go better on my home field.

She stopped and looked right at me. "You keep referring to this as if it were a battle or a contest of some kind. That's not what it is, Gene. If you can't bear to be with us in our home, I don't think it would help for us to come to yours." Then she turned and walked on.

The sharpness of her last comment sank me. I felt empty. The weekend had been a roller coaster of emotions, and at that moment I was definitely in the lowest dip.

I knew that I had lost my father, but it shocked me to realize that my mother had followed him so far away from me. But then as my mother had just said, "When had I given them the chance to love me in the last twenty years?"

*****

I didn't find my way back to my family that weekend.

I spent a few hours with my sister, Elizabeth. She was more sympathetic with me than my mother had been. She, too, felt that my father had gotten more difficult to live with over the years. Her own relationship with him had its rocky moments. She insisted that they still missed me terribly. And like my mother, she maintained that it was my own continual absence that had sealed the doom of our familial tie. She said that he now simply refused to talk about me when they were together.

    I spent my entire flight back to California running the week's happenings over and over in my mind. The death of Pastor Jim Bob at the hands of a distraught vet and my visit with Stick's parents had brought the anger and despair of the Vietnam War back with a sharpness that shook me.

    Its mark on me was obviously still very close to my heart. I considered my mother's assessment that it was a change in me that had drawn us apart. If that was true, and I suspected that it was, that change had festered the year that I spent in Vietnam and mutated as I stood above the bloody body of my boyhood pal.

    After Pastor Jim Bob's funeral I had watched as each of my parents walked away from me. But deep down I knew that it was I who had walked away from them long ago. And for every mile I now flew away from them, it felt like ten thousand. By the time I landed in California I was sure that I had lost them forever. Sadly, it turns out I was right.

2004

Coming back to Chandler for my father's funeral was easier than coming back for my mother's the year before. Then, I anticipated I would be faced with my father's scorn as well as my own guilt.

My father had not been as belligerent as I thought he might be. His grief had overwhelmed him so completely, that he had no emotion left to expend on me. He accepted my hugs and condolences numbly, much as he accepted those of practically every person in Chandler.

It surprised me how deeply my mother had touched nearly the entire population of the town. She was a quiet, unassuming woman, but as people began to tell their favorite memories of her, I became aware how much I had missed about her. It seemed that when anyone in Chandler had a personal tragedy, my mother found some quiet way to offer comfort.

At the funeral, when he needed comfort, my father had turned to Tom and Elizabeth, as well he should have. I stood aside like some member of the community who had a passing acquaintance with this woman who had given birth to me.

~Boomer~

After the funeral I returned to California without any attempt to cross the chasm that had grown between my father and me over the years.

So, I came back to Chandler this time with the expectation it would be the last time. My father was the final thread connecting me to my hometown, and with that gone, I would have no reason to return.

I doubted that I would be included in any estate my father left behind, and certainly felt that I had no claim to anything. In the end, it had been my decision to not be a part of my family. I had decided that if, despite our separation, my parents left me something, I would have it redirected to Tom and Elizabeth's five children.

So, with all of the ends neatly tied off, I could make my final exit and leave my anger and guilt and Chandler behind. Or so I thought.

The flood of emotions that greeted me in Chandler surprised me. Every corner of town seemed to raise a memory in a way it hadn't in earlier visits. All of my last visits had been clouded by the frustration of conflict with my parents. With that now absent, the fond remembrances of my past rose like a cloud of colorful balloons.

It had begun with my visit to my boyhood home, a gentle walk through my memories, guided by an incredibly friendly stranger, Mrs. Hemseth. It continued in a warm reunion with Elizabeth, my sister. Between these I spent hours walking the streets of Chandler, reliving the first eighteen years I had spent there, realizing that they had been far and away the happiest of my life. How had the place which supplied me so much joy in my youth become a focus of my anger and resentment afterward?

I am a city person now, and tell myself I could never

~2004~

easily move back to the slower pace of small town, Midwestern life. But that day I realized Chandler had been the best possible place in which to grow up. If my life had gone differently and I had children of my own, it is the kind of place I would want them to have experienced as well. I struggled to solve this paradox of my past.

A visitation had been scheduled that night before my father's funeral. As with my mother's, Elizabeth had made all the arrangements.

She had tried so many times to reconnect me with our parents. And when I failed to respond, without seemingly a moment of resentment, she had shouldered the burden of their care. I came to realize that she considered this, like so many other things, something I had missed, not something into which she had been forced. Instead of anger and resentment, she felt genuinely sorry for me. When this was over, I had to somehow show her how much I appreciated her unconditional love.

The line of people who came to say goodbye to my father seemed endless. This I dreaded with my usual selfishness. What would these people think of me, a son who had time for his parents only when they died?

In this, too, I was mistaken. No one treated me with anything but fondness. The older ones shared happy memories of my father and me. A former neighbor recalled the night I had played catch with my dad in the back yard and had cracked the side window of his car with a wild throw. I remembered it clearly, but also remembered that my father had blamed himself for standing where the car might be in danger.

No one seemed to believe that I had been anything but a loving, dutiful son. Person after person brought me their

~Boomer~

comfort with glowing stories of the man I had dismissed.

It wasn't that I hated him or resented him. I had simply given up on him, and evidently, he on me as well. The more stories people helped me to recall, the more I began to realize my mistake, and to realize that my lifetime in Chandler wasn't about to end at all, would never end.

And then from the back of the line a pair of eyes met mine, and my resolve to forget Chandler was lost. Fud. It was definitely the eyes that caught me. The body might have fooled me, for it was slim and firm, not the pudgy Fud I had always known.

I hadn't seen him since the day of Pastor Jim Bob's funeral, and even our yearly birthday greetings had faltered. He had sent his condolence after my mother's death. He had been traveling and had missed the funeral. I handed over the last few people in the line to my brother and sister and ushered Fud to some chairs at the side of the room.

"I'm sorry about your dad, Boomer," he said. It was going to take us some time to find comfortable conversation.

"How are your folks doing?" I asked, trying to find common ground.

"I lost my dad last winter. My mom is in the nursing home in Clearview. Her sister is there as well, and it is a little closer for me to visit."

My embarrassment at knowing nothing of Fud's recent past set the conversation back even further. "Well, what are you doing now? Are you still in Rochester?" At least I remembered that he had been once.

"Not only there, I am the mayor of Rochester. How's that?" he half whispered. "The first fag mayor south of Red Wing."

We laughed together, but mine caught in my throat

and turned almost to a sob.

"God, Fud, how did I let all this get away from me? Why didn't I know you are mayor? Why didn't I know your father is gone? What the hell is the matter with me, Fud?"

"We've just had a little temporary blackout is all. It's nothing we don't have time to fix if you want to, Boomer. Maybe it is time to reconnect."

"Temporary. Right. Like twenty years. Listen, I hadn't planned to stay around after the funeral, but I'm finding that there are really some things here I need to take care of. Have you got some time in the next few days? I really would like to get back together."

"I think that can be arranged. But before it is, there is something else to which you need attend. There is somebody out in my car that wants to see you. I was just sent in here to break the ice. She's the main attraction."

The "she" took the mystery from Fud's surprise. There was only one she from my past that came into my mind. As we walked across the parking lot of the funeral home, Gracie stepped out of a car and rushed toward us.

She and I collided in a hug which lasted minutes. When we broke, it was only to reach out to include Fud.

Finally, I stepped back to look at my once best friend. Time had been very good to Gracie. She looked thirty-nine instead of fifty-nine. I couldn't get any words from my brain to my mouth. "Gracie," I finally blurted.

"Boomer."

"John. Marsha," mocked Fud. "Listen, kids, I'd love to stay and see how this turns out, but I've got my mom in town with me, and I have to pick her up from a friend's house. Boomer, do you suppose that I can trust you to get this young lady home at a reasonable hour."

~Boomer~

"Home?" I asked.

"I live in town again. I'm back with my mom. Guess I'll never grow up."

The three of us made arrangements to meet for dinner the following evening and then Fud left Gracie and me staring at one another in a kind of uncertain ecstasy.

I knew for sure where the conversation had to start. "I know that I am thirty years too late for this, Gracie, but I've got to say it. I'm so sorry." I grabbed her into a hug once again.

She didn't ask, "What for?" I had done only one thing in our lives for which I needed to apologize, but it was such a grotesque, ugly thing, that after thirty years, it wouldn't have surprised me if she had again kneed me in the groin.

I started to realize that some of my negative feeling toward Chandler in the past thirty years had been wound up in that single, drunken, inexcusable moment when I had attacked her. It was that stupid act which had turned our years of mutual joy to emptiness. That's what I had felt whenever I had let myself think of Gracie since that time.

For a long time I had tried to justify my action as an understandable response to her jilting me, but somewhere along the line I had grown up enough to admit that I had in fact attempted rape that summer night in 1967. I didn't know what time had done to Gracie's memory of the incident.

"Listen, Boomer," she said. "Let's not start there."

"All right," I said, a bit relieved, but also uncertain what else we had to talk about. I wasn't entirely sure I was standing across from an old friend or a stranger.

She felt like a friend as we walked hand in hand to the boulevard and sat beneath a tree that shaded us from the light of a nearby street lamp.

~2004~

"How long have you been back in Chandler?" I asked.

"About ten years. It took me a long time to stop being mad and decide that this is really where I want to be."

"Who were you mad at? I wasn't around."

"Something else I'd like to postpone for a bit. Tell me about your life, Boomer."

And so we talked about me. We talked about Vietnam and she cried when I mentioned Sticks' death. We talked about my failed marriage. She said that she was sorry, but that she had predicted the breakup. She had known Deanna enough in school to suspect we were incompatible.

"It really was your fault, you know." I said it as a joke, but immediately recognized some truth in what I was thinking. "After those summer nights with you, no female could ever measure up."

"Oh, don't be ridiculous, Boomer." She pushed me away

We talked of my escape to California and my life there. "Are you really happy there?" she probed. She asked it as if she had some concrete evidence that I was not. I always said that I was happy there, and in many ways it was true.

Professionally, I had found my niche. Personally, I was contented with the uncomplicated status of my life. My friends were mostly business associates, so I kept some distance to avoid job/personal conflicts. I had been in and out of relationships with women on several occasions, but didn't feel the need to add the complexities of marriage to my life once again.

"Yes," I told Gracie, "I'm relatively happy. And what about you?"

And then we talked about her. She had left Chandler

suddenly and without much of a plan, taking a waitress job and living near the University of Minnesota campus. She had earned enough to take some art classes and had dabbled in the technical aspects of drama with some of the University plays. Then she had gotten a job as a costumer at the Children's Theater in Minneapolis.

It was her mother's condition that had brought her back to Chandler. Her alcoholism had reached a life-threatening stage, and Gracie had moved home to try to save her. She had succeeded. Her mother had been dry almost since the day of Gracie's return.

"That's terrific," I said. "I wish that I could say I gave something back to my parents. My mom, especially. I really feel like I let her down." And then we talked about me again, and the feelings that pulled me further and further from my parents.

"I've always blamed my dad for pushing me away. I'd even come to think of him as an unreasonable, mean-spirited person. I don't know. Then tonight everyone has been telling me what a prince he was. And I think back to when we were kids, and he was a very good father. And then I blame him for not understanding me, and I blame myself for not understanding him. And now it really doesn't matter, because he's gone, and whatever was wrong between us won't get fixed."

Gracie took my arm and hugged it. It surprised me that after all these years she still cared about any pains I might have.

"You know," I said, "we're a lot alike in that way. Both of us lost our fathers along the way and were never able to get them back. Is there any chance for you yet?"

"No more than you, Boomer. No more than you."

~2004~

She pressed her head to my chest. We held each other quietly for a long while.

"Boomer, don't you wonder why I decided to come tonight?"

I hadn't. I had been so overwhelmed at seeing her that any question of her motivation had not entered my mind.

"I don't know. Is there a special reason? I guess that I figured it was for old times sake."

She sighed deeply and tightened her grip on my hand. "Oh, Boomer, things were so easy when we were kids, and now they are so hard."

"What is it Gracie? It's all right."

"He was my father, too." She buried her face in my jacket.

"Who? Your father? Who was your father, too?"

"Your father, Glen Boomer. He was my real father, too."

It still took a moment for what she was saying to sink in. I tried to pull back and look at her face, but she clung tightly to my chest. "What are you talking about, Gracie? That's crazy. How could that be?"

"While your mother was pregnant with you, my mother and your father had an affair. It wasn't really even an affair. They spent a few nights together. And afterward she got pregnant - with me."

A load of memories rushed into my head, as I tried to comprehend the possibility of what Gracie was telling me. Was there something that I could latch on to that would say to me for sure, "Yes, this is true, or no, this couldn't be true?"

I remembered that once my mother had told me that her pregnancy with me had been the most difficult time of their marriage. Was this part of that difficulty? My mind spun on, but nothing took hold. Gracie was holding me so tightly, as if she could physically press this truth into my body with hers.

"How do you know this?"

"My mother told me."

"But how could she even be sure. Your father - or her husband was still living with her at that time. How can she be sure you're not his child?"

"Their marriage had been in trouble for quite a while by that time. He hadn't touched her for months before she got pregnant. Afterward, she tried to convince him that we could still be a family, that the two of them could raise me as their child. For a while he went along, but when I was born, it was too much for him and he took off. Sometimes after I found out about this, I felt sorry for him. In Chandler he has always been seen as a cad for abandoning his wife and newborn child."

I pulled from Gracie's grasp, stood up and moved away. I didn't know what I was feeling. It felt like anger, but I didn't know with whom I should be angry. I sounded angry when I spoke again.

"I don't believe this, Gracie. You're trying to tell me that my father got your mother and my mother pregnant within the same year?"

"Six months apart, to be exact. Your father and my mother have always been close friends. She says that she loved him long before anything happened between them. Your dad was having a tough time at home, and my mother was right there in his station for comfort. And then it became something more than just comfort."

"Yeah, right. Poor Dad," I thought, thinking more of my mother.

~2004~

"My mom says that she has been in love with him ever since. For years she was able to stay close to him by working at the station, but it was as much torture as it was pleasure, and it kept driving her further and further into her alcoholism."

Everything made sense. I couldn't think of a single fact to counter Gracie's story, but I still resisted. I couldn't believe that this secret had hovered in the happiness of our childhood home. I kept prodding, trying to find some flaw in Gracie's story which would deny the whole thing.

"How long have you known about this?"

"Oh, Boomer, that's the important thing. That's why I'm really here tonight. To tell you that. And if nothing else will make you believe me, maybe this will."

"I don't understand."

"Do you remember our last summer, how close we got?"

I saw instantly where this was taking us. I remembered vividly how close we had gotten. Into my mind came our nights in the boat when we had nearly given everything to each other. I had fallen in love with Gracie that summer. I started to feel sick. I bent at the waist and wrapped my arms around my stomach.

"When your father found out how serious we were becoming, he came to my mother and told her she had to do something to put a stop to it. He knew that he couldn't talk with you about it. He made my mother promise to not tell either of us why it was necessary to break up. He didn't want you to know he had been unfaithful to your mother."

I had this momentary urge to march into the funeral parlor and strike my father across the face. But what had he done, compared to me. He had temporarily abandoned my mother. I had done it to her dying day.

All of the pieces fit so tightly. I remembered how my father had been uncomfortable and had tried to steer me away from a relationship with Grace.

Grace continued. "At first my mother just tried to get me to stop seeing you, but her reasons were all weak and I would have no part of it. Finally, she told me the real reason, who my real father was."

"You should have told me," I almost shouted at her.

"I couldn't. My mother made me promise that I would never ever tell anyone. I believe her, that she really loved your father, and that she would do anything to protect him. The one thing that I couldn't do was tell you."

"And so you just stopped seeing me."

"I went crazy. I didn't know what to do. The whole thing just overwhelmed me. Suddenly I had not just been left behind by one father, but by two fathers. Suddenly all of the things we had ever shared in our whole lives took on a different feeling, and I didn't know how to be with you. I was just hoping that week would end, that you would leave and I would have time to figure out a way to reconnect with you."

"But couldn't you just have seen me until that happened?"

Gracie stepped to me and reached her arms around me. I stood stiffly, but let her hold me. "I was afraid to. Boomer, those nights in the boat. We were so close. I was falling in love with you. I couldn't trust you. I couldn't trust me to keep quiet. It broke my heart to have you leave the way you did. Vietnam was so hard for you anyway, and then to have to leave that way. It was so unfair."

My resistance finally gave way. The truth of it and all

of the things that it meant for us overwhelmed me. I put my arms around her shoulders and buried my head in her neck.

"Oh, Gracie. That awful night." All of the guilt that I had felt for my treatment of her that night by the river suddenly doubled. She had been in such confusion and pain, and I had added to it immeasurably.

"Boomer, I never hated you for that night. I understood why it happened. I even felt that I somehow deserved what happened."

"Oh, Gracie, no."

"I know how it looked that night. Like I had just thrown you over for someone else. But I swear to you, Boomer, that wasn't it. I loved you, and I didn't know what to do about it. That night my mother just kept pestering me to be sure to end it with you. She kept after me until I finally just blew up at her. At that point I just needed a friend, someone to get me out of the house, and Sticks was really the only one available. We only talked. We never touched each other. Boomer, I'm so sorry that it took me so long to tell you this. There have been so many times when I have wanted to get in touch. When you were in Vietnam, I even wrote you a letter explaining the whole thing, and then I tore it up. You had enough to deal with over there without another mess back home. And then you just sort of drifted further and further away from me, and I gave up ever telling you. I'm so sorry."

"It doesn't matter. It's all over now." I leaned back and took her gently by the shoulders. I looked into her dimly lit face. "You're my sister Grace."

"You're my big brother Bing."

Why had I resisted this so? Now it felt so very right. None of this could hurt my mother or my father. Gracie and

I had acted like brother and sister most of our years together. Why shouldn't we slip back into that comfortable state?

We sat back down and talked about what this would mean to our futures. We talked about the kind of relationship we would like to grow between us.

We discussed who should know this news and who shouldn't. We planned how we might tell Tom and Elizabeth of their surprise sibling. Finally, the chill in the night air was finding its way to our middle-aged bones.

"Hey, Sis," I said, "you want to go inside and pay your last respects to the old man?"

"I would love to, Bro. Especially with you at my side."

We entered the darkened funeral chapel, long empty of any other visitors. The only lights left on, were dim ones, shining on our father's body. We walked through the darkness and stood by the coffin, our arms around each other.

"It's odd," I said. "Our father has died, and yet the sense of loss that usually goes along with that isn't here for either of us. Is it?"

"I don't know. Don't you feel anything, Boomer?"
I paused, trying to see if, in fact, I did feel anything.

"It's like I had two fathers. The one I loved and got along with the first eighteen years of my life, and the one I fought with for the last forty years. I guess we were both just too stubborn to give the other a chance. How about you? What do you feel? Did he ever once acknowledge that you were his daughter?"

"Not that I recognized. I've thought about that ever since I found out he was my father. I had very few contacts with him, but I've gone over the ones we had, trying to remember if there was something he said or did where he was reaching out to me. But I've never found it. Of course, he never knew that I knew who he was. If he had, it might have been different. He was always really nice to me. When we were kids, and I spent time at your house, he always laughed and joked with me. He never seemed uncomfortable with me that I can remember."

"Maybe that was the tip-off. As I recall, he hardly laughed and joked with anybody."

"Well, one of us has got to say it eventually. Ain't life strange?"

We turned and started to make our way down the dark aisle. I reached out and took her hand. "God, Gracie. I'm in a daze. Part of me feels so happy to know this, and part of me feels so unbelievably cheated. I just can't help wondering what I missed by not knowing."

"You git what you git and you don't raise a fit," Gracie said with a silly southern accent.

"What!" I stopped and laughed a loud hoot.

"It is something Mrs. Tomlin told us in 1st grade, and it has just stuck with me. I use it all the time."

"Gracie, you are something else. You git what you git and you don't raise a fit."

"Boomer, let's just enjoy thinking about some wonderful things ahead now that you know."

We walked off into the parking lot. I had to admit that I felt better than I had for a long time. I had lost my father, but in the process had gained a sister.

In the next weeks I would spend time thinking about how earlier knowledge of that sister might have changed my relationship with my father, but for now it felt just fine to have her hand in mine.

~Boomer~

*****

We had arranged to have dinner the following night, forgetting that we would be together for another event before that, my father's funeral.

My sister looked questioningly when I insisted that Gracie sit beside me with the family. Sometime soon I would explain the reason, but I would let the wound of her lost father begin to heal first. Elizabeth was taking it harder than I expected. It wasn't only losing her father, but also the realization that she no longer had any parent, and that our lives were moving rather quickly forward.

Both Elizabeth and Tom were really decent to me. It really felt like we were a family again, and the more I felt it, the more stupid I felt for having given it up along the way. I vowed to myself that I would make up for lost time with them, and that I would help them to understand and accept the additional family member in their midst.

For the very first time I even thought that I might investigate job opportunities back in Minnesota. I wasn't too old for yet another shakeup in my life. What fun to be near Fud and Gracie once again.

Fud, too, must have wondered about Gracie's position amongst our family, for Gracie had not told him the real reason she had wanted to see me the night before. He sat alone, several rows behind us.

As I looked back to wave at him, my eyes settled on two women sitting side by side in the back row. One was Joyce Hemseth, the charming young woman who now lived in my boyhood home. Her eyes caught mine and she flashed a slightly embarrassed smile before looking down. "How exceptionally kind of her to come to my father's funeral," I thought. Perhaps the spark I had felt as she guided me through the house was real. I resolved to see her again in the next days to find out exactly what it was we shared.

My eyes moved to the other woman. Later, when I got closer to her, I would see that the years of alcoholism had taken a toll on Cherry Maculum. But from across the church, she was still a strikingly beautiful woman. Even in mourning clothes, her taste outshone every other person in the room. She caught me staring at her and gave me a warm smile before looking down as well. I wondered what she must be feeling at my father's funeral. And I wondered if anyone else in the church knew why she was feeling that way.

As I sat waiting for the service to begin, I found myself wishing it would really capture my father. I wanted the pallbearers sitting up front on blocks of cement in blue striped overalls. Instead of Bible verses, I wanted platitudes of wisdom, the kind he handed out to customers at the gas station so freely. Instead of roses, I wanted the smell of kerosene, and steaming wet mittens. And at the reception I wanted someone serving up slabs of bologna, and handing out cold bottles of beer.

By the time the service began, my father was so alive for me that it wouldn't have surprised me if he had stood up out of his coffin and asked if anybody wanted to go uptown for coffee.

But of course, it didn't go that way. Those who eulogized him were younger members of his church that praised him for acts of which I had no knowledge. The singer was the church soloist, who was only a little younger than my dead father, and warbled her way unsteadily through *Rock of Ages*.

Only with Elizabeth did I feel the speaker really knew who my father was. But then, who was I to judge? I hadn't known my father for decades. I had spent the last two thirds of my life creating an image of my father as the cold, uncompromising tyrant. I spent the last half of the service replacing that with the stern but totally reliable guide of my youth. I was so engrossed in my reverie that when time came for the family to follow the coffin out of the church, Gracie had to take my hand and gently pull me to my feet.

The first thing I saw at the grave was my mother's headstone. *Marion Elizabeth Boomer.* I had forgotten that she had given one of her names to her daughter. *1911 - 2003. You have to live life to love life.*

I realized that I had never seen that headstone before. It must have been erected after I had returned to California. While the minister led us through the final rituals, my eyes kept returning to it.

At one point I whispered to Elizabeth, "Did you pick Mother's epitaph?"

She glanced at the grave. "No."

The minister began a prayer. "Who did?"

"I don't know. Maybe Dad. Or maybe she picked it herself."

I knew that my dad was so distracted after her death that he never could have made such a choice, so my mother must have arranged it ahead of time.

The minister was now reading scripture. I leaned toward Elizabeth one more time. "Did she ever say that to you?"

"Not that I remember. Shh."

"She said it to me all the time."

The grave side ceremony ended without me hearing much of it. People wandered back toward their cars and stragglers stopped by to give their final condolence to

Elizabeth, Tom and me.

Everyone else wandered away, Tom and Elizabeth's children with other relatives, Gracie with Fud, leaving the three of us standing at the open grave. We held hands, and Elizabeth sobbed softly between her two brothers. I momentarily wished that Gracie were holding my other hand where she had every right to be.

Finally, I said, "I can't tell you how much I appreciate the way you two have treated me this week. I know that I don't deserve it. I haven't done anything to deserve being a part of this family for decades, and yet you two have gone out of your way to include me, and I can't even begin to understand why."

"Ours is not the reason why, Gene," Elizabeth said. "In a way we were just following orders."

"Whose?"

"Theirs." She nodded her head toward our parents' graves.

"She's right," said Tom. "Mom always let us know that it was not acceptable in her house to speak badly of you. And I never heard her criticize you either."

"What about Dad?"

"Dad too, in his own grumbling sort of way."

"That's amazing. It seems like when we were together, all Dad ever did was criticize me."

"They loved you, Gene," said Elizabeth, "and I probably shouldn't say it just now, but it hurt them deeply to not see you."

I hugged her tightly, "Oh, Elizabeth, how could I have let them die without giving us another chance?" She held me and rubbed my back.

"Listen, kid," Tom said. "Some things happened in

your life that didn't happen in ours. We had life really easy and things went our way. They didn't always for you."

"Thanks for trying to let me off the hook, but my life has not been so tough. I just blew it with the folks. But if you'd let me, I sure would like to make some of it up with you two."

"That would be great, but you'd better get going. You've got a whole bunch of nieces and nephews who need uncling."

We walked toward the limousine, picking Fud and Gracie up along the way. I smiled at Gracie and said to Tom and Elizabeth, "Before we all leave town, I need to talk with you again. I've got something to tell you that will just blow your minds."

*****

That evening, Fud picked me up for dinner. We then moved on to Gracie's house. From there it felt like we should have moved on to Pastor Jim Bob's house and then to Sticks'.

It was Gracie who first said how much she felt their absence. Yet as the night went on, and we talked of our past, our two lost friends seemed to rejoin us. It was an unbelievably strong bond that held the five of us together. We had hardly seen each other in thirty-five years, and yet it felt like we had been in continual contact.

From the back seat I noticed Fud's grey hair, and when Gracie turned to talk with me, there were a few wrinkles in a face that was for the most part defying her fifty-nine years. We were more than half a lifetime beyond those silly kids who used to fight for the front seat and goad the driver into peeling out. We all fastened our seatbelts, something that had not even existed in our first cars. We had felt perfectly safe in those days, but perhaps it had more to do with the condition of life than the technology of cars.

I felt sorry for the other customers who had to share dinner with us that night at the Road House. For one thing, Gracie had worked there off and on through the years and held somewhat of celebrity status. Some cook or waitress was always leaving his or her post to come visit with us. We had other company as well. Leonard Marks, one of our high school classmates, was having dinner with his wife and stopped by when he recognized us.

I was somewhat uncomfortable, as I recognized other people from the funeral, and I imagine they thought it unfeeling of me to be out having quite so much fun on the day I buried my father.

But all else was dwarfed by the sheer joy of the reunion with my two close friends. The next two hours were punctuated frequently by our uproarious laughter as we relived old times.

Fud and Gracie had both brought picture books, and we pored over them hungrily. Most of the shots contained Sticks or Pastor Jim Bob or both, and it moved us all to laughter and tears to see us back together.

A newspaper clipping showed Sticks scoring a basket to send Chandler to the State Basketball Tournament. A classroom shot showed Mr. Baldwick with his arm around the shoulder of Fud, who was holding his stuffed duck. My favorite was of Gracie receiving her "most valuable fan" award at the boys' basketball banquet. Story after story we recounted, helping each other to fill in the details.

While we ate, we decided to each share a favorite memory. Gracie's was the night we had gone out to sabotage and obliterate all of the snowmen and forts built that snowy day in Chandler. We had armed ourselves with baseball bats and hockey sticks and shovels. At one site a huge dog had attacked us and chased us into a tool shed where he kept us captive most of the night. We had huddled in a big lump in the corner of the shed to keep each other warm. Hours later, when we could no longer stand the freezing temperatures, Pastor Jim Bob had ventured out to face the growling beast, only to discover that he was really very friendly and that our only danger was being licked to death.

Fud recounted the time we had tried to burn a C C, for Chandler Cardinals, into the middle of the Lakeland football field. We tried to spell it with gasoline. The grass was so dry that we lost control of the blaze. By the time we were able to stomp it out, we had just burned two big black blobs. From them the Lakeland student body would never recognize what rivals had besmirched their home field.

My vivid memory was the day we had decided to walk across the railroad bridge at the Black River. It crossed a wide canyon, so that the bridge was probably an eighth of a mile in length and stretched high above the treetops. Gracie had been most hesitant to follow, certain that once we reached the middle, a train would arrive, forcing us to leap to our deaths to avoid an even worse death under its wheels. Fud had insisted that there were very few trains still using the line, and that he knew none of them traveled at that time of day. I suspect that he knew no such thing. Gracie managed to get herself halfway across by staring at Pastor Jim Bob's back and taking baby steps from one tie to the next. Near the middle, Fud had convinced Gracie to look down to the spectacular view, a grave error. Gracie had frozen. She didn't get hysterical. She didn't cry out. She just became totally incapable of movement. The four of us had to literally carry her to the other side of the bridge, at which point she did become hysterical and ran around beating on any of us she could catch.

Amidst all of the laughter and joy that night at the Road House, each of us had a serious story that captivated the others. Mine was of Sticks. Gracie had no idea that I had been with him when he died, and they both hung on my every word as I recounted the events of his final day. I had told the whole story to no one, since telling it to Stick's mother seventeen years earlier. When I finished, my two friends got up from their chairs and held me.

Fud's story was of Pastor Jim Bob. They had been the only two to keep a close and continuous relationship. Fud told us things about Pastor Jim Bob that Gracie and I never suspected. Behind his jovial exterior lurked bouts of depression. On occasion Pastor Jim Bob had expressed doubts about his own sexuality. He had been frustrated by a failure to find a female mate in Chandler. Fud recounted the phone call from Jim Bob the night before his death. Again Fud laid out his guilt for not steering his friend away from the awaiting danger. Now it was Gracie and I out of our chairs holding Fud.

The restaurant was closing. The owner said that we were welcome to stay and talk, but we had already imposed on his hospitality. We returned to Fud's car and drove back into Chandler.

And then Gracie began to tell Fud our strange story. At the announcement of our shared parentage, his mouth dropped open. He actually pulled the car to the side of the street and stopped to avoid running a red light or rear ending another car. For the next half hour we sat there filling him in.

When his amazement had subsided, Fud returned to the jovial approach with which he met most things in life.

~Boomer~

"I always knew there was something about you two," he said. "I should have guessed that night at the Chinese restaurant when neither of you could handle chopsticks." He actually made us put our heads together to see what common facial features he could spot. When we got to the part about our romantic nights in the boat, he said, "Oh, Ish. And people think I'm a pervert."

"You can't tell anyone about this," I warned him. "We haven't really decided how we are going to handle this news with people."

"Don't worry. Mum's the word." Fud paused. "Speaking of which. I think I will pay a visit to my mum. I'm wondering if she ever had anything to do with your dad."

"Fud!" scolded Gracie.

"You're no brother of mine," I said, laughing and slugging him on the arm. He started the car and we continued onward.

We didn't want the night to end. We cruised the streets of Chandler as we had in high school. We parked and walked around the school, which had since been converted into a community center. Stories continued to resurface, and as we recounted each one, we drove to the sight where it had happened. In the end we purchased a bottle of wine and returned to the cemetery to toast the graves of our two lost group members.

I wondered if we could actually find them in the dark, but Fud had visited both quite often and found them easily. At each grave we spent more time reminiscing. We each told the others what we liked best, what we missed most and what we found the funniest and strangest about our former mates.

By the time we finished our tales, we had finished the

wine as well. We started back for the car. On the way we passed near to my parents' graves. My father's was now enclosed with a headstone already in place. I stopped.

"Do you guys mind going back without me? I'll walk back to town in a little while. I think I have a little more work to do out here." I indicated my mother's grave.

Gracie hugged me and Fud took my hand and then followed her toward the car. Fud turned to say, "You all right?"

"We'll see." And then I was alone with my parents. For a while I just sat on the grass pondering what a turbulent week it had been.

When I had arrived in Chandler this time, I had expected it to be the end of something. Now it seemed it was more of a beginning. If nothing else, maybe it was the beginning of facing my own shortcomings.

I had a successful career, but after fifteen years in California, I had little to show for it but work. I had no strong friendships, no causes that I championed, no activities about which I was passionate. I had left my old family behind, and done nothing about making a new one.

I looked at my father's new gravestone. My feelings about him were still hopelessly confused. I wondered what other things I didn't know about him.

I wondered if his relationship with Gracie's mother and the guilt he must have felt from it influenced the way he felt about and treated me. I wondered how he could have a daughter living that near to him and never take any part in her life. But if I looked backward far enough, I could still remember the man who always had time to play catch with me, who would always come to Ashcroft Park and who pulled my kite down when I let out so much string that I couldn't retrieve it myself. He had been a good father to me, and I knew that it was partly... probably mostly... certainly mostly... entirely my fault that the relationship had died.

"I'm so sorry, Dad," I said aloud to his grave.

I moved two steps to my right and stared at my mother's grave. The guilt I had felt at my father's mushroomed. I sank to my knees and cried the tears I had neglected to cry at her funeral.

How could I have been so selfish as to give nothing back to this kind and gentle woman who had given me so much of her life? I wondered if she had ever just given up on me, said, "Oh, what the heck, two out of three ain't bad." No. I was sure she hadn't. I was sure that her love never faltered, and so the pain I caused her by my absence must have been as acute at the end as at the beginning.

I wiped my eyes. I thought, "How seldom I cried as a child, but how often as an adult."

Again I looked at her gravestone. *You've got to live life to love life.* Was I the only one to whom she said that? Was I the only one to whom it needed saying?

At that moment I missed my parents more than I could ever have imagined possible. I suddenly saw them to be truly wonderful people, maybe even more wonderful than they really were. But I had squandered them. And with them I had squandered my gentle, happy childhood.

Maybe it had been too gentle and happy. Maybe it didn't prepare me for the harsh realities, for the Vietnams that were to follow. Maybe I shunned my mother and father because I still needed them so badly, because I had never really grown up.

I spent the next hour with them. It may have seemed a pitiful compensation for the neglect of many years, but by

~2004~

the end of it, I had talked through a multitude of issues, and it was almost as if they had guided me. I felt that somehow I was now ready to start living life.

*****

Printed in the United States
107726LV00002B/12/A